SCREEN

by Joe Randazzo

A Sprezzatura Book

from New Renaissance Press

Sprezzatura Books
New Renaissance Press
8 Woodside Drive
South Burlington, VT 05403

ISBN 978-0-615-23158-7
Library of Congress Control Number: 2008906253

This book is a work of fiction. Character names and incidents in the plot are products of the author's imagination. Any resemblance to actual events or persons, living or dead, is entirely coincidental.

Front and back covers: Photo by Chris Koch of an installation by Michael Kuk
Author's photograph: Chris Koch

Printed in the United States of America

Dedicated to:

Rita Randazzo
My everything

CHAPTER ONE

The Crown Victoria's trunk was cavernous. There was plenty of room for the four boxes of vital evidence, three notebook computers, and a projector.

Senator Mario McGuire and his staff of three were well prepared but tired. They had been up most of the night at Rosa's apartment getting ready for their presentation. Media trucks from all over the world were parked next to the Capitol, waiting to see what McGuire would say at the Vermont hearing, which was scheduled to begin at 10:00 a.m.

The senator was in the front seat, sitting next to his chief of staff, Nadene Johnson, who was driving. Right behind him was Sethos Azizi, and next to Sethos in the backseat was Rosa Montez. Her home was at the top of the hill, two miles from the Capitol. Nadene pulled out of Rosa's driveway and turned onto State Street. She gently braked at the corner, but the car didn't slow down.

"Mario, Mario, we have no brakes!" She tried to use the emergency brake, but nothing happened. They were moving downhill at 30 miles an hour on a twisty two-lane road with parked cars on either side. A BMW pulled out in front of her and she swerved into the opposite lane to go around it, just missing an oncoming SUV. Her speed was now 45 miles an hour. She narrowly avoided two more vehicles.

"The bastards cut the brake lines!" Mario shouted. "I don't believe it, last night the bastards cut the brake lines!" He grabbed the wheel and tried to scrape against some parked cars to slow them down, but Nadene shoved his hand aside.

"That won't work, we're moving too fast!"

The two-ton behemoth picked up speed quickly and was now going 60 miles an hour. State Street turned sharply to the left, and the car skidded around a 90-degree turn with all four tires squealing. Nadene used the whole road. The steepest part was directly ahead. It was a little over a mile and a half long and ended right at the Capitol steps. She narrowly missed two children on bicycles. She was driving like she was on a ski slalom. Rosa and Sethos slid back and forth in the rear seat until he managed to fasten both their seat belts. Mario's foot hit against the FM radio, and suddenly they were listening to the rapper DawgLeg at top volume.

I had me a bitch who didn't know the score,
till I gave her my tall man,
then she begged me for some more.
I finished with the bitch cause I got tired of goin' round,
so I jumped on her mama and throwed her to the ground.

"Oh great," Sethos yelled, "I'm going to die listening to this shit!" Rosa shut her eyes and said a prayer to Saint Teresa, her patron saint.

Suddenly, they were going uphill. There was a slight incline before the road again went downhill. Nadene tried to put the car in low to slow it down, but it was stuck in drive. Their speed was now 25 miles an hour. She scraped against a row of four cars parked closely together, and the Ford came to a complete stop against the last car in the row. The side air bags had been sabotaged and did not deploy.

"Thank you Jesus, thank you Allah, thank you Saint Teresa."

"Thank you Nadene, great driving," Mario said.

She relaxed her grip on the wheel. They all sat dazed for a moment. Mario tried to turn off the radio, but accidentally pressed the select button and changed the station to WVPR,

Vermont Public Radio. A Vivaldi guitar concerto was playing. They tried to get out of the car but none of the doors would open. The locks were frozen in child-safety mode. Sethos kicked at his window as the car started rolling again but couldn't break it. There were no more parked cars and solid traffic raced toward them. They were again moving downhill at 10, 20, 30, 40, then 50 miles an hour.

"Are we going to die?" Rosa sobbed.

"Put your arms in front of your face!" Nadene shouted. Mario tried again to grab the wheel, but she knocked his hand away as she wove around cars in both lanes. The last half-mile was a steep downhill straight with a very sharp turn at the bottom. No one looked at the speedometer, which now read 85 miles an hour. Nadene screeched around the last turn and yelled at everyone to brace themselves. Mario put both feet on the dashboard.

~ ~ ~

Six weeks earlier at Stanford University, behind an ivory-painted wall with a ten-foot-long mural of surfers on Ventura Beach, two scientists sat in a small conference room. Usually the pace was slow here, nothing like the ER in any major hospital, but not today. For the last week researchers at the Neuro-Sciences Center had been finding abnormal brain cells in Iraq war veterans with head wounds. Nine percent of the patients had been exhibiting the early signs of occipital lobe tumors, and business-as-usual had been put aside.

"Holy cow, look at this. Steph, did you enter this data?"

"That's the reason I asked you here, Don."

Dr. Stephanie Morrison grabbed a medical file and showed it to Dr. Donald Satowski, head of the department.

"What have you found, Stephanie?"

"Corporal Sandoval has all the classic symptoms of a tumor in his occipital lobe. Difficulty speaking and swallowing, hearing loss, morning headache, muscle weakness on one side of the body, vision loss, and vomiting."

Doctor Satowski, a short, wide man with very small silver-rimmed glasses, wasn't alarmed.

"Stephanie, this is unfortunate, but as you know, 20 out of 100,000 people do develop occipital-lobe tumors. But why are four other soldiers' records in this folder?"

Dr. Stephanie Morrison was an unusual woman. She was both a veteran researcher and a top brain surgeon. She wore her unruly hair in a bun, had freckles everywhere, and had been divorced twice. She told her best friends that she was now married to her work. When she wasn't at the center, she wrote and published mystery novels. Slightly over five feet tall, she was roughly the same age as Don Satowski. They had both graduated from MIT in 1972 with degrees in physics. They lost touch, went to different medical schools, and didn't meet again until 1985 when she went to work with him at Stanford.

She took the file from Don and asked him to sit down. A photo of the new Krayton MRI prototype scanner was on the wall right above the couch. Earlier in the day, the scanner had taken images of eight soldiers, including the corporal. It had been in use for only two weeks.

The Krayton scanner was one of three prototypes that had taken five years to develop, and was the first to be tested. Thanks to the new Intel R242 chip, designed specifically for this unit, spectral and 3D image data was processed instantly. There were two sensors that looked like inverted pie plates, mounted on two parallel cantilevered arms. X and Y axis travel was controlled by a joystick, and when the arms rotated they made a whirring sound like an electric toothbrush. Gone was the need for a patient to pass through a claustrophobic tunnel for MRI readings. The

Krayton images were of such high quality that they could be enlarged electronically to ten by twelve feet with perfect detail. The resolution was 50 times greater than had been previously possible. The researchers could now distinguish neural activity at locations separated by as little as .004 millimeters.

"This is what I've got, Don. Here are the photos."

"Steph, you don't need the new Krayton MRI to see the corporal's problem. He has terminal brain cancer. Are you telling me that you found occipital lobe tumors in the other soldiers in this file? Holy cow, is that what you're saying?"

"Not yet, but look at these, Don. To summarize, they haven't yet developed into tumors, but early evidence suggests pre-cancerous cells are present in nine percent of all the people we've scanned in the last two weeks. We expanded the tests to include returning soldiers who had injuries other than head wounds. Seven-point-five percent of them also exhibit the same signs."

Don quickly did the math. "This doesn't mean that they will all develop the disease, but there has to be a cause for such a dramatic increase over normal incidence. Holy cow, this absolutely can't be a random event. Steph, are you sure these results are accurate?" Don looked at the files and then at Stephanie. She responded with obvious annoyance.

"How long have you known me and my work? I've been over these results four times in the last twenty-four hours. I sat in on today's scans and compared the results with what we've done all week."

"And?"

"And we found two more cases."

"I wonder if they've been exposed to vinyl chloride. That's the only thing I can think of that would cause brain cancer in multiple cases. It's a known carcinogen used in manufacturing plastic products, pipes, car parts, stuff like that. God knows what they've been exposed to in Iraq. Please Steph, not a word to anyone. I

5

don't know what's going on here, but we don't need any publicity. We especially don't want the Veteran's Administration snooping around just yet. We need VA approval to continue this research program."

"It's probably too late, Don. Lynch was with me during the testing and he saw the data. He could have spoken to someone about it."

"Call David Feinstein. He's also been working with the Krayton scanner, and he told me he's found something interesting, but he wouldn't say what it was. I'm going to see Lynch right now and tell him to keep quiet. Notify David that we're all going to meet in my office tomorrow morning at eight to discuss our findings and decide what to do next. Make sure all data, both on computer and paper, is secure and protected."

~ ~ ~

David Feinstein was six feet two and one-half inches tall but weighed only 160 pounds. He walked with a slight stoop and generally had a smile on his face. He was thirty-five years old and was the junior researcher on the staff. As he walked into Satowski's office, he wasn't smiling.

The office was large and so cluttered with electronic testing equipment that he had to watch his step. Don was at the far end of a dark mahogany table that had once belonged to the previous department head. His predecessor, now deceased, sat by the window so many times that his elbow wore a two-inch-wide indentation in the finish on the left side of the table. Satowski sat in the same spot but was left-handed, so his elbow rested on the right side. There were eight shabby but very comfortable chairs around the table. Five of them were occupied. Doctors Lynch and Feinstein sat on one side, and Doctor Morrison sat on the other along with Carol Morrison, her daughter, who was the departmental secretary.

Don Satowski had frequent meetings in his office, and he always controlled the tone and content. He was moody; sometimes the tone was light and everyone told jokes. Other times he was displeased, and his staff had better stick to the topic at hand or he could get very testy.

"Thank you all for showing up on time. I hope you've had breakfast; we had no time to pick up doughnuts and coffee. I've asked Carol to record and print out everything we say, and the minutes will be kept here for now. I want this on permanent file because we don't know where it will lead, and it will be very hard to remember who said what later if we have to piece it all back together. Carol, please stop us if you need clarification or explanation on any of the issues; you know how it is when we get going. And please don't rely on that tape recorder. Take notes in case it craps out. Everybody, let's not all gab at once so Carol can keep up. Steph has already filled David in about the brain cancer, and I've told Bob to keep our findings quiet. So, David, what the hell is going on at your end?"

David passed copies of his notes around the table.

"Long story short, I've noticed disturbing changes to brain cells on a basic molecular level. As you all know, I've been using the 4.7 T Bruker/GE CSI Omega MR system for animal and in vitro research to measure brain waves in mice and rats. We linked the Bruker with the new Krayton MRI to expand its range, and I've done random testing of human volunteers. I've been using the scanner at night after you've finished your testing. I believe I've uncovered an important new way that the brain performs complex functions such as pattern recognition. At the molecular level this involves finding the balance between the minus and plus inputs on individual neurons. This allows me to measure the results of moving images in the brain."

7

"What *are* the results?" Satowski asked.

"Bottom line, we've got trouble. The primary visual cortex, where neurons are tuned to the vertical, horizontal, and diagonal lines, gives shape to moving images. Stimulation from moving images evokes different patterns of synaptic inputs, causing the brain to compensate."

"But we know all that, David," Satowski said. "Why do you say there's trouble?"

"Well, I combined my scans with a computer mockup of the visual cortex before and after stimulation with moving visual images, and I noticed basic molecular changes in the cells. I have no way of knowing yet if the changes are permanent or what effect, if any, they are having on the striate cortex."

"Could you repeat that?" Carol asked. "What does this mean in English?"

"The most important thing I learned is that these mutant cells could be deadly. I suggest that we expand the testing so we can understand the relationship between moving images and these changes. I would like..."

"David, hold on a minute," Don interrupted. He was extremely worried. What else was this scanner going to uncover? Don prioritized on the spot.

"Holy cow, David, this is extremely disturbing. Obviously we must look deeply into your findings as soon as we can, but there's something else we have to do first. Why are soldiers returning from Iraq with cancer cells in their fucking brains? I don't want any of you working on anything else. Don't eat, don't sleep, don't wash, don't drink, don't shit until we know what's going on. All right, I have to go. I'll leave all of you to work out the cah-cah. Stay here until you finish. If any of you lets this leak out, I'm going to beat your ass until you think you're a drum."

About fifteen seconds after he shut the door, they all burst into laughter. Carol took out a small red spiral notebook. Steph laughed the loudest.

"*Cah-cah*? Isn't that a new one?" she asked Carol, who was checking through the book.

"It's a new one, but remember our rule, he has to say it at least three times for it to become official. We've already got *beat your ass until you think you're a drum*. This week we also have *get with the program, he's a flaming jerk, holy cow, craps out, everybody wants to get into the act, another rocket scientist*, and *too many chefs spoil the soup*. That counts, doesn't it, even though he didn't say *broth*?"

"Of course it does," David Feinstein replied. "It's a fractured cliché, which is perfectly acceptable, perhaps more desirable."

"I don't understand it," Dr. Robert Lynch commented. "Here's a man with an immeasurably high IQ, who's published six books that have been translated into nearly every major language, and he can't speak a sentence without using some stupid cliché. If I hear 'holy cow' one more time, I'm going walk out of the room."

The rest of them stared at him without saying anything.

"I have to go, got to teach a class in fifteen minutes. Let me know what you need from me." Lynch closed the door with moderate force.

Carol had a guilty look on her face. "Maybe we shouldn't do this."

Stephanie countered, "Don't let Lynch bother you, Carol. He's mad at Don because he didn't get the go-ahead for his project, and his book has so far been rejected by the major houses. Don is basically good-natured. He'll laugh when he finds out about our little list. Remember our bet, the person who comes in last in our baseball pool has to give him the red book as a birthday present along with a bottle of his favorite Bowmar 17-year-old single malt."

David sighed. "I can't get a word in when Don decides to shut down the conversation. I also found the possibility that these mutant cells could migrate to other parts of the body. Steph, you know about the University of Pittsburgh studies showing the cellphone-cancer link. They actually put out warnings that cellphones shouldn't be used by children. My research has also corroborated their data. With the Krayton MRI we can see the first signs of damage. This new problem with screens is going to make cellphones seem insignificant. This is one thousand times worse. "

Stephanie advised him to hold the data for now. He would have a chance to advance his theories later.

~ ~ ~

Robert Lynch made a phone call to Washington and discussed the day's events with the person who was overseeing the treatment of returning soldiers for the Veterans Administration. Lynch suggested that he might want to visit Stanford and have a look for himself. He asked him to keep their conversation confidential. He hung up the phone and felt good that he had gone against his boss's instructions, felt good that he had the power to make his own decisions. It didn't disturb him one bit that his co-workers would be horrified if they knew what he'd done.

Lynch was in his mid-forties, although he looked ten years younger. He was married to the actress Jennifer Wheelan. She had just landed an important role in a new evening soap and wanted to live closer to LA. He was uneasy because she would be making over one million dollars a year, and she was starting to act very independent.

~ ~ ~

Two days later, Stephanie called her brother in Vermont.

"Hello, Steph, I knew it had to be you."

"How did you know?"

"Because it's midnight."

"Oh shit, I did it again. I'm sorry Mario, but it's only 9:00 here."

"Tell me something, Steph. How can such a brilliant woman also be such an airhead?"

"Be nice to me, I haven't talked to you in three weeks. You would make it much easier for me, and everyone else for that matter, if you would only buy a cellphone so I could call you during the day. How can you get along without one? You're supposed to be accessible, but you act like a hermit. Mario, I'm sorry I called so late, but I need your help."

"Cellphones? I hate them. Do you want me to get cancer? What's wrong that you need my help?"

Stephanie gave her brother a complete rundown on the Stanford discoveries. She told him that someone must have contacted the VA, because they were sending a team to California. There was talk that the VA wanted to stop all testing and send returning service men and women elsewhere for treatment.

"Mario, you're the senior senator from Vermont. You're also a ranking member of the Armed Services Committee. Why would the government want to stop our project? This research has got to continue until we find the cause of these altered cells."

"I don't know, Steph. Wow, you have my undivided attention. You know how I feel about these wars in the Middle East. It's always the soldiers and their families who lose out. Suicide rates among veterans are way up. We'll do anything but face the fact that our policies have failed. I think it's possible that the government is hiding something. Maybe our soldiers are being exposed to chemical contamination, what is it again, vinyl chloride? I'll fly out tomorrow morning with Nadene, my chief of staff. You remember her, don't you? When we saw you last year, she drove me to the airport. Do you have any idea who called Washington?"

"Yes, I do. I'll tell you when you get here. By the way, when are you going to renew your driver's license? You don't use a cellphone, you don't drive, you don't own a television, and Nadene has to handle your e-mail for you."

"Steph, do you always wear your big straw hat when you go outside in the bright sun like the doctor told you to?"

"No."

"Then lay off my habits. Besides, I'm older than you are and you should have some respect."

"Older by seven minutes. Because you were born first you want respect. Listen Mario, you can't demand respect. You can demand compliance, you can demand obedience, but not respect. Respect has to be earned."

"Steph, why do you always have to get so heavy and start trouble? You're the only person I know who asks me for help and insults me at the same time."

"It's good for you, Mario. No one else does. Everyone thinks you're perfect. You got sixty-eight percent of the vote in the last election and beat that Republican, what's-his-name. Next time I'm going to tell the voters what you did with Rebecca in the fifth grade, and I'm going to send our home movies to the networks. You know, the one where you lost your bathing suit in our backyard pool."

"Ha, ha, Steph, love you too. How's my lovely niece Carol doing?"

"Fine. She likes her job as departmental secretary."

"Nadene will let you know when we're arriving."

"Of course she will, she's the only one who knows how to use a telephone."

~ ~ ~

David Feinstein had remained in close contact with his college roommate, Takeo Arai, who was now on the faculty of Keio University. He was part of the research team headquartered at the Shinanomachi Campus School of Medicine in Tokyo. Like David, Arai had been studying the effects of moving images on the brain.

Earlier Japanese research had proved that rapidly moving cartoons could cause fits and seizures in children. The Keio team had found evidence that corroborated what David now suspected. The team had conducted extensive tests that showed people who watched more than four hours of television, or played more than four hours of video games, every day for a period of three years or more, exhibited altered cellular structure in their brain. The team needed to use the Krayton scanner to determine if these cells had the potential of becoming cancerous and then possibly migrating to other parts of the body. Takeo was putting pressure on David to arrange a conference and working session between their two groups. Arai's team desperately needed to use the unique scanner to finalize their research. David promised him that he would have things set up in a few days and hung up the phone.

"Oh shit, now I've done it. Don will kill me."

David turned on his stereo. He had burned a disk of the Dave Matthews Band, Norah Jones, and a Vermont group called Grace Potter and the Nocturnals that Carol told him about. He liked their bluesy sound. Carol had been on his mind constantly and he was often distracted. She was twenty-five years old and much taller than her mother, almost five-eight. She had deep auburn hair with red highlights, green eyes, and had inherited her mother's freckles. Carol was not curvy, but he paraphrased what Spencer Tracy once said about Katherine Hepburn: There's not much meat on her bones, but what there is, is choice.

He poured himself a cup of chamomile tea and remembered Columbia University Medical School. He and Takeo had been starting point guards on the basketball team as undergrads. Takeo, who was only five-seven, would rather die than lose. He was second on the team in scoring, so he considered his playing a failure. Everything he ever tried, he attacked with abandon. He had learned English in four months and was immediately writing papers that earned straight A's. He had finished fourth in his graduating class and wouldn't talk about that either. David found it very difficult to say no to Takeo, so he had put himself in a box. He decided to call Stephanie.

"You did what? David, Mario is arriving today with his chief of staff, the Veterans Administration group arrives the day after tomorrow, and you want to schedule a meeting for joint research. Just call Takeo and tell him we have a crisis here."

"Steph, I really want to do this now because I feel we're going in the wrong direction. I believe nothing is happening in Iraq to cause cancer in our troops. I've got to meet with Don and convince him to do this joint research, and I need your help."

"You'll have to convince *me* first. I've got to pick up Mario and Nadene at the San Jose airport, so ride with me and tell me what you've found out. By the way, are you in love with my daughter?"

~ ~ ~

As her twin brother Mario could tell you, Stephanie was an unpredictable mixture of confusing elements. She never used a two-syllable word if she could use a four-syllable one, but she always wore torn jeans. She did the *New York Times* Sunday crossword puzzle in twenty minutes, but often forgot to pay her bills on time.

After insisting that David buckle his seat belt, Stephanie started her Toyota convertible and pulled out into the heavy traffic. She turned left on Galvez Street headed toward El Camino Real. She had big-city driving skills, never made eye contact with other drivers, and kept the small car revved above 3,000 rpm while she made perfect downshifts. She kept a mint-condition restored Jaguar 140 in her garage and took it out for a run every once in a while.

Under her relentless questioning, David admitted that he was in love with Carol, then quickly switched the conversation to his puzzling findings.

"Takeo and I have been comparing our research data. He can't discern images with separations of less than 3.5 millimeters. That's why he needs the Krayton scanner to confirm his findings. But I believe we've both found the same thing at the same time. Exposure to images flashing across a television or computer screen is causing genetic changes to cells on the most basic molecular level.

"In certain people these cells could become cancerous and travel to other parts of the body. I don't have all the answers. If Takeo and I are right, it means that you accidentally discovered the same thing while you were examining the soldiers. You've got to tell Mario and Don not to jump to conclusions until we know more. I believe this has nothing to do with the military, so Mario shouldn't start a witch-hunt in Washington."

Stephanie was so rattled that she popped the clutch at the next light and left a small patch of rubber. She pulled off the road and stared at David.

15

"Call Takeo now on this cellphone and tell him to bring his people over as soon as he can. I will, no, *we* will go see Don right after I brief Mario."

~~~

After inspecting the Stanford facilities, the Veterans Administration made its decision. Returning service personnel would now be treated at the Universities of Georgia and Illinois. Don Satowski was under fire from the Stanford administration for letting the lucrative program slip away. He knew that he'd have to do some hard selling to get the university to back the joint research project, but he thought he could pull it off. David and Takeo's findings were now his top priority. Scientific truth would always come before politics or his own convenience.

~~~

Robert Lynch received a call from John Peterson, head of the Government Office of Domestic Security. "Doctor Lynch, we feel that the Stanford research team may be working against the country's best interests. We would like to discuss several options with you, and we want to move quickly. Can you be here tomorrow at 3:00 Eastern time?"

Lynch agreed to go to Washington.

~~~

Takeo Arai, seven other researchers led by Dr. Ichiro Kobayashi, and two translators arrived at The Richard M. Lucas Center for Magnetic Resonance Spectroscopy and Imaging to begin work with Satowski and his team. Don was upset that Lynch had to leave town due to an illness in the family, and he snapped at David.

"How long have you two been working on this, and why the fuck didn't you tell me earlier? This may be the most important medical discovery of the last 50 years, and you lollygag back and forth with Arai in Japan without saying a word to me."

"I'm sorry, Don, but that's not fair. It all came together at once. I tried to tell you at our meeting. Takeo and I have known each other since college, and we compare notes on just about everything."

"Yeah, yeah, from now on I want to know all the details or you'll be up the creek without a paddle."

~ ~ ~

For the next two weeks, three rooms full of brilliant men and women concentrated, investigated, and confirmed their findings. The scientists, completely gowned in particle-controlling white suits and facemasks, worked at consoles that rivaled the command center of the *Starship Enterprise*. The Japanese shouted back and forth at each other, and the Americans raised their voices to match. Half-eaten pizzas and stale doughnuts still in their boxes were piled on desks in the outer office.

At the end of the session, Doctor Kobayashi and Doctor Satowski issued a joint report to Jerome Pritchard, President of Stanford University. Pritchard assured the team that the university would back their research and vowed to give them whatever they needed. A news conference was scheduled for 10:00 a.m. two days later. The Stanford Public Relations Office contacted all the major media and informed them that this was the most important discovery the university had ever made.

~ ~ ~

At 10 a.m. there were dozens of cameras and two media trucks outside the Sherman Fairchild Auditorium on the Stanford campus. Every cable and wire service was represented, as well as reporters from the *Los Angeles Times* and *New York Times*. The PR group had done its job very well. The research team and about 120 other interested parties were also present in the room. Standing at the ten-foot-wide podium were President Pritchard, Doctor Kobayashi, and Doctor Satowski. Two computers were hooked up to projectors and flashed still photos on large screens on either side of the podium.

Pritchard introduced Doctor Satowski, who read from a prepared statement.

"Thank you for coming, ladies and gentlemen. We have made a very important discovery that will impact the future health of millions of people. With Doctor Kobayashi and his Japanese colleagues, we have conducted and corroborated research that proves that watching moving color images on either a television or computer screen over a period of three years or longer is causing cells to undergo changes in the brain. These cells become pre-cancerous, then cancerous, and travel to other parts of the body."

The audience gasped in shock, and Don had to pause while people made comments to each other.

"It's possible that there is a genetic imprint and the disease could skip a generation before surfacing. People who have been watching television the longest will start to exhibit signs of the disease first. We are already beginning to see a rise in cancer deaths in the United States, since we were the first to have both television and computer screens. We have also found lesser abnormalities in brain tissue as the result of watching moving black and white images, but so far, we do not see the same results in movie theaters using projected images. More study will be needed."

Don cleared his throat and raised his voice. "It is our recommendation that everyone stop watching their screens immediately."

Pandemonium broke out, and it took a full five minutes to restore order.

"A complete report of our technical findings will be published this week in the *New England Journal of Medicine, Australian Medicine,* and the *Journal of the Japan Medical Association.* My colleagues David Feinstein and Takeo Arai, who were first to discover this link, are filing a report with the United Nations World Health Organization. They are scheduled to appear before WHO next week. It is our recommendation that an international medical conference be held at the UN, with the best minds in the world, to continue this research. Right after we take questions, we'll provide a slide presentation with some of the technical details. Doctor Kobayashi and I will try to answer your questions now." Ichiro Kobayashi joined Don at the microphone.

"Doctor Kobayashi, Sid Hersch, *New York Times.* Do you honestly think that people are going to turn off their televisions and stop using computers?"

"Mr. Hersch, we have presented the facts. We have no control over what people will or will not do. These are our recommendations based on those facts."

"Come on, get real!" Metro Media reporter Kalie Kohn shouted. "You're asking the world to stop running. It's absolutely impossible, it's totally ridiculous."

"Look, Ms. Kohn," Satowski replied, "what we're looking at is an epidemic five times larger than the AIDS epidemic. It will start very slowly, but if nothing is done, in a few decades the death toll will be in the hundreds of millions. It will appear first in the developed countries, starting with the United States. It may happen to you or your children. Like it or not, these are the facts."

Kohn said angrily, "Who cooked up this research? Isn't it possible that you're wrong and your conclusions are in error?"

Pritchard responded calmly. "The research is thorough and accurate.   Stanford and Keio Universities stand behind the findings. We must....."

Kohn interrupted. "The last thing we need is..."

"The last thing we need is any more cah-cah from you, Ms. Kohn," Satowski cut her off. "Next question."

"Mario McGuire, U.S. senator from Vermont. Why did the VA stop using Stanford as a treatment center for returning service men and women?"

Pritchard replied that the VA had not yet given them a reason.

McGuire said, "Is there anything that you would advise the United States government to do?"

"Same thing we're going to do when we get back to Japan, tell them to pass a law to ban screens," Kobayashi responded.

"Sal Cataldi, AP. Is there any way people can minimize the danger and still watch their favorite shows?"

"There's no way," Satowski answered. "There are no filters, mirrors, or other devices that will protect the viewer. It doesn't matter how the images reach the visual cortex. When they get there, they do the damage."

The news conference continued for another half-hour. Veteran, hard-boiled reporters who had seen everything were suddenly very quiet and frightened. Some shook their heads in disbelief; several were weeping.

Kalie Kohn shouted, "This is bullshit! You wait, everyone will know it's bullshit!" She led her camera crew out of the room and called her boss, Harold Slokov, President of Metro Media.

~ ~ ~

Stephanie, Mario, David, Carol, Takeo, and his wife Sara sat in Stephanie's living room on two long couches placed at right angles to each other. In the corner, where the couches met, was a square table holding a lamp made from an old brass alto saxophone. Alongside the lamp were four tickets to New York City.

Mario said, "Now remember, don't spend all your time working. After you make your presentation at the UN, drive up to Vermont and spend a few days. We can put the four of you up, no need to use a hotel. Besides, I've decided to try to implement something on a local level, and I could use your help. I'll give you the details when you get to Vermont. Your plane leaves in two hours, so you'd better get moving. Security screening is tight because a new terrorist alert has just been posted. It'll probably take you an hour to get through the check-in."

The two couples said goodbye to Mario and Stephanie, then departed for the airport.

"Steph, are they serious about each other, Carol and David?"

"David is in love with Carol. I asked him if she was in love with him, and he said no. But when I asked her if she was in love with him, she said yes. Which proves yet again that men are stupid."

"Here we go, don't you ever let up for a minute, Steph? I happen to think it's great."

"He's ten years older than she is."

"So what? I'm ten years older than Julie."

"And you two fight all the time."

"I know we have our problems, but it has nothing to do with our age difference. We would both fight no matter who we were married to. Some people are calm, composed, and quiet. Others are not. Besides, you should talk. You've had two marriages and three other serious relationships that went on longer than five years, including your on-again, off-again thing with Don. Why the hell don't the two of you get married and get it over with?"

"Because it would ruin our working relationship."

"Okay, Steph, it's really none of my business anyway. Thanks for the slide presentation disk. I'm sure Nadene can get a projector and we can present your findings when we get home. Oh, one other thing, in all this excitement I forgot to ask you. Who do you think tipped off Washington?"

"It was Lynch. David is 100% trustworthy. So that leaves me, Carol, or Robert Lynch.

"Do you have proof?"

"Oh, I have proof, all right. The day after he came back from 'visiting his sick brother' we had a nice chat. I could tell that he was lying. Besides, his story was so easy to refute. There were no planes flying from Fargo to San Francisco on the day he was supposedly traveling. No planes from Fargo to Chicago and on to San Francisco or San Jose either. He should have picked a place that was better traveled. There's your proof. He's about as forthright as that VA administrator. I'll bet they have been in contact all along. I'm going to ask Don to fire him."

"Steph, you be careful. I don't want you locking horns with the people in Washington. If a department head or cabinet member is doing something shady, or even illegal, he can cause trouble."

"You can't be serious, Mario! Who the hell is afraid of them?"

"I know how they operate, Steph. Remember the CIA leak that put Valerie Plame in danger? They'll plant evidence to discredit you and start rumors to undermine your career and family life. They're very skilled at thwarting people who go against their agenda."

"Who the hell are *they*?"

~ ~ ~

American Airlines flight 2375 touched down at Kennedy Airport, runway number two, and the plane taxied to the terminal. Takeo and David both smiled. David hadn't been to New York since he left medical school. Sara Levine was from Queens, so she and Takeo visited her family there three times a year. Carol Morrison had never been to the Big Apple. David and Takeo reminisced about the great meals they used to have at Sammy Wo's in Chinatown.

"Do you remember B.B. King, John Hyatt, and Cassandra Wilson at the Apollo?" Takeo asked.

"Best concert I ever saw," David responded as he took his and Carol's carry-on luggage from the overhead compartment. Three rows behind them were two casually dressed men quietly watching them. They strained to listen as Takeo told Carol how they would get to the hotel. Carol glanced at the men, and they both looked away.

The four friends got into a yellow cab. The two men got into a waiting Volvo station wagon and followed discreetly behind the cab. They were in radio contact with two other men in a dark blue, windowless Ford van with "Crazy Marvin's Used Cars, Astoria, Queens" painted on both sides. It was traveling alongside the cab on First Avenue. Carol and Sara were laughing as the foursome left the cab at 304 East 42nd Street and entered the Crowne Plaza Hotel lobby. A tall, distinguished-looking Catholic priest stepped from the van and entered the lobby directly behind them. He stood next to Carol alongside a brown velvet rope attached to two silver posts. David handed a Platinum Visa card to the hotel clerk.

"Here are your keys, rooms 702, 703, and 704, non-smoking. The lounge is open until 2:00 a.m. and both restaurants close at midnight. Enjoy your stay." The clerk passed three keys across the desk to David.

"Good evening, Father," Carol said, turning to look at the priest.

He flashed a broad smile and said, "And top of the evening to you, miss."

She noticed a strong smell of garlic coming from the priest as he walked away from the desk and out of sight. He waited a few minutes in the lobby, nonchalantly reading the sports pages of the *Times*, then walked outside and got into the Volvo.

~ ~ ~

Robert Lynch recognized the voice at once as his new contact in Washington, John Peterson, director of Domestic Security. "Six million dollars has been deposited in Cayman Island account D457947. The password you will need to access the money is grefab723uio. Remember the account number and password. You don't need to give them your name. The IRS has no record of the transaction, so there will be no taxes to pay. I've fulfilled my part of our bargain, Robert. What have you got for me?"

It was Friday, 8:00 p.m. Eastern time. Every Friday there would be a call at 8:00 p.m., and every week Lynch was expected to have fresh information. This week it was easy.

"You already know that Feinstein, Arai, and two women are in New York. They're headed north after they appear at the UN, to meet with Morrison's brother, Senator McGuire. I overheard him tell his sister that he's going to introduce legislation in Vermont to ban TV. The Japanese delegation has finished their work and they're headed back to Tokyo tomorrow afternoon."

Lynch hung up the phone, took the piece of paper on which he'd scribbled his account number and password, and made a copy of it. He placed the copy in his wallet and the original in the first book on the second shelf of his library, *The South Beach Diet*, between pages 22 and 23.

He called his wife Jennifer and teased her. "Hello sweets, I just bought you a present, but I'm not going to tell you what it is until Saturday night."

~ ~ ~

The World Health Organization of the United Nations had its offices in Geneva. Most meetings were held there, but occasionally the director and his staff were at New York headquarters for other business. David and Takeo had made special arrangements to meet with the director and team scientists, due to the critical nature of their discovery. The group would meet in the Economic and Social Council Chamber, which was a gift from the people of Sweden.

The team was in David's hotel room planning their presentation. Sara went over the inventory of slide-show equipment while Carol called the desk to arrange for a dry-cleaning pickup.

"While you're at it, have them send up a bottle – no make that two bottles – of Sebastiani Zinfandel. 2005, if they have it, but 2006 is all right," Takeo said. He and David were nervous. Neither of them had ever given such an important presentation. A thump against the door made both men start. Sara looked through the peephole but saw nothing. Takeo opened the door to find the evening edition of the *New York Times*. On page one was a large article about them and their mission. This made him even more uneasy.

"I was hoping we could slip in and out of New York without any publicity, but it ain't gonna happen," Takeo said. "I'm glad no one saw us check in here."

Carol picked up a brochure about the United Nations and read aloud to help break the tension. "Hey, listen to this, here's a paragraph about the room you'll be using tomorrow."

A special feature of the Social Council Chamber is the exposed pipes and ducts in the ceiling above the public gallery. The architect believed that anything useful should be left uncovered. The 'unfinished' ceiling is commonly seen as a symbolic reminder that the economic and social work of the United Nations never finishes; there will always be something more that can be done to improve the living conditions of the world's people.

David forced a smile. "Or maybe they just ran out of money to finish the ceiling." He asked the others whether they had watched their TVs to see if there were any other media reports. They all looked at him with alarm. "Oops, it's going to take me a while to get used to this."

Sara walked over to the 30-inch Philips flat-screen set, stretched out her hand, but didn't touch it.

"My God, what do I tell my mother? She watches *The Guiding Light*, *The Today Show*, *Oprah*, *Wheel of Fortune*, *American Idol*, *Dancing with the Stars*, and *The Tonight Show*. It's been a comfort to her since she's been sick."

Takeo shouted at her. "Our findings will have to be accepted by everyone, including your mother. What's the big deal? Tell her to just turn the fucking thing off and read a good book. What did people do before they had TV, sit on the floor and play with themselves?"

"Takeo, that's not fair, and don't shout at me because you're nervous. I'm not your personal punching bag."

"I'm sorry, Sara. Listen, the two of you can't stay with us all day. We're going into several closed-door meetings that will last for hours. Take off on your own and do some shopping."

"Bad idea," Carol objected. "Just tell them we're part of your research team. Mario told Sara and me not to go wandering around New York by ourselves."

"Sounds paranoiac," David said, "but unfortunately, Mario is usually right. Okay, stay with us just to be safe."

~ ~ ~

David moved to the small lounge in front of the TV. There was a vase of white daisies on a kidney-shaped glass table, between two loveseats. Above one seat was a copy of *Woman in White* by Picasso. The color theme was continued with a large, fluffy white comforter tucked neatly around the king-sized bed, and two fat pillows. A single small, square red pillow with fringe was tastefully placed in the center.

The room was remarkably quiet, with only the occasional sound of a car horn leaking through. The Crowne Plaza had been built in 1931 and was originally named the Tudor. It had 300 rooms on 20 floors and had housed heads of state from every continent. The staff spoke fifteen languages. They got to use all of them.

At 9:30 that evening the quartet had just finished a round of Taboo, a word-association game that Carol had recently discovered. It was the girls against the boys. The final score was girls 23, boys 16.

"I'm glad you brought this game along, Carol," David said with gratitude. "How did you know we would be able to... how did you know we would need to..." He stopped talking and just looked at her.

Carol waited for him to say something else. When he didn't speak, she said, "It's late, I'm going back to my room and get a good night's sleep."

"Yeah, right." Takeo stood and stretched. "I guess we'll try to get some sleep, too. Good night, see you at 6 sharp. "

Carol looked over her shoulder at David as she walked out of his room. Alone, David crawled onto the right side of the huge bed. He absentmindedly grabbed the remote and turned on the TV. He recovered quickly and turned it off before the sound came on. He felt vaguely guilty. He should be thinking about tomorrow, but all he could think about was Carol. *I don't think she likes me. Not that way.* He took a copy of Stephanie's latest mystery from his suitcase, *The Beckwith Murders*. David marveled at how well she did the sex scenes, but his eyes were weary, so he put the book down and donned his headphones. His iPod played *Concierto de Aranjuez* by Rodrigo. John Williams was the guitarist.

Carol was in her room, reclining on the left side of her bed. She had on a green silk teddy that was designed to be removed by a lover. She had said quiet prayers for everyone: for David, for Mario, for Takeo and Sara, for her mother and Don, for everyone but herself. Out of nowhere, she had a flashback of the blond priest at the hotel desk, the one who smelled of garlic. She was not sure why, but she knew he wasn't a priest. Perhaps it was the way he looked at her when her group walked away. And his voice just didn't match his face. The newspaper was probably a prop. Why didn't he have any luggage? Tomorrow she would ask the desk clerk if any priests were registered at the hotel.

She was suddenly irritated at herself for thinking like a frightened little girl, and got out of bed. It was time for grownup Carol to make her move. She slipped into her matching green satin robe and sprayed some Norell perfume between her breasts.

David heard a soft knock on his door and looked through the peephole. He opened the door wide, and Carol jumped on him so hard that he staggered backward and fell onto the bed with her in his arms.

~ ~ ~

New York in May can be very beautiful. The tulips in Central Park were in bloom. This morning, there was a northern breeze that had cleaned the air. The temperature was sixty degrees and a red, pink, blue, and purple sunrise framed the buildings and reflected everywhere off the skyscrapers. The moon was setting, and both the sun and the moon were clearly visible in the dawn sky.

It was 6:45 a.m., and Sara marveled at the sunrise as the four walked outside to hail a cab for the UN. A blue van appeared suddenly at the hotel curb. The doors burst open, and four hooded men grabbed them and tossed them onto bench seats right behind the driver. Sara screamed. Takeo kicked one of the attackers but was quickly subdued by the other men. They were handcuffed and gagged, and hoods were yanked over their heads. Carol was crying. None of the four knew whom they were sitting next to. None of the attackers said a word. There were clicking sounds as ammo clips were snapped into position.

They had traveled for about ten minutes when the faint sound of two-way communications through a headset was heard.

"Fox Leader Two, this is Fox Leader One, do you copy?"

"Copy, Leader One, go ahead."

"Abort, complete abort, Leader Two. Copy?"

"Roger, Leader One."

Carol smelled garlic. The van's driver slammed on the brakes and stopped at First Avenue and Nineteenth Street. Their handcuffs were removed, and the four captives were shoved out onto the sidewalk along with their computer cases. David and Takeo tore off their hoods in time to read "Crazy Marvin's Used Cars" as the van sped away.

"Is anyone hurt?" Takeo asked, trying to keep his composure. Sara's knee was bloodied. He took a bandage from his small pocket medical kit and dressed the wound. They clung to each other, and Carol took out her cellphone to call the police.

"No," Sara begged, "let's get a cab and go straight to the UN How do we know that wasn't the police? Who can we trust? My God, they might be the military, the CIA, or some other government agency. I heard someone called Fox Leader give them the order to abort."

"So did I," Carol agreed. "David, do you remember the priest I said good evening to last night? He had a peculiar smell of garlic, not like on a pizza, but more like people who take garlic pills. I smelled the same thing just now in that van."

"I smelled it too," David said. "Do you think you would recognize him?"

Takeo said, "I don't get it, I noticed that van riding alongside us yesterday when we were in the cab on our way to the hotel. They go to all the trouble of tailing and kidnapping us. Then they let us go and don't even take our computer cases? Why? David, I kicked one of them, and I think I broke his arm. Perhaps he'll go to a hospital for treatment."

"Not around here, he won't," Sara replied. "They'll completely disappear. Calling the police will just make us look stupid. It was too early in the morning for there to be witnesses, and we can't prove anything. I'll bet there is no Crazy Marvin's Used Cars. Do you think they were just trying to scare us?"

"It worked," David said in a strained voice. "But I don't understand why they didn't threaten us, like 'Go to the UN and you're dead.' Or 'Stop this research or we'll kill your family'."

"Please don't talk like that," Carol pleaded. "Let's do this and then go to Vermont."

David kissed Carol and said, "I was afraid our lives were over just when mine has finally begun." Takeo and Sara looked at them and smiled.

~ ~ ~

The four gathered themselves, took a cab to the United Nations, and apologized to the World Health Organization for arriving forty-five minutes late for their meeting. The presentation was successfully made and recorded at the Social Council Chamber. Copies of the slide presentation were given to the WHO liaison to the United States. Sara was afraid to return to the Crowne Plaza and didn't want to leave the UN.

Takeo reassured her. "It will be okay to go back now because there are people everywhere. The doorman will be out front. Let's go outside and just select a random cab. I know, I'll tell the press where we're staying. There'll be an army of reporters outside the hotel waiting to interview us. No one will dare try to hurt us with so many people around."

"Let them follow us to the restaurant, who cares about privacy now?" David suggested. "We can fly to Vermont in the morning."

~ ~ ~

They had finished their meal and were back in David's room. Takeo had just opened a bottle of Zinfandel when they were surprised by a phone call from Nadene Johnson, Mario's chief of staff, who was in the lobby. David told her to come up, and waited by the door to let her in.

"Hey guys, which one of you has an extra bed? This place is full up," Nadene said as she entered the room.

"You can have your own room," David said with total happiness in his voice.

"Mario sent me to drive you back to Vermont tomorrow. He doesn't want any of you hanging around in airports. I'm going to take you and Carol to Montpelier, and continue on to Montreal with Takeo and Sara." Nadene turned to the Arais. "You two are booked on a flight back to Tokyo. We're scared to death after that incident this morning."

"Nadene, how did you hear about it?" Sara asked.

"Carol called her mom from the UN, and Stephanie called Mario," Nadene responded.

~ ~ ~

The friends were together listening to WINS all-news radio at exactly 8:00 p.m. when the lead story was broadcast.

"American Airlines flight 3358 with 117 people on board has crashed into the Pacific about 80 miles southeast of Yokohama, Japan. It was on its way to Tokyo International Airport. Among the passengers was the delegation of scientists returning to Keio University from their historic joint research project at Stanford University in California. There are unconfirmed reports that the pilot of a Japan Air flight outbound for San Francisco believed he saw a missile hit the plane. It is not known if there were military aircraft or ships in the area. There are no other details at this time."

Takeo picked up the bottle of Zinfandel, drank what was left in one long gulp, then shattered it against the television screen.

CHAPTER TWO

Metro Media was huge. It owned a sizeable percentage of everything that controlled what people watched, heard, or read: 127 television stations, the Universal Cable Network, 229 radio stations, 32 major newspapers, 109 Balcony Theaters, and 19 wireless telecommunications networks. Their main office was in Dallas. The Metro Media building was the largest glass-fronted building in Texas and would still be considered large if it were in New York or Chicago.

On the thirty-ninth floor was a conference room with armed guards at the entrance. Today, eight people sat at an olivewood table with Italian marquetry inlays around all the edges. The leather chairs, twenty on either side plus two at each end, were fully adjustable in every direction. On the walls were original paintings by Andrew Wyeth and Norman Rockwell. The group was clustered at the right end of the table near a wet bar and two carts loaded with French and Austrian pastries. There were six different kinds of blended coffee available. The one-way windows were made of a specially designed glass that could be seen through only from inside. There was soundproofing on all surfaces. There were no tape recorders or video cameras. What went on in that room, stayed in that room.

Harold Slokov was at the head of the table. Sitting close by were members of the Wenman family, owners of the WenCo retail giant, and the CEOs of Supreme Oil of Houston and Eagle Claw Security Systems. A special representative of the Government Office of Domestic Security was also present.

Beatrice Wenman, CEO of WenCo, spoke first. "We are very concerned about what Harold and, what's your reporter's name, Kalie, told us last week. If this thing gets out of hand we stand to lose billions of dollars. We depend on television for our advertising, to create a demand for our goods. I'll get right to the point, Harold. We'll do anything to stop this movement from going any further."

Slokov asked John Peterson of Domestic Security to fill everyone in on the latest developments.

"I want to hear only one thing," Ludlowe Wenman, Beatrice's son, interrupted. "I want to hear a plan that shuts these people up permanently. Do you understand what I'm saying? They're about to ruin the country. Do I have to remind you that WenCo is the sixteenth largest economy in the world? This is war."

Peterson said, "We agree with you, Ludlowe, so we've already taken care of a few things. We've got an informant at Stanford who's working with us. We're going to try to discredit the scientists. For now, the Japanese delegation is no longer a problem, although they may regroup and have to be dealt with later. We've prepared information on the people we have to bring down."

"Why not just kill them and get it over with?" Beatrice Wenman asked.

"Good question. We don't want to provide the 'ban TV' movement with any martyrs. News of the ban is sweeping the country; it's actually sweeping the world. We have to be creative on how we're going to stop it."

Harold Slokov informed the group that he had used his vast fact-finding network along with Peterson's government resources to prepare information packets on the people they had to neutralize. He passed them around the table.

"So far, there is one main group of troublemakers, headed by Senator Mario McGuire, the only Independent in the U.S. Senate.

He's trying to get the Vermont legislature to ban TV. He's 58 years old and was born in New York City. His mother, Sophia Bavetta, is Italian and his father, Patrick McGuire, was Irish. The family moved to Vermont when he and his twin sister Stephanie were nine years old. His family ran a weekly newspaper, the *Barre-Montpelier Clarion*. In the late fifties, circulation dropped because advertisers went to the local television station instead of advertising in the *Clarion*. His father's health deteriorated, and in 1970 he died a bitter, impoverished man. So his son Mario has an anti-TV agenda. A man with a vendetta is a vulnerable man, remember that.

"McGuire had to work hard to support his mother and sister, and he also put himself through college. He served two years in Vietnam as a MedEvac chopper pilot. His wife Julie is ten years younger, and I'll talk more about her later. His sister Stephanie is one of the researchers who discovered this time bomb. She and her colleague and sometimes-lover Don Satowski will also have to be neutralized. I'll have more on their backgrounds next week. Peterson and I are planning to deposit money into their bank accounts and trap them with accusations of fraud.

"Nadene Johnson is McGuire's chief of staff. She was born in Greenville, South Carolina and moved to Vermont in 1995 after serving three years in the U.S. Marines. She's a 38-year-old African American, and was a former sergeant with the Burlington Police Department. She quit when she earned her master's degree in music. She always carries a gun and is the most capable person they have.

"Rosa Montez is 22 and has been working on McGuire's staff for a year. She was born in Mexico, moved to Vermont, and graduated from Saint Michael's College.

"Sethos Azizi was born in El Minya, Egypt. He's 25 years old and is the newest member of McGuire's group. He attended the

University of Vermont on a basketball scholarship and stayed in the US. He's an information specialist and an electrical engineer.

"There are two others that need to be watched, but we don't have much info on them as yet. One is David Feinstein, a Jewish researcher, and the other is Carol Morrison, Stephanie's daughter."

"What about that Jap scientist who got away?" Lyle Sinton of Supreme Oil asked.

"He's headed back to Japan and is not a major concern for us at this time, but we're watching his movements," Peterson answered.

"So, look at this shit," Ludlowe Wenman said. "There's a yid, a jap, a wetback, a towelhead, and a spook. How fucking international."

"My son has a point," Beatrice interjected. "Perhaps we can discredit them because they aren't really Americans."

"That will be very difficult," Peterson answered. "This isn't the same country it was in the 1940s. *We* will soon be in the minority. We have to go in another direction. McGuire and his staff have formed a music group. They play some sort of rock and roll together to unwind before staff meetings. Since they are weird, we can exploit their eccentricities. We need to emphasize that 'different' isn't better, if you know what I mean. We need to show people that they're wackos who are trying to take over the country."

"What do they call themselves, The Mulattos?" Ludlowe chuckled as he dripped whipped cream on his blue tie. Pieces of rum cake were stuck to his chin and he belched loudly. Beatrice kicked him under the table.

Harold Slokov, clearly annoyed, slapped his hand on the polished tabletop.

"We're dealing with Super Mario here, folks. Only he's not an action game hero. He is a super pain in the ass who has to be taken seriously. In this game our job is to give him a permanent dungeon hazard." They all laughed loudly, and Ludlowe spat crumbs on his mother.

Slokov said, "We'll meet again in seven days and report on what we've accomplished." He then deferred to John Peterson, who presented the action items.

"Eagle Claw will put a bug in Montez's apartment. She will be easiest to get to, and she has the same knowledge as the rest of them. They won't make any moves without our knowing what they are.

"Lyle and Beatrice, you are to use your best lawyers and prepare a team to defend TV at the Vermont hearings. It's also a good idea to have a topnotch quick-response legal team in place in case they're needed in other states. Harold, you're going to approach Julie McGuire and see if she can be persuaded to side against her husband. Word is out in Washington that they may have separated, and she could be angry with him. We can try to discredit him through her. We may also be able to trump up an affair between McGuire and Montez.

"Harold, I want you to use your photographic resources to shadow them at all times. If you can get pictures of them taking dumps, I want you to do it. Be prepared to offer Julie McGuire whatever she asks for. We've just bought a seven-million-dollar home in the Virgin Islands. Use that as part of the bait if you have to. Every person has a price. Just make sure she does what we want her to. I'll continue my weekly calls to Lynch, our informant at Stanford.

"Harold, you're also to prepare a series of infomercials blasting the Stanford findings. Don't forget, the audience is the same people who are shopping at WenCo, so don't get too fancy or philosophical. 'Don't let them take away our TVs,' something simple like that. We'll talk about it at our next meeting. My job is to get additional data on Feinstein and Carol Morrison, and my boss has another related project that I'll discuss later." Peterson took a sip of coffee.

"Who is your boss?" Sinton asked.

"Let's just call him Best Friend," Peterson replied.

Ludlowe grabbed a Danish, wrapped a napkin around it, and stuffed it in his pocket. They all exited past the guards, except for Slokov and Peterson, who remained in the room.

"Harold, Best Friend gave me the order to abort the New York mission. There was too much publicity. We didn't have enough time to arrange for hits to look like random violence, so we had to call it off. There will be other opportunities if he gives us the order. For now, let's pursue the options we discussed. See you next week."

~ ~ ~

Nadene was driving a beige Crown Victoria across the Tappan Zee Bridge, on her way to the New York Throughway, then north to Burlington, Vermont. It was a big car that her boss liked because ever since he got back from Vietnam, his stomach became queasy whenever he rode. For McGuire, smoother was better. The smaller the car, the worse he felt.

Takeo had not shed one tear. He looked at Sara calmly, and said, "I should have been on that plane. Kobayashi was like my favorite uncle. He did everything for us. He gave us credit for our discovery and let us make the presentation to the UN rather than doing it himself. It should have been me on that plane." Sara said nothing, but squeezed her husband's hand.

"Yo, hold on here," Nadene scolded. "Number one, you can't bring them back. Number two, fate, God, call it what you want, was on your side because you're still alive. Somebody is telling you that your work isn't finished. When you get back to Japan, you assemble a new team and keep right on truckin' in their memory."

Takeo pumped his fist and gave a loud "yes!", then put his head on Sara's shoulder and began to weep. David was sitting in the front seat. He reached back and patted his friend on the shoulder. Twenty miles down the road Nadene broke the silence, turned, and looked at David.

"Were you raised in California? Is that where your parents live?"

"No, I grew up in Massachusetts. My father is a cardiologist at Mass. General Hospital."

"Is that why you became a doctor, to be like your father?"

"I guess so, but for a long while my parents were disappointed in me because I became a researcher instead of a heart specialist. They're always trying to make me feel guilty about something."

Carol laughed.

"But look what you've done, look what y'all have done," Nadene said. "I'll bet your dad never had his photo on page one of the *New York Times*."

David asked Nadene what she wanted to do next with her life.

"Simple, hon, I'm going to make a CD of songs I write and sing. If I don't become rich and famous, after all this is over I'm going to teach music in some high school. I'm also going to continue to take care of my husband and kids."

"That doesn't sound so simple," David said.

After passing Saratoga Springs on Highway 87, Nadene pulled into a rest area so she and Carol could use the restroom. Carol was unable to open the car door because the child locks were activated.

"Sorry, Carol," Nadene said. "I have them on all the time because I'm always driving my kids around. I have to unlock your door from the outside."

Sara asked David if there were any tissues on the front seat. He found none so he opened the glove box. There were none there either, but there was something else that startled him, a Ruger 45 automatic pistol with Hogue rubber grips and two extra clips. There was also a box of CorBon PowerBall 165 grain ammo under the clips. Nadene saw him close the compartment as she walked back to the car.

"That's my backup weapon, David," she informed him.

"I was just looking for some tissues."

"No problem." She opened her purse and handed him some.

"What's your primary weapon?" Takeo asked.

"Same thing." She lifted up her overblouse to reveal another Ruger P90, 45 caliber auto in an Uncle Mike's inside-the-waistband holster.

"Oh my God," Carol said, "I hate guns."

David said, "Neat, can I look at it?"

"No. Hands off, shut that glove box," Nadene barked.

~ ~ ~

Rosa Montez had an apartment in an old three-story building with a 40-foot covered balcony at the top of State Street in Montpelier, Vermont. It was about two miles from the Capitol and had a phenomenal view of the city. In the winter, when there were no leaves on the trees, she could see the top of the golden dome below. Tonight she was cleaning the house in preparation for an important meeting. Mario, Sethos, Nadene, and the others would arrive at 7:00 that evening. They were going to plan their strategy and present their case to Governor Howard and the General Assembly at 10:00 a.m. tomorrow. Rosa was listening to Los Lobos, and then to the Neville Brothers. The volume was high so she could hear over the noise of the vacuum cleaner: "One world, one heart, let's get together and feel alright."

Rosa was five-four, exactly a foot shorter than Seth. She and Seth could be mistaken for brother and sister. They both had black hair, dark brown eyes, and olive skin. Rosa had a body that should be registered as a lethal weapon. She was braless, and she danced and swung her hips as she salsaed the old Hoover around the dining room rug. Rosa's apartment was large, about 1,800 square feet. It took up the entire third floor of an old house that had been used as a cooking school until 1983, when it was converted to three separate units. The landlord lived in Florida.

Seth would arrive at 6:30, ahead of the others, so Rosa wanted to look hot. She planned on sitting next to him on the couch and flirting as shamelessly as possible. She wondered if it could work, a Muslim and a Catholic. *He doesn't seem very religious; perhaps he won't care.* She fantasized about being married to him and traveling to Egypt to meet his parents. Would they make her wear a black burkha whenever she went outside? The phone rang, so she turned down the music to talk to her mother in Burlington.

"Hello, Ma."

"Rosa, I haven't seen you in two weeks, why do you forget about me?"

"Ma, you know I was in Washington."

"Washington, Washington, when am I going to meet that boy you told me about?"

"I don't know, Ma, give me a chance. I have to go out with him first."

"Let me tell you something, I know what your problem is. Ever since you were fourteen, you cause trouble because you're too timid. There have been a fist fight, two broken marriages, and remember that fat one who bought you a new Chevrolet. You hated him, and got in big trouble when you wouldn't give the car back. You're not married yet, and you're almost 25. You are a good girl but men see how you look and they get horny. You have to pick them. You don't have to be sexy, not right away. First you

41

find a good professional man with a future. What's this boy's name?"

"Sethos."

"Sethos. What is he, Greek? That can be okay. So, listen to me. You pick him but you have to make it seem like he is picking you."

"Thanks, Ma. That may have worked for you in Mexico, but not here in Vermont."

"Ay, por Dios. Men are the same everywhere."

Rosa's mother, Elena, was right. Rosa had been chased by nearly every man under 50 that she'd ever met. She had given in a couple of times, but was always unhappy with the men she picked, or as Elena said, who picked her. She decided to change into a loose-fitting black cotton dress that ended six inches below her knees. She added a silver necklace and two-inch matching silver dangle earrings. There, Mom, she thought to herself, I'm very proper.

She prepared canapés of focaccia bread with rosemary olive oil, and three types of cheeses. There was a bottle of sweet orange muscat wine and a tray of tiny tulip-shaped cordial glasses. She had found the beautiful flower-painted tray at a flea market in Charlotte last summer.

As Rosa had hoped, Seth was first to arrive. If there were an Egyptian or Greek God look-alike contest, he would win it. He had a charming accent. His R's were slightly rolled and his consonant sounds were softer than the average American's. He was modest and spoke softly, which added to his appeal. He had been working on a new program for Mario, putting in twelve-hour days for the last week, and was very tired. He handed Rosa a box of Champlain Chocolates and took off his jacket. She thanked him for the chocolates and tossed the jacket on the couch.

"Would you like some wine? I made some canapés."

"Coffee would be better, if you have some. I've got to try to stay awake." Seth yawned and smiled at the same time.

He watched Rosa walk across the living and dining rooms to the kitchen. He liked the way she looked but thought that she was trying to hide in that dress. It wasn't working. Every time she turned or bent down, the supple cloth filled and gathered in places that stirred his imagination. He suddenly found it easy to stay awake.

Rosa heard footsteps coming up the stairs and knew that the rest of her company was a half-hour early. This made her unhappy, but she forced a smile as Nadene and her four passengers arrived.

Nadene smiled at Rosa, but then became brusque. "Listen, I'm going to pick up Mario. Here's a list of what he wants to accomplish this evening. Please set up the slide presentation, we have a lot of work to do, folks."

~ ~ ~

Mario was at his mother's house. She lived on College Street in Montpelier. Her house was a charming Cape that her son and daughter had bought for her. She rarely used the upstairs anymore, even though Mario had one of those lift chairs installed. Mrs. Sophia McGuire was 83 years old. She hugged Mario hard as he was about to leave.

"Nadene will be here in a few minutes, Mom, so remember what I told you. Let Greta help you with the housework; don't do it all yourself."

"I know, I know, Patrick," she replied. "Where's Julie? I haven't seen her in a long time."

"She's in Boston, shopping with her friend Paula."

"You don't spend enough time with that girl. She's a beautiful woman. You neglect her. Don't be stupido."

Mario saw the car outside and gave his mother one last hug before he got in the Crown Victoria. "How was your trip?" he asked Nadene.

She filled him in. "They're all waiting at Rosa's."

"That's fine. There are some new developments, and we may be looking at an all-night meeting. Did you eat dinner?"

"No, we were all supposed to go to Sarducci's, remember?"

"We can't spare the time. I'm going to need everyone's full attention. This can't be a party, this is a work session. When we get to Rosa's we'll call Sarducci's for some pizza."

"I don't think they deliver, but we can call for pizza, manicotti, whatever, and someone can pick it up," Nadene suggested. "How's your mom?"

"She's fine, but she sometimes calls me by my father's name and she repeats herself a lot."

"Give her a break, she's 83."

"I know, but it hurts me. She misses my father a lot. It's been thirty years since he died. She never thought of remarrying. They had a strong love that she could never replace. How are Oscar and the kids?"

Nadene told him that her husband was anxious to get back into the field. Oscar Johnson worked for Homeland Security in Cambridge, Vermont. He was a Special Agent with ICE, Immigration and Customs Enforcement. She and Oscar had met when both were in the Marine Corps. ICE had him bottled up in a desk job, and he wanted something more active. She asked Mario if he could help. He didn't promise anything, but said he would try to pull a few strings to get Oscar moved from office work.

"Where's Julie?"

"She's in Florida with her friend Alice."

"How long has it been since you two got it on?"

"Nadene!"

"Listen Mario, you've been looking at me funny lately."

"I have not!"

"Yes, you have, and you know I'm true blue."

"I have not. Of course I know you don't play around, that's a terrible thing to say."

"Maybe so, but you gotta do something."

"I wish you'd stop saying things just for shock value. But you're right, I'm beginning to feel like a priest."

~ ~ ~

Back at Rosa's apartment, Mario was glad to see everyone safe and expressed sympathy to Takeo and Sara. He threw his arms around Carol and lifted her off the ground as he wiped away tears.

"Uncle Mario, we were scared."

"I'm so sorry that happened to you. I never would have let you go to New York if I thought you would be in danger. It caught me by surprise."

He asked Nadene to set things in motion.

"Okay people, first of all we need food. We planned on eating out but plans have changed. We could be here all night."

Seth looked up at the ceiling.

"Rosa, you call Sarducci's, pick up the food, and bring back a couple of six packs of Long Trail Ale."

Mario handed Seth a box. Seth opened it and pulled out a CF220TYR electronic wireless device detector. Mario said the batteries were included. A feeble joke, but it lightened the atmosphere a bit.

"Where did you get that?" Nadene asked.

"My contact at U.S. Naval Intelligence. He's also done work for the National Security Administration. Seth asked me to get it. There are no instructions or manual with that thing."

45

"No problem." Seth immediately put it to work. He turned up the sensitivity control and got multiple readings and a confused display on the LCD screen. "Could everyone take their cellphones out of the living and dining rooms, please."

"What are you doing?" Rosa asked when she returned a half-hour later with two brown bags of food and beer.

"It's a bug detector," Nadene responded.

Seth turned on the two-inch-by-three-inch black box with a six-inch-long rubber coated antenna and got a single point source. He turned down the sensitivity control as he got closer. He swept it back and forth. Finally, stuck to the back of Rosa's end table drawer he found a sub-miniature microphone taped in place. He removed it, and held it up to inspect. Rosa dropped the food and put both hands over her mouth.

"This is a 2.8 Gigahertz device, .375 x .250 x .200 mm. The battery lasts for about ten days. It has a range of only 250 feet, at most. That means whoever is listening has to be very close. Have you noticed any strange cars or people outside, Rosa?"

"There's only one other building that's close enough, that one." Rosa pointed to a brown-shingled raised ranch.

"Who lives there, and who lives downstairs?" Nadene asked.

"The Thomas family lives in the house. I've know them for two years. They're wonderful people. He's a retired minister."

"How about the other two apartments?" Nadene asked again.

"They were both occupied when I moved in. Below me is Suzy, a graduate student. She's going to teach English. On the first floor is the LeClair family. They have two kids. He's a fireman and she's a nurse. They are all good people, it *can't* be any of them."

"I'll be right back." Seth asked Nadene for the car keys and headed outside. He swept the entire car, plus two others nearby. Nadene came outside and asked him what he had found.

"Nothing, the car's clean. I don't get it, there has to be someone around here listening."

"How about some*thing*?" Nadene asked. "Could they record our conversations and take the recorder later? Maybe they stuck it in a tree or behind the building."

"It's possible, but unlikely. Usually there's just a receiver with a person listening to headphones, but it wouldn't hurt to check. Do you have a flashlight?"

First Seth scanned the juniper hedges. He then checked every tree, gradually expanding his radius outward.

~ ~ ~

When he returned to the meeting about twenty minutes later, everyone had finished eating.

"I saved some manicotti for you, Seth," Rosa told him.

David was setting up the slide presentation, and Nadene asked Seth if he'd found anything. Seth was smiling as he threw a ten-inch-long black box with a one-foot-long whip antenna on the kitchen table. It was covered in plastic.

"This is how they did it." Everyone stopped what they were doing and gathered around the table. "Nadene, you were right, it was in a tree in front of the house. This is quite ingenious. It's a battery-powered 2.8 gigahertz repeater."

"What the hell is that?" Rosa asked. She was very upset that someone had been listening to all the intimate details of her life. She was in a rage, and the anger had no place to go. Seth squeezed her hand, and she began crying. He hugged her, and this made her cry even harder. She finally stopped, and they just stood there with their arms around each other. They suddenly realized that everyone was watching them. Seth stepped back, and Mario asked him what the range of the device was.

47

"A repeater is both a receiver and a transmitter. It receives the signal from this bug and re-transmits it in every direction. The range is one-half to three-quarters of a mile."

"Forget it," Nadene said, "that's too big an area. They could be listening anywhere."

~ ~ ~

It had been three weeks since the Stanford news conference. Brian Howard, the governor of Vermont, and Senator McGuire were good friends. Howard strongly supported McGuire's ban. The governor was a Republican, but the senator often referred to him as a closet Democrat. Normally, a bill had to go through two standing committees before it made its way to the floor for a vote, but in this instance the governor moved quickly to bypass the committees and place the ban on the agenda. He saw to it that the papers were filed, and the Democratic majority in the Vermont House and Senate backed him up. They moved so fast because Howard had invoked the rarely used Emergency Management Clause. When the public safety was threatened, he could cut corners. Mario called it legislative triage.

~ ~ ~

Seth and Rosa lingered in the kitchen. From the living room, Nadene saw them kissing. She turned to David and Mario, who were sitting on the couch.

"Ooowee, tin-to-one they make some beautiful babies."

David laughed. "I love your accent, Nadene."

"What accent, I don't have an accent, you have an accent."

"Oh," David teased, "what's the number after 9?"

"Tin."

48

"And what metal is a can made out of?"

"Tin."

"What object has ink in it and you write with it?"

"A pin."

"What is that gold thing on your blouse?"

"A pin. Hold on, hold on, you'd have to be pretty dumb to use a pin that you write with and stick it on your blouse."

Mario laughed and said, "Dis is good, David, you've proved your point."

Nadene said, "*Dis*? What is *dis*? Is it like *dat*? Mario, you have to put your tongue behind your top teeth. It's a *th* sound, not a *d*. Try it: *this, that, these, those*. I know you moved from New York a long time ago, but every once in a while *your* accent sneaks out. You sound like a street heavy. *Dis*?" Mario cracked up.

"Wait a minute, David." Nadene raised her voice. "Come back here. You were raised in Massachusetts."

"Yes."

"Well, does a horse gallop or gollop?"

"It gallops."

"And what do you eat, a scallop or a scollop?"

"A scollop."

"Is a loose woman a trallop or a trollop?"

"A trollop."

"I have an accent? You Yankees are so confused you don't know whether you're eating shellfish or servicing whores."

Seth, Takeo, and David were talking basketball. Seth became very animated. "Hey, UVM beat Syracuse in the first round of the NCAAs, what's Columbia done?" Takeo responded that Columbia's players are more intelligent. Seth and Takeo had a great time gibing back and forth, and they became friends.

~ ~ ~

There are people who, when they walk into a room, make everyone cringe. Such a person has a negative aura about them, and a pall floats over the gathering. Laughter and merriment come to a dead stop. Other people have joy written on their faces. It doesn't matter what they do for a living, or whether they are having a good day or a not-so-good one. You are glad to see them, and everyone in the room is lifted. When there are several people with this magic quality in the same place, an ordinary occasion can turn into a party. Sethos, Rosa, David, Carol, Takeo, and Sara were all blessed with this gift, and they quickly became fast friends. They started making plans to meet. Mario got caught up in the gaiety and told everyone about the new Fender Deluxe Player's Stratocaster he had just bought.

"It's a fabulous blues guitar. I can't wait to play it in our group," he said with excitement. That got Nadene's attention, and she asked him which amp he would use. He told her his Fender Super Reverb should be perfect. Nadene stopped herself from exploring any further into musical territory. Time was short.

"Hold on, hold on, people. We have to get busy."

They got down to work. Earlier, Takeo had persuaded Nadene to take him to a car rental office. He said it wasn't necessary for her to drive them to Montreal. He volunteered to drive David and Carol back to Burlington after they finished their work session tonight, so they could catch their flight back to San Francisco at noon tomorrow. But David elected to postpone his departure for a day so he could help with tomorrow's hearing. He told Takeo to get going as early as possible.

"Are you sure you can drive to Montreal? You must be exhausted," Carol said to Takeo.

"It's only three hours. Sara's been there a dozen times and knows the way. Don't worry, I'm fine."

At 11:00 p.m. Takeo and Sara left for Montreal.

~ ~ ~

Mario gathered the others together. "I didn't want to say this in front of Takeo and Sara, and I know it's also going to upset you two, David and Carol. When he gave me the detector, my Naval Intelligence contact told me something in confidence. Please don't repeat this until I know what action I'm going to take. When that plane went down in the Pacific, an aircraft carrier task force including two Ticonderoga Class guided missile cruisers, the *Thomas B. Sturget* and the *Richard S. Nichols* were in the area."

"What does this mean?" Nadene asked. "Did that missile come from one of *our* ships? Who would give such an order? What are the Japanese going to think?"

"I don't know yet if the missile was fired from one of those ships, or who gave the order, or how high up the chain of command it started. It's beginning to look like some important government people may not want us to continue our work. I have to tell this to you now. We may all be in harm's way. I don't want any of you to get hurt, and I will fully understand if you want to quit. It's not worth your life."

"What about the lives of all those people who will die from cancer?" Nadene asked. "Shoot, count me in."

"Same here." "Me too." Seth and Rosa spoke up without hesitation.

David and Carol both said yes. They were fully committed to the cause.

51

~~~

Julie McGuire was a classic beauty. She was the kind of woman who got prettier the more time you spent with her. Some people, male and female, look good from the outside, but as soon as they open their mouths, click, the light switch turns off. Not so with Julie. She was one of those rare people whose face, voice, mind, and body combined into one beckoning force. You simply wanted to spend more time with her.

She had so many talents it would take hours to list them all. She was an established mixed-media artist. Her work had appeared in the Boston Museum of Fine Arts, the Portland Museum, and in Burlington's sister city, the museum in Yaroslavl, Russia. She had had a show at the Whitney in New York, and at the Place des Artes in Montreal. The Place des Artes was currently negotiating with her to purchase a major work. She was thrilled about the prospect of having a piece there because it was her favorite space. She was also an accomplished violinist and played with the Vermont Symphony Orchestra on occasion. Two years ago she had published a cookbook on Italian food. Sometimes she liked to disappear for three days at a time. When her husband was in Washington she couldn't be counted on to just stay at home and feed the cats. Julie had one major fault. She was totally unpredictable.

~~~

Harold Slokov had money and power. They were the only things he needed because he had both of those in abundance. He was worth twenty-three billion dollars. He owned eighty percent of the stock in Metro Media, and the total area from his worldwide real-estate holdings was twice the size of Delaware. Like most men who are all-powerful, he seemed to enjoy life. He owned three yachts, a PBY seaplane, and had a complete two-lane bowling alley and an Olympic-sized swimming pool in the basement of his home. He dated three voluptuous women who pretended to adore him. None of them knew of the others' existence.

Slokov's main character traits were largely predictable. He enjoyed winning more if it was at another person's expense. He was a combination of four main forces: sadism, sexual conquest to prove he still had it, empire building, and raging ego. He was also brilliant. He spoke seven languages, and with no prior knowledge could remember the names and bios of twenty people who had introduced themselves around his conference table.

Harold had one major flaw. Sometimes he deliberately put himself in danger. Psychiatrists would call it a death wish. Some thought that he just enjoyed a challenge. Or perhaps, just perhaps, he was bored. When you thought you had him analyzed, he would surprise you. None of his associates knew that every week he traveled to an inner-city elementary school. He was part of a mentor program of executives who spent an hour reading to children. His mentee was an at-risk ten-year-old boy who was now doing very well. Harold loved children.

~ ~ ~

It had been three days since Slokov's personal secretary, the Eurasian beauty he saw on Thursday and Sunday nights, placed a call to Julie McGuire. Now Julie was sitting in his office, which was actually the entire top floor of Metro Media Towers. They were sitting alone in a forty-foot-long greenhouse. It was completely glassed in, and temperature and humidity controlled. There were dozens of varieties of orchids, a fifteen-foot-tall miniature banyan tree, and swarms of butterflies filled the air with color and movement.

They were sitting on a bench placed perfectly so you would swear that you were in the tropics instead of in a modern office building. Julie was not easily distracted, but even she was mesmerized by the rare copper butterfly that landed on her left shoulder. Julie had curly chestnut hair and stood five feet eleven inches tall, about an inch taller than her husband. She was wearing a snug-fitting, caramel-colored wool skirt, and a dark-brown satin blouse under a matching caramel jacket. Her blouse had a low neckline and her only jewelry was a gold Etruscan horse pin on her jacket, and a gold wedding ring.

"I wanted to meet with you because I urgently need your help. Your husband is about to embark on a course of action that will be disastrous for this country and very dangerous for him and his associates. Like it or not, television is controlled by the twenty-five largest corporations in the country. Many CEOs have already told me that if TV and computer screens are banned, their companies could go out of business. Without the steady exposure that constant television advertising provides, people will no longer buy new cars, home furnishings, or designer clothes, to name just a few products. We will be economic sitting ducks for the rest of the world's powers, who will continue to make and market these goods. How do you feel about what he's doing?"

"I make it a point to never get involved with his decisions. Our marriage works only if I stay out of his business and he stays out of mine."

"But you didn't answer my question. Do you want to see this country destroyed?"

"No, but what am I supposed to do about it, and what gave you the strange idea that I would help you?"

Slokov gave Julie a carefully edited explanation of his plan and how she could help him. He admitted that he had heard talk about her marital troubles and figured he'd try a long shot. He wondered if it was possible to convince her to play by his rules. Julie admitted to having marital problems that would probably result in eventual divorce.

"I've got a number of grudges against my husband, but they're none of your business."

After two Grey Goose l'Orange martinis she also admitted that she strongly disliked the senator's new quest, or as Slokov referred to it, witch-hunt, and agreed that it was dangerous for the country.

"What's in it for me?" she asked.

Slokov handed her a sheet of paper and told her to read it now and memorize it, because he wanted it back.

"That's not acceptable," Julie responded, and took a small notebook and pen out of her purse. She copied down everything that was on the sheet.

Slokov had expected her to do that. He even had a pad and pen ready in a small walnut end table near the bench, in case she didn't have any. He studied Julie for her reaction.

"Where in the Virgin Islands is this house, and why do you think I would want to live there?" *He's a good-looking man but much too sure of himself,* she thought.

"It's on St. John Island, where you have vacationed alone for the last two years."

"I'll say one thing for you, your research is good. So is your nerve. You are asking me to betray my husband."

"Your husband is a nut case. I'm asking you to help save your country. Don't give me an answer now. I will personally call you in three days. We can meet again here."

Slokov's eyes moved from Julie's eyes to her mouth, and then from her mouth back up to her eyes. He didn't want to telegraph how much she appealed to him, but couldn't seem to help himself. He didn't understand his attraction to Julie McGuire. It certainly wasn't her looks, although they were fine. He had met hundreds of talented, intelligent, more beautiful women. Perhaps it was because she was the senator's wife. He walked with her down the hall to the elevator. He noticed her perfume. He had thought he knew them all but didn't recognize hers.

"It's best if you return to the lobby alone."

~ ~ ~

It was three a.m. before they finished compiling their evidence. Seth was asleep in a La-Z-Boy recliner, Rosa and Nadene had the bed, David and Carol were in a two-person sleeping bag on the dining room floor, and Mario was on the living room couch. Carol and David giggled.

"Knock it off and get some sleep," Mario ordered.

~ ~ ~

"It's showtime." Nadene shook Mario, who grunted. She clapped her hands. "It's seven-thirty, everybody wake up, let's get crackin'. We have to be at the Capitol, fully prepared, by nine. The hearing starts at tin."

Rosa put on some coffee, and the aroma of dark French roast combined with toasted onion bagels. Seth leaned backward on the La-Z-Boy and went back to sleep.

"Poor baby is so tired," Rosa crooned. She walked behind the chair and gently shook it. Seth didn't move. She rocked it harder, but he just groaned and changed his position. Nadene watched her.

"Rosa, darlin', I'm not going to enjoy this, but I've got to do it." She went to the back of the chair and tipped it forward. Seth was still on the cushion when she slid it and him onto the living room rug.

They all finished breakfast and loaded the four boxes of evidence and their computer equipment into the Crown Victoria LX's trunk. Everything about the Ford was oversized. It held over seventy dollars worth of gas. It got only about fifteen miles to the gallon in the city, and everyone chided Mario about it. He declared that it was his only *public* vice.

"Here's the plan." Nadene had center stage. "David and Carol will remain here to finish the foils on genetic mutations. This is an important part of the evidence. I will come and get you at 9:30 sharp. David, you have to be ready to comment on these yourself, since you are the discoverer."

"We'll be ready at 9:30," David promised.

"And stay out of that sleeping bag," Mario joked.

"Okay, B Team, let's go," Nadene shouted.

"B Team?" Mario asked.

"We're going to *Ban* television, aren't we? We're the B Team."

~ ~ ~

After the harrowing descent down State Street with cut brake lines, Nadene careened around the last turn. The Vivaldi concerto was still playing but was drowned out by screeching tires. She told everyone to brace themselves. Mario put both feet on the dashboard.

The road had now leveled off in front of the Capitol. There was a three-hundred-foot-long, four-foot-high stone wall separating the road from the flower gardens. Pedestrians and news-people saw the car jump off the road, and they ran to safety. Nadene scraped against the wall and managed to blow both tires. Sparks were flying. The car flipped onto its side and slid to a stop about thirty feet from the end of the wall. It ended up right in front of the TV production trucks, there to cover the hearing.

Help arrived instantly. Two Montpelier police officers climbed up the underside of the car and used a crowbar to open the back door. The passengers quickly unbuckled their seat belts. There was a strong smell of gasoline, and Nadene yelled at everyone to get the hell out fast. She pressed the trunk release before she exited the car. Seth reached into the trunk and threw out the cartons of evidence. One of them had burst open, so he frantically grabbed the loose papers and handed them to Rosa. EMTs had arrived at the scene to help treat their wounds. Everyone was bruised and bleeding, but they refused to go to the hospital. Mario vomited on the lawn and then shouted at the police.

"Check the brake lines, check the brake lines! Someone cut the lines!"

Reporters had now mobbed the senator, who was bleeding from a gash over his right eye.

"Senator, are you saying that someone tried to kill you?"

"That's exactly what I'm saying."

Nadene shouted for everyone to get away from the car. Someone had tossed a lit cigarette and it was about to ignite the spilled gasoline. They all grabbed the evidence and ran away from the car. Seth dropped one of the computer cases and had to run back for it. At that moment the car exploded, throwing metal and glass in all directions. Everyone hit the ground. The back of Seth's shirt and his pants were on fire. He rolled around on the grass, and Mario threw his jacket over him to put out the flames. Seth had been burned, and his clothes were ruined. He tied Mario's jacket around his waist. A well-dressed man who Mario didn't recognize told all the lawmakers who were milling around that the hearing should be cancelled.

"No way," Mario responded. "We will conduct this hearing."

Nadene shouted at the police and pointed to the same well-dressed man. "Arrest him, that's the guy who threw the cigarette." By this time, the fire department had arrived. Rosa's neighbor, firefighter Tom LeClair, recognized her immediately and asked if she was all right. The fire team hosed down the car, and in a few minutes all that was left was a charred hulk. The water hissed as it hit the metal, and the steam had the rancid smell of burnt rubber and plastic. The B Team walked up the Capitol steps. Mario asked police lieutenant Walsh if he had picked up the guy who threw the cigarette.

"That was deliberate. I want to know who he is."

"We thought it was an accident, Senator, so we didn't detain him."

Mario spotted his friend Francine Bouchard, a reporter with the *Barre/Montpelier Times-Argus*. Francine became bored after retiring at 62, so now she was back working part-time at the newspaper. She helped them carry their evidence into the Senate Chamber.

"Francine, you're the best reporter I know. Please find out who that bastard with the cigarette is, and who he works for. I'm sure it's the same people who bugged Rosa's apartment."

"They did what?"

"Francine, we have to talk after the hearing. I need your help."

~ ~ ~

It was 9:15. Media coverage of the explosion had brought hundreds more spectators to the scene. The entire gallery was already full, and most of the legislators were in their seats. A select team of lawyers representing the pro-TV group was sitting on the left side of the podium. The pro-ban team was on the right side. Satellite trucks from every major network were parked outside. There were hundreds of reporters from the U.S. and many foreign countries. Mario had a two-inch bandage over his right eye, his shirt was badly torn, and he was without a tie or a jacket. He was the last person of his group to enter the chamber.

CHAPTER THREE

Montpelier is the smallest state capital in the country. Representatives Hall, where the General Assembly meets, is the oldest hall in America still in its original condition. There are red drapes on all the windows, and the tables and chairs are arranged in four horseshoes around the center podium. Above the podium, where the governor will soon call the meeting to order, hangs a huge portrait of George Washington, an 1836 copy of Gilbert Stuart's original, painted by George Gassner. Above the portrait is the Vermont coat of arms, carved, painted, and gilded pine.

A polite woman in a blue dress stopped in front of the State House and handed a box of clothes to the guard. She asked him to please give it to the young man whose clothes had burned. The garments in the box had once belonged to her son, an Army National Guard sergeant who was killed in Iraq last year, she explained. She couldn't bring herself to throw his things out, and now she had finally found a good use for them. She drove away in her Subaru wagon. Seth was handed the box by an officer, and left the floor to change. The late sergeant was also a tall man, so everything was about the right size. He selected camouflage pants with two large cargo pockets, and a sweatshirt with "Green Mountain Boys" across the chest.

Nadene looked at Mario. "I'm angry, Mario. My arms and legs are still shaking."

"My *insides* are still shaking."

~ ~ ~

Nadene had borrowed a car, picked up David and Carol at the apartment, and the three of them were now at Mario's table with Seth and Rosa, busily preparing their data. Across the aisle the opposition lawyers were whispering to each other. Mario looked at them and spoke in a very loud voice. "What's the matter, ladies and gentlemen, didn't expect to see us here?"

There were 150 representatives and 30 senators in the Hall. Most of them heard Mario shout, and they too were whispering to each other. The opposition lawyers were uneasy. The intensity and focus of Mario and his team were intimidating.

Both sides were prepared. Each had its bishops, knights, rooks, queen, and king at the ready. The black king had sent out his pawns, but they were no longer on the board. Nadene had neutralized them.

~ ~ ~

The gavel was dropped, Governor Howard called the session to order, and immediately made a statement.

"Before we debate the contents of this proposed bill, I would like to comment on events that occurred this morning. There is evidence to suggest that Senator McGuire's car was tampered with. Lieutenant Walsh of the Montpelier Police Department informs me that the brake lines had been deliberately cut. The senator and his staff were nearly killed. An electronic listening device was also recovered from the home of one of his staff, who lives just a few miles from this building.

"I have asked the FBI and the State Police for their help. It is obvious to anyone who understands power-politics that there is a conspiracy loose, the sole intent of which is to stop Senator

McGuire by unlawful means and criminal acts. This will not be tolerated in the State of Vermont. I want all the lawmakers present in this room to factor in these disturbing recent events when they weigh the evidence they are about to hear.

"Senator McGuire, please make your opening statement, and describe the contents of the bill before this Assembly."

"Mmm, mmm," Nadene said to David and Carol. "My Grandpappy once told me, make sure you take your gun out of its holster before you squeeze the trigger. Looks like our buddies over there just shot themselves in their collective foots."

David tried to cover his mouth as he smiled.

Mario made the opening remarks, and then pointed out an interesting fact to the lawmakers.

"I want the learned people in this chamber to be aware that counsel for the opposition has been selected from two organizations. Four of these lawyers are employed by the WenCo Corporation, and the other three work for Supreme Oil of Houston. This is hardly a team that represents the people of Vermont or the best interests of the American people."

"How the hell did he know that?" Seth whispered to Rosa.

The evidence was presented fast and furiously by the B Team. The opposition was poorly prepared and was caught flatfooted. Four hours later the issue was decided. The General Assembly overwhelmingly passed the "Cancer Prevention Act." Governor Howard signed the bill, and it became law.

The Speaker of the House read the summary provisions aloud.

"In order to safeguard the people of the State of Vermont, and prevent untold deaths due to malignant tumors caused by moving imagery, the citizens are hereby directed to dispose of all existing television sets and computer screens. It is also hereby stipulated that the seven television stations, both UHF and VHF, in the State of Vermont, cease transmission immediately. It is hereby illegal for any retail establishment or private party to sell or give away

63

television sets or computer screens. It is unlawful for any Vermont resident to import television sets or computer screens by mailorder, or any other means. Portable devices that are used to play video games are also prohibited. Penalties for refusing to comply with this law are to be determined."

Checkmate.

Mario shook hands with Governor Howard, thanked him for his courageous support, and agreed to cooperate with the FBI inquiry into the sabotage of his vehicle and the bugging of Rosa's apartment. Rosa glared at a WenCo attorney, a woman in a sharp white pantsuit, and made a side comment to her as she left the hall. This greatly disturbed the woman, who sped up and looked over her shoulder several times as she exited.

"What did you say to her?" Nadene asked.

"Nothing."

"What did you say?"

"Nothing."

"Come on, girl, I want to know what you said to that bitch."

"I told her that she shouldn't pee in her pants unless she's wearing a dark suit."

~ ~ ~

Mario ordered that there be no celebrating until they left the hall. He instructed the team to shake hands and act very dignified. They controlled themselves except for Nadene, who threw out her arms and did a quick shimmy.

There were several thousand people outside, with a police line between the crowd and the Capitol steps. David suddenly felt a dull thud against his chest. He looked down to see egg yolk running down his shirt. More eggs were thrown at them, with several hitting their targets. Young men were shouting at them; some gave them the finger.

"Go to hell, McGuire, you can't have my TV!"

"Eat shit, McGuire, I'm gonna watch all the baseball games and no one is gonna stop me."

"Sex and the City, Sex and the City, Sex and the City," four fraternity brothers chanted.

The police made several arrests. The hecklers resisted, and had to be handcuffed and forcibly placed in patrol cars. Many others were shouting against the newly adopted law. Several were holding signs, including one woman who had "HOW DO I FEED MY FAMILY?" crudely printed on a piece of brown cardboard.

Mario was also egged and had yellow slime all over his clothes. "I didn't expect *this*." He turned to a police sergeant who told him that the men who threw the eggs and who were making the most noise were from Marshfield Military Academy. "I can tell by the short haircuts," the sergeant said. "We can't arrest them all. We don't have enough officers."

~ ~ ~

"Hey, why don't we call our group 'B for Blues'?" Rosa suggested. "If we're the B Team because we want to ban TV, why not B for Blues for our music group?"

Nadene laughed and said, "Sure, why not, most of my songs are B sides anyway."

It had been two days since the historic Vermont vote. David and Carol were back in California. As was their newly created tradition, the B Team had a music session in the senator's Burlington office to get in the mood for making future plans. The room was small, about 15 by 25 feet, and there was foam soundproofing on the walls.

Mario laughed and said that he had hired Seth only because he could play the drums. Seth said he was not a drummer, he was a percussionist. In addition to his Ludwig drum kit, he had Middle-Eastern dumbeks, African shakers, and South American rattles to complement the kit. He had soft hands and didn't overpower the other players. Rosa had a Fender Precision bass. It was very heavy, so she didn't like to stand when she played. She had a custom made wooden glider that was designed for guitar players. It was covered with blue denim fabric, and rocked backward and forward with no up and down movements. Every time she started rocking, Seth was distracted and sometimes he missed a beat.

Nadene had a Yamaha keyboard and was a first-rate player. She was classically trained, and as part of her master's degree she had given a Bach recital. Her voice was smoky. She sounded like a combination of Sarah Vaughn, Billie Holiday, and Janis Joplin. She had the range of Sarah, the phrasing of Billie, and the fire of Janis, yet her style was completely unique. She had saved a long time for a Newmann condenser microphone that cost over two thousand dollars. Her PA system had several choice special effects, and with just a slight bit of echo, she sounded good enough to sing for anybody.

Mario was a guitar and amp nut. He owned five Fender Stratocasters including a sunburst 12-string, four Martin flat-tops, a Gibson Les Paul Custom, and four amplifiers. His favorite Super Reverb and Princeton amps were powered by tubes, and he liked the sound of the original Jensen speakers. Mario had started playing when he was six years old. At sixteen he was the lead singer and guitarist for a rock band called Shake. His voice was adequate, but his guitar playing was excellent.

The B Team tried to keep their sound at low levels, but by the end of the session the volume controls had climbed a couple of notches.

Guitar, drums, and bass gave a short blues intro and then paused. Nadene sang,

If you ever need me baby, you'll know just where I'll be.

She repeated the phrase, this time joined by the entire band including her piano.

If you ever need me baby, you'll know just where I'll be. I'm going back to Chicago, cause you're so damn mean to me.

They had been playing for almost two hours when they heard a knock on the door. It was the accountant and his secretary who worked in the next office.

"Hey, you're really starting to sound good, Senator."

"Hope it's not too loud."

"Not at all. I like 'Back Break Baby Blues'," the young secretary said. "You guys should record it."

After they left, Seth opened a box and handed each person a CD. "What's this?" Nadene asked, and then answered her own question. "This is us."

"I told you that digital recorder is good," Seth said. "I made this disk from our last three sessions. There are twelve songs." He'd even added a photo of the four of them that he had taken last month with his self-timer.

Mario was delighted and complimented him on being so sneaky.

"There is something else," Seth sheepishly volunteered. "I sent the CD to Colossal Records."

"You did what?" Mario said, horrified.

"I sent it to Colossal Records, and they want to release it. They love our sound."

"Hold on, Sethos Azizi, this is a very bad idea," Mario responded.

"I think it's a good idea," Rosa said. "You and Nadene have written some fine songs, and two of them are about our work to ban TV. This is a great way to get our message out. If we can win friends through our music, maybe it will be easier to convince Americans that television is bad."

"What, no television contract?" Mario sniped back.

Nadene looked at Mario. "You know something, Senator, I think Rosa may have a point. Tell you what I'm thinking. Oscar and I like my buns just the way they are. I think our enemies are less likely to want to rearrange them if we become celebrities."

"Not to mention all the fame and money you will have," Mario countered.

"That too."

"You people are impossible."

"Can we sign a recording contract?"

"Impossible."

"Oh come on, can't we sign a contract? Pat Leahy was in a Batman movie."

"Impossible." Mario paused, looked around at the three eager faces, and relented.

"Yeah, yeah, sign the contract."

~ ~ ~

Harold Slokov looked again at his gold Omega watch. Julie McGuire was now an hour late for their meeting. He was prepared for her to be late, about half an hour was his guess. He knew that she understood power, and that every gesture and decision conveyed a message. He thought about all the different ways he could try to impress her. He could have picked her up in his seaplane. He could have sent a limo with dark-tinted glass on all windows, and a bottle of her favorite Grey Goose in the small refrigerator. He had elected not to do either of those things. He would not even be waiting for her to get out of the elevator. He would be sitting at his desk when she walked in, and they would talk on the couch next to his table. This time he wouldn't take her into the greenhouse.

Now he was beginning to get annoyed because she was really late. Finally the door opened. She stumbled as she entered the room.

"Scuse me, I had a previous engagement." Julie appeared to have been drinking. She was slightly disheveled, and there was a pink glow on her cheeks. Her speech was less crisp than usual. "I haven't had enough time to think about your offer, Harold."

"What's to think about?" Slokov asked with irritation. "Did you see the footage of that motley crew, pelted with eggs? That's what the people of Vermont think of your husband, and it's going to get a lot worse. Julie, fifty million dollars is a lot of money, you can't want more money."

"I didn't say that I wanted more money. I said I needed more time. Tell me more about what you expect from me. I want everything on the table. I want nothing omitted."

Any hopes Slokov might have entertained about Julie not being at her best were utterly dashed. Though not entirely sober, she was still pretty sharp, and was proving very difficult to manipulate. He would have to go into more detail about their agreement, and try to convince her today. He answered a lot of her questions, and after about forty minutes' conversation she reiterated her intention to think about it some more.

"Fine," Slokov said with resignation. "We'll meet here next week. Is the same time okay? I want a definite answer then, no more waffling."

Julie nodded her head and picked up her purse. When she raised her head to look up at him, Slokov was again drawn against his will to stare at her mouth. Her lips were the most sensuous he'd ever seen.

Julie started to rise from the couch, but tripped on the carpet. Slokov moved to steady her, and it took all the control he could muster to keep from pulling her against him and kissing that mouth. He collected himself at the last possible millisecond, and helped her up, instead.

"You lost your balance. See you next week."

~ ~ ~

Mario put Seth's CD on the stereo system. He had to admit that they really did sound good. Mario suggested that they could dub in a sax, or background vocals, but Seth insisted that they already had their sound. It was not overly processed, and was straight-ahead "B Team" blues. They closed the music room door and sat around the small conference table. Seth was perspiring from two hours of drumming.

Nadene said, "Listen guys, I know we've done well, even done what most people said was impossible, but don't go to sleep. We had great success in Montpelier. But Mount Peculiar isn't like the rest of the country. You can shoot fish in Vermont, carry a concealed handgun into a bank, and pass across a double yellow line on any highway. It was the first state to allow civil union for gays, and the only Independent congressman in Washington, our very own Senator McGuire, is from Vermont. Vermont is not South Carolina or Montana. What do we do next, Mario?"

"Nadene, there's one thing about you that I'm really beginning to dislike. You're always right. Yes, Vermont is different, and yes, it's going to be very tough in the other states, especially in DC. I must try to convince my colleagues in the Senate to form a committee to study the issue. Our goal is to have the full Senate vote on the ban. This won't be a quick process like it was in Vermont. Many bills die in committee, and we'll be in the lion's den. People in high places are going to turn up the heat, and quite frankly, I don't know how far they will go to stop us."

70

Seth had been wondering about something. "How did you know that those lawyers worked for WenCo and Supreme Oil? Somebody has to be controlling them, somebody higher up."

Nadene and Rosa smiled at each other, remembering the woman in the white suit.

"Seth, you're right on. I have a friend in the FBI who told me about the lawyers. I can't prove it, but I believe there's a link between WenCo, Supreme Oil, and whoever did the dirty work to our car and Rosa's apartment. My FBI contact says that the lead man could be Harold Slokov of Metro Media. I also know that someone in the Government Office of Domestic Security is involved. That's another reason I'm staying in Washington for a while. I'm going to try to find out who's responsible.

"Nadene, you will come with me to Washington. Rosa and Seth, your job is to spread information in two places, Missouri and North Carolina. Both governors have contacted me and want all the details of our Vermont bill. There's a good possibility they will try to enact the same ban. You may have to visit both places and do all the prep work. Let me know the best time for me to make an appearance. We're getting a lot of hate mail and threatening phone calls. Keep these doors locked at all times, and be careful when you travel. I've asked the Burlington Police Department to give you extra security, and they promised me they would be available 24/7 if you need help."

~ ~ ~

"What have you got for me, Robert?" It had been a quiet week in California and Lynch didn't have much to report. Peterson told him that they were going to bug Stephanie's phone. They wanted him to listen in from his office, which was across the hall.

"But that's very dangerous! What if somebody finds out?"

71

"No one will find out, just pretend you're listening to your iPod. I like it when you have news for me, and this will give us something to talk about. There's so much electronic equipment in that building, bug detectors would be useless. They'll never find our devices."

"Devices?"

"Yes, we're also going to bug the phones of David Feinstein and Don Satowski. Just pretend you're at a cocktail party and take notes."

"Very fucking funny, I didn't sign on for this."

"What did you think you were going to have to do after we gave you six million dollars, tell us who's going on vacation? We demand you increase your involvement or we want all our funds back, immediately. I will let you know when everything is in place, and I will see that you get the receiver with instructions on how to use it." Peterson hung up the phone.

Robert Lynch was worried. He had already spent four hundred thousand dollars, and it would take him a long time to replace it. *They probably know that, the bastards.* He couldn't go through with it. He had thought the money would make it work for him, but it didn't. He was caught in dangerous quicksand, a queasy middle-ground of not being either kind enough or ruthless enough. He was not their friend, but he found it impossible to further victimize his coworkers. He panicked.

~ ~ ~

Jennifer Wheelen had been working all week on the set of *Wicked Loving Lies*. She usually came home on Saturday afternoon, spent a short weekend with Robert, and left again on Monday morning for LA. This Saturday she did not arrive at the usual time. Robert's calls to the studio and to her apartment went unanswered. Finally at eight that evening, the phone rang.

"Hello, sweets, what happened? I was really beginning to worry, are you at the airport?"

"Sorry Robert, I should have called you earlier."

"I've got a very special present for you. Let's just say it's a moving object that you've always wanted."

"Robert, I'm sure that's nice, but I have to talk to you. This isn't easy for me to say, but we've been going in two different directions for a long time. I feel bad that we have to end it, but such is life. I'm not coming home at all. Sorry about the car, but you can give it to someone else."

"But Jennifer, I love you. I have six million dollars now because of some really good investments I made, and we can buy a fine house in LA."

"That won't buy much out here," she responded with boredom in her voice.

"Sorry Robert, I know this is abrupt. I'll send someone up for my things. There's no need for you to pack them, I left instructions." She hung up the phone.

Jennifer had been sleeping with her producer, and he had promised her a role in his next movie. He was worth about three hundred million dollars, and she thought he would marry her after the divorce was finalized.

Robert Lynch had lost the only woman he ever cared about, and lost the good-will and respect of his coworkers. He had caused the deaths of all the Japanese researchers, and was about to lose his career and make an enemy of John Peterson, a merciless, corrupt man who would not hesitate to destroy him. For Lynch, there was only one way out.

~ ~ ~

Why do people commit suicide by putting their mouths around a handgun? Perhaps it's because they come into the world sucking on a woman's breast, and once they've embraced the dark side, they must leave it sucking on Satan's breast.

Don Satowski heard the shot and came running into Lynch's office. There was a short note: "Don, Steph, I'm sorry you have to clean up this mess. The government is going to bug your phones. I was supposed to listen in and report back to them. My contact in Washington is John Peterson. He works for the Government Office of Domestic Security. I couldn't go through with it. Tell Jennifer I love her."

~ ~ ~

Stephanie called Mario and told him that Robert Lynch was dead. She faxed him the suicide note. Mario pleaded with her to be careful, and told her to handle the note by its edges only. It was important that Lynch's prints be found on the paper. He instructed her to call the FBI.

"Steph, don't say anything important to me from that phone. Your phone, car, and house could all be bugged. I will call the FBI and have them on the Stanford campus immediately."

News of Lynch's death spread fast, and both Mario and the Government Office of Domestic Security were moving quickly. Mario contacted the FBI in California and in Washington. He told them what had happened and demanded that they arrest John Peterson.

Domestic Security had already created a team of bogus Federal Marshals, who were in reality their own agents, and had them on

74

the scene at Stanford before the FBI arrived. Eight agents exited from three government cars. They were in plain clothes, but some carried advanced weaponry and electronic equipment. They closely resembled a police SWAT team.

The agents introduced themselves to Satowski and Morrison and thanked them for reporting the note. They would process it for fingerprints, and carry it back to Washington under armed guard as evidence against John Peterson. Don handed them an envelope containing the note, and the agents left the campus. The government cars traveled about three miles before the ninth member of the team, a man who had remained in vehicle number two, spoke. "I had a feeling Lynch would unravel." He took out a cigarette lighter and set fire to the note.

John Peterson then gave orders to return to Washington.

~ ~ ~

Peterson was arrested when he arrived, but was immediately released. Mario phoned his friend, Rocco DiAngelo, and asked him why. DiAngelo was third in command at the FBI, and had served with Mario in Vietnam. Mario was piloting the MedEvac chopper that lifted Rocco and his platoon out of the jungle. They had suffered heavy casualties near Qhe Sahn, and Captain DiAngelo was wounded twice leading his men to safety. He received a Silver Star and two Purple Hearts.

Mario flew the chopper back to base, and was so focused on the mission that he was on the ground for twenty minutes before realizing he'd been shot in the leg. The chopper had over a hundred bullet holes in it when it was examined later. Mario was awarded a Purple Heart and two Special Commendations. Don't say anything against the FBI to Mario. He will not listen. He had worked closely with the agency on many occasions, and thought they were the finest law enforcement professionals in the world. Rocco would likewise do anything for Mario.

"Orders from above, Mario, I'm sorry."

Mario was told that Lynch's original note had disappeared. The Federal Marshall's service said they were not on campus yesterday, so some other group must have impersonated them and grabbed the note. Mario's faxed copy was blank. He hadn't loaded the ink cartridge properly.

The FBI had checked all the offices at Stanford and found no electronic surveillance devices.

DiAngelo said, "We interviewed Lynch's wife. She had just dumped him, and it's possible that he fabricated the 'bug' story for shock value just before his death. There's no proof yet that John Peterson or the Government Office of Domestic Security was planning to bug the researchers. So far no one has found any evidence, but Lynch did buy a new Mercedes convertible and a very expensive emerald necklace for his wife, the poor bastard. We're trying to find out where he got the money. I don't think your sister or her team is in danger. If additional operations were planned by some rogue agency, especially Domestic Security, they will be completely aborted now."

Mario was upset. "Come on, Rocco, you know it's them, who else would have the resources to pull off something on that scale? I don't believe no one got the license numbers of those cars. They'll just try something else. You know Peterson is dirty."

"My advice, Mario, is for you to call the president of Stanford and ask him to post 24-hour campus security around the researchers' offices. Don't worry, we'll get Peterson eventually."

~ ~ ~

For the next week, Mario talked one on one with his fellow senators. He didn't have the money, time, or inclination to hire a team of lobbyists. Actually, he hated lobbyists and rarely spoke to them. He was trying to accomplish two things at once. He was attempting to link Peterson with the Vermont and Stanford crimes, and was also trying to get his proposed bill before a Senate committee.

When the Senate reconvened, Mario was recognized to speak for the record. He didn't have a speech prepared, and was not reading from notes. He was at his best that way.

Mario McGuire was of average height with brown eyes and thinning brown hair. He was wearing a rumpled, dark gray lightweight suit and an unmemorable tie. Although he was in good shape, his physical appearance wasn't imposing, but it wasn't his looks that had earned him the name "Super Mario."

"Thank you, Mr. Vice President. In the last three weeks, an attempt has been made on my life and on the lives of my staff, and electronic listening devices have been recovered from one of my employee's home. There was also extensive electronic surveillance planned for the offices of the Stanford research team, including that of my sister, Stephanie Morrison, who is a noted neurosurgeon. The plane carrying the Japanese scientists who were working with my sister and her team mysteriously crashed into the ocean, just after it passed directly over elements of the US Pacific fleet. An outbound pilot saw a missile hit the plane. There were no survivors. My niece, Stephanie's daughter Carol Morrison, and the scientific delegation that discovered the image-cancer link, were abducted at gun point and terrorized in New York City. I want everyone to listen and listen good. I will find the person or persons responsible for these reprehensible acts. I will find them, and I will destroy them.

"How dare they abuse their power and victimize the citizens of this country? How dare they attack me and my family? How dare they kill innocent civilians from another country? The Cold War is over; is the administration conducting a new one against the American people? Waging a new war against those people in foreign lands who disagree with their agenda?

"Our lives and the lives of our children are in mortal danger. We are all in danger of dying from cancer due to watching television and computer screens. It is our duty to lead the nation, to find ways of safeguarding everyone's health. It is our duty to develop an image system that does not harm those who have to use it. It is our duty not to let the covert and overt actions of greedy corporations and corrupt government officials undermine our efforts to safeguard the population. I'm asking the Senate to let us debate these issues. Let both sides talk about what's at stake."

Mario took a drink of water and then continued. "It is unacceptable that in this great nation, violence, threats, and counter-threats are ruling the debate. We need, instead, a dialogue by which sane men and women can work out their differences and reach a solution for the common good. I am asking the Senate to approve Resolution 16-3 and allow a committee to be formed to study my proposed bill, The Cancer Prevention Act. Thank you, ladies and gentlemen."

After he finished speaking, there was lot of cross-talk in the Senate chamber. The senators' mumbling sounded like a congregation intoning prayers. "Good job," the senator from North Carolina praised Mario. In a private aside, Senator Cyrus Whitcom of Texas cornered Senator McGuire. He told Mario that the economy of the country would come to a grinding halt if he was allowed to continue with this television ban.

"American business will do anything to stop you, and I do fear for your safety, sir."

Mario had an "aha" moment. He wondered if this was the man behind it all. "Is that a threat? Tell me something, Cyrus, don't you own twenty percent of Metro Media and thirty percent of Supreme Oil of Houston?"

"My stock holdings are none of your business and are not the issue here, sir. Your irresponsible actions are."

"As you know, Senator Whitcom, we're not permitted to use profanity on the floor of the Senate. This is a hallowed body in what I consider to be a sacred building, so I will refrain from telling you exactly what I think of you. I would ask you, however, to remember the worst, most degrading and disgusting gutter insults you have ever heard and apply them liberally to yourself. If you want to step outside to discuss this further, please be my guest."

Whitcom said nothing and just glared at Mario McGuire.

~ ~ ~

Mario was happy. "Bingo, Nadene! We got our bipartisan committee. There will be eight Republicans and six Democrats, but I don't yet know who they will be. A simple majority is all we need to send our bill to the floor for a vote. This is going to be one hell of a fight. If they vote along party lines we won't win, but I'm hoping to open their minds. Let's fly back to Vermont tomorrow and make plans. The hearing starts next week."

~ ~ ~

Back in Burlington, everyone was tired. Mario had kept them working until after 8:00 p.m. It would take another day just to recap what had already been done, before any new plans could be made. Finally the conference room light was turned off, and everyone exited through the music room. Mario said goodnight first, and Seth was right behind him. Rosa grabbed Nadene's arm. "Do you have to get right home? Can I talk to you for a few minutes?"

"Sure, is there something bothering you?"

"Nadene, how long did it take before you and Oscar, you know, got together?"

"About seven seconds," Nadene laughed. "Actually, it took way longer than we liked. We were both in the Marines, and at first it was rough to get any time to see each other. What's the matter, hon, you and Seth having trouble?"

Rosa began crying. "He doesn't love me that way."

"What do you mean? I saw the two of you kissing, and believe me, he is one hot and bothered young man."

"But that's as far as it went. I'm so unhappy, I wish I was dead. I know what's wrong, it's our religions. Nadene, you know I majored in Theology at St. Michael's College. I want to teach it someday. I love being a Catholic. Seth is a devout Muslim, five times a day he prays to Allah. I love him, and I know he loves me, but it's never going to work."

"Did you two talk about it?"

"I tried to last week, but he got angry and walked away. He hasn't talked to me since, except about our work."

"Hon, you're going to have to try harder. Sit him down and ask him if he loves you. Ask him if he feels he has a future with you, and if not, why not. If you don't talk about your religions, they will definitely keep you apart. I'll tell you one thing as sure as I know the sun will rise tomorrow. If you both want to be together, you'll find a way. Don't be afraid to mix it up, shout a little, get everything out in the open."

"Thanks, Nadene."

"Let's go home."

Nadene and Rosa got into their cars parked on level one of the Main Street garage. Rosa exited in her Toyota Corolla, but instead of pulling onto the highway toward her home in Montpelier, she turned left on South Union Street toward Seth's apartment. She had never been inside, although he'd described parts of it to her.

She knocked on the door, but there was no answer. She heard music playing, so she knocked harder. Finally Seth answered in his bathrobe.

"Come in, I was taking a shower. I'll get dressed, be right back, sit down, sit down. Do you want coffee? I have some almond nut tarts I baked yesterday."

"That will be fine, but I've got to talk to you."

"I know, I haven't been able to sleep, I'm also upset. I'll be right back."

Seth disappeared to change his clothes, and Rosa listened more closely to the music. It was a haunting sound she'd never heard before, an old vinyl recording of the classical music of Iraq. The instruments included a santur, jaoza, and darbuka, and the vocals were mesmerizing. She studied the album cover and then glanced at the titles in Seth's bookcase. Filling the top shelf were books on religion, in both English and Arabic. Among the English titles were the Koran, two different Bibles, the Torah, Talmud, and books by Thomas Aquinas and Saint Augustine.

In the bedroom, Seth put on the pair of army pants he had worn at the Vermont Assembly. He always wore a top with something written on it. His tee said "Zildjian Cymbals." The writing and brass colored high-hat were worn, but still readable. *Why did she have to wear that black dress and those silver earrings? She thinks it makes her look less sexy, but she is so wrong.* Seth turned the volume down when he came back into the living room. Rosa was sitting on the couch, but he didn't sit next to her, choosing instead a chair next to the stereo.

"I'm glad I finally see where you live. Seth, I want to know more about you. You met my mother, you know about my family. You never talk about yours. I know you're from Egypt. Where in Egypt? Are your parents still alive? Did you ever have a girlfriend?"

"I was born and raised in El Minya, and yes, my parents are both alive. I'm afraid to talk about myself because we are from different worlds. I don't know if those worlds can ever come together."

"Well, let's find out, shall we? Nothing can be worse than the way it is now. We are being kept apart by things neither of us will speak about."

"You're right, but I don't know where to start."

"Tell me about your hometown, about your childhood, about your parents, about your religion, especially, your religion. I want to know everything about you."

"El Minya is on the Nile, about 150 miles from Cairo. I'll bet you didn't know that the world's biggest cemetery is there. It's called Zawiyyet al-Mayyiteen which means 'place of the dead.' Muslims and Christians are both buried there."

"Isn't it sad that they lie next to each other in death, but cannot stand to be next to each other in life? I do not accept this, Sethos. What does your name mean?"

"Sethos is the name of a prince, and Azizi means 'precious.' My mother is Greek and my father Egyptian. My mother stays at home and my father has a company that manufactures soap."

"Does she wear a burkha when she goes out in public?"

"No, she doesn't, many women don't. They live in a nice house that used to belong to a cotton baron. She is Orthodox Catholic but converted to Islam. I was raised a Muslim. When I was little, my father took me to the El-Umra Mosque. I memorized the entire Koran, and parts of the Bible, by the way. When I was thirteen, I was a teacher there and would instruct children in the ways of Islam."

"I had no idea you knew so much about religion. Did you have any girlfriends?"

"A few, but only one was serious. My parents knew her parents, and they did everything they could to bring us together, but it didn't last long. Finally she married a doctor and moved to France."

"Why do you say we can never be together?"

"I will not convert to your religion. You will not convert to my religion."

"I didn't fall in love with your religion, Sethos, I fell in love with you. Your religion is nothing but trouble for me."

"See, this is what I mean. For you Islam is trouble, for me it is life."

Rosa walked over to Seth's bookcase and grabbed the Koran. She had studied it and written several papers on its contents. She turned to Sura 5:51 and read from the book.

Have nothing to do with Christians or Jews, who are evil people – O you who believe! Do not take the Jews and the Christians for friends; they are friends of each other, and whoever amongst you takes them for a friend, then surely he is one of them; surely Allah does not guide the unjust people.

She turned the pages and read another passage from Sura 9:5.

Kill the unbelievers – So when the sacred months have passed away, then slay the idolaters wherever you find them, and take them captives and besiege them and lie in wait for them in ambush.

"Is this what you believe, is this what you embrace?"

Seth said nothing for an uncomfortably long while. He got up and selected a book from his library. He walked over to Rosa, handed her a Bible, and took back the Koran.

"I have two versions of the Bible. Look in the front, that is the Catholic version. It says Imprimatur. The other, on the shelf, is the King James version. Look at Revelation 2:7. It says: *He who has an ear, let him hear what the Spirit says to the churches. To him who conquers I will grant to eat of the tree of life, which is the paradise of God.*" Seth raised his voice. 'To him who conquers.'

"Shit, this will get us nowhere. Let me tell you something, Rosa, Osama Bin Laden does not speak for me. Did George Bush speak for you when he invaded Iraq?"

"No, but Islam is responsible for violence around the world."

"And who started the Crusades, the Swami of Hindustan? Look at the Irish. They kill each other in the name of the same Jesus Christ."

Rosa raised her voice in turn. "And what about the Sunnis and the Shiites? They enjoy slaughtering each other all over the Middle East." She put the Bible down on the couch and folded her arms.

Seth hung his head. "See what I mean? It will never work. You are beautiful, but we are doomed before we can even begin."

"Seth, the problem is that extremists in both our worlds are causing all the trouble. There are people who use these ancient texts and follow them literally. This is a disaster, because the old language and customs do not fit our modern world. They are not a blueprint, they are guidelines. Look at Christians. It says in the Bible, Mark 16:17, *they shall take up serpents and if they drink any deadly thing it shall not hurt them.* So there's a church in Tennessee where people in the congregation pick up rattlesnakes during the service."

"This is true?"

"Yes, and years ago one of the ministers was bitten and died. Moderate Christians and Muslims have no hatred for each other. Do you hate Christians and Jews?"

"Of course not."

"Sethos, you listen to me.   Jehovah, Allah, God the Father, Jesus, the Great Spirit, and many others are all the same. There is only one God, but we call Him by the name that we learned from our own culture. We'll all end up in the same Paradise; we just have different ways of getting there.   There isn't some office building in heaven with Gods in cubicles. Can you see it now, the Jewish office, the Catholic, Protestant, Muslim, and Buddhist offices."

Seth smiled and joined in. "And across the hall by the cloud-making machine, there's the Hindu, the Brahmins, and the Zoroastrians. But Allah is the President."

"He is not, Jesus is," Rosa giggled as she picked up the Bible.

Seth walked over to the couch and sat next to Rosa. He wore a playful smile as he read from Sura 36:55.

☾ *On that day the dwellers of Paradise shall think of nothing but their bliss. Together with their wives, they shall recline in shady groves upon soft couches. They shall have fruits and all that they desire.*

"See if you can top that in the Bible."

Rosa smiled and turned to the Song of Solomon.

† *Let him kiss me with the kisses of his mouth: for thy love is better than wine.*

They continued to read to each other, alternating verses from the Koran and the Bible.

☾ *Virgins as fair as corals and rubies. Which of your Lord's blessing would you deny?*

† *His left hand is under my head, and his right hand doth embrace me.*

☾ *Each bears every kind of fruit in pairs. Each is watered by a flowing spring. Which of your Lord's blessing would you deny?*

† *My beloved is like a roe or a young hart: behold he standeth behind our wall, he looketh forth at the windows, shewing himself through the lattice.*

Seth paused and grabbed Rosa's hand.

☾ *They shall recline on couches lined with thick brocade, and within their reach will hang the fruits of both gardens. Which of your Lord's blessing would you deny?*

† *I opened to my beloved; but he had withdrawn himself, and was gone: my soul failed when he spake: I sought him, but I could not find him; I called him, but he gave me no answer.*

Rosa dropped the Bible and burst into tears. Seth put one large hand on either side of her face, pulled her to him and kissed her mouth over and over again. Rosa turned toward Seth, slid one leg across his body, and sat on his lap facing him. She kissed him ardently. He put his hands inside her dress and lifted her off the couch with her legs wrapped around him. They held their kiss as he carried her to his bedroom and opened the door with his foot. He placed her gently on his bed, lay next to her, and they took off each other's clothes.

I am my beloved's, and his desire is toward me.

CHAPTER FOUR

Stephanie and Carol Morrison were going shopping with Don Satowski in the car he had just bought. There was a new status symbol in California: the hybrid car. People who could afford most anything they wanted were now driving these vehicles. Instead of trying to one-up each other with how much their vehicle cost, people now argued about which car got the best gas mileage. Big cars still turned heads, and many doctors drove luxury models, but Don had traded in his Land Rover SUV for a Toyota Prius. This made Carol happy, and she'd been chiding her mother about her Jaguar 140.

"I use it only every three weeks or so. I put about two thousand miles a year on the Jag," Stephanie tried to defend herself.

"But it gets about twelve miles to the gallon. Or is it twelve gallons to the mile?" Carol kept teasing her. "Gas is going to cost eight dollars a quart soon."

"You'll never ride in it again, you ungrateful little worm." Stephanie smiled as she hit Carol with a rolled up newspaper. Don was laughing.

"That'll teach you, Carol. Insult my lady's Jaguar and she'll beat the cah-cah out of you." Don continued to laugh as he pulled into the shopping mall. Carol had to go to the bookstore, and Steph and Don were headed for the furniture store. He needed a new recliner, and she wanted a new bed for the guestroom.

Saturday mornings were always busy at Stanford Plaza. For hundreds of shoppers, it was the major activity of the week as dozens of teenagers cruised trendy shops. Carol decided to use the Rite Buy entrance into the mall. The huge store was a wholly owned subsidiary of the WenCo Corporation. Row after row of giant screen TVs marched through the store and lined the entire back wall as well. *How can anyone work here, the noise is deafening.* Carol stopped and read the manufacturers' names: Sharp, Sony, Toshiba, Westinghouse, Magnavox, Samsung, Sylvania, Pioneer. *This store uses more electric power than a medium-sized African city.* With each passing month, the manufacturers upped the ante with features to lure the buyer. Digital-cinema-ready, next-generation high-definition DLP chips, memory-stick slot for viewing still images directly on your TV, IEEE 1394 FireWire DV interface that allows high-speed digital communication with camcorders, digital video recorders, and computers.

There were stacks of ads and flyers advertising direct TV: "Receive hundreds of channels. Watch four baseball games simultaneously on our split screen. We also carry the adult entertainment network." *That's the first station these kids are going to tune in when their parents aren't home. Trying to shut this down is going to be like trying to reverse the flow of a river.*

Carol noticed a group of high-school kids sitting on benches as she entered the mall from Rite Buy. The girls had tattoos on their lower backs, visible above their belts. Naturally they were all wearing midriff-bearing, cropped tees. Some of the boys were carrying skateboards and were wearing their baseball caps backwards.

Fifteen minutes later, a tremendous explosion was heard in the parking lot. A bomb had been planted in Don's car and detonated remotely. Human and metal parts were hurled over a half a mile. Three young shoppers who had just arrived at the mall, and parked next to Don Satowski, were killed instantly.

One hour later the phone rang at Senator McGuire's Burlington office. The B Team was in the conference room, planning tactics for the Senate committee hearing. Seth walked to the outer office and answered the phone. The office was on the other side of the music room, far enough away that the others couldn't hear him speak. The caller was Rocco DiAngelo of the FBI. Seth heard the news that Stephanie Morrison, Carol Morrison, and Donald Satowski had been killed by a car bomb. The FBI had found a human female foot and part of a man's hand. They had made positive identifications on all three victims based on human body samples and DNA evidence.

Rocco asked to speak to Mario, but Seth said that he would rather break the news in person. Before he hung up Rocco gave Seth a message. "You tell my friend that we will find the people who killed his sister and niece. I will not rest until I find them."

Seth was still in the outer office, wondering how he would tell Mario. He came back into the conference room, gray-faced.

Mario looked at Seth, knew instantly what was wrong and said, "Stephanie is dead, isn't she?"

"How can you think that? What do you mean?" Nadene asked.

Seth was fighting back tears. He hugged Mario and told him they were all dead, Stephanie, Don, and Carol.

~ ~ ~

Twins share a special bond. Mario and Stephanie had been even closer than most twins. No one can explain how Mario knew she was gone. Perhaps she spoke to him. It had to have been something spiritual, because there was no other explanation. Hundreds of thoughts passed in fast-frames through Mario's mind. He had lost a piece of himself. He remembered that he had kept putting off reading her new book, *The Beckwith Murders*. When she'd called him two days ago and asked him what he thought of it, he said he had been too busy to read it. He remembered his speech on the Senate floor. Why had he mentioned Steph and Carol? He had set them up for murder with

89

his big mouth. He remembered Carol at Rosa's apartment, the very last time he saw her.

She was so scared. I lifted her off the ground and she looked at me with trust. She felt safe. Rocco told me not to worry, that Steph was safe. Everyone was safe. Everyone is now dead. How do I tell my mother? Where's David? Was he with them?

Mario still had not spoken, even though Seth, Rosa, and Nadene were sobbing. He stood up, grabbed his black umbrella, and walked out the door. Rosa tried to follow him, but he held up his hand to stop her. "Thank you, I need to be alone. You will have to work without me for a few days. Call Rocco DiAngelo and tell him to watch out for David. They may try to get him next."

It was a chilly day in Vermont for this late in June, and there was a light drizzle falling. Mario left Court House Plaza and walked down Main Street. Most stores were closed for the day, and there were few pedestrians braving the weather. He moved quickly. The repetitive act of putting one foot down in front of the other freed his thoughts. Suddenly he wanted to visit Barre and see the house where his family used to live, and St. Francis Church where they went to Mass every Sunday. He always sat next to Stephanie and made jokes about the pastor with the great big belly. Once he used the word "stupid" instead of "sacred" when the congregation was praying, and Steph laughed out loud. Everyone in the church heard Steph, so they both got punished.

He remembered what the punishment was, no TV for a week. The next Sunday his mother separated them. His mom and dad sat between him and Steph. He still managed to make her laugh by making funny squeaks with his freshly shined shoes while they were kneeling. This time he was the only one who was punished. No TV for two weeks. No Mickey Mouse Club, no Lone Ranger, no Ed Sullivan. It was the worst thing they could have done to him. He was heartbroken. He remembered that Steph wouldn't watch

TV either, until he was again able to. That's the way she is. That's the way she *was*.

He stopped in a liquor store and asked the man behind the register to bring him a bottle of Redbreast Irish whiskey. He handed the clerk his credit card, and stuffed the whiskey into a brown paper bag. Imprinted in green on the bag were the words "Drink Responsibly."

Mario walked another two blocks to the Lake Champlain Cab Company. The dispatcher recognized him and said hello. Mario asked to be taken to Barre. The dispatcher had just heard the news of Stephanie's death on the radio and gave Mario her condolences. She refused to charge him anything, and a driver took him to the cemetery behind Saint Francis Church.

He visited his father's grave, took the foil off the bottle of Redbreast, twisted the cork out with his teeth, and spat it to the left side of the grave. He poured some out on the soil as a tribute. He had not cried, and tried somehow to connect with his sister. His thoughts were only of her, Carol, and his family. He talked to his sister and prayed out loud, but was answered only by silence.

It was almost midnight and Mario was wet and cold. The bottle was more than half gone. He was carrying it by the neck with his left hand as he walked toward the church.   He tried the side entrance and found it open. No one was inside, and the lights were turned off except for offertory candles that were stacked like bleacher seats on an eight-foot-long wrought iron table to the left of the altar. They illuminated the entire front of the church. He hadn't been inside this building in over forty years. It was exactly the same as he remembered it, except for one thing. On the right side of the altar there was now a life-sized statue of Saint Francis. Mario stumbled up the aisle to row seven and sat in the exact spot where he and Stephanie had always sat. He cried for half an hour before getting up. He staggered over to the statue of Saint Francis, took another long drink, and dropped the bottle of whiskey. It shattered on the marble floor. He began talking to the statue.

"Ooops, look here, Frank. You don't mind if I call you Frank, do you? I dropped m' bottle, all gone. Tell me something, Frank, is all of this bullshit? Are you up in heaven or is your dust long gone? How 'bout giving me a sign. I'm waiting, Frank ol' buddy. How 'bout a shaft of light, make a white dove appear. How 'bout piping in some Robert Johnson music. I didn't think so. You tell your boss that he's a phony. You tell him that if he really existed, he wouldn't let beautiful souls like my beloved sister and my beloved niece be slaughtered. You tell him that, Frank, ol' buddy. You tell him that, Frank. You tell him..."

Mario stood up with his arm around the statue. He passed out and fell, dragging the statue down with him. Saint Francis shattered when it hit the marble, and Mario sprawled unconscious next to the broken pieces.

~ ~ ~

Ludlowe Wenman grabbed a Napoleon and poured himself a cup of rare Colombian coffee. His mother Beatrice addressed him just as he sat down at the conference table. "I'd like a cup of coffee with cream and sugar, you know how much I use, and I would also like two of those lemon Linzer tarts."

Ludlowe was clearly annoyed. "Yes, mother."

There was one additional person present at this week's Metro Media conference room meeting, Senator Cyrus Whitcom of Texas.

Harold Slokov brought the meeting to order and asked John Peterson for his report. "We have had several 'corporate dismissals.' McGuire's sister, and the other top Stanford researcher, Don Satowski, were neutralized yesterday."

"Why did we kill them?" Slokov asked. "This is going to make my job much tougher, trying to get Julie McGuire to go along with us. What if she now feels sorry for her husband?"

Peterson responded, "We don't think it will make one bit of difference. We believe she will come on board. She's just being coy. The very minute she agreed to come up here to talk to you, that's when her decision was made. She's just playing you like a big trout."

"Fuck you, Peterson," Slokov said. "She wouldn't give you the time of day if you had a diamond watch stuck up your ass."

"That's enough, gentlemen." Cyrus Whitcom raised his voice. Whitcom was tall, clumsy, without much muscle mass, and had sandy hair. He was not good-looking like Harold Slokov, but Whitcom was the richest man in the U.S. government and was one of the highest-ranking senators. He had been selected by the Vice President to sit on the committee that will evaluate Mario McGuire's ban-TV bill. He put events in perspective for the others.

"Now see here, this was a good move for several reasons. Number one, Mario McGuire will now be off his game. He was closer to his sister than he is to his wife. He will now be minimally effective, at best. His staff will try to fill in for him, but I seriously doubt if they can convince any of the Republican members of this committee. Number two, I like the idea of instilling fear in all the others. We've learned a few things from the terrorists we've been chasing. Strike into the heart of your enemy. Let them wonder who's going to be next. Which researcher at Stanford is going to be brave enough to apply for Satowski's job? I'll bet there aren't any."

Beatrice Wenman said, "We need a new legal team. I've fired the lawyers that worked for me. They did an abysmal job in Vermont. I don't want the Supreme Oil lawyers, either. We must bring in a new team and pay them top dollar. I don't want to contract with a company full of hot-shot partners, who have other work going on. I want the highest paid people with the best track records to concentrate solely on this hearing. Let them hire a hundred paralegals to fetch for them. Who cares how much it costs? We can't afford any more performances like the one in Vermont."

"I agree," Slokov said.

"Why don't we just kill Mario McGuire?" Ludlowe asked.

Cyrus Whitcom was clearly annoyed. "Beatrice, why can't you leave Ludlowe at home? Tell you what I'm going to do, son. It will be your job to kill Mario. Do you have a gun with a silencer, and know how to use it?"

"No, I didn't mean that *I* should do it."

"Then what exactly did you mean?"

"I want someone else to do it, a professional."

"Who would you recommend?"

"I don't know."

"Precisely, Ludlowe, you don't know. Since you don't know anything, please shut the hell up."

Beatrice laughed out loud. "Please get me another tart, son."

Ludlowe didn't move.

Peterson said, "I agree with Beatrice that a new legal team is a top priority. Harold, we want you to concentrate on finding experts who can refute the researchers' medical evidence. We're going to need them at the hearing. Again, pay all people top dollar. There is a cardinal rule here, lady and gentlemen, everything and everyone we use must be the absolute best. If not, we're going to have a rough time."

Whitcom spoke. "There is another disturbing item. Skip Walsh of Eagle Claw told me he has so far been unable to successfully plant listening devices on any of McGuire's staff. I've asked John Peterson to get authorization to intercept cellphone messages. McGuire has an electronics expert on staff who can spot bugs in land-line phones. We can monitor all their cellphone frequencies, but that may not be enough. Their expert, that towelhead Sethos Azizi, may know that cellphones are vulnerable, and try something different. We will also intercept their messages at the phone company's relay points. There's no way that can be detected. We can use national security as the reason."

"Why not just kill Azizi?" Ludlowe asked.

"Normally, I would agree to that," Peterson said. "But they have just released a blues-music CD which has sold millions of copies. Azizi and the rest of those bastards are becoming rock stars. McGuire's team is much too visible to be eliminated. We have to beat them at the committee hearing. His bill will never get out of committee, and the issue will be dropped."

The meeting was adjourned. Ludlowe Wenman was the first person to leave. He didn't wait for his mother, who called after him.

Whitcom stopped Peterson and Slokov. "We'll have to keep on eye on Pudge; he's becoming a problem. We can't afford any internal strife. And that goes for the two of you as well. If we work against each other, we might as well be working for Mario McGuire. Do I make myself clear?"

Slokov and Peterson shook hands, and the three of them walked out the door past the security guards.

~ ~ ~

Mario woke up in a small bed, in a simple but tastefully decorated room in the church rectory. He moaned and held his head. Everything was spinning, and his left forearm was wrapped in a large bandage. Father Raymond Messier heard Mario and fully opened the door, which had been left open a few inches.

"How do you feel, Senator McGuire?" the priest asked. "I'm so sorry about your sister and niece. I know how much they meant to you."

Father Messier was seventy-one years old. He was frail looking, like an Indian Marharishi, but was deceptively strong. He had been at St. Francis for over thirty years, and knew Mario's mother Sophia very well. She still came to church every Sunday.

"Thank you, Father, I guess I passed out. Did you put this bandage on my arm? What happened? What did I do?"

"Yes, I did, you broke a bottle of whiskey on the floor, good stuff, I might add. You must have been leaning on the statue of Saint Francis because it fell over with you. You cut yourself when you fell."

"Is the statue broken?"

"Quite."

"I'm sorry, Father, I'll pay for a new one." Mario stood up. His head was pounding like there was a wild animal trapped inside trying to get out.

"Your mother called me last night. Nadene went to see her and comforted her. She's very upset."

"Father, shit, I should have been the one to tell her. She's so old, this will probably kill her." Mario shouted, "You can't tell me that God is merciful, this is bullshit! Why does he allow such suffering?"

"I know how you feel. Sometimes I'm angry at Him too. But He doesn't create suffering. He's made us with free will. It's what we do to each other, that's the problem."

"What about Carol and those three innocent teenagers who were also blown up? What about little children who die in car and plane crashes?"

"Perhaps He is involved with the larger picture. No human can understand His divine plan. That's where faith comes in."

"I'm glad it works for you, Father. Please let me know how much my damage cost the church. I would like to give a donation over and above that as well, and I can never repay your kindness. May I use your phone to call a cab? I must see my mother."

"You may not," the priest answered sternly. He took car keys out of his pocket and handed them to Mario. "It's the white Buick parked near the cemetery."

"But I don't have a driver's license, Father."

"You know how to drive, don't you, and you have an expired Vermont license, right?"

"Yes."

"Well, the Lord told me to let you use my car. I won't need it until Tuesday. All you have to do to repay me is go to the Motor Vehicle bureau, get your picture taken, and get a current, valid license. Oh, and fill the tank with gas.

"The Lord told me something else. He wanted me to smash my television set, not just throw it away. I had a good time heaving it into the dumpster. The tube made a very loud pop when it hit the bottom, almost as loud as a firecracker. Reading a good book is better than watching any sitcom; I won't miss it. We ought not to expose ourselves to the physical health risks; the researchers proved how dangerous they are. Mario, please look at something else. The risk to our spiritual health is even greater. You must talk to religious leaders and get their support."

Mario listened intently to the last thing Father Messier said. For the moment he was thinking about something other than the death of his sister. He had a flashback to his family's newspaper and how all the advertisers had left for the TV station. "That's a wonderful idea. Let's talk about it when I return your car. Car, what am I doing? Father, it makes me nauseous to ride in a car."

"It makes you nauseous to *ride* in a car, but not to drive a car. This isn't physical, Mario, it's psychological. When you have to drive, you'll forget all about getting sick, although I must admit that this morning you may have a good reason to be sick. If you have to throw up, try to do it out the window. If a cop stops you, I guarantee that you'll be given clear passage. Just tell the officer to call me at this number." He handed Mario a piece of paper with the phone number on it. "You're Mario McGuire, and you have important things to do. Go with my blessing. Go with Stephanie's blessing."

~ ~ ~

Harold Slokov answered his phone.

"Hello, Harold, I'm not able to meet with you as we planned."

"You know something, Julie, I'm beginning to think that you aren't interested in my offer."

"I didn't say that I wasn't interested, I said I couldn't meet with you as planned."

"Julie, I've had enough of these put-offs and delays. Are you going to work with us, or not? Just answer yes or no, and answer right now!" Slokov had raised his voice.

"There's no reason to come unglued, Harold, all I want to do is make it another day. We can meet two days later if you want to. I'm going to see my husband and have dinner with him in Washington on Friday night."

"Isn't that nice," Slokov said sarcastically.

"Do you, or do you not, want to know what is going on?"

"We do, but it sounds to me like you *are* working with us."

"Harold, we can discuss it when we meet. How about Monday evening at 8:00?"

"You had better be here or the deal is off. By the way, what restaurant are you eating in?"

"Why do you want to know?"

"Just curious, I guess."

"Bistro Bis. Mario and his staff like to eat there. It's next to the Hotel George near the Capitol."

"I know exactly where it is," Slokov said. "See you Monday night."

Slokov placed a call to John Peterson and instructed him to have agents at the restaurant with hidden directional microphones recording every word of the conversation between Julie and Mario McGuire. He wanted to listen in on Mario's staff as well, so it would be wise to have several agents who could roam freely in case they were sitting in a different area.

Peterson liked the idea. "Piece of cake, Harold, about the easiest assignment an agent could have. We should learn a lot."

~ ~ ~

Bistro Bis was frequented by senators, congressmen, and power brokers of every persuasion. The atmosphere was upscale French bistro. It was warm and intimate but decidedly modern. The interior was paneled with natural cherry, and it had a zinc bar with tall columns. The tables were located on multiple levels divided by translucent screens. You could see through the glass and observe diners on the other levels.

The restaurant was nearly full, and Mario was waiting at a table in the center of the largest level. The table next to his was empty because he also expected his three staff members to show up a half-hour later than Julie. That would give the two of them some time to talk privately. He hadn't seen her since Stephanie died, although he had spoken with her on several occasions.

He was also hungry because he had skipped lunch. Mario loved the pommes frites and the bouillabaisse, and was anxious to eat. He called the waiter over and ordered for himself and Julie. He knew she liked the braised veal stew. He ordered her a vodka martini and himself a Redbreast straight up. Julie arrived about ten minutes late and kissed Mario before she sat down. The waiter delivered their drinks.

"I'm so sorry about Stephanie and Carol. I knew this would all end badly. Why are you continuing a fight you can't win, and probably shouldn't even be trying to win? What are you waiting for? Are you waiting for them to kill me? Perhaps that's what you wish would happen."

Mario glared at Julie. "Don't be so melodramatic, this has nothing to do with you. You've never been involved in my work. That is your choice. Admit it, you don't give a shit whether I'm successful or not."

"I'm very impressed, Mario, that you want to save the world. Did you ever think of trying to save your fucking marriage?"

"I knew this would happen. I haven't seen you in weeks and we're together for less than five minutes and already we're fighting."

The waiter brought the food and asked them if they wanted another drink. They both said yes. He filled their water glasses and left to get their drinks.

"You don't need a wife, you need a doormat you can wipe your feet on. I've had it. People I've never met are cursing at me because you want to take away their televisions. Why should I have to be afraid? Do you think that's fair?"

"We all have to make sacrifices. Think of all the people who will die if we're not successful."

"You should be thinking of Stephanie, Don, and Carol. They are dead, remember, you bastard!"

"Why don't you go back into your own selfish world and leave me alone?"

"You and this marriage can go straight to hell," Julie screamed at Mario.

Nadene, Rosa, and Seth arrived just in time to hear her last comment, and watched in dismay as she shoved Mario's dinner across the table onto his lap. She threw a glass of water in his face. She also splashed the wife of a congressman from Pennsylvania who was sitting directly behind Mario. The woman was startled and jumped up. All the diners were watching this spectacle with interest. Julie raced past Mario's staff without making eye contact. She walked out onto the street and down the block. Seth told Rosa and Nadene to sit down with Mario, and he left to follow Julie.

A Domestic Security agent stepped into the women's room to use her cellphone in private. "Pigeon out of the coop, flying east." She repeated the message.

"Got her," was the response. A black limo with tinted glass pulled up alongside Julie. John Peterson was in the middle seat and Harold Slokov was sitting in the rear. He opened the door and told Julie to get in. Seth was standing in the perfect spot to see a reflection of the limo interior on the rear-window glass. He saw Slokov grab and kiss Julie McGuire, just before the door closed. Seth ran back to Bis and found Mario and the others standing outside. He told Mario what had happened.

"You have to divorce her, you can no longer trust her. She got into a black stretch-limo and kissed the guy who was in the back seat. I don't know who he was."

"I don't care who he was," Mario said, and then he raised his voice. "She can't hurt us, we have more important things to do."

"Rotten bitch," Rosa said to Nadene.

"You're better off without her," Nadene told Mario. He was obviously upset, but refused to discuss it any further and immediately changed the subject.

~ ~ ~

Mario was in his Washington office at the Capitol. He was expecting the B Team to arrive in twenty minutes. He opened his desk drawer and removed what looked like a black wallet. But instead of a wad of cash, he pulled out a Beretta Tomcat automatic from a black square holster. Because of recent threats on his life, Rocco DiAngelo had been able to get him full carry-and-concealment privileges that could be used in any government building or airline. All he had to do was show his special ID and he could go anywhere a Federal Marshall could.

The weapon was a small, stainless steel, 32-caliber automatic. It held eight shots of high-powered Cor Bon ammo, the same company that made Nadene's 45-caliber ammo. In knock-down power, it was about the same as the old snub-nosed .38, but the .32 was much more concealable. The square wallet-holster hid the gun's profile in his pants pocket. Mario could draw and fire the Tomcat in less than half a second, and he could place three quick shots inside a four-inch circle at thirty-five feet. He kept one Beretta in Washington and another in Burlington. He was never without one in his pocket.

A week earlier, he had decided to drive to the National Forest in Lincoln, Vermont. He went for a long walk in the woods carrying a micro tape recorder and a small canvas bag. In the bag were hearing protectors, a box of 50 .32 ACP shells, and paper targets. He did some bull's-eye shooting. He had always been very good with a handgun. In Vietnam, no one could outshoot him with a .45 or a 9mm auto. He brought the tape recorder with him because he often got his best ideas when he was in the woods. He spoke into the recorder of violence and death, and of his decision to write a book when this was all over.

Now Mario's team was just about to arrive at the office. He looked at his new driver's license. He managed a slight smile, thinking about Nadene. She was actually upset that she didn't have to chauffeur him everywhere. He had thought she'd be happy.

They were on time, and the first thing Seth did was to make a scan with the bug detector. He found nothing.

Mario often bought presents for his staff. This time he gave them a book called *Material World*. It was a beautiful collection of photographs and articles about how an average family lived. Countries from all corners of the earth were represented. It showed compelling pictures of each family and all the possessions they owned. It showed a gold-plated bathroom in Kuwait, and the total lack of bathrooms in Ethiopia. It showed the rugged, simple faces of a family in Nepal, their possessions able to fit on a tabletop. Contrasted with their poverty were families from Europe, America, and the Middle East, possessing astonishing material abundance.

Mario had always had a global world-view. He loved America, and had been ready to die for his country, but he knew that the future of mankind depended on embracing other cultures. He had always fought against outrages to the human spirit. He often quoted the great missionary, Albert Schweitzer: "The quality of a culture is based on its reverence for all life." Mario hated the stranglehold that big corporations had on the American people. The CEOs got richer as our precious resources disappeared into their pockets, and into the pockets of war profiteers. He feared that corporate interests would defeat his efforts to ban TV, in spite of all the evidence of harm being done.

Mario sometimes took himself too seriously, and could be a real prig. He could always find a soapbox and would rant and rave at the slightest provocation. He could be intolerant of people's shortcomings, especially if the person had a different view of life than he did. He had a quick temper and had made hundreds of enemies in Washington. *Compromise* was a word that eluded him. Nobody knew these things about Mario better than Mario himself.

Last year, Mario had taken a group of seniors on a bus to Canada so they could buy affordable prescription drugs. None of his colleagues would have had the guts. Or perhaps none of them had the same world-view. Mario would always champion the cause of the honest little guy trying to make it. He would also kick the absolute shit out of you if you were one of those people trying to victimize that honest little guy. If you were a government liar, a corporate liar, a military liar, or a member of any other sub-human species, he would work hard against you. He would rally others against you. Mario McGuire was a man who liars couldn't beat one-on-one. They had to use other means.

The heat was being turned up by the dark side, as Obi-Wan Kenobe referred to Darth Vader and his band. Mario liked the old *Star Wars* movies because they were clear-cut morality plays about good and evil. He was approaching this week's senate hearing the same way. This was clearly a battle between good and evil.

~~~

They all got a surprise when David knocked on the door. "What are you doing here?" Mario asked as he greeted him.

"I have come to testify at the hearing. Takeo and Sara are arriving tomorrow." David gathered himself and looked at Mario. "You know that Takeo hardly ever loses."

"I'm against it, you're both at risk. I put an FBI tail on you, how did you elude them?"

"I didn't even know they were following me, and it doesn't matter. Now that I've lost Carol, I don't care what happens to me. She was my everything. She will never be replaced. I'm not afraid to die, because then I would be with her. I will testify and hold up her picture. You have to let me."

The phone rang. "Hello Mario, this is Rocco. As you know, David arrived safely at your office. Do you want us to continue keeping tabs on him, or will he be working with you?" Mario excused himself and asked everyone to leave the office. Seth started frantically waving his hands and said, "No, do not speak."

"What's going on, Seth?"

Seth told him that his phone was probably bugged. Mario relayed this news to Rocco and asked him not to call his number. He would be in contact with him by other means.

Seth reminded everyone that telephone communications of any kind were very risky. The Government Office of Domestic Security, GODS, had the capability to intercept cellphone messages, and was probably listening to the other phones at the network level.

"What do we do?" Mario asked.

Seth would tell them his plan, later.

Nadene handed Mario two hand-written sympathy cards. They were from Vermont's junior senator and its lone representative. He rarely met or worked with either of them. They were both Democrats, and were usually more conservative than Mario, who was an Independent. Mario had managed to alienate both of them. They usually voted on the same side, but Mario had heavily criticized them for not supporting his Ambassador Corps proposal. He had also refused to support their military pay cutbacks. Mario couldn't count on his colleagues' enthusiastic support for his bill, but thought they would probably vote for the ban in the end.

~ ~ ~

Mario outlined his agenda for the next week. "The hearing starts in only four days, so we will be very busy. I just learned that Governor Thompson of Missouri wants us to appear before their state hearing tomorrow."

"Tomorrow?" Nadene showed surprise.

"That's right. There's an excellent chance that they'll pass the ban. Rosa, make the flight arrangements. Nadene, make all the appointments and on-the-ground itinerary. Seth, gather our presentation material. I'm going to contact Governor Thompson. David, you need to stay here and meet with Takeo. Use this office."

Seth reminded everyone not to use the phones anywhere in the building. "If you have to make a call, go into a restaurant, a gas station, anywhere but from here."

"Whoa, wait a minute, there's a lot more," Mario said. "Seth and Rosa have to fly from Missouri to North Carolina and talk with the governor about their hearing. It's the day after the Missouri hearing. While you're there, it's vitally important for you to talk with the Reverend Virgil MacKenzie. He's pastor of the largest Baptist congregation in Charlotte. Father Messier from Barre met him at a National Council of Churches, Synagogues, and Mosques convention. He's the president of that organization, and he's passionately anti-television and wants to testify on behalf of the ban. I can't go to North Carolina because I must get ready for the hearing. Please bring Reverend MacKenzie back with you.

"Nadene, when you get back here from Missouri, I want you to try to get other religious leaders to work with us. If we can get their support, we will erode our opponents' traditional power-base. Republicans started out as the religious right's darlings, but lately they've fallen out of favor with their lies and immoral

106

behavior. It's time for us to flash, in bright neon lights, in the biggest letters possible, that America doesn't belong to those who are now in power. Our leaders are actually the Antichrist, if I may use their term."

"Is that all you want me to do?" Nadene said sarcastically.

"I know it's a big job, but just get started. Let's see if we can recruit some divine help. In the meantime, let's get packin' and crackin', we're off to Missouri."

~ ~ ~

The next morning at 9:00, the B Team was driving down Highway 70 in a rented beige Ford Taurus, traveling from St. Louis to Jefferson City, the capital of Missouri.

Nadene was driving and she asked, "Has anybody heard of the 'Memphis Blues'?" She waited for a response. "No? Okay, how about another song written by the same composer. Here's your clue: W.C. Handy wrote it in 1914."

"Oh, I know," Mario said.

Nadene looked at Seth and Rosa in the back seat. "Still don't know? Well, here's my version." Nadene belted out the first verse of "Saint Louis Blues."

"Oh, I hate to see the evening sun go down..."

Rosa clapped rhythmically, and Seth used the back of his computer case as a hand drum. Everyone was singing and stamping their feet.

Nadene added a few verses of her own to the song.

When we get to Jefferson City, we're gonna have our say,

When we get to Jefferson City, we're gonna have our say,
Missouri is gonna vote with us
And then the whole U. S. of A.

Then it's on to North Carolina, we're really on a jelly roll,
It's on to North Carolina, yes we're on a jelly roll,
Gonna stick it to the government,
Cause they're out of control.

"How can you be *on* a jelly roll?" Seth asked playfully, "Wouldn't you squash all the juice out of it?"

"Never you mind about that, Mr. Azizi, you're too young and inexperienced to know about that." Nadene winked at Seth.

This was the first time since the death of his family that Mario had shown any joy, or interest in music. Nadene pressed the scan button on the AM and then the FM radio. She was looking for one of their songs. She finally found "Broke Back Baby Blues." First Mario said, "Oh, my God," then he smiled.

"They're playing us here, chillins, that's a good sign," Nadene said.

~ ~ ~

The Missouri hearing was over even more quickly than the Vermont hearing. There were only two dissenting votes in the entire Legislature. The Missouri wording was a bit different, and their bill was called "The Public Protection Act." For the first time since he had introduced the ban, Mario and his team believed it was possible to win. They were still afraid for their lives, and for the lives of David and the others, but now they were not alone. If

North Carolina passed the ban the next day, the entire nation would take notice.

Mario said, "Seth, you were a good basketball player. You know about momentum. It's hard to know what makes it work. All of a sudden your team starts to play good defense, and everyone hits his three-point shots. The opposition calls a time-out to try to stop you. Sometimes it works, and sometimes it doesn't. If you come back from the time-out, and continue to play with momentum, you can put the game out of reach, and even beat teams that are better than you. Catch my drift here?"

"Oh yeah," Seth replied, "I got it, but what if we go cold and miss our shots?"

Rosa playfully hit him on the head.

The B Team split up and headed for North Carolina and Washington.

~ ~ ~

Mario's first stop was to visit Rocco DiAngelo at the FBI. Rocco had some news. "We can't say for sure yet if they are all dirty, but we have a real good lead on who's behind your sister's death, and possibly all the other crimes. We know where they hold their weekly meetings."

"Fantastic! For Christ's sake, tell me."

"Mario, I know what a hothead you can be, so I don't want you to do anything to mess this up. Do I have your word?"

"Yes, you do."

Rocco DiAngelo had a pristine record of public service. He was six feet two inches tall, and still had jet-black hair. Even though he no longer worked in the field, he always carried his issue weapon in a shoulder holster under his jacket. Mario had seen him in action many times. He would joke with Julie, when they were on speaking terms, that Rocco *always* got his man.

"Okay, buddy, here's what we've got. I checked the movements of Lyle Sinton of Supreme Oil, Beatrice Wenman of WenCo, and Skip Walsh of Eagle Claw Securities. We know that they all have close ties to Harold Slokov of Metro Media. They prepared the legal team you faced in Vermont, and they have worked together on other things."

"Yeah, sure. Working on ways to rob the American people," Mario said.

"We monitored all their flight schedules and knew when they would be in Dallas, so I set up surveillance outside Metro Media's offices. We've got photographs of all the people I mentioned, plus, and you're going to like this, two other scumbags wandered into our camera range."

Mario shouted out, "John Peterson and Cyrus Whitcom!"

"You got it, baby."

"Were they all there on the same day?"

"More than once. They meet every Friday night at 9:00. The nightcrawlers think that the dark gives them protection."

"Rocco, how did you get the photos of them at night? Let's go in there and arrest them all!"

"Mario, here's where you have to have patience. We can't arrest ordinary citizens just for meeting. We need to know why they are meeting and what they are saying. When we broke up an organized crime syndicate in Connecticut, we had video cameras planted at the hotel. They were all caught with their pants down, and prosecution was easy. We can't do this at Metro Towers, because the conference room is completely isolated."

"So they meet and plot, and we can't touch them?"

"Not exactly. Mario, if you breathe a word of this you will compromise the entire FBI, do I make myself clear? Do not tell Julie, do not tell Nadene. I want you to sleep with a gag in your mouth, just in case someone is listening. I want you to put a metal pail over your head in case someone is trying to read your mind."

"Rocco, you have my word that whatever you tell me, stays right here."

"All right, here's what's going down. The photos outside the hotel were no problem. We didn't even need to use infrared or night-vision technology. We have ultra-fast films that work great at close range, much better than low-light digital cameras. The conference room is another matter. It's on the 39th floor, the glass is completely opaque and can't be penetrated from the outside.

"Here's what we're going to do. We have a newly developed long-range camera. It is infrared and sits in an anti-shake housing. We can get a perfect shot of a human face through the glass from a distance of three miles because the camera is highly heat-sensitive. Because of the anti-shake technology, the images are always sharp. We've rented an office under an assumed company name, in a building just half a mile from Metro Media. It's about level with the 39th floor conference room. I made some test photos and here's what they look like." Rocco turned on a laptop computer.

"Wow, these aren't still photos, you got motion. But what good will these be? You already know who's in the room. We can't hear what they're saying."

"You and I can't hear them, Mario, but Agent Maria Perez can. She's been deaf since birth, and she's an expert at reading lips. I admit that a person has to be facing the window or be in profile for her to read him." DiAngelo enlarged the computer image. "Notice how the person at the head of the table is always in profile. Here is what Maria transcribed. It's a sales meeting that took place a few days ago, and the sales manager is talking."

Mario took the sheet of paper and read while he watched the computer. "It is important for you, Ralph, to sell every minute of the game. I don't care what they want to advertise, as long as they're willing to pay. So she flashed her tit, who cares? Nancy, do you have the new projections for me? (pause) This is shit, this is total shit. We are down, down, down. We're losing market share. (pause) I don't care about the ban. (pause) I know what she did, but I don't care about that either. We will just have to raise our rates in other markets to compensate."

"Dis is absolutely amazing!" Mario was very excited.

"You'll notice that there are pauses. That's because the sales manager was responding to questions from someone whose back was to Maria. We still got want we wanted. We know what the meeting was about, and if they were doing something illegal, we could trap them. We will be able to understand every word of the person sitting at the head of the table, and I'll bet that person will be either Harold Slokov or Cyrus Whitcom."

"Rocco, did you get a court order?"

"Not yet, it's just a test."

"Thanks for sticking your neck out."

"I told you we're going to get Peterson, and it looks like a whole lot more. I'll get the court order later."

Mario knew how precarious it was for Rocco to walk the thin line between doing his job effectively, and tipping his hand to corrupt judges. They both believed in the Constitution and to a citizen's right to privacy. But this was a case in which the government itself was engaging in criminal acts. Mario couldn't follow correct procedures, get court orders, play by the book, and expect to defeat them.

The Government Office of Domestic Security had a small, elite group of agents, helicopters, and other aircraft at its disposal. At most, there were a few hundred GODS agents. They were no match for the FBI, but Domestic Security had immense power. They could wiretap at will, they could arrest people and make them disappear, and they could conduct any covert operation without legal approval.

Rocco was right when he said that the FBI had to use some of Domestic Security's own methods against them. Mario only hoped they could use these tactics without becoming dirty themselves.

CHAPTER FIVE

It was 10:01 a.m. in Room SD-325, Russell Senate Office Building. The Senate committee was now in session. This was the same room that had held the Clarence Thomas/Anita Hill hearings of 1991. It also saw the Iran Contra Affair in 1987, and in 1973 it heard testimony on the Watergate break-in. The room was big, 74 feet long by 54 feet wide, and was furnished with several hundred simple metal and wood chairs that could be moved about. Right now they were in perfect rows, but by the end of the day they would be rearranged into clusters. The room boasted two Corinthian pilasters and the ceiling was decorated with classical motifs, rosettes, and a Greek key, all of which had been recently gilded. Besides the six windows looking out on the courtyard, light came from white globes etched with emblems on American themes.

The gallery was full, and the entire session would be televised, an irony that many people had noticed. Chairperson of the committee was the Honorable Nancy Hollister, Republican senator from Iowa. Also present on the committee were Senators Whitcom, Heller, Sanchez, Klein, Giulini, Radkiss, Snowdon, Connor, Bruch, Pappas, Lowenstein, Burton, and Caulfield. Six of the senators were Democrats and seven were Republicans. The chairperson would not vote.

Senator Hollister spoke into her microphone. "This meeting is now in session. I'm going to ask the Capitol Hill Police to maintain order and decorum in this room. Anyone who disrupts this hearing by any means will be escorted out of the committee room.

"Today this committee is meeting to hear evidence on Resolution 16-3, The Cancer Prevention Act. It will recommend, by a simple majority vote, whether or not this bill will be brought before the full senate for further debate and final vote. Since there are no abstentions allowed, and since thirteen senators are voting, there can be no tie.

"This hearing is scheduled to last for ten days. During that time we will hear from those who are for, and those who are against, The Cancer Prevention Act. I will direct this hearing to allow only those questions that are relevant to the subject at hand. I will not permit grandstanding, or long-winded dissertations that do not directly speak to whether or not moving images on a screen pose a health risk to the American people.

"My primary job as chairperson is to be fair, and to give every witness who acts in good faith the time to present her or his evidence. This committee will explore all avenues to find the truth. I will not allow members of this committee to inhibit or thwart legitimate discussion. I will overrule any speaker who is not presenting facts, or who is taking advantage of his or her position, either on the committee or as a witness, to obfuscate the issues. No one will be permitted to subvert our search for the true facts of this case.

"I will ask proponents of the bill to speak first. They will have two hours. I will then allow opponents to speak for two hours. During this time, members of the committee will refrain from asking questions. At the end of the four-hour period, we will take a short break. Then my esteemed colleagues may question the witnesses. At the beginning of each session, members of this Committee will be allowed to call any witness they choose. I will alternate between those who are for, and those who are against the bill. Cross-examination will then be allowed before the next witness is introduced. Everyone who speaks in this room will be required to take a solemn oath to tell the truth.

"The issue before us is whether or not the health of the American people is endangered by watching television or computer screens. It is up to this committee to decide whether or not further study is needed, and whether or not the bill should be brought to the Senate floor for a vote."

Mario was already nervous. He liked Chairperson Hollister's opening remarks but didn't like the wording of her last statement. If the committee voted that further study was needed, they could bottle the bill up for months. *What the hell did you expect?* Mario chided himself. *They're not going to roll out a red velvet carpet from here to the Senate floor.*

Nancy Hollister had decided that the bill's supporters would speak first. She called Senator McGuire to make his opening statement. "The chair recognizes the Independent senator from Vermont."

"Thank you, Madam Chairperson, and distinguished senators. I thank you for the opportunity to present what we will prove to be a crisis facing America that is greater than any in living memory. We will prove that immediate action is needed to safeguard the citizenry. We will further prove that medical research is urgently needed to address disease that is already developing in our citizens as a result of exposure to television and other moving images.

"I'm not going to make a long-winded speech on the dangers. There are people present who can speak to the issues far better than I can. As you have so correctly stated, Madam Chairperson, our goal is to arrive at the truth. I accept your guidelines, and will conduct myself according to your stated objectives. We hope the opposition will do the same. We will not respond to rancor with additional rancor. Let me assure members of this Committee that we will conduct ourselves with the utmost decorum.

"We will hear from Dr. David Feinstein and Dr. Takeo Arai, the two researchers who discovered the link between moving images and cancer in the human body. Doctor Arai is a distinguished scholar and researcher from Keio University in Japan. We are fortunate to have this corroborative evidence from a highly qualified, impartial source. We are fortunate that they were able to document and finalize their research before an unspeakable outrage was perpetrated. Before I turn this microphone over to them, I would like to speak of crimes committed by some opponents of this ban.

"I am one-hundred percent certain that there is an organized conspiracy comprised of people both from within our government, and from key entities under government control, to try and influence the actions of this Committee. These are not idle charges, ladies and gentlemen. When I spoke on the Senate floor, asking that The Cancer Prevention Bill be referred to this committee, I mentioned that attempts had been made on my life, and the lives of my staff. Since that speech, my sister Stephanie Morrison, her close friend Donald Satowski, and my niece Carol Morrison, were killed by a car bomb. A hand-written suicide note by Dr. Robert Lynch, another Stanford researcher, was discovered after he had killed himself. He directly implicated John Peterson, from the Government Office of Domestic Security, in a planned illegal surveillance. The original note was destroyed by a clandestine raid on the Stanford campus by bogus agents posing as federal marshals. They have not yet been identified, but they are almost certainly part of this same Office of Domestic Security. This agency has run amok, and we must speak of these abuses as part of this hearing."

"Senator McGuire, please confine yourself to the issues at hand," Senator Whitcom interrupted. "Madam Chairperson, can you not advise the senator from Vermont to stick to the issues?"

"Senator Whitcom, I do not need you to remind me of my duties. I will remind *you* that you are not to question the witness until both opening statements are completed."

"Excuse me, Madam Chairperson, I wasn't asking a question, I was commenting on the direction of the witness, since it did not seem to relate to health issues, or your other criteria."

"Senator Whitcom, I will remind *you* a second time, do not interrupt the witness. I will decide when he is out of order, and I will direct the flow of this discussion. Thank you for your cooperation." Cyrus Whitcom nodded his head, and forced a grin.

Mario McGuire continued. "Thank you, Madam Chairperson. On the senate floor, I promised that I would find those responsible for the attempts on my life, and for the deaths of Takeo Arai's colleagues in an as-yet unexplained missile attack over the Pacific. I will renew that pledge on behalf of my sister and niece, and Doctor Satowski. Investigations are now underway that will impact this hearing. I ask you to allow the evidence to be presented. It will show that criminal acts have been committed by high-ranking officials of the United States Government. There is another health issue, Madam Chairperson, the health of our Republic. I pray that honest discourse be allowed, even though the facts that will surface may be disturbing, and potentially horrifying to the American people.

"I would now like to introduce David Feinstein and Takeo Arai. Doctor Feinstein and Doctor Arai were college roommates at Columbia University. Doctor Feinstein was engaged to my niece, the late Carol Morrison, before she was murdered. They will give you an overview of their research. We will get into more detail in days ahead. Our final speaker will be Lee Sun, Director of the United Nations World Health Organization. He will speak of the worldwide threat posed by television and computer screens. Doctor Feinstein will speak first."

David wore an elegant tweed suit. The fabric was much too heavy for late June in Washington, but it had been Carol's favorite. On the last night of her life, she had brushed it and hung it lovingly in his closet.

He walked to the witness chair and put a small leather briefcase down on the table by the microphone. He opened the case and took out his notes, and also removed an eight-by-ten-inch photograph of himself and Carol, mounted in a desk frame. Stephanie had snapped them standing with their arms around each other in her backyard. The late evening sun reddened Carol's hair, and if you looked closely you could see her freckles.

The fourteen senators were sitting at a twenty-five-foot-long table, covered completely with a floor-length green cloth. Nancy Hollister was in the center, and each senator had a microphone. David spoke into his mike.

"I want everyone to see what I have lost, what the world has lost." His voice was very shaky, and he could barely control himself as he wiped away tears. He turned around to face the TV cameras and held up the photo. He then shouted into the mike. "Her killers are somewhere in this room! They are sitting among us in this very room!" He walked to the senators' table, and slowly passed directly in front of them, holding the photo in his outstretched hands.

Senator Snowdon said, "I'm sorry, she was lovely."

Senator Lowenstein said, "I pray for justice."

Senator Whitcom, sitting second from the end on the left, didn't look up. David stopped in front of him and said, "Does this make you uncomfortable, Senator?"

Whitcom couldn't hide the annoyance in his face, even though he said, "I'm sorry, son, I sympathize."

David walked back to his seat and paused for a minute before he began to read. Even though the room was full of people, there was not a sound to be heard.

Mario was suddenly aware of the intense quiet. He looked up to see one of the globe lights gently swaying from the natural air currents in the room. He remembered his family's newspaper, *The Clarion*. When he was eleven years old, his job was to help set type. Their biggest advertiser was Crescent Department Stores. They always brought in their full-page ads on Wednesday. One Wednesday, he couldn't remember what year it had been, they didn't bring the ads. They went to the TV station instead. His father pretended that Crescent was just late. He then disappeared into the back room. That was the beginning of the end of *The Clarion*, and of his father.

Mario looked at David.

"I would like to call Takeo Arai from Keio University to share this time with me," David said, as he placed Carol's photo upright on his table. Takeo walked like a Samurai warrior. He was so light on his feet that he seemed to glide from place to place. He sat next to David. For the next forty-five minutes, they gave the senators an overview of their discovery. The two scientists listed the highpoints, and stated their intention to present medical evidence in great detail in the days to come. Takeo was last to speak.

"Madam Chairperson, distinguished senators, ladies and gentlemen, I would now like to introduce Dr. Lee Sun, Director of the United Nations World Health Organization. On our way to make a presentation to the United Nations, David and I, along with my wife and Carol Morrison, were abducted at gunpoint in front of our New York hotel. We were later released unharmed, and we could hear over their radio that they were ordered to abort the mission. Ichiro Kobayashi was the director of my research team, and Donald Satowski was the director of David's research team, and now they are both dead."

"My God, what is loose in this land?" muttered Senator James Connor, Republican from Kansas.

Takeo continued, "These two fine men gave us credit for our discoveries, and asked us to go to the United Nations to present the findings. That is why I wasn't on the plane that crashed. It is in their memory that I proudly introduce Dr. Lee Sun.

~~~

"I didn't expect this," Carl Goodman whispered to Kalie Kohn. "They've really got the senators going by asking them to identify with the researchers' tragedies. They gained more points with sympathy than they did with the facts. We will have to show how lack of television is causing distress, hunger, and pain. Let's get workers to testify about losing their jobs, and not having enough money for medical care because of the television ban. It's already happening in Vermont and Missouri, and North Carolina has just passed its ban."

Carl Goodman was the lead man for the opposition. He would be working closely with Kalie Kohn, who until recently had been the top reporter for Metro Media's national desk. She had been seeing Harold Slokov on Mondays and Tuesdays, and had just been promoted to Vice President in charge of Cable Television Operations. She was an abrasive woman with a rapier-sharp mind, and was good at exploiting others' weaknesses. Goodman was the best lawyer in America. In addition to practicing law, he had a master's degree in psychology. The first thing he had done on his way to the top was to change his name from Godowski to Goodman. He had a genuine smile, and could sell you gasoline if your pants were on fire. He would do all the talking for the pro-TV opposition.

Kalie Kohn would not speak, but she would act as liaison between Goodman and the rest of their team. She had been captain of the U.S. softball team that had once won an Olympic gold medal. She wore people out quickly, and few could stand to be around her for longer than a couple of weeks. Soon, Harold Slokov would probably reach the same conclusion. She was very effective, however, in two-hour spurts. She approached everything as if she were still pitching, and relied heavily on her fastball.

~ ~ ~

Lee Sun had completed his talk. The bill's supporters finished seven minutes early. Senator Hollister asked Mario if he would like to use the remaining time. He had to think fast; he didn't want his time to go to the opposition. Mario thanked the chairperson and asked, instead, that the room be silent for seven minutes in memory of all those who had died, and who would die from this new disease.

"This guy is slick," Goodman said. "Now he's got silence working for him. I'm going to enjoy this."

~ ~ ~

"Back break baby, you got me workin' round the clock,
back break baby, you got me workin' round the clock,
I can't stand it baby, you've taken everything I've got.

You got six diamond rings, and two Cadillac cars,
you got twenty new dresses, and four gold-filled jars,
you got a brand new sofa, and a hundred pair of shoes,
all I get from workin' are these back break baby blues.

Back break baby, you got me workin' round the clock,
back break baby, you got me workin' round the clock,
I can't stand it baby, you've taken everything I've got.

You got twelve designer handbags, and a new chinchilla coat,
you got three miniature poodles, and a forty-two foot boat,
you got a vacation in Hawaii, I pay your country club dues,
all I get from workin', are these back break baby blues.

Back break baby, you got me workin' round the clock,
back break baby, you got me workin' round the clock,
I can't stand it baby, you've taken everything I've got."

"I think we've started another tradition," Rosa said, as she turned up the radio. "Every time we win, they play one of our songs."

Seth and Rosa were traveling from Raleigh, the capital, to Charlotte, North Carolina to meet the Reverend Virgil MacKenzie. Earlier in the day, the North Carolina Legislature had passed the ban. It was closer than the Missouri vote, but sixty-seven percent voted affirmatively. There were now three states in favor.

Rosa had kept her apartment, but she had been living with Seth. They were very happy together and were making plans to get married. Religious differences remained, but the couple was trying to work them out.

"Sethos, so far we have no trouble. You go to the mosque, and I go to my church. When we have children, then there will be trouble."

"I know what we can do," Seth said. "When we have a boy, we can have him bar mitzvahed. Then we will both be happy. We can raise Jewish children and teach them the Koran and the New Testament."

Rosa laughed as they turned into the parking lot of the First Baptist Church of Charlotte. "They will probably be less confused than we are. You know, you have a point. Why not let *them* choose what they want to be?"

"Of course, the Koran will be placed under his or her pillow."

"No, the Bible."

"Koran."

"Bible."

"Koran, okay, okay, we will put both books under the pillow, but the Koran goes on the right side."

123

"Left side."

"Right side."

"Left side," Rosa said as she hugged Seth very hard.

~~~

The First Baptist Church had a congregation of 3,500. They had four full-time ministers and a vast complex of buildings. The main church was constructed of brick, with white columns and a white steeple. Reverend Mackenzie was glad to see them. "How do you like Charlotte?"

"I love Charlotte," Seth said.

Rosa kissed the preacher on the cheek and said, "We won, we won!"

Mackenzie blushed and said, "We kicked their butts, pardon my French."

Seth was driving the reverend and his wife Clara to the airport for a flight to Washington. He and Rosa had to leave for Maine directly after that. Clara noticed how Rosa pronounced the name of their city. "Rosa, you say Char*lotte*, with the emphasis on the *lotte*. We say *Char*lotte, with the emphasis on the *char*. Do you have a town in Vermont called Char*lotte*?"

"Yes, we do."

Reverend Mackenzie sang, "Oh you say either and I say ayther, you say neither and I say nyther, either, ayther, neither, nyther, oh let's call the whole thing off." The others laughed. "You know, Father Messier is a fine man. We've kept in touch. I can't tell you how helpful he's been to us. He was a guest speaker here last year. People are still talking about his sermon," the reverend said.

Mackenzie was only thirty-eight years old, and had fire in his belly.

~ ~ ~

Carl Goodman walked to the witness table. He was six feet tall and wore a casual cream-colored summerweight suit and cordovan wing-tip shoes. He held a simple, school-type, marbled copybook, with loose sheets stuck inside. He also carried a blue celluloid Pelikan fountain pen.

He opened the pen and the copybook.

"Before we begin our testimony, I would like to thank Senator Mario McGuire for all he is doing on behalf of the families that have been impacted by these recent, unspeakable tragedies. Our hearts go out to him, and to those who have died, and also to those who have become sick. We may disagree as to the causes of the disease, but we also care very deeply about these losses.

"We intend to show that Senator McGuire and his group are fighting a non-existent enemy. Everyone is shouting 'the sky is falling, the sky is falling.' But unlike Chicken Little, who was merely foolish, my opposition is traveling on a ruinous course that will destroy this great country."

Mario was thinking, *This guy is good, baby-faced Goodman. He glossed over the murders without skipping a beat, and immediately changed the subject.*

Goodman continued, "For our first order of business, we would like to discuss flaws in the Stanford data. I'd like to call Dr. Emily Beech, from Harvard Medical School, who will speak to the specifics. Doctor Beech is one of world's leading neurologists, and has just written a book titled *Imagery and Cognition in the Human Brain*. Doctor Beech."

"Thank you, Mr. Goodman. The main problem I have with the Stanford data is that they have used only one advanced scanner to take all the samples. Ninety percent of the people studied were service men and women returning from Iraq. Only ten percent of those studied were non-military. It is entirely possible that there are other causes of the conditions that were found in their tests. The soldiers could have been exposed to vinyl chloride, used by enemies of the United States. There simply isn't enough data to extrapolate yet into the general population. We need months of study, in different parts of the world, using the Krayton scanner. I read the specifications on this machine and it's very impressive. Actually, I wish we had invented it at Harvard (everyone laughs), but we need to manufacture additional units and do further tests. What if there's an unfound defect in this particular scanner? It could be giving us false readings."

Doctor Beech concluded her talk and the opposition's time was up. Senator Hollister informed the audience that there would be a fifteen-minute break before the committee would begin questioning.

Takeo Arai and Senator Cyrus Whitcom were standing next to each other at the men's room urinals. Whitcom was about seven inches taller and he glanced down at Takeo, who had a maniacal grin on his face. "Looks like your medical evidence is not as bullet-proof as you thought, son," the senator said.

"Suck a fat rat's ass, you bloated piece of garbage," Takeo responded very quietly, so only Whitcom could hear. "You're going down."

"Hope you can swim, Jap boy."

If the men's room were empty, Takeo would have kicked Whitcom to death right then and there. Takeo finished first, zipped his fly, and started out the door. He stopped, walked back to the senator and whispered again, "Going down."

David walked into the men's room as Carl Goodman was leaving. David clipped Goodman with his shoulder and knocked him against the door. "Please excuse me," David said.

Goodman knew it had been deliberate. Goodman and Whitcom conferred in the hall just before the break ended.

The hearing resumed and questioning began. Very little new evidence was presented except for questions about the statistics.

Senator Caulfield began the questioning and asked David to the witness stand. "Doctor Feinstein, Doctor Beech questioned the validity of your statistics. How do you respond?"

"Thank you for giving me the opportunity to respond, Senator Caulfield. Doctor Beech is correct in saying that additional scanners are needed, and we have built them. Several hundred more people have been tested. We're no longer testing soldiers at Stanford, but we have continued testing volunteers. The latest data is here for your study."

David stood up and handed each senator three stapled sheets of paper. "As you can see, the percentages have altered slightly. Instead of nine percent showing pre-cancerous cells, as was the case in our original study, the Stanford scanner now shows nine-point-two percent. This is an increase of point two percent. A second unit was built and is also in use on campus. Three hundred and ninety-seven subjects were studied by that scanner. The percentage of pre-cancerous cells remains at about the same level, eight point seven percent. A third scanner was shipped to Japan. The Keio University study shows that seven-point-one percent of their subjects had the same pre-cancerous cells. We theorize that their figures are slightly lower because Americans have been watching television for a longer period of time than the Japanese. These three studies are nearly identical. We now have enough data to call the evidence incontrovertible."

The senators studied the material. Senator Hollister asked if anyone wanted to question a witness from the opposition. None of them moved forward, so she asked if there were any other proponent witnesses that they would like to have testify.

Whitcom called Takeo Arai to the stand.

"Your Honor, I would like to ask Doctor Arai why he just threatened my life in the men's room during our break." Everyone began talking at once. Mario's face did not show his anger.

"Order, order!" Nancy Hollister rapped her gavel. "Please explain your charges before I instruct Doctor Arai to answer."

"I will not be intimidated by a bunch of thugs, Madam Chairperson. Doctor Arai whispered an obscenity to me and said that I would be targeted for violence."

"What obscenity?" Takeo said.

Everyone started talking again.

"Order, order!" Nancy Hollister again rapped her gavel. "If there is another outburst I will clear this room. Senator Whitcom, what was the obscenity?"

"I will not repeat it, Your Honor."

"Repeat it for the record, or it will remain a non-event."

"I will not repeat it, Your Honor, but I would like to call Carl Goodman to the stand. Please tell the committee what happened to you in the same men's room."

"Madam Chairperson, I was deliberately knocked into the door by Doctor Feinstein as he was leaving the room. Senator Bruch saw what happened."

"Is that right, Senator Bruch?" Hollister asked.

"Yes, I saw Doctor Feinstein shove Mr. Goodman into the door."

"The Chair also calls Doctor Feinstein to the stand. I will ask the questions. Doctor Feinstein did you deliberately shove Carl Goodman?"

"I nudged him, Your Honor, but accidentally. I said 'excuse me.' Surely Senator Bruch heard me say that?"

"I did not hear him say that, Madam Chairperson."

Hollister questioned Takeo. "Did you, or did you not, curse at Senator Whitcom and threaten his life?"

"I did not, Your Honor. I am a doctor, not an assassin. I'll leave that to others in this room. Perhaps the senator is projecting."

"How dare you!" Whitcom shouted.

Hollister raised her voice. "Welcome to kindergarten 101. I'm ending this hearing one hour early because it seems that neither side can conduct itself with proper decorum. If there are further outbursts from *anyone*, I will permanently disqualify that person from further testimony. You will also face criminal charges if you attempt to intimidate other witnesses or members of this committee. I will not stand for it. Do I make myself perfectly clear?"

Mario sat impassively, but inside he was boiling. *I'm going to kill both of them.*

~ ~ ~

Takeo and David apologized to Mario for their behavior. Mario made one brief statement. "If either of you do anything like that again, we will lose." The subject was then dropped. The three of them drove out of town, and found a good Italian restaurant.

"How's Sara?" Mario asked Takeo.

"She's in New York staying with her parents. She refuses to watch the hearings on TV, even though her mother has it on."

They were sitting in a booth in Casa Napoli. Mario used David's cellphone to call Francine Bouchard of the *Barre/Montpelier Times-Argus*. He talked to her weekly about the pulse of the print media. Nobody knew newspapers like she did.

"Hello, Francine, this is Mario, you asked me to call you."

"Hi, Mario, I finally found out who that man is."

"You mean the guy who tossed the lit cigarette in Montpelier?"

"His name is John Hopper, and he's a photographer for Metro Media. His office is in Springvale, Maine."

"Fantastic work, Francine. Could you do me another favor? Is it possible for you to tail this creep? Seth and Rosa will be in Maine

129

tomorrow. They'll be staying at the Ridgeway Motel near Augusta. In two days, Maine will decide if they will ban television. He may try some dirty work. If you have any trouble with your publisher, just call me."

"No trouble, Mario, it's my nickel. Don't forget I work only part-time."

"Keep a record of your expenses, I'll pay every dime."

~ ~ ~

Francine also checked into the Ridgeway Motel, and re-introduced herself to Seth and Rosa. Rosa said Francine looked like Miss Marple in the Agatha Christie stories, and was very cute. They would only be at the Ridgeway for two nights, so Francine had a suspicion, call it simple intuition, that Hopper would try something that evening. Francine had patience, and she loved to read. She parked her car in the well-lit parking lot to read her novel, and waited. She had Seth and Rosa's room in view, about one hundred feet away. There were cars on either side of hers, so she was well hidden.

Francine's hunch proved right. At 11:30 p.m. she saw a man stop right outside Seth and Rosa's motel room. He took out a camera and started shooting through the window. Francine raised her camera and took pictures of him. She used her telephoto lens and got good pictures, very good pictures indeed. Hopper then walked around the building, climbed into a pickup truck, and drove away.

~ ~ ~

Julie McGuire was back at home in Vermont. She paid her house-sitter and told her to come back in two days. Both cats were happy to see her and began begging for food immediately. The McGuires lived in a 2,400-square-foot ranch house on Spear Street, in South Burlington. They had a magnificent view of Lake Champlain, and had spent many hours sitting on their back deck watching the sun set across the lake, behind the Adirondack Mountains in New York. They had no children, so there was more than enough space for his music room and her studio, and plenty of room for the frisky cats to play in. When she and Mario were together, Isis always sat on her lap and Figaro always sat on his. They even had his and hers cats; Isis never sat on Mario's lap, nor Figaro on hers.

Julie wanted to finish a mixed media piece that she'd been working on for a month. It was acrylic, painted on wood, 20 by 30 inches. The focal point was a television screen made of clear Lucite, surrounded by a plastic frame. Julie had taken the Lucite into the woods and shot three holes through it with Mario's Winchester 30-30 hunting rifle. Behind the Lucite was a collage of found objects and photographs including the White House and the Capitol building. There was a carved marble goddess about four inches high, placed on a pedestal in the lower left corner. It was broken in half and glued to the surface. To the right of the television screen was a thickly painted garden with a trio of two-inch-long quartz crystals imbedded in the paint. All she needed to do was add some metallic silver, darken the blue sky in the upper left corner, sign her name, and the piece was done. She wondered what to call it.

Before leaving the house, she grabbed five photographs of Mario, and two of herself and Mario, and placed them in an envelope.

~ ~ ~

After warning everyone present that she would not tolerate a repeat of yesterday's disruptions, Chairperson Hollister brought the hearing to order. She informed the panel that she would allow opening statements for one hour before they could call witnesses. She felt this change in the original schedule was important, because new evidence could be presented early, and the senators could prepare questions for later in the day. Hollister informed the opposition that they would speak first. She also reminded everyone that they were still under oath.

"Thank you, Madam Chairperson, distinguished senators," Carl Goodman said from the witness stand. "I would like to call, as my first witness, Margie Bolton, from Rutland, Vermont. Margie, please tell this committee how the Vermont ban has affected you and your family."

Senator Lowenstein asked Senator Hollister if this type of testimony should be allowed. "It doesn't speak directly to the question of whether or not TV should be banned as a health hazard. The *effects* of the ban are a totally different issue."

Goodman said, "This is about threats to the health of Americans as a result of television being banned. You can't separate these two things."

"Mr. Goodman," Hollister said, "the question was posed to me. Please do not respond to a question asked of the chair."

"I'm sorry, Madam Chairperson."

"I do agree with Mr. Goodman. There may be bone fide health issues as a result of the ban. We can't exclude threads or avenues of discussion without knowing what their final relevance will be. Please continue, Mr. Goodman."

"Thank you, Madam Chairperson. Please go ahead, Margie, you can say anything you want."

Margie Bolton was a small, mousy-haired woman of limited means and average intelligence. She was one of those people who often fall through the cracks. She now had no health insurance, and had a diabetic daughter who needed constant treatment. Her abusive husband had abandoned the family three years ago. She had been caring for three children and working for Crescent Department Store in their appliance department, selling washing machines and televisions. When the ownership and sale of televisions was outlawed in Vermont, she was laid off. She lost her job and her health insurance, because she couldn't afford eleven thousand dollars a year for a basic COBRA policy.

Her voice trembled as she spoke.

"I honestly don't know how I'm going to make it. I'm trying to get another job, but so many people have lost their jobs, there's not much out there. Vermont supplemental insurance is paying for my daughter's treatments, but I won't even be able to afford that in a few weeks. The price of gas, food, and heating oil are going up so fast, we have to choose between being cold or going hungry. All I want to do is be able to support my family. I'm not asking for any handouts. I really don't have much more to say."

"Thank you, Margie," Goodman said. He put one arm around her shoulders as he helped her rise from the witness chair. "Ladies and gentlemen, this story is being repeated all over Vermont, Missouri, and North Carolina. Who is going to support all these displaced workers? How is the country going to cope with double-digit unemployment? We could see it rise to levels higher than those in the Great Depression. Many people will die of malnutrition, of disease, because they can't afford medical care. Is this not a health risk? Our vulnerability to foreign competition will intensify, and the results will be catastrophic. Without these basic communications networks, we will become a third-world country within a decade."

Goodman produced two more witnesses who had similar stories of hardship. He also introduced a young woman who had recently earned her degree in informatics, medical software, and computer technology. She had completed the entire course of study online, because she lived seventy miles from campus. Because of the ban, she would not have been able to do that today.

"Do my learned friends who are so sanctimoniously pressing for the elimination of television have any idea how much *good* has been accomplished as the result of watching the screen? The screen isn't our enemy, the screen is part of our way of life. I believe in American science. I believe in the skills of Lee Sun and the international community. They will quickly find a way to counter possible ill effects, if indeed there are any.

"We didn't kill a child who developed polio, did we? No, we found a vaccine that prevented the disease. Why should we kill our TVs and computers, because there is a *possibility* of ill effects? No, ladies and gentlemen, the answer is to put our efforts not into destruction, but into working with our existing systems. It's defeatist to pull the plug. It's like pulling the plug of a baby on a respirator before he or she even has a *chance* at life."

"Mr. Goodman, your hour is up. Do you have a closing statement?"

"No, Madam Chairperson, I just want people to understand what they will be throwing away."

~ ~ ~

Reverend Virgil Mackenzie was sitting with Mario McGuire and a third person, Hanna Stein, Professor of Sociology at Columbia University. Mario heard Chairperson Hollister call for his witness, and he introduced Reverend Mackenzie.

"Reverend Virgil Mackenzie is Executive Director of the National Council of Churches, Synagogues, and Mosques. He gave the inaugural benediction for the last two Presidents of the United States. We appreciate your counsel, Reverend."

"Thank you, Senator McGuire, Madam Chairperson, distinguished, and I might add, patient senators. I would like to apologize to you all for what I am about to say, but say it I must.

"Before I hear any objections to my 'thread' or 'avenue of discussion,' as Senator Hollister so aptly put it, I would like to remind everyone here that spiritual health is equally as important as physical health. There is a direct relationship between physical, emotional, and spiritual health. When one is compromised, the others often are as well. I would like you to listen to something. The speaker is actress Jennifer Wheelen, and the dialogue is from the evening soap opera called *Wicked Loving Lies*."

Reverend Mackenzie handed each senator a fat envelope. "Distinguished senators, you have much data in those packets. We could not possibly cover all that material during this hearing. Please read it at your leisure. The first sheet is the transcribed dialogue that you are about to hear. Jennifer Wheelen plays a character named Lavinia Stone, and she is talking on the telephone to her boyfriend. According to a study completed by the University of Kansas, the market share for this show is forty million households. It's rated number one in the eight-to-nine p.m. time slot. Thirty-seven point three million children aged 11 to 17 watch every week." He turned on a large portable CD player and pointed it directly at the senators. The sound was clearly heard throughout the room.

"Calvin, I'm thinking about you. Calvin, do know what I'm doing to myself as I'm talking to you? Calvin, I'm touching myself. Calvin, I'm thinking about you as I touch myself. You want to be near me, don't you? Can't you do that one thing for me? Just do it, and it will be finished. Then we can be together."

"The *thing*," Reverend Mackenzie said, "that Lavinia wants Calvin to do for her is commit murder. She wants Calvin to kill her husband. This is what those thirty-seven point three million children are watching. Y'all remember the Super Bowl in 2004, when Justin Timberlake 'accidentally' ripped off a piece of Janet Jackson's top, exposing her right breast. It was bettered at the 2008 MSC Music Awards when rap artist Fontina grabbed DawgLeg's crotch and said, and I quote, 'Is that thing ready to (she uses the 'F' word) me, baby?' This is a music show that is especially targeted to teens and pre-teens.

"If you read the material that I just handed you, you will find three hundred and eighty-seven similar incidents on prime-time television in the last ten months. This is by no means all-inclusive, because the Kansas study targeted only sixty percent of all available shows. *Wicked Loving Lies* and the MSC Music Awards were both shown on the Metro Media Cable Network.

"Sitting at that table, next to Carl Goodman, is Kalie Kohn. She is Vice President and Director of Metro's US Cable operations. Please ask her to testify, and explain why she is permitting this filth to enter the minds of our young people. I'll tell you what she won't have the courage to tell you. It's because Metro Media, and the other major networks, have put profits ahead of ethics in any programming they decide to produce. Senator Connor, I might add that this marvelous Kansas University study and the actress Jennifer Wheelen are both from your home state. I applaud you for one, and sympathize with you for the other."

Senator Connor laughed, and remarked that Jennifer Wheelen was not one of his state's favorite daughters.

"Dr. Hanna Stein, who will speak to you in a few minutes, is an expert on the social ramifications of these aberrations, so I won't attempt to get scientific. I will say that sex isn't the only thing that is perverted. It is the combination of sex and violence, just as you heard on this TV show, that is affecting the spiritual health of our nation.   According to a study by the American Psychiatric Association, by age 18, a U.S. youth will have seen 16,000 simulated murders and 200,000 acts of violence on television. Is it any wonder that violence is such an issue now in our nation's schools?

"At the beginning of my testimony, I spoke about the relationship between the spiritual, the emotional, and the physical. It's unanimous among all 3,500 researchers studying the relationship between watching media violence and committing real acts of violence, that there is an undisputed link. So you see, we dare not exclude spiritual health when we talk about the deleterious effects the screen has on our culture. My Catholic and Jewish friends agree with me. My Muslim friends agree with me. Distinguished senators, we stand united on this issue. The spiritual well-being of America is in great peril. I will speak further as this hearing progresses, and I invite you senators to call me to testify if you want clarification or embellishment." The reverend laughed. "Testifying is something I try to do very well."

As Virgil Mackenzie got up from the witness stand, forty people stood up, shouted, and applauded. This startled the committee members. Chairperson Hollister didn't need to ask for order because the clapping stopped quickly. She did remind people in the audience not to clap or talk during the hearing. Mario shook hands with the reverend as he arrived back at his table. He spoke into the mike to introduce Hanna Stein.

"Doctor Stein is professor emeritus, Columbia University. She shared the Nobel Prize for Medicine with two Columbia colleagues for their work in understanding and quantifying the causes of urban mortality rates in developing countries. She is an expert on the relationship between disease and social systems."

"Thank you, Senator McGuire. Good afternoon, everyone. I just love this time of year in our nation's capital. Madam Chairperson, and distinguished senators, I'll get right to the point.

Watching television is hazardous to your health. Not only does it change the cellular structure in the brain, but it is transforming society in negative ways. According to a RealVision study, the average American household has at least one TV on for seven hours and forty minutes every day. Forty percent watch TV while eating.

"According to the American Psychological Association, in addition to promoting violence, TV desensitizes viewers to real violence. Television dulls the emotional response to violence and its victims. According to the A.C. Nielsen Co., the average U.S. household owns 2.24 television sets. The number of hours per year the average American youth spends in school is 900 hours. The average number of hours per year they spend watching television is 1,500 hours. The number of 30-second commercials seen in a year by the average child is 20,000. The percentage of shows devoted to crime is 53.8. The percentage devoted to public service announcements, 0.7. The percentage of Americans who can name The Three Stooges is 59. The percentage of Americans who can name at least three justices of the Supreme Court is 17.

"There was a prophetic book published back in 1978. The title of this book is *Four Arguments For the Elimination of Television,* by Jerry Mander. He spoke of the alienation television causes by separating the viewer from his or her family and community. The television becomes its own community, the sole purpose of which is to create consumers. Commercials are aimed at children as young as two years old. Parents park their children in front of the sets while they go about their business. The TV becomes a surrogate babysitter, and those young minds, in their most impressionable and vulnerable state, are then exposed to violent images and relentless advertising. The children then become confused about what is real and what is not. We must look to TV as one of the major causes of school violence and even death. Juliet B. Schor, who wrote *Born to Buy* in 2004, states that advertisers try to tap into children's innermost psychological needs. This is accomplished by sensory stimulation, which often causes sensory overload.

"Jerry Mander was a pioneer who spoke of this danger, decades before the Stanford and Keio researchers did their studies. He observed that children store energy when they are watching rapidly moving cartoons. They become aggressive and irritable afterwards when all this pent-up energy is randomly released.

Doctor Stein paused and took a drink of water. "The most important thing Mr. Mander discussed, ladies and gentlemen, is the TV-cancer link that is being debated in this room. Mander often quotes Dr. John Ott, the scientist who first developed full-spectrum light bulbs. Dr. Ott discovered that certain colors of light would cause plant growth to be severely retarded. Other colors would cause the plants to die. When he placed bean plants in front of a color TV, they grew misshapen and twisted. Mice that were placed in front of color television sets for long periods of time developed cancerous lesions. The pink fluorescent light found in television screens was responsible for causing the highest rates of cancer in rats.

"Dr. Ott found that natural, full-spectrum light was beneficial, so he then concentrated on the mal-illumination we are discussing now. He discovered that it causes lowered resistance to disease. The scientific community did not take him seriously when he theorized that watching too much television could lead to violence, heart disease, and cancer. He warned that the body would break down on the *cellular level*. We are beginning to see this effect with cellphones as well. The Pittsburgh University study that you senators have in your packet, is further proof that there may be a high price to pay for misunderstanding the forces of nature. Sometimes it's years or decades later that the harmful effects are finally known, and for so many people it is then too late to undo the damage.

139

"Ladies and gentlemen, Jerry Mander, Juliet B. Schor, and John Ott are three prophetic voices who have not been heard by a large audience, but with the Krayton scanner, we can now document the damage they wrote about. Distinguished members of this committee, you may, or may not, vote to ban television, but there is one fact that is beyond any debate. Moving images on television and computer screens are harmful for all of us. Perhaps some of you will find the ban so inconvenient that you will rationalize away the dangers. Each of you has to decide, by looking inward to your own conscience, whether you can support a technology that will ultimately cause the disability and death of millions of people. Thank you very much."

~ ~ ~

Reverend Mackenzie and Hanna Stein were such powerful speakers that no one on the panel realized that Doctor Stein had gone over her time limit by four minutes. Finally Nancy Hollister looked at the clock. "Thank you, Doctor Stein. You went over your allotted time, so I will add four minutes to the opposition's time on Monday."

The senators questioned the witnesses, with ninety percent of the questions going to the last two speakers. The ban-TV movement had scored a decisive victory today. Mario McGuire knew it. Carl Goodman knew it. Nancy Hollister knew it.

She spoke at the end of the session. "We will recess for the weekend and resume at 10:00 Monday morning. This meeting is adjourned."

CHAPTER SIX

Mario was back in his Washington office, and Nadene handed him a peculiar-looking telephone. It was about twice the size of the average cellphone and was not hinged in the middle. It had a small half-inch-wide LCD readout and looked like a miniature walkie-talkie, but instead of putting the phone directly to your ear, you plugged headphones into the side. There was a mike built into the top that picked up your voice from a distance of five feet or less.

"Seth gave each of us one of these," Nadene said. "I have no idea how or why it's safe, but we're to use *only* these phones. He said there's no way anyone can bug them. Seth has been working with the FBI, and they developed it together. Speaking of the FBI, call Rocco, he says it's important."

"Thanks, Nadene," Mario said as he dialed his new phone. "Seth amazes me. Hello, Rocco, what's up? How does this phone work?"

"Hey Mario, look, I don't have much time, about ten minutes. I'm in Dallas with my team, including agent Maria Perez. We're going to tape the Metro Media conference meeting tonight. Yeah, the phone. Seth came up with the idea. Look Mario, when this is over I'm going to hire that guy. I want him to be in charge of FBI communications. He came up with a scrambler/de-scrambler circuit with two million different combinations. We decide beforehand which two combinations we'll use. Even if another person has the exact same phone, if he doesn't know those combinations, there's no way he can unscramble the conversation. And unlike normal cellphones, where the radiation causes a hotspot in the human brain, these phones are safe because they use an ultra-high frequency. The signal is relayed using standard cellphone technology, except that anyone listening in won't hear human voices. All they will hear is a high-pitched squeal, sort of sounds like two bats screwing.

"Reminds me of a submarine movie I saw," Mario said.

"We continue to gather evidence against Peterson. One of our agents found a scrap of paper in Lynch's wallet, with the name and password of a Cayman Island bank account. When we accessed it, we found that Lynch withdrew over four hundred thousand dollars, enough to buy his slut wife a Mercedes and an emerald necklace. My first idea was to get a court order and monitor the withdrawals of Supreme Oil, Metro Media, and WenCo. I didn't, for two reasons. Number one, it will take too long. Number two, they're smart. They would never withdraw a large sum of money that could be traced back to them.

"So I called Max Glock. Let me tell you about Max. Max is a money launderer. He funnels money from Colombia, Sicily, Russia, China, Israel, the U.S., anyplace where people don't want to leave either a paper or an electronic trail. He gets a percentage for his trouble. Naturally he's worth mega-millions for his good deeds. The FBI and Max have an interesting relationship. We don't arrest him, and he lets us look over his shoulder. When we learn who is sending money to whom, that gives us important clues."

"Rocco, where is this guy, Max?"

"Our agents talked to him in Stowe, right in your neck of the woods. One of his homes is a modest forty-room chalet near the ski slopes. Listen, Mario, the six million dollars came from WenCo."

"No shit!"

"Oh yeah. They make more than two hundred million dollars a day, so it was easy for them to simply hold back some of the receipts and not deposit the money in their conventional accounts. They gave the six million to Max instead, and Max set up the Cayman account. All we have to do is find out who told them to do it.

"Mario, I have only a few minutes. At 3:00 a.m. on Sunday, we're going to arrest Ludlowe Wenman. We're going roust him out of bed, and charge him with money laundering and conspiracy to commit murder. We can hold him for a few days before his mommy bails him out. We'll offer him immunity from prosecution if he'll name the person running the show. We want the guy who gave the order to send the money. We want him to name Peterson. We're going to go at him hard and rattle him. He's got the maturity of a twelve-year-old, and I'll bet he cracks like a dropped egg. Mario, got to go. There are five of us here, and we have to finish setting up."

"Thanks Rocco, please call me after the meeting is over, and let me know what's going on."

"It will be very late. I know, I know, call you anyway. Ciao."

~ ~ ~

The RD 750 PT forward-looking thermal infrared camera cost the American taxpayers ten million dollars. It had a 630x zoom, and the scanning frequencies could be dialed between 14,434 kHz and 16,784 kHz. Resolution capability was 4250 K pixels, and the minimum illumination needed for video input was 0.3 Lux. Agent Bradley set up the thermal imager and CCD TV camera, and connected them both to the attached computer. Every optical and electrical component had battery backup in the event of a power failure, and the entire unit was contained in a sophisticated anti-shake housing. Otherwise, a vibration half a mile away and half the width of a human hair would blur the images.

The agent set the gain and sensor level, dialed in the pan-parameters, and established a computer link. Everything was being recorded on hard disk. "Ready to roll, Rocco," Bradley said with a wry smile.

The monitor was twenty-one inches, measured diagonally. Agent Maria Perez was directly in front of the screen, while the others watched from the side. The camera was focused on the door so the FBI could monitor arrivals.

Harold Slokov held the door for Beatrice Wenman, the first to enter. She was followed by Slokov, Ludlowe Wenman, Skip Walsh, and Lyle Sinton. A sixth person, unknown to the FBI, also entered. He was a robust looking man in his thirties. Neither John Peterson nor Cyrus Whitcom were in Dallas. Slokov activated the speaker-phone in the center of the conference table, and then sat down at the end. Beatrice and Ludlowe Wenman were facing the window, and Sinton and the unknown man were on the other side, with their backs to the window. The FBI could not bug this conference-room phone because Slokov had ordered Eagle Claw to route the line through a maze of Metro Media circuitry. The FBI never knew where the point of origin might be.

The pastry carts were empty, and only coffee was available for this meeting.

Slokov spoke. "Best Friend will phone us in half an hour. First order of business, Beatrice, did you give the fifty million dollars to Max Glock?"

"I took care of that," Ludlowe said.

"Good. Max will give the account number and password to Peterson, and we can reel Julie McGuire in for good."

"Is she or isn't she part of our team?" Walsh asked.

"Does this answer your question?" Slokov tossed some photographs on the table. "This is what we're going to do. Julie has provided some excellent photos of McGuire, including a few shots of him in swimming trunks. We have another photograph taken by John Hopper, who is here to talk about what he's going to do with it."

The man now identified as Hopper held up a photograph of Seth and Rosa making love. "I shot this from outside their motel room. They are very enthusiastic, as you can see. Luckily for us, they weren't under the sheets."

"She's a nice piece of tail," Sinton commented.

Slokov smiled.

"I'm going to take this photograph, crop out Azizi, and superimpose McGuire's image on top of Montez," Hopper said.

Slokov said, "We have the most advanced digital processing software in the world at Metro Media. We can put a giraffe's head on you, Ludlowe, and there isn't an expert in the country who could tell that the photo was doctored."

"It would probably be an improvement," Beatrice said, and they all laughed.

"Go to hell, Mother dear."

Slokov said, "We will have a completely believable photograph of Mario screwing Rosa. At the right moment in the hearing we'll present it, destroying his credibility with the religious leaders who are now rallying around him."

A warning light flashed on the speaker-phone. Slokov pressed a button on his remote and said, "Harold Slokov, go ahead."

Best Friend was on the line. "Harold, we are going to switch priorities. I've already informed Peterson, Whitcom, and Bruch. We won't be using the photograph at the hearing. We'll save it for the future. By all means go ahead and get it ready, but we're putting it on hold."

"Hey, I know that voice," Ludlowe whispered.

Beatrice clamped her hand over his mouth and hissed, "Shut up!"

Best Friend said, "California, Oregon, and Maine are all about to pass the television ban. There are hearings upcoming in sixteen other states over the next two months. Our research indicates that it will pass in those states as well. If we bottle up the bill in committee, the states will pass the ban individually, and we will be out of business. The only chance we have of beating them is with a full Senate vote. Our research indicates that the majority of senators are still against the ban. I've instructed Whitcom and Bruch to send the bill to the senate."

Everyone in the conference room was clearly agitated. They could see their empires slipping away.

Beatrice Wenman said, "Sir, we control over 450 billion dollars of trade and assets. If the committee votes to send the bill to the Senate, it will take several months before it can come to a vote. We can't afford to wait that long. We will lose billions.

"If television is taken away from the populace, we're all in trouble. We are already seeing a sharp sales decline in those states that have passed the ban. The one hundred largest corporations in America, and the administration in Washington, depend on television to pacify the citizens. If Americans don't get their opiate, they are going to start getting involved in other things. They will get agitated, and then they will start asking questions. The next thing you know, our employees will want medical care and retirement benefits. We're not ready to give them that. What if they try to unionize?"

Lyle Sinton said, "America without entertainment will be a time bomb waiting to explode in the administration's face. What if the senate decides to pass the ban?"

Best Friend had been listening passively. He was very calm and thanked everyone for their feedback. "There is an additional plan that we are going to implement in each state where the ban has already been passed." He described the plan and then hung up the telephone.

Those sitting around the table clapped and whooped. They all congratulated each other.

"This may give us total control," Slokov said.

Beatrice said, "This country has been going downhill since Franklin Delano Roosevelt. We've become weak and impotent. Until a short time ago, our leaders were no better than a bunch of granola sociologists. Lately, with the present administration, we've turned things around and we're starting to return to our former greatness. I'm glad to see that we won't have to give up the ground we've gained."

~ ~ ~

"You know something, Mario," Nadene said, "Peterson reminds me of a critter I used to play with when I was a little girl. We had some woods behind our house in Greenville, and one day I saw this black snake. It wasn't very big, but it was fast. I grabbed a stick and was going to bop it on the head, but it slithered away. So I said uh, uh, can't catch that snake, and turned away. You know what that snake did? It came back after me. So I chased it again, and it ran away again. We did this for an hour, back and forth. My daddy later told me it was a black racer. They're harmless, but they like to play tag with you. Peterson is not harmless, but that's what he does. We chase him and he disappears. Right now he's quiet. But as soon as we turn our backs, he will chase us again."

"He's a black snake all right, and I'm going to cut his head off," Mario said.

~ ~ ~

It was Saturday morning. The B Team was back together. David and Takeo were with them, and Sara had flown from New York City to join her husband. Mario congratulated Seth on the fine job he had done with the new telephones. He told Seth that

147

Rocco had a top job waiting for him if he wanted it. The team was going to compare notes and plan strategy for the final week's hearing. Nadene brought in three boxes of Dunkin' Donuts, and Seth made a pot of coffee and put hot water on for tea. Mario had still not heard what happened at the Metro Media meeting. Rocco had called him at midnight and said it would be morning before they could transcribe the conversations. Mario was still anxiously awaiting that call.

Takeo asked Mario, "How do you think the senators will vote?"

"I'll tell you something," David said, "Bruch is in their pocket. He was three feet away, and looked right at me when I said 'excuse me' to smiley Goodman outside that men's room."

"I agree," Mario said. "He's on the take, but I've been trying to figure out how the others will vote. Can any of you say for certain?"

No one could.

"That's the way I feel; I haven't a clue. They're all so God-damned poker-faced. Some may act like they're going to support us, but who knows what they're really thinking? You can bet outside pressures and special interests are going to control their vote."

~ ~ ~

The call finally came in from Rocco in Dallas. Mario excused himself and shut the door.

"Hello, Mario. I'm in my hotel room, I've been up for forty-eight hours, and I need some rest. We learned some important information, but are missing key details. Here's what happened.

"The big news first. They have a new strategy. They now want the Senate to vote on the ban. I don't know which senators they

148

are controlling, or how they are going to do it, but look for a change in tactics."

"That's because they're getting beaten in the states," Mario said. "That means that Whitcom and Bruch will vote 'yes.' My God, Rocco, you have done a remarkable job. We'll just be going through the motions for the next week; the issue is already decided. You know, I should have been a cab-driver, a studio musician, a wine-taster, *anything* but a senator."

"The only people facing the camera were Mommy and Sonny Wenman and Harold Slokov. They had a speaker-phone on at the center of the table and it was someone important. It could have been Whitcom or Peterson, but I don't think so. Beatrice Wenman called him 'sir,' and she doesn't usually use that term for those other guys, but it is possible. They have some photographs of you, including some in your swimsuit. They're going to doctor them to look like you and Rosa are making love." Rocco didn't mention the photos Julie had supplied, or the fifty million dollars given to Max Glock. He did ask Mario how Julie was. "You don't talk about her much."

"She's okay, I guess. Lately we've both been very busy."

"When is the last time you saw her?"

"We had dinner together in Washington,"

"Mario, everyone in town knows that your dinner wound up in your lap. What's going on?"

"It's just business as usual for us, nothing to worry about."

"I wouldn't trust her if I were you, Mario. Watch your back. I have some bad news. We can't use Maria Perez's transcriptions as evidence to get warrants. We may be able to use them in court, but the federal judge ruled against the warrants."

"Who appointed that asshole?" Mario said.

"Who do you think? We learned that something big is going down, but unfortunately we don't know what it is. Whoever was speaking on the phone gave them the details. They called him Best

Friend. Whatever he said, he gave Mom Wenman an immediate orgasm. She got all teary-eyed remembering the good old days before Franklin Roosevelt was in office.

"They're up to something. I sense that Slokov and company are about to up the ante. Perhaps we can learn more at their next meeting.

"I suggest you increase your safety awareness, don't make any unnecessary trips, and keep close tabs on each other. This is going to get more dangerous. We have agents round the clock a few minutes away. You know the number to call. Make sure your staff has the number. God bless you, and may Stephanie and Carol rest in peace. I'm going to get some sleep." Rocco hung up and there was only silence on the line.

~ ~ ~

Mario didn't tell the team about the opposition's change in tactics. He feared it would blunt their intensity, and tip off the opposition that his side knew they were about to cave. He wanted the B Team to act as if the issue were still in doubt. He hoped that *he* could be convincing.

Mario said, "The opposition is planning something big, but so far the details aren't clear. Rocco advised all of us to be careful in our movements. The danger level may rise."

"Don't worry, we're ready for them," David said and looked at Takeo.

"What's that supposed to mean?" Nadene asked. Her police instincts told her that something was up. "Wait, let me guess. You both have guns in your cars, and are carrying them with you when you are not in federal buildings. Is that right, David?"

"Yes."

"You two are going to get yourselves killed, do you hear me?"

"I think it's a good idea," Mario said. "Just don't get caught."

"Mario!" Nadene raised her voice and turned to David and Takeo. "Have either of you ever shot a handgun? You'll blow your own feet off."

"We practiced twice in the woods, and we can both hit targets. My ears are still ringing," David said.

"You're supposed to wear hearing protectors," Nadene said. The former Marine was pissed. She turned again to Mario. "This is a very bad idea."

Mario showed Nadene his special ID, and told her he that was permitted to carry a weapon anywhere a federal marshal could.

"You mean you have one here, now, in this building?"

"Yes."

"How about you, Seth, and you, Rosa? Do either of you have any spare machine guns you'd like to share?" Nadene said, with both hands on her hips.

"Neither of us knows how to shoot, but I'd like to learn," Seth said.

"Me too, I guess," Rosa said. She wasn't quite sure.

Nadene was unhappy, looked at Mario and said, "Don't you trust me anymore? Why didn't you tell me? It's my job to handle security."

"I'm sorry, Nadene. I should have mentioned it. Looks to me like everyone wants to help you. Why should you be the only person in harm's way? Besides, I'm a much better shot than you are."

"Oh yeah? How much do you care to wager? Soon as we get back to Vermont we'll go to the range, and we'll see who shoots better. Come on, how much?"

"The loser has to bake cookies and brownies for our meetings for an entire month," Mario said.

"I want Mario to win; Nadene is a much better cook," Rosa said.

~ ~ ~

Mario instructed his staff to be vigilant, and to go after the opposition with full force. He wanted the enemy to believe that its tactical shift had gone undiscovered, and he also feared a turnabout. Perhaps the opposition would change strategy again. Best to play out the hand one deliberate move at a time.

For another five days, evidence went back and forth at the hearing. There was some shouting by witnesses who got very emotional. At least once a day, Chairperson Hollister had to pound her gavel and ask for order. Everyone was growing weary.

Maine, California, and Oregon voted to ban television and computer screens. California was a real surprise for Mario. He had thought, because of the huge entertainment industry, that the vote would be close, but it wasn't. Seventy percent of the state's legislators voted in favor of the ban. Pro-ban forces had all the momentum now, and Mario realized that the opposition had had no choice but to send the bill to the senate floor. But anti-ban forces were determined to win in the end. Mario wondered what they were planning.

~ ~ ~

"I would like to thank everyone who has taken part in this historic hearing," Chairperson Nancy Hollister said as the senators entered the room after deliberations. Testimony had ended at 2:00 p.m., and the senators were allowed to either remain at the table, or leave the premises for an hour, before handing the chairperson a slip of paper with their vote. In addition to the written vote, Chairperson Hollister would call each senator by name and ask for their voice vote.

It was 3:00, and all the senators were seated at the table. They had all given the chairperson their written votes. A "yes" vote meant that the senator wanted to send the bill before the full Senate. She called them by seating order, from left to right:

Senator Radkiss (Republican) from Delaware	No
Senator Lowenstein (Democrat) from New York	Yes
Senator Klein (D) from Michigan	Yes
Senator Bruch (D) from Pennsylvania	Yes

"You have got to be fucking kidding me!" Takeo whispered to David.

Senator Connor (R) from Kansas	Yes
Senator Giulini (R) from Maryland	No
Senator Snowdon (R) from North Dakota	No
Senator Sanchez (R) from Colorado	No
Senator Pappas (D) from Maine	Yes
Senator Burton (R) from Nebraska	No
Senator Heller (D) from New Jersey	Yes
Senator Whitcom (R) from Texas	Yes
Senator Caulfield (D) from Oregon	Yes

Nancy Hollister was not surprised that Whitcom and Bruch had voted "yes." She was a veteran politician, and knew that it would take a federal vote to stop the states. She had intended to vote no in the Senate, but now she was not sure.

She announced the final vote: yes 8, no 5. Mario and his team were already celebrating; they had been counting as each senator voted. Mario glared at Whitcom as he left the room. Mario knew that if Whitcom and Bruch had voted no instead of yes, they would have killed his bill right then and there. He explained everything to his team, why they changed their votes.

"They didn't give us anything," Takeo said. "We kicked their asses in the states, and they had to send it on."

"Just remember one thing," Mario reminded them all. "Whitcom and Bruch will vote 'no' on the Senate floor."

Nancy Hollister rapped her gavel for order. "I have been informed by the vice president that the bill will be brought before the full Senate on September fourth in a special session."

Mario walked over to Nancy Hollister and shook her hand. "I hope the republic holds together for that long, Nancy."

"So do I, Mario, so do I."

~ ~ ~

There was a raucous celebration at Casa Napoli. Mario and his staff often drove to Rockland, Maryland to get away from the capital. Bistro Bis in DC was always full of lawmakers, and privacy was hard to come by. Even if they were recognized in Rockland, and they almost always were, the crowds were small. Mario warned everyone not to discuss private business in this public place, and they all sat down to eat pizza and drink too much Chianti.

Mario said, "There is nothing that can't keep for a week, so I want everyone to unwind. Try to forget about me, if you can, and go do something honest and meaningful instead."

Everyone laughed. Nadene and Rosa both said, "Oh, poor baby."

Mario said, "We all have Seth's phones, so please remember, that is the *only* way we should communicate with each other. I have some business with the FBI, and will let you know if anything important comes up. I don't want any of my staff to live in fear that your phone will ring, so please, have a good time. One week from today we will meet at the Burlington office for a music session. Three state hearings are scheduled in the following two weeks including..." Mario looked at Seth, "...drum roll, please... including, New York and New Jersey."

Everyone cheered.

Rosa said, "I'd like to propose a toast to two people who could not be here to celebrate with us. To Reverend Mackenzie and Doctor Stein; you were beautiful."

Everyone cheered again and clinked their glasses together. Mario wanted to toast Stephanie, Don, and Carol, but decided against spoiling the joyful gathering.

Takeo said, "Here's to my friends." He named every one of the researchers. He then named Steph, Don, and Carol. Takeo was crying; he and David were quite drunk. David clumsily dropped his automatic pistol on the restaurant floor. Mario quickly picked it up and stuffed it back in David's belt before anyone noticed. They were at Casa Napoli until closing time.

~ ~ ~

Mario flew home to Vermont on the shuttle with the others, except for Takeo and Sara, who flew to New York. Mario took a cab back to his home in South Burlington. He paid the house-sitter and fed the cats. He sat down in his favorite chair, and Figaro jumped in his lap. Isis batted at his shoelaces. Before sitting down, he had put a frozen braised beef dinner in the microwave oven, and set the timer for six minutes. When the timer dinged, Mario was fast asleep. He didn't move for nine hours.

The next morning after breakfast, Mario walked through the house. He noticed the Winchester rifle propped against his guitar amplifier, instead of in the closet where he usually kept it. On top of the amp was a box of 30-30 shells with three missing. *What the hell was she doing with my rifle?* He finally got the answer when he walked into Julie's studio. Her mixed-media piece, with three bullet holes through the Lucite television screen, was still on her easel. He smiled. *Hope she never decides to use me as a subject.* He really liked her latest piece. He thought it should be titled *Wicked Loving Lies.*

Mario planned to spend the next three days in the woods. He picked up the 30-30 with the box of shells and decided to take it along in case he wanted to do some target shooting. He packed his tent, enough freeze-dried food to last a week, his gas stove, a small chemical toilet, and a large sleeping bag. He packed a box full of other belongings including a small shortwave radio, and his telephone with an extra battery. He also brought a notebook, two pens, and his micro tape recorder.

Mario was headed for Bristol Pond in the national forest near Lincoln. He can park his Cabrio about two hundred feet from the pond so he will have to make just three trips with his gear. Mario never traveled light. Once he and Julie had gone camping with an aluminum casserole full of lasagna. They had also brought a guitar, three bottles of wine, six books, and two aluminum beach chairs. It made him very happy to remember that trip. He was now camped in the exact same spot about fifty feet from the water's edge. He was completely alone. The only manmade sound he heard was an occasional plane at high altitude. Mario put on some insect repellent and sat at the water's edge. He spoke into his tape recorder, starting to outline the book he had been planning to write for ten years. He recalled the law of inertia: A body at rest tends to stay at rest, and a body in motion tends to stay in motion. He was surely in motion now.

Mario was so wound up that it was almost impossible for him to relax. Yesterday he had been exhausted, but he had lost the ability to spend quiet time meditating. All he could do was crash when he passed his limit. Now he heard a car door close nearby.

Julie was right on time and she ran to Mario. They hugged and kissed passionately. They didn't speak as they fell down upon a bed of pine needles. Mario picked her up and carried her inside the tent. He placed her gently on top of the double-sized sleeping bag and kissed her breasts through her satin blouse. He had been waiting so long, so very long to loosen his belt, and to loosen her belt, to take off his clothes, and to take off hers.   They lay there with their arms around each other. She had on his favorite red underwear, and he had on her favorite black underwear. A flock of wood ducks splash-landed on the pond, and spring peeper frogs started singing as dusk approached.

"Tell me something, I've got to know," Mario said. "Did you sleep with Slokov?"

"Does that matter to you, right here, right now?" Julie asked.

"No," Mario answered as he gently slipped off her tiny garments.

Their lovemaking lasted only a short while because Mario had been under so much pressure, and he hadn't touched her in weeks.

They cuddled in the sleeping bag now and Julie said, "No, I did not sleep with him. There's only so much I will do for the cause, Mario." She giggled, but then got serious. "I have never been unfaithful to you. I've never wanted to. I may be wild at times, but you're the only man for me."

"Seth saw Slokov kiss you when you got in that limo."

"He kissed me all right, and started to unbutton my blouse, but since Peterson was in the car, he backed off. Mario, those men are evil. They are evil, dangerous men."

"I believe you." Mario reached around Julie and smacked her hard on her bare bottom.

"Ow, what was that for?"

"You were only supposed to throw the drink at me at Bistro Bis, remember? Why did you also push my dinner onto my lap?"

Julie laughed at him. "I just wanted to see the look on your face."

Mario said, "I'm glad you took those acting lessons when you were in college. You made a good drunk. Your troupe did *Taming of the Shrew*, right?"

"Yes, among others."

"That was an appropriate play for your personality."

~ ~ ~

Mario and Julie had worked out a careful plan to infiltrate the opposition. It was Julie's idea. Mario was totally against the scheme, but he knew that she would have found a way to do it in spite of his objections. She always got her way. She would shout, beg, plead, threaten, and if all that didn't work, she would put on a satin gown and some Obsession perfume, and rub up against him. Everyone knew they occasionally fought, but the truth was, they had never been closer than they were now. Not even his mother knew what had been going on between them. Mario's staff was convinced that they were estranged, and Slokov and Peterson thought Julie was firmly in their camp. They talked every day about strategy, and managed to do that without blowing her cover. Mario wanted to change course now, however.

"Julie, we can't go it alone any more. It's never been safe, and I'm a complete basket case worrying about you. I'm calling a halt to it. Let me tell you why. When you gave those photos to Slokov, he must have showed them to the others. Remember I told you that Rocco was taping that crud pack at their Friday night conference? I could tell Rocco was holding something back from me. He asked me how you were doing in a way that showed he's suspicious. He told me not to trust you. I'll bet he knows that you gave the photos to Slokov, and probably a whole lot more. I'm

158

going to call him right now, and tell him what we've been doing. I don't want you to contact Slokov or anybody else, and I want you under FBI protection."

"I already called Rocco this morning. I also figured that he probably knew what I've been up to. My God, did he yell at me! He said that I had rocks in my head to even attempt such a stupid thing without backup. I told him that was the only way it could have worked. Rocco said that I deserved a good spanking. You'll have to tell him that you gave me one this afternoon. No more shoptalk for a while," Julie said as she turned on the LED lamp. "Did you bring my clothes? How's poor David doing?"

Mario and Julie spent joyful hours talking about people, places, even food. They renewed their argument about how cannoli should be made. He said that orange rind was part of his late aunt's recipe, and she said it didn't belong in decent cannoli. She liked to use Frangelico liqueur in the filling, and he said that was a sacrilege invented by non-Italians who drove big SUVs.

Mario shared his fear that the country wouldn't hold together much longer. He was convinced that the "dark side" was much too strong. Julie knew how to soothe her husband. She had magic fingers, and when she ran them through his hair, over and over, it made his troubles disappear out the top of his head. Mario couldn't envision life without her. He considered himself the luckiest man alive.

~ ~ ~

If you want peace and quiet, don't camp next to a beaver pond in summer. Mario and Julie finally grew weary of talking and settled into each other's arms. Mario used the remote to turn off his new Cabella's LED lantern hanging from the tent's peak, and they began to drift into sleep. Suddenly Mario heard a rustling on the pine needles next to the tent, so he grabbed his flashlight and shined it toward the sound. It was only a field mouse, but it had certainly sounded larger. They again glided into that hazy zone between awake and asleep, that time when the day's thoughts recede and the night's dreams begin.

Thwap! It sounded like a rifle shot right at the water's edge.

"What was that?" Julie sat up, startled.

Mario shined his light and saw a beaver swimming away. They tried to get back to sleep, but every ten minutes the beaver swam by and slapped the water with his tail, right in front of their tent.

Thwap!

Julie laughed. "Somebody doesn't want us to be here."

Finally the beaver stopped tormenting them, and they fell asleep once more. Mario was again awakened by a sound on the pine needles, but this time it wasn't a mouse. He switched on his flashlight and saw the side of the tent moving as an animal rubbed against it. A porcupine looked at them through the screen, and then slowly waddled away into the woods.

They fell asleep once more, but were soon awakened by the sound of several animals. Mario grabbed his flashlight and saw a family of raccoons climbing the tree where he had secured their food. Mario always kept his food outside the tent, so bears wouldn't decide to have *him* for dinner. He had placed the food in a backpack and hung it from a rope thrown around a high branch. One of the coons was trying to bite through the rope. Mario shouted at them and banged a spoon against a pot bottom. The raccoons ran away.

"I'm going back to Washington, where it's quiet," Mario said.

They finally got to sleep, this time undisturbed. Undisturbed, that is, until the bear showed up. At midnight a black bear nosed around their tent. Julie had never seen a bear before in the wild, and Mario hadn't either, although he'd told Julie that he had.

"What do we do?" Julie asked.

"I don't know," Mario said.

"Where's your rifle?" Julie asked.

"In the car."

Mario shined his flashlight at the bear as it climbed up the food tree. It took one swipe at the cord and the backpack fell to the ground. As the bear ripped open the nylon pack, Mario and Julie jumped out of the sleeping bag and tried to find their clothes in the dark. Julie put her jeans on backward. They lifted up the side of their tent and were laughing as they ran back to their cars.

"Quick, open the door, I think the bear is following us," Julie said.

"I can't."

"Why the hell not?"

"Because the keys are back in the tent."

They both sat on top of Julie's Subaru wagon and tried not to move. The bear walked around both vehicles, sniffed the air, and finally ambled back into the woods. They both tried very hard not to laugh.

~ ~ ~

The McGuires were back home. Julie was annoyed that she hadn't remembered to bring her camera along. Mario knew that Julie would forever torment him with the bear incident. He could see her now at some future cocktail party, ".....and guess where his rifle was, and guess where the car keys were, guess what happened to our food?"

They were sitting on the deck on a clear evening, temperature about 77 degrees. The sun was setting behind the Adirondack Mountains in New York. Cumulus clouds were lit from below as the sun disappeared behind the mountain. It was half visible, then a crescent, then completely gone. The underside of the clouds glowed with a dozen colors. God had filled his canvas with gun-metal gray, orange, and blue-green halos around the higher clouds. They had watched thousands of sunsets from their deck.

Mosquitoes started biting so they moved back inside the house. They drank a toast to Stephanie, Carol, and Don. Mario was having a hard time coming to grips with their deaths. He was sad and troubled, and talked to Julie for comfort. "What are we going to do about Stephanie's things, about her will? I can't bring myself to go to California. I can't bear to see her house, to go through her possessions. She left the bulk of her estate to Carol. Since Carol and Don died with her, it will probably all go to me. I just don't know how to handle this. I don't want Stephanie's stuff."

"Don't think about it for a while, Mario. You have too many responsibilities right now. I'll help you when the time comes. I know you will keep a few items, only because they're part of the memories you shared. We can give the rest to charity."

"Perhaps we can give most of it to David?" Mario suggested.

"I don't know, Mario, let's wait and see what happens. I'll call the lawyer and ask for the details. You are still grieving; don't worry about the estate. She had no pets, and David is taking care of her plants. Everything else can just sit there until we're ready to deal with it."

"Thanks, baby," Mario said with gratitude.

~ ~ ~

Rocco didn't call Mario Monday morning as they had planned, and Mario was wondering how the Ludlowe Wenman arrest had gone. Mario knew that Rocco would be pissed at him, but he called anyway.

"Hello Rocco, this is Mario, did you get Ludlowe Wenman?"

"Mario who?" Rocco responded. "I used to know a Mario McGuire. I thought he was a forthcoming, honest man. The Mario I knew was a man who would never withhold information from me, and would never let his wife talk him into the most stupid, dangerous stunt that's ever been attempted by a sane couple. Let me tell you something, Mario. You are pussy-whipped. You let her do anything she wants. You aren't smart enough to have cooked this up. She's the chef, right?"

"I'm sorry I didn't mention it. Julie and I agreed we would keep it quiet. We thought it would be best if nobody knew. If it makes you feel any better, no one on my staff knew either."

"No, it doesn't, and I will say only one thing more. Please tell her to come see me next week; I've got a job for her as a special undercover agent."

"Ha, ha, Rocco, very funny. She did do a good job, but it's over. The risk is too great, and I don't want her hurt."

"Mario, the risk to her will be greater if she quits. Don't tell your staff. Now that we know, I'll have a ring of protection around her. Don't worry, we'll keep a low profile."

"Forget it, Rocco, she's not going back."

"Okay Mario, I understand, but at least let her talk to Slokov by phone for a while. Let him *think* she's still on his team. She'll learn what they want her to do next, and this may give us an important clue as to what's going down.

"So, to answer your question. We didn't get Fatso yet. He's been sunning himself in Puerto Rico, and gets back home tomorrow. We want him to be nice and comfy in his own bed. He bought a new girlfriend a few months ago, and she will probably be there with him. Hopefully she will scream, and further agitate and embarrass him."

"Rocco, you've been doing this too long. You sound like you're actually going to enjoy rousting him."

"I am. Are you going to enjoy putting a noose around Peterson's neck, Mario?"

"Only if I can pull the rope so tight that his eyes pop out."

"I think we both need a long vacation."

~ ~ ~

She called herself Lulu Brightstar. She had been surgically enhanced in the two places sexually immature men always preferred, the right one and the left one. Ludlowe met her at a Bazookas Restaurant in Miami. She recognized him as one of the Wenman family, and made it known she was available for anything he wanted. She didn't dance on tables anymore, not since Ludlowe had her move in with him. When the two of them had visited his mother in Monaco two months ago, Beatrice belittled her and laughed at him. Beatrice said she knew it was a mistake to bottle feed him when he was a baby, because he's been trying to find a milk-cow ever since.

~ ~ ~

The FBI had no trouble disabling the Eagle Claw security system around Ludlowe's mansion. Rocco knew that very large homes, with few people inside, are the easiest to enter without being detected. They knew exactly where his bedroom was. At 2:45 a.m., four FBI agents shined their powerful flashlights in Ludlowe's and Lulu's faces.

"Don't anybody move!"

"Hands up or we'll shoot!"

"If either of you so much as twitches, we'll blow your heads off!"

All the agents were shouting at the same time. Ludlowe and Lulu sat up and the covers fell off. Lulu's breasts stuck straight out

164

as if they were made of hard rubber. Rocco had orchestrated this grand entrance for shock value. Of course Lulu started screaming. Ludlowe screamed even louder.

"Don't shoot, don't shoot, I've got money! Don't shoot, I'm worth billions, and I'll take care of you. Please don't shoot!"

"Ludlowe Wenman, put your clothes on, you're under arrest for conspiracy to commit murder. Ma'am, you stay right where you are, and don't make any trouble or we'll arrest you too." Lulu didn't stop screaming for the entire three minutes it took to get Ludlowe dressed, handcuffed, out of the house, and into the car. As soon as she knew they had gone, she quieted down and said, "Shit, bummer." She then looked through Ludlowe's desk and dresser for any cash that might be lying around.

At the FBI lockup, the agents read Ludlowe his rights and allowed him one phone call. He woke up a WenCo attorney who told him to just sit tight until he found out what was going on. The lawyer would call Beatrice.

Rocco worked the classic good cop, bad cop routine on Ludlowe. The agents who arrested him said he was going to jail for a long time. The interrogation room was stark and intimidating.

"Did you murder Lynch?"

"No, he committed suicide, I never touched Robert Lynch."

"How come you know his name is Robert?"

"It was in the paper?"

"The six million dollars has your name written all over it."

"I know nothing about it."

"We have photos of you at Metro Media in Dallas. What were you doing there?"

"I wasn't doing anything."

"What about the fifty million for Julie McGuire? How did you get that money?"

"It wasn't me, I didn't do it."

165

Finally the interrogators let up, dimmed the lights, and left the room. Ludlowe sat there alone for fifteen minutes and let out a whimper or two before an attractive, large-breasted female agent sat down next to him. She had on a business suit, and she brought Ludlowe a cup of coffee and a piece of very sweet coffee cake.

"I think I can help you, Ludlowe. You've gotten yourself in quite a fix. It's my job to see that both you and the FBI come out ahead here. I know you don't want to go to jail, and we want some very simple information. I will personally guarantee, and put it in writing so you can show your attorney, immunity from prosecution if you will name the person who told you to put that money into the Cayman Island account."

"But I didn't put it in the Cayman Island account, I just gave it to the person who put it in the account."

"Bingo!" Rocco said as his team watched and listened from the one-way glass in the next room. "Great work, Donna."

"Yeah! Way to go, Donna."

Agent Donna Clark continued to work on Ludlowe. "I'm glad you told me that, Ludlowe. Do you mind if I call you Ludlowe? You may call me Donna. This information makes a big difference. How did you get the money, and who did you give it to? Was that the same person who set up the Cayman account?"

"I got the money from our California receipts and gave it to my mother," Ludlowe replied.

"Sheesh! Do you believe this guy?" Rocco said.

His colleague shook his head. "Doctor, Doctor, sonny has a mommy fixation."

"Come on, Donna, press him on that," Rocco said to his agent. Donna wore a miniature ear-bud receiver under her hair and could hear Rocco's instructions.

"Beatrice didn't handle these funds," Rocco said to her.

"Ludlowe, how did she set it up? Are you sure your mother has the contacts to do this? It sounds like a government job to me."

166

"Yes, I'm sure."

"Are you willing to testify to that in court?"

"You said I would have immunity if I cooperated."

"I said you would have immunity from *prosecution* if you cooperated, not from testifying. We must all testify to the truth. Are you sure no one else is involved?"

"It was my mother. I don't know if she worked with anyone else."

"Okay, Donna, bag it, he's not going to name Peterson. Good job." Rocco turned to his associates and outlined their next moves.

"We have successfully driven a wedge between Ludlowe and Beatrice. We have enough to go on from his testimony to arrest her. She won't talk, and we won't be able to book her because we have no additional proof, but she and Ludlowe are going to go for each other's throats. They may get sloppy and make some indiscreet moves. Let's monitor those two very carefully. Ludlowe can't be prosecuted for moving funds from his own company to his mother, so we have to release him."

CHAPTER SEVEN

Mario was playing his new Fender Stratocaster, plugged into a Princeton Chorus amp. He had changed the stock speakers for two Eminence Ragin' Cajuns' and although the amp was solid state instead of tubes, it sounded very good. With the headphone jack, he could play without disturbing Julie. They could both be in the same room doing completely different things; all she heard was a quiet un-amplified solid-body electric guitar. He could rattle his brains in total privacy while she designed her next mixed-media piece. He had the white button pressed in on the guitar pick guard and the five-way selector set all the way up. This gave him the neck and bridge pickup combination, not usually found on a standard Strat. There was a Telecaster-type twang to it, a great sound for country, rock, and blues.

Julie looked up from her work and smiled at Mario. Whenever he played, he made funny faces. He raised his eyebrows and turned one side of his mouth down in a half-scowl. Then he'd close his eyes and make his lips disappear. She could almost tell what he was playing by his face.

Mario was a very bad liar in person, although he could be quite convincing on the phone. Even if he had a good reason, like keeping information from an enemy, he found it difficult to fabricate a story, or mislead an adversary when they were there in front of him. It was his face. It was easier to read than a large-print children's book. That was just one of the three dozen reasons Julie had fallen in love with him.

She had once read an article in *Northeast Psychology Journal*. Researchers had posed the question: "Are couples eventually repelled by the same things that originally attracted them to their mate?" Two therapists interviewed people who were recently divorced and asked them what had attracted them to their spouses in the first place. They then asked them the reasons for their divorce. It was a small sampling, only one hundred couples, but the results were suggestive. Seventy-two percent said that they broke up, not because their partner had changed, but because *they* had changed. They were no longer attracted to the same qualities that had brought them together in the first place. The spontaneous person had suddenly become an annoying, irresponsible child. A good, conscientious provider had turned into a bore.

Julie felt sorry for such people. *Perhaps I'll divorce Mario because he's too honest. He is also a fine lover; that attracted me as well. He's also very brave.* They had been married for twenty years, and she hoped for another thirty. *If I grow dissatisfied, I could always find a lying, cowardly slob who's lousy in bed.*

~ ~ ~

Mario had an unusual political belief system. He was either liberal or conservative, depending on the issue. He hated to be labeled as one or the other. He was passionately against abortion, but he believed in a woman's right to choose. He was not anti-gun, or even anti-concealed-weapon. He thought there should be no restrictions on gun ownership. He was for universal health care, no exceptions. He wanted a 100,000-troop quick-strike military force with full air support that could be anywhere in the world in seven hours. He was a strict environmentalist, especially since he'd sold the Crown Victoria and bought a used VW Cabrio. He was for civil unions for gays, but admitted it made him uncomfortable to see two men holding hands.

169

Mario finished playing his Strat and sat down at his computer to work on a pet project. The television ban would soon be settled, and he would finally have time to find co-sponsors in the Senate for a new initiative he'd created. It had all started one day when he'd noticed a group of teenagers listening to dirty rap lyrics. They were just hanging out at the mall with nothing to do, mindlessly sucking in all this filth. He despised what our culture was doing to its children. He thought many Americans were spoiled and greedy because they never had to be poor, or go without food. He wanted one-year, compulsory non-military service for all teenagers when they reached 18 years old. After high school, they could choose where they wanted to work, the Peace Corps, Department of the Interior, or Agriculture, to name just three. They would get college credit for their service. As the economy worsens, this option becomes more attractive. Jobs are hard to find for students who want to work before going to college.

There were dozens of agencies in need of intelligence and labor. The majority of work would be in foreign countries. Our young people would see true hardship, and they would be better people as a result. They would enter college, not as pampered materialistic children, but as young adults with a consciousness of other cultures. Each person would have three choices, but there would be no guarantee that they would get their request. He wanted to call this group "The Ambassador Corps." Unlike the Peace Corps, this would not be a voluntary program. Mario often quoted from the book *The Ugly American*. He didn't like our image in the rest of the world.

~ ~ ~

Mario turned to Julie and said, "Which is better, using the creative energy of America's brightest people for international

170

projects, or exporting pornography and cigarettes? No one would dare to call us the Great Satan if we had the Ambassador Corps."

Julie had heard all this before. Many people had told him that he was nuts for suggesting the Corps. "Mario, you're going to have to make it a volunteer program, or it will be as unpopular as the draft."

"How many volunteers do you think we'll get?"

"Nine," Julie said.

"Thank you for your unconditional support," Mario joked, as his special phone rang. He kept it in a battery charger on their kitchen table. "Hello, this is Mario."

"Put up or shut up," Nadene said.

Mario laughed. "What's the matter, can't stay away from me?" Nadene told Mario that she, her husband Oscar, Seth, and Rosa were going to the national forest tomorrow to do some target shooting. If he did not come along, he would automatically forfeit their bet, and would have to bake brownies and bring them to the music session on Friday.

"My honest belief, Senator McGuire, is that you may have somewhat overstated your prowess with a .45."

"Okay, tomorrow will be fine," Mario said.

"We'll pick you up."

Mario hung up the phone and then remembered that Julie was home. He told her that the staff was coming over, and she agreed to end the deception. He didn't care what Rocco wanted; she was finished putting herself in danger.

"You are out of the spy business. When they come in here, let *me* tell them about our little plot," Mario said.

~ ~ ~

The next morning Mario took out his Kimber .45 automatic pistol. It was a stainless Gold Match II model with an adjustable rear sight, target trigger, and hammer. He felt sorry for Nadene because she had her double-action duty weapon, which was nowhere near as accurate as his .45 Kimber. He loaded hardball ammo into two clips, and put the gun and box of shells in the canvas bag he always took to the woods.

"Don't forget your hearing protectors, and bring some for me too," Julie said. Ordinarily she didn't go shooting, but she wanted to be with him. She wouldn't admit it, but now she was frightened to be alone.

"Dis should shake up the B Team," Mario said. "I can't wait until they see you."

~ ~ ~

Nadene's red Volvo station wagon pulled into their driveway. Julie's car was in the garage, and only Mario's Cabrio was visible. Seth got out of the car to fetch Mario, but Mario opened the front door and beckoned all of them to come in. He completely trusted Oscar Johnson. Nadene's husband was a fine Immigration Customs Enforcement agent, and Nadene told him everything.

Julie was sitting on the couch when they came into the living room. Before Mario could speak, Julie stood up and walked over to Nadene.

"My cover is blown, Nadene. I've been working with Mario the whole time. We are very much in love, and that scene at Bistro Bis was completely staged. We waited until you arrived before we performed the final act. Don't be mad at Mario, it was my idea. We didn't tell you because your anger at me in the restaurant was

172

real, and was being recorded by Domestic Security agents. If any of you had known beforehand, you would have had to fake it. It would have been almost impossible to pull off convincingly."

The B Team was stunned and quiet until Nadene walked over to Mario. "Do you have any more surprises, a dinosaur in the back yard, a harem in the basement, a mummy of the president in your coat closet?"

Julie laughed and said, "No more surprises."

Mario finally spoke. "She did an incredible job of finding out information about Slokov and what his crud pack were going to do next. I know what you're thinking, Seth, but Julie pushed Slokov away in that limo. Peterson was also there."

Rosa looked at Julie and said, "My God, woman, that was brave."

"That was stupid," Nadene said. She was sulking because Mario hadn't let her in on the plan.

Julie could sense that his staff was upset at being excluded, so she said, "Mario loves all of you. He didn't want the team to be in any more danger."

"That's what I'm paid for," Nadene said. She was still cold and unfriendly.

Oscar put his arms around Julie and said, "Thank you both for looking out for my wife. She isn't half as tough as she thinks she is."

Nadene turned to Mario and said, "There's been a change in plans. The stakes aren't high enough for our contest. If I beat you, you have to write, one thousand times, 'I will never deceive my staff, even if I think it's for their own good.' You will also have to bake brownies. If I lose, I just bake brownies. Deal?"

Before Mario could answer, Julie laughed and said, "Deal, absolutely, a deal."

Mario just smiled and in a very soft voice said, "I'm just thankful that we are all alive and in this room together. I pray that God protects all of us. Let's go have a shootout."

~ ~ ~

The Johnsons' Volvo had a fold-down rear seat, so it could easily accommodate seven passengers. It took a half-hour to drive to the forest, plenty of time for Julie to make friends again. Oscar was driving, while Nadene asked Julie question after question about her adventures. Julie answered everything. She said, "Do you know that Slokov has a tropical forest in his office, complete with a banyan tree, butterflies, and orchids? He has a seaplane and several huge yachts. He has a complete bowling alley and an Olympic-sized pool in his basement. He's totally ruthless, and will commit murder to expand his wealth and power. In my opinion, he's even more dangerous than Peterson."

They arrived at Mount Abraham Valley, a beautiful area of old logging roads and abandoned homesteads. When it was declared a national forest, all the roads were blocked off. They grabbed their equipment and hiked to a natural shooting range Mario remembered. A short walk down the road brought them to a meadow twice the size of a football field. At the end of the meadow was a fifty-foot rise of sandy soil. Behind the rise was a trail that went to the top of Mount Abraham, over four thousand feet high. Mario had come shooting here ever since he had graduated from high school. There were raspberry bushes everywhere, and the fruit was mostly ripe. Nadene said, "Oscar, we've got to buy some jelly-making supplies. Look at all the bushes. We can pick gallons of berries."

Mario put two thumbtacks through a paper target and stuck it to a dead branch, then wiggled the branch into the soil. The tacks were off center, so there would be less chance of blasting the stick that held the target. He removed a fifty-foot wind-up tape from his canvas bag, measured off thirty-five feet from the target, and made a line in the dirt with his foot. Nadene placed several weapons on top of their nylon cases on the ground in front of the line. There was one small aluminum case engraved with her name. She pulled out a customized Colt Government, Gold Match .45 auto that she had bought when she was a Marine. She had replaced the barrel, bushing, ejector, and recoil spring because she'd worn them all out. She had won many matches with this pistol.

Uh oh, Mario thought. "I thought you would be using your Ruger."

"Nope. This one is sighted in for the ammo I loaded."

"You load your own shells?" Mario asked.

"185 grain copper-coated match bullet pushed by 5.5 grains of Unique powder. The muzzle velocity is a very controllable 750 feet-per-second. I like Hornady brass. I buy my supplies at Datillio's on Shelburne Road."

Uh oh, he thought again. Mario had underestimated his chief of staff. He removed the custom Kimber .45 from his canvas bag.

Nadene became really animated. "Look here, the Senator has a custom .45. He was ready to challenge me and my regular duty weapon with his custom .45. I want everyone to see how unfair this would have been. My boss is trying to take unfair advantage of me."

Mario was having a really good time and said, "I refuse to lose to a woman."

"Good luck, Senator McGuire," Seth said with a grin.

Oscar said, "I have a pen and lots of paper in the car for that list you'll have to write."

Nadene laid down the rules. "The target is clearly marked. A bull's-eye is worth twelve points. All the other rings are marked

175

from five to nine points. We each get three shots. Rosa, don't you worry about scoring. My job is to teach you how to shoot. Rosa, Seth, and Julie, you will use this Smith & Wesson .38 with a six-inch barrel. I've got wad-cutter target ammo in it, and it doesn't kick nearly as much as these .45s. All shooters will wear hearing protectors, and everyone else will stand at least ten feet behind the shooter. Put your hands over your ears, because guns are very loud and will damage your hearing."

Seth shot first and got a score of 20. Julie shot next and got a score of 19. Oscar shot a 25 with his service issue .40.

After each shooter, Mario placed a piece of masking tape over the holes in the target so it could be re-used.

Rosa said she wanted to shoot last; she was clearly intimidated. Mario and Nadene both shot a 27.

"We'll have to shoot again to break the tie," Nadene said, "but first Rosa has to shoot."

Rosa grabbed the revolver with both hands and closed her eyes as she snapped the trigger.

"No, girl," Nadene said. "You don't close your eyes. Just squeeze the trigger, don't jerk it or you'll pull your shot off."

Rosa shot again, but closed her eyes and jerked the trigger. She shot the same way for her third shot.

"That's okay, hon, you'll get the hang of it."

Oscar inspected the target. "Holy shit, she got three bull's-eyes. She scored a perfect 36."

"Those are her measurements," Seth said happily.

Rosa picked up some pinecones and threw them at Seth. She chased him through the woods. Seth was running around in circles shouting, "Help, help, mad woman!"

Rosa shouted, "I won, I won!"

Mario took out his tape, measured 75 feet from the target, and made another line in the dirt. He and Nadene each shot three more rounds. The score was again tied, 26 to 26.

Mario measured back to one hundred feet. They would try once again to break the tie. Nadene was getting ready to shoot when Mario's phone rang. It was Rocco DiAngelo.

"Hello, Rocco, how's it going?"

Rocco said he needed to talk to him and Julie in detail about Harold Slokov and Beatrice Wenman, and he had some important news. Mario must return home because there was information on his computer that Rocco needed. Mario apologized to everyone and said that they had to leave the forest right away.

"Saved by the bell," Nadene said.

Mario said, "You're shooting custom made target ammo, and I'm only using standard hardball. Plus I haven't shot my .45 in almost a year, and you practice every few weeks. Next time I'll use target ammo. I absolutely love pecans in my brownies, Nadene."

~ ~ ~

They were sitting at Mario's computer. Rocco was in Washington on the special phone, and Mario and Julie were sharing the headset.

"Julie, did Harold Slokov ever mention George Huntington?" Rocco asked.

"No, he didn't."

"Wait a minute, I know that name. He's director of the Federal Communications Commission," Mario said.

"That's right. There have been two meetings between Peterson, Slokov, and Huntington. I'll bet they aren't talking about football."

"Miserable bastards, those miserable bastards," Mario said.

"What, what?" Rocco asked.

"There's legislation before the House and Senate, a bill that gives the FCC new powers to regulate communications in a national emergency. When national security is threatened, Huntington will be able to shut down entire networks. Holy cannoli, I've totally ignored that bill, because all my efforts have gone into our Cancer Prevention Act."

"Since Huntington is meeting with Slokov and Peterson, we can assume he's dirty. What exactly is this bill about?" Rocco said.

Mario opened the computer file with information on the pending legislation and read it to Rocco and Julie. "It's called the Emergency Communications Act. When the President of the United States declares a communications-specific emergency..."

"What is a communications-specific emergency?" Rocco interrupted.

"It's defined as an emergency in which the national security of the United States is threatened, and must be safeguarded by regulating internal and external communications. This includes all media that could impact national security. In other words, they can shut down every newspaper, radio and television station, and even control telecommunications. Now here's the scary part, Rocco. Any member of Congress can request that the president declare such an emergency. The House and Senate then vote on the measure. If it passes, the president can authorize these wide-ranging controls."

"Do you think this bill will pass?" Julie asked. "When is the vote?"

"There's a special session next week to vote on this bill and another one, an emergency defense appropriations package. As a matter of fact, the Republican leadership has linked the two bills together. This is a sneaky device. If anyone votes against the communications bill, they are also voting against needed military funds. The Republicans are also trying to push it through at the last minute, when many in Congress are preparing for recess."

~ ~ ~

Mario called his team together and told them that there was a new crisis. They would leave for Washington immediately. The B Team was to contact every senator and representative and lobby against the bill. He asked Julie if she would help, and she said yes.

Mario's staff worked tirelessly, calling mostly Republican congressmen and senators. The American Civil Liberties Union and other groups were also lobbying against the bill. Mario hated this part of being a lawmaker. He wouldn't even take calls from lobbyists, and here he was exerting pressure himself.

~ ~ ~

Voting day arrived and Mario made a speech asking the senators to vote against the Emergency Communications Bill. Unfortunately, the day before it had passed in the Republican-controlled House by seventeen votes. Mario's speech was good, but he felt he was preaching to the converted rather than breaking new ground. Senator Bruch, a Democrat, also made a good speech telling everyone why he was in favor of the measure.

"Now is the time," Bruch said, "to put partisanship aside and do what's best for America. There is too much division in the land. We all have a common goal to safeguard our national security. None of us wants the republic to be picked apart by terrorists, or by those who want to put an end to our way of life. If we don't have the capability to monitor communications, we won't know where or when the enemy will strike."

Mario had heard these platitudes so many times that he wished he'd brought a barf-bag to the Senate. How often was he going to have to listen to some crooked politician tell the American people that he was going to take good care of them, if only they would give him power? *They always play the fear card. All a citizen has to do to be safe is give up his or her firstborn child, two gallons of blood, all their personal letters, and half their worldly goods. That's not too high a price to pay, now is it?*

He remembered the Benjamin Franklin quote: "They who give up essential liberty for temporary security, deserve neither liberty or security."

Mario knew that this Emergency Communications bill, like the Patriot Act before it, was a carte blanche for the erosion of liberty. He made one last comment before the vote.

"The Speaker recognizes the Independent Senator from Vermont."

"Thank you, Mr. Speaker. I'm not going to repeat myself. I have just one additional point. We respect the present administration, both houses of Congress, and the Supreme Court. We all have the best interest of the country at heart. This does not mean that any one group should have *legislated* control, in writing, that can be used against the very people we are trying to protect."

Mario raised his voice. "We must *always, always, always* be very suspicious of any legislation that can be abused by those who govern this nation. We should not give ourselves, or the president, a blank check to control aspects of citizens' lives that should be private, and under a citizen's own control. We must have safeguards in place to thwart those in power who may have evil intentions. There are no guarantees that the motives of those in our three branches of government will remain pure. I say again, we must never enact legislation that can be used against the American people. The Emergency Communications bill is dangerous. There are no safeguards. Please defeat this measure and separate it from the Defense Appropriations Package. We can vote on that in another session. Thank you."

Two Republicans voted against the bill, but it passed in the Senate by four votes. The president would sign the measure.

~ ~ ~

The television ban passed in New York, New Jersey, and in six other states. There were so many votes taking place that Mario and his staff had abandoned plans to travel to each state. They had made their case brilliantly at the Senate hearing, and momentum was still very much with them.

Rocco was on the phone. "I blew it, Mario. We picked up Beatrice Wenman and we questioned her just like we did Ludlowe. She didn't say a word. Guess who she brought with her as her attorney?"

"Carl Goodman," Mario answered.

"You got it, buddy. We couldn't pin anything on her, so we had to let her go. When we set up for this Friday's meeting at Metro Media, nobody showed up. I reviewed the transcript of our questions to Ludlowe and Beatrice Wenman. We had asked Ludlowe why he was in Dallas, at Metro Media. Duhhh, he isn't totally stupid. Obviously he told the others. We spooked them with that careless comment during interrogation. But don't worry, they have to meet somewhere. I have almost one hundred agents tailing all of them 24/7. Eventually we'll find out where.

"You should see these agents, Mario, you'd get a kick out of them. We have grandmothers pushing baby carriages, complete with babies, I might add. We have young guys who look like kids on skateboards. We have plumbers, sanitation workers, pizza delivery drivers, and all of them are FBI agents. Did you know that we have a special makeup department?"

"No shit."

"You bet. The person in charge used to work for Titan Studios. They could make you look nineteen again."

"God no," Mario said, "I couldn't live through my teens again."

"Has Slokov tried to reach Julie?"

"Not yet."

"Tell her to be ready for him. I guarantee he will contact her. Let's see what he wants her to do next. That's all I have for now. Ciao."

~ ~ ~

It had been days since any major activity. The ban passed in Alaska, making a total of seventeen states that had voted in favor of the Cancer Prevention Act. There was an eerie quiet in Washington.

Mario remembered the history of World War II. War was declared on Germany by England and France, but nothing happened for seven months after Hitler invaded Poland. They called it the Phony War. Neither side mounted an attack. Mario hoped the present lull in the action wasn't a foretelling of what had happened in World War II.

The FBI had nothing more to report. The FCC was quiet. Whitcom, Bruch, Slokov, Peterson, all quiet. Even crank calls from pro-TV forces had subsided. They still got e-mails, but those too had fallen off in the last few days. There were thousands of them stored in two computer folders.

Mario asked Seth to invent a program to count the messages, both for and against the TV ban. Seth said it wasn't totally accurate, but he devised word recognition technology that scanned each message. If a message contained key negative words, it would be considered a message against the ban. If positive key words showed up, the message was put into the pro-ban folder.

The team created a separate mailbox just to handle e-mails about the ban, cancerpreventionact@worldlink.com.

Mario was disturbed by the totals. Using Seth's system, which had a margin for error of about five percent, 434,848 messages were in favor of the ban, and 435,432 messages opposed it. The opposition was almost 600 votes ahead, but the race was very close. If Mario's totals were a good cross-section of what was also going on in each state, the lawmakers' actions were not reflecting what people actually felt. Mario had no trouble accepting that, because it furthered the cause he believed in. But when Missouri lawmakers voted almost overwhelmingly to ban television, they were not honoring the wishes of over half the state's population.

That same situation happened over and over again in Washington. People fought in wars they didn't want, and didn't get the medical care they did want. Everyone seemed to know what was best for the people while they ignored what the people told them they wanted. Mario felt as if he were a part of some kind of conspiracy and had a dark night of the soul. For the first time in many years, he was actually praying to God for guidance. He kept giving himself positive affirmations, but sometimes he felt that his shoulders weren't wide enough to hold his own big head, let alone the problems of the world. *What right do I have to try to safeguard the population if they don't want the safeguards?* Mario questioned what he was doing, and it was keeping him awake at night. *The people are so easily manipulated, someone has to look out for them. But isn't that what my opposition is also saying? But they're murderers!* His resolve and determination were playing ping-pong with his fears and uncertainty.

"I should have been an anarchist musician!" Mario shouted as he passed Nadene and Rosa in the hall.

~~~

Two hundred feet below Roundback Mountain, a secret complex had been built back in 1955. The Cold War was then challenging the Eisenhower administration, and three bunkers were constructed on the Maryland-Pennsylvania border for top government people to hide in should there be a nuclear attack. Roundback was the largest of the three and had been expanded several times. It was now a complete underground city. It stocked enough food and water to sustain two dozen people for a year. The air was filtered to remove any biological or nuclear contamination. It would survive a direct hit from an atomic bomb. It generated its own electric power, and had complete communications links, including encrypted satellite relays to all branches of the government. A small elevator took people back and forth to the surface, but a secret code was needed to activate it.

Although the facility was part of the Government Office of Domestic Security, it used Marine guards, like most other government installations. There was a permanent detachment of ten guards stationed there who rotated out every month. Six were topside and four were underground. It was better than submarine duty, because there was more room and more recreation. It was boring, however, for the Marines. Females were not part of the detachment, for obvious reasons. No liquor or drugs were allowed, but when the guards were alone, some had a beer or two.

Roundback's total area was almost thirty thousand square feet. There were several good meeting places, two recreation rooms, and a suite for the commander-in-chief. The rooms were small, about the size of an average living room. The command center had a twelve-foot-long table with eight chairs. The chairs were adjustable open mesh, comfortable but very simple. The center was well isolated from the other rooms.

There were portraits of the President and Vice President of the United States on one wall. Emergency safety procedures were posted on another wall, with instructions on what to do in case of nuclear attack, and a large first-aid cabinet alongside them. On a third wall were special safety evacuation procedures. The only decoration was two photographs: one of the cherry blossoms in bloom at the Capital, and one of the aircraft carrier Kitty Hawk, out at sea, with a deep blue sky above her and a full complement of jets on her flight deck. The recreation rooms had televisions, stereos, video games, and were decorated with homey touches. They also had comfortable couches, and there was a good library in one rec room.

The Command Center, however, was a serious room. Slokov, Peterson, Huntington, Whitcom, the Wenmans, Walsh, and Sinton got down to business.

Peterson said, "No doubt the FBI knows that we're meeting here, but they can't do anything about it, nor can they bug our conversation. We are totally protected."

"Speaking of bugs," Huntington said, "one of your Domestic Security agents found one in my car. He said it was definitely an FBI microphone. Looks like they're playing dirty. No judge is giving them court orders, or I'd know about it. If the FBI is working with Mario McGuire, we have big trouble."

"I completely agree," Peterson said. "There is no way we can fight the FBI. They are totally independent and uncontrollable. It's not that they are working for Mario McGuire, they just get their jollies chasing criminals."

"That's us, remember?" Ludlowe laughed as he spilled coffee into his saucer.

No one else laughed, and Peterson continued. "McGuire is close friends with Rocco DiAngelo. We all know what DiAngelo is capable of. My advice is to stay clear. We don't have enough power or enough agents to challenge them directly. We can only lose, head to head."

"Why not kill Rocco DiAngelo?" Ludlowe Wenman asked.

No one answered him.

Slokov said, "So we have a cat-and-mouse game going on with your agents and the FBI agents."

"That's exactly what it is," Peterson said. "We're tailing McGuire's team. The FBI is tailing our agents who are tailing theirs. We have agents tailing those agents. And the same goes for us. The FBI is watching every move we make, and our agents are watching the FBI watching us. It's kind of like the Cold War with nuclear deterrent. Neither side can win or lose, because everybody's nose is up everybody else's rear end."

"What about our plan?" Whitcom looked at Huntington to get the meeting back on track. "Who was supposed to get the medical evidence?"

"That was Beatrice and Harold," Peterson answered.

Slokov said, "We've got testimony and reports from three medical researchers who will swear that cellphones and radio waves cause cancer in humans."

"How much did we have to pay them?" Sinton asked.

"Ten million dollars each," Slokov answered. "The testimony is absolutely fabulous. After I read through it, I was scared to use my phone or turn on the radio."

"But a radio is just sound waves," Whitcom said.

"It isn't the sound coming out of the speaker that supposedly causes cancer," Slokov said. "It's the radio waves that are transmitted from the antenna. They are all around us and weaken the autoimmune system and make our bodies susceptible to disease."

Whitcom gave a rare smile. "This is called using the enemy's own tactics against him. Very good, lady and gentleman, very good indeed." He slapped his hand on the table in delight.

Huntington gave further details of the plan. "We're going to call it Operation Signoff. First we're going to have the surgeon general issue a warning about these new dangers. It shouldn't be too hard to get congress to agree to invoke the Emergency Communications Act, due to this new health threat. The momentum is with us now in both houses since McGuire got his ass kicked in the senate on that one.

"Then we're going to target those states where the television ban has passed. Our reasoning to congress will be that the bureaucracy is already in place in those states to eliminate television. It's logical to piggyback the elimination of radio and cellphones on their current screen roundups. We are going to send in a federal team to each state comprised of FCC and Domestic Security agents to shut down the radio stations and disable the cellphone relay towers. Nothing could be easier. There are very few towers to disable, and once the radio stations are silenced, radios themselves will be useless."

Whitcom said, "Our goal, Best Friend told me, is to infuriate the population. When kids can't play with their cellphones, and people can't listen to the radio when they are driving, all hell will break loose. It will be the old proverbial straw that breaks McGuire's back. They will put pressure on their senators and congressman to stop the FCC. We can link the television ban with the radio and cellphone ban and write legislation to bring them all together. If the senate passes McGuire's bill, it's our ace in the hole, if you will forgive the cliché."

Harold Slokov gave a report on newsreel preparation. "We're going to get copies of the latest episodes of the top ten TV programs and put them in our Balcony Theaters this week in every state where television has been banned. We won't charge anything, and we will highly publicize the free shows as a public service from Metro Media. As part of the package, we will run some of the old cartoons. Right after the cartoons, before the main TV features, we will show newsreels about the hardships of doing without our beloved screens. We will not run movies, either current or classic, only TV programs. The studios continue to shoot, because they know it's just a matter of time before McGuire's witch-hunt fails."

George Huntington said, "There's something else we need to discuss. We are going to try to get control of telephone networks using the Emergency Communications Act. We can cite subversive activity, or perhaps the threat of internal terrorism. John Peterson has a good idea. Why don't you tell us about it, John."

"We plan to dynamite several movie theaters...."

"None of mine, I hope," Slokov interrupted.

"Sorry, yes, some of yours as well. We want to have a solid reason to declare a state of emergency. We have plans in place to agitate the population and even commit acts of sabotage, if necessary. We will pressure some of the governors to call up their National Guards. In actuality, there probably will be very little violence. A few dozen people may get killed here and there, but the *perception* of widespread chaos will give us an excuse to seize control of telecommunications. The average person will need to schedule an appointment days in advance to make a phone call, and each call will be monitored by anti-terrorist personnel. This plan is going to be difficult to enact and could backfire, so we have to be very careful. We don't have all the details worked out yet."

"It's something to consider," Beatrice said, "because it will give us total control in all the states that passed the ban. It will also serve as a warning to the other states that if they follow suit, they will not only lose their televisions, but radio and phone communications as well. That should make them think twice."

"There is one last item, before we return to the surface," Whitcom said.

"Good," Ludlowe said. "This place gives me the creeps."

No one responded to Ludlowe.

"Harold, would you please show everybody the finished photograph of Mario McGuire and Rosa," Whitcom said.

Slokov took a rolled-up 16-by-20 color photo from a cardboard mailing tube and passed it around. It showed a perfect image of Mario making love to Rosa. Mario's head and the side of his face were clearly visible. Everybody clapped and laughed.

"At a strategic moment, just before the final vote on the Senate floor, I'm going to produce this photograph to humiliate Mario McGuire and decimate his credibility. I guarantee the presence of this photo will influence those senators who may be undecided," Whitcom said.

~ ~ ~

The President of the United States was holding a news conference. It was covered by all media, including those television stations that were still operative.

"Good evening, my fellow Americans. Much has happened in the last twenty-four hours. Three oil refineries in Texas and Louisiana have been destroyed by terrorist bombs. Forty-five Americans and twelve foreign workers were killed, and dozens injured. The Islamic group El Jaride has claimed responsibility and threatened that other, even more destructive explosions will follow. At the same time, the FBI has foiled a terrorist plot in Los Angeles to bomb a major sporting event that was attended by over fifty thousand people. The terrorist plan would have completely destroyed the stadium with an unspeakable loss of life. In New York City, the Port of New York Authority Police arrested ten members of El Jaride who were stowed away on a Liberian freighter. Two police officers and four terrorists were killed. It is still not known what they were planning, but FBI and Domestic Security agents have been dispatched to the scene.

"I want those responsible for these horrendous acts to understand that America will never be intimidated by violence. We will do whatever is necessary, within the law, to bring the members of El Jaride to justice. We will hunt them down wherever they may be hiding. My fellow Americans, nothing is more cowardly that an act of terrorism. These evil human beings take innocent lives and then go back and hide among their women and children.

"Their behavior is shunned by all godly people, be they Muslims, Christians, or Jews. I ask for help from every one of you, and from our friends overseas. We must be vigilant because we are at war. There are people living among us who want us destroyed, and they will stop at nothing, including sacrificing their own lives, to advance their cause."

~ ~ ~

Mario phoned Rocco. "Are you listening to the president's news conference? Is all of this true?"

"Yes, it is, Mario. Peterson and I have both been called to New York. This should be interesting. I'll talk to you later."

~ ~ ~

The president continued, "There is another danger to our country. We must not let the proposed ban on television divide us. We must work together and find solutions to our problems without using threats or violence. If we weaken ourselves, we will be more vulnerable to threats from outside our borders. I'm asking the American people and our leaders, especially our leaders, to set a good example by working together to find answers. I will now take questions."

"Yes, Mr. Hersch."

"Thank you, Mr. President. Are there other terrorist plans that have been uncovered, and are you at liberty to discuss them?"

"We have intercepted some communications that speak of other planned terrorist activity, but we have yet to analyze them. It is a common device of El Jaride's to try to confuse us by giving us false information. They have done this in the past just to raise our terrorist alert level. When we do see an actual threat, we will immediately let the American people know. Yes, Ms. Kohn."

"Mr. President, do you feel that it's bad for the country to eliminate television and computer screens?"

"It depends what you mean by 'bad.' It's a very good thing if we can prevent our people from developing brain cancer. It's not a good thing if we have to completely rebuild our communications infrastructure. Commerce will suffer. But we will get through it. We've had greater challenges and have prevailed. I have tremendous faith in the American people. Yes, Nancy."

"Thank you, Mr. President. Do you and the First Lady still watch movies on television?"

"I suppose I should lie to you and say no, but I made a vow to never lie to the American people, so the answer is yes. But we cut way back." The president laughed. "Yes, the woman in the second row."

"Francine Bouchard, *Barre/Montpelier Times-Argus*. Thank you for taking my question, Mr. President...."

"Oh yes, Senator McGuire's home state. How are Vermonters adjusting to a life without television?"

"Some are adjusting very well, and others aren't, sir. Many people have lost their jobs, and as you said earlier, we're trying to pull together and solve our problems. Mr. President, there are elements within the government that are engaging in criminal acts. It has even been rumored that an American missile hit the plane that was carrying the Japanese researchers back to Tokyo. How do you respond to that, sir?"

"I've heard the same rumors. There is evidence that some group, so far still unknown to us, is responsible for criminal behavior, including murder. Senator McGuire's own family, as well as his staff, was targeted. I've asked both the FBI and the Office of Domestic Security to investigate. As far as the report of a missile hitting that plane, I've asked U.S. Naval Intelligence to investigate. Senator McGuire knows Admiral Bonner very well; he is heading up the inquiry."

"What have they told you, sir?"

"I can't comment on the details, but Domestic Security is exploring the possibility that an outside contractor is responsible for the acts. This contractor may or may not have ties to people in this government. Let me assure you, and the Japanese people, that if a link is found to a person or persons in my administration or to anyone else in Washington, that person will be immediately prosecuted for his crimes. You, sir."

"Mr. President, Joe Pike, *Milwaukee Journal*. Do you plan to veto the television ban if it passes the Senate?"

"I'm going to wait until I hear all the evidence before I decide. As you know, this is going to be a lively debate and a very tough decision both for the senators and for me."

"Mr. President......"

"Thank you, ladies and gentlemen," the president's press secretary said as the commander-in-chief left the podium.

~~~

"Nice try, Francine," Mario said as he and his staff listened to the radio.

"She came close to finding out some solid information," Nadene commented.

Mario said, "The president doesn't have many answers. There's a lot going on behind his back. About New York, yeah, I just called Rocco and he confirmed that he and Peterson will both be investigating the sabotage on that Liberian freighter. Peterson will act like a choir boy. Rocco won't be able to nail him."

"Are all these terrorist threats real, Mario?" Rosa asked. "If you want to control the people, it's very effective to make up stories and fabricate outside threats. Perhaps the president's cabinet is lying to him."

"These threats are real and aren't coming from Americans, but Rosa, you make an excellent point. If those in power want a cover for their dirty work, they will use these terrorist acts as camouflage. We saw it after the 9/11 attacks, and we could see it again."

"Why don't we launch a pre-emptive strike of our own?" Seth suggested.

"What do you mean, like what?" Mario asked.

"I don't know, can't we prepare a mailing for the senators, representatives, and governors to watch out for new restrictions on our liberties?"

"I understand where you're coming from, but what do we say, watch your backs, the government is on the loose? Wait a minute, why the hell not? Seth, you may be onto something here. We know that Huntington, Peterson, and God knows who else are planning some move against our communications networks. Let's put out bulletins warning everybody. Let's do exactly what you suggest. We'll brainstorm it right here and now.

"Rosa, turn on both tape recorders in case one of them fails. Who wants to start?"

Three hours later the B Team had an excellent document. It was very short, only one page. They were aware that lawmakers had very little time to digest long-winded mailings. The B Team was going to spread the word two different ways. They were going to hand-carry the message to all the senators and representatives who were in town, and they were going to mail the letter to the state governors, lieutenant governors, and to members of Congress who weren't in town.

CHAPTER EIGHT

"Get your fucking hands off that door! Who the hell let you in? Beat it or I'll arrest you for obstructing justice," Rocco DiAngelo shouted at a man in a navy blue trench coat. A dozen FBI agents were searching for clues aboard the freighter *John Darby* in New York. "Who the hell are you?"

"I'm with Domestic Security," the man answered.

"Then you should know better than to put your God-damned fingerprints all over a crime scene, or didn't they teach you that in college?" Rocco was angry, and was in no mood to entertain members of an agency he despised. "Tell your fucking boss I want to see him, now!"

The *John Darby* was built in 1956. It had been renamed twice, which sailors consider bad luck, and had changed ownership five times. She now sailed under the Liberian flag. Every year, hundreds of rusting old freighters arrived in New York. The waterfront was not the kind of place you wanted to go strolling through at night. Truck heists were common, and contraband flowed back and forth in spite of the Port Authority police.

Immigration and Customs Enforcement special agents had arrived onboard the *John Darby* at the same time as the FBI, finished their work, and left. They were a tight-knit group and very capable. Rocco DiAngelo worked with them every time a foreign national was involved in a crime scene, which was often. Nadene Johnson's husband Oscar had been assigned to this case. He was one of the ICE special agents sent by the president to interrogate suspected members of El Jaride in New York. The agents questioned the terrorists and determined that they were all from Saudi Arabia. ICE already had files on two of the men who had been previously deported for illegal entry. The FBI shared the ICE data, and they were working together to create new files for the other terrorists.

Six people, including two police officers, had been shot and killed on this ship, in two rooms and in the companionway leading to the forward metal stairs. Ten members of El Jaride who were arrested by the New York Police were being questioned by an FBI interrogation team back at the precinct. The captain and crew of the *John Darby* were also being questioned. The Government Office of Domestic Security had been late in getting its agents on board the freighter because they had to travel from Washington. The FBI and ICE already had a large presence in New York City.

The FBI had been dusting all surfaces for prints, and searching all the hatches and companionways for evidence. They found false passports and visas, and several automatic weapons. The team moved quickly and immediately returned to the precinct to join their colleagues.

"My boss told me that we should have access to the same evidence that the FBI does," a Domestic Security agent said to DiAngelo as they walked across the *Darby's* deck.

"You and your boss can both pound sand up your butts."

Later that day, DiAngelo showed up at Precinct #42. Peterson and five of his agents were there arguing with the FBI agents. Rocco had suspected this would happen, so he'd instructed his team to exclude the GODS agents from the investigation. Peterson was irate and threatened the lead FBI interrogator. "We are the department responsible for coordinating all domestic anti-terrorist activities. The FBI and ICE are just two of the agencies that should report to us in times of national emergency," Peterson said.

"Is that a fact?" Rocco DiAngelo heard Peterson's last comment as he entered the room. "Would you excuse us, please?" DiAngelo asked the other agents to leave. The FBI agent walked away and turned to the Domestic Security agent. "That means you too, out, they want privacy."

"Tell me something, John Boy," DiAngelo said to Peterson. They were now alone in a small holding cell down the hall from where the terrorists were being interrogated. "Did you naturally evolve into the consummate vermin you are today, or did you inherit this character trait from your mommy?" Peterson didn't speak or move. "I am going to arrest and convict you for murder, do you hear me? If you so much as drop a fingernail clipping in the wrong place, I'll make sure you get the electric chair for treason. If you just twitch around me, asshole, you're dead."

"As soon as you have proof, hotshot, you come get me. Until that time back the fuck off."

DiAngelo slammed Peterson with his left fist so hard that he knocked him over a desk. Peterson landed in a trash barrel and a couple of his teeth bounced on the desktop. Rocco walked back into the hall and shouted to one of the Domestic Security agents. "Hey buddy, get in there and take your boss out of the garbage can. On second thought, take him out with the garbage."

DiAngelo called Frank Clancy, the director of the FBI, and told him what he had done. Clancy yelled at him, but promised to protect DiAngelo when Peterson whined to the president.

~ ~ ~

"Hello Mario, this is Rocco. I lost my temper and popped Peterson. Knocked out some of his teeth. My boss is very perturbed, but I've done this kind of thing before. Remember when I tipped over the table at Bistro Bis?"

Rocco sounded like he was proud of himself. "Rocco, how can I say you were wrong? I'm afraid to run into the prick because I would do even worse. He isn't smart, he isn't tough, he's just

197

ruthless and cagey. He killed my sister and my niece. I'm glad you belted him. I just wish that he'd hit his head and died."

"His days are numbered. I've got some bad news, and some good news, Mario. The bad news is that the criminals are now cavorting at a Domestic Security bunker on the Maryland-Pennsylvania border. I didn't get anything on the last meeting because the facility is impenetrable from the outside. We do know that Huntington is the newest member of the organization."

"What's the good news?"

"The good news is that we will be recording their *next* meeting. As you know, Marine guards are placed in most sensitive federal facilities, and this bunker is no exception. The FBI's major training center is in Quantico, Virginia at the Marine base. One of the generals there is a personal friend of mine. I've worked with him for many years. The general and I often 'dress up' FBI agents in Marine uniforms. We gave my agent a sergeant's uniform, and I've placed him with the group inside the bunker. Our agent is an ex-Marine, three times tougher than I am, and he knows military procedures very well. He will plant a device that will record all the festivities. It's a new digital recorder about the size of a credit card, and a quarter of an inch thick. It's completely indestructible and can record up to seven hours of conversation. The mike is so sensitive it can pick up a whisper at twenty feet. And listen to this, Mario, they can't detect the recorder with a scanner. I will personally review the tape."

"Hey Rocco, remind me never to get you mad at me."

"Has Slokov contacted Julie yet?"

"Not yet."

"I was thinking of something. Tell her to withdraw some of her Cayman funds. Let her take out a million and buy something really expensive. I want them to think that she's active. It will make them nervous if she withdraws a large sum of money, and they will want value for their dollar, if you get my drift. Tell her to buy an expensive car. Everybody buys a flashy car as soon as they come into money. Under no circumstances should she meet with any of them. There's a good possibility that they have been tailing her, and know that the two of you are working together. She might be able to get away with saying that she's still spying on you for them, but they may not buy it. I'm going to tell you again. Do not let her meet with them under any circumstances."

"You bet, Rocco. I agree, thanks a million."

~ ~ ~

Alan Drawler, the surgeon general of the United States, held a news conference. He cited disturbing new evidence showing that radio waves and cellphone communications were harmful to the immune system. Naturally, he had been pressured by Best Friend to make the announcement.

Domestic Security, and the National Security Administration, could uncover uncomfortable facts about a person's past. The surgeon general's wife had had an abortion when they were first married, and his son was a transgendered prostitute living in New Orleans. The surgeon general was very afraid that these facts would be made public, so it was easy to get him to make an urgent request that the radio wave and cellphone evidence be acted upon at the congressional level.

In another news conference the next day, Margaret Zelkie, the director of the Department of Health, Education, and Welfare, announced that television and computer screens would be banned from the nation's elementary and secondary schools. She distributed literature that HEW had prepared to warn teachers and students of the dangers. The students would also be forbidden to play video games anywhere on school property. The HEW announcement came as a complete surprise to everybody.

Unlike the surgeon general, Zelkie hadn't been blackmailed; she was acting from conviction. Whitcom, Slokov, Bruch, Peterson, Best Friend, and their group were furious. Mario and his team were elated.

"As Jackie Gleason used to say, 'How sweet it is'. I love Health, Education, and Welfare," Mario said. David was in the office, nodded his head in approval, and gave a "V" sign with his fingers.

Mario's phone rang. "Hello Mario, this is Rocco. I want to see you and your entire staff in my office immediately. Traffic will be heavy in an hour so hotfoot it out of there now."

"Wait, let me guess, you can't tell me what's going on until we get there, right?"

"Right."

Mario told his staff that they had been summoned to Rocco's office.

"All of us," Nadene asked, "including David and Julie? Isn't that kind of unusual? Did he tell you why?"

"He wouldn't say. We'll take two cars. Nadene, you know where FBI headquarters is, don't you?"

"Yes, I do. It's on Pennsylvania Avenue, between 9th and 10th."

"Rocco's office is on the fifth floor. Okay, let's go see what this is all about."

"I like the mailing the B Team created," David said. He was riding in the car with Mario and Julie and read from the handout. "Our liberties are in danger. Do not let anyone shut down radio communications or try to eliminate telecommunications in your state. There exists a right-wing conspiracy whose purpose is to undermine the Cancer Prevention Act by illegal and criminal means. Unlike the advanced research and proven technology that discovered the cancer/moving-image link, there has been no documented research to prove that radio waves are harmful. Please contact your local law enforcement or FBI agent if anyone attempts to interfere with your right to communicate."

"My God, Hillary was right," David said, "there *is* a vast right-wing conspiracy."

Mario said, "Senator Lowenstein of New York spoke on the floor of the Senate asking, actually it was more like begging, his colleagues to put through a measure to keep tabs on Domestic Security. He was completely correct when he said that they are allowed to access any data in any facility with complete impunity. The Republican majority and several Democrats voted not to act on his proposal. There you have it, David. There you have it."

~ ~ ~

Nadene, Seth, and Rosa arrived at the same time as Mario and his party. They took the elevator to the fifth floor together. Two agents greeted them at the door and walked them into Rocco's office. Mario was surprised, because this had never happened before. A small table had been set up with coffee, tea, and fancy Italian cookies. A big, burly man was seated at the end of the table next to Rocco; he got up and shook Mario's hand.

"Hello Frank, how are you, sir," Mario said. "Folks, this is Frank Clancy, director of the FBI." Clancy shook everyone's hand. Mario couldn't imagine why the director was in Rocco's office.

Rocco said, "We asked you to come here because we are essentially going to have to place you all under house arrest." Rocco smiled as he spoke.

"What?" Julie was aghast.

"Don't put it that way, Rocco," the director said. "It's not house arrest at all. I think you enjoy yanking Senator McGuire's chain." The rest of the B Team sat motionless, except for Seth, who almost choked on an anisette cookie.

Frank Clancy continued, "There are new developments that cause us to strongly recommend that you and your team change your plans, Mario. A high-ranking official in Washington spoke to me in confidence yesterday. There are elements of the government, as yet unknown, who may be involved in a criminal conspiracy. Most of you know what I'm talking about. Our agents have intercepted communications between some department heads..."

"Please forgive me for interrupting, Director Clancy," Nadene said. "Are we talking about Mr. Huntington, Mr. Whitcom, and Mr. Peterson? If we are, can't we just put our cards on the table?"

Frank Clancy smiled, "Rocco, you were right, she *is* good. Mario, you better treat Nadene right or we'll double her salary at the FBI.

"Some of the people you mentioned are involved, and others who you did not mention are also involved, and that's where the trouble is. Rocco, why don't you tell them the rest? It was your group that did the legwork."

"Thanks, Frank. The FCC and Domestic Security have been recruiting agents, mostly from pools of private security personnel, including many from Eagle Claw. Private security agencies are the next big business in America. They are already major players in Iraq and other countries. During Hurricane Katrina, Eagle Claw had over three hundred men protecting homes and businesses, because the local police were in disarray. We also have evidence to suggest that elements of the National Security Administration may also be linking with the FCC. Mario, let me ask you a question. Do you need to stay in Washington at this time? Aren't most of the senators and representatives home for the summer?"

"Yes, they are, and we just completed a mailing and hand-delivered it to those who are still in town. I guess that work is finished. We were going to stand by in case we needed to travel to any of the state hearings."

"That's not wise," Director Clancy said. "We want all of you to go back to Vermont as soon as possible."

"Why, what's going on? You still haven't told us what's happening," Mario said.

Rocco said, "We fear that there will be attempts at violence and sabotage. If this group has changed tactics, they may try to get you and your team. We don't know who else is involved in the plot, so it will be impossible to protect you here in Washington. We have no trouble when you are in the Capitol, but as soon as you leave the building, you are exposed and very vulnerable. I strongly suggest that all of you work from Vermont for the time being. We'll increase the number of agents in Vermont. It will be much safer for you in your home state, and much easier for us to protect you. David, I contacted your friends Takeo and Sara Arai, and told them the same thing I'm telling you now. They are on their way from New York to Vermont. Sorry, Julie, looks like you've got houseguests."

Director Clancy said, "We are expecting a cadre of Domestic Security and FCC agents to attempt to shut down communications, but we don't know where they will strike. I'll get right to the point. In my forty years of government service, I've never seen this country in so much trouble. Not since the Vietnam era have we faced such a crisis.

"We are on the brink of civil war. The only way to avoid it is to stop any attempts at sabotage that will undermine legitimate business and communications. I've asked the president for his help, but he doesn't give me answers or advice. He keeps telling me that he will meet with his cabinet and national security adviser, and they will find ways to keep the country safe. It is my honest belief that few people in government, including the president, realize how serious the threat is to our stability. The president has been totally ineffective at controlling his own cabinet. He follows advice from people who have their own agendas, and who don't have America's interests at heart."

"Is the military involved?" Mario asked.

"Not so far," Clancy said. "If this group is successful in creating disturbances in the states, the governors may call out their National Guards, but regular units of our armed forces are not on alert."

Mario stood up. "I want everyone in this room to understand what is really going on. The people in power, those who own the corporations and their political stooges, would rather see every liberty we possess destroyed before they let go of one bloody nickel that really belongs to the people in the first place. This is about money and power, nothing else." Mario was waving his arms.

"There are only three billionaires in Canada, only one in Great Britain, and seven in Germany. There are over four hundred in the United States. And thousands more fat-cats have over half a billion dollars each. They don't want to see television and moving computer images eliminated because they can't sell their useless products without them, and it may make a dent in those fortunes. Our children's lives are in danger, while they subvert and destroy the country with their greed."

"Have a cookie, dear." Julie handed Mario an almond wafer to calm him down.

~ ~ ~

It had been two days since the B Team returned to Vermont. Everything was quiet. There was no ban-TV activity at the state level until a vote on the ban in Minnesota, four days away. Mario had two large maps of the states on his office walls, one in Washington and one in Vermont. Rosa had already highlighted Minnesota in green. The state was expected to unanimously approve the ban. Mario reminded her not to color in any more states until the actual votes took place. Sometime in late August, on dates yet to be determined, Texas and Michigan would vote.

Neither of these two states were sure things. Mario was worried about both. A defeat in either could put an end to their momentum going into the Senate hearing on September fourth.

Mario had called a meeting of his team to discuss what they could do from Vermont to help the pro-ban forces in Michigan and Texas. They were in their music room to unwind before getting down to business. Mario said, "Neat, looks like the B Team has grown by three people." Takeo was dressed in shorts and a Hawaiian shirt, Sara had on a halter-top and sarong, and they were both wearing sandals. They were in the conference room with David, who also wore a Hawaiian shirt. They were comparing notes on genetic imprinting. Julie entered the outer office with a tray of cannoli.

"Do they have Frangelico in them?" Mario asked.

"Ungrateful, spoiled husband," Julie answered. "I didn't make them for you; I made them for everyone else."

Mario had brought his new Strat from home and plugged it into his Super Reverb amp. He had the reverb turned up to three, and the treble, bass, and mid controls set to seven. The volume was all the way up to eight, but he controlled it from his guitar. Seth was warming up and Rosa sat on her guitar player's rocking chair. She looked over her shoulder at Seth and smiled as she playfully moved back and forth. Seth had confessed about watching her on the glider, and she was purposely teasing him. Nadene knew exactly what she was doing and said, "Cut that out, girl."

Julie said, "This may be the only band in history that has sold over two million copies of its CD without making one single personal appearance."

"But all the sales have been to family and friends," Sara shouted from the conference room.

They were in the key of A, and Mario played an intro. He bent the strings as he worked the neck from high A all the way down to an open A chord. The rest of the band joined in on the open chord, and Nadene sang a blues she had written, the third cut on their CD:

I don't know what's wrong with me, baby,
There's a hurt down deep inside.
I don't know what's wrong with me, baby,
There's a hurt down deep inside.
You better love me while you can,
or I won't be satisfied.

I'm going to testify in the mountains,
going to testify by the sea.
I'm going to testify in the mountains,
going to testify by the sea.
Going to tell everyone about it,
'cause it means so much to me.

I've got the TV blues,
got them from my head down to my shoes,
I've never had so God awful much to lose,
I've got the TV blues.

Well, that old box is quiet,
There's no need to turn it on.
Well, that old box is quiet,
There's no need to turn it on.
Gonna throw it in the garbage,
all my pain will be up and gone.

I've got the TV blues,
got them from my head down to my shoes,
I've never had so God awful much to lose,
I've got the TV blues.

The entire band harmonized on the chorus. People from nearby offices swarmed in the hall outside Mario's outer door. Four FBI agents suddenly appeared. They were dressed in full camouflage uniforms, and they politely asked the people to move back. They thanked everyone for their cooperation. The accountant from next door asked one of the agents if he could tell the senator something.

"Of course, sir, go ahead."

"Hey senator, 'TV Blues' is my favorite song."

"Thanks, Lester," Mario said as he shook his hand. "Sorry for the extra security, but as you can imagine, we have to be careful."

"I understand, sir," Lester said.

Mario turned to the FBI agents, "Where did you guys come from?"

"We have an office down the hall, senator. We were going to introduce ourselves tomorrow morning. It's probably not a good idea to play music, senator. We don't want to attract crowds if at all possible. Sir, could you do one thing for me?" the agent asked. She handed Mario four CDs. "Could you sign these for us, sir?"

Mario invited the FBI in for coffee and cannoli, but they were on duty and regretfully declined the offer. Mario passed the CDs to the band and all four of the musicians signed each disk.

"Thank you, sir!" The agents were very happy.

"Does anyone know how much money we've made on our CD?" Nadene asked.

"Dis thing is selling good," Mario responded.

"Dis, Mario?"

"*This* thing, *this* thing, okay. This thing is selling good."

"This thing is selling well, dear," Julie said.

"I will ignore the disrespectful comments from common ordinary women who should know better..."

"Say what?" Sara yelled from the next room.

"Mario, you're going to start a war," David said.

Seth explained that he had an attorney taking care of all the financial arrangements for the group. So far they had sold almost two and a half million CDs and had made two dollars and twenty-five cents on each one sold. This did not include the song royalties for their original material that would be covered by other artists. They had agreed to split everything four ways.

Nadene put both hands to her face. "Seth, are we millionaires?"

"Before taxes," he answered.

"I'm worth fifty million dollars, and I have a seven million dollar house in the Virgin Islands," Julie said. "I did what Rocco wanted and withdrew a hunk of cash. I had them wire the funds to a Vermont Municipal Bank account that I opened. I'm going to buy a hot red Mercedes convertible, and ride around with the top down."

"Too conspicuous," Mario said. "Don't get too used to that car, you'll just have to give it back. It's government property, remember? It will be part of their evidence."

"Okay, then I'll get a dark gray one."

~ ~ ~

The B Team settled down to business. Mario grabbed a cannoli and said to Julie, "Mmm, this is delicious. I can tell that you didn't add Frangelico. That stuff doesn't belong in the filling."

Of course, Julie did add the liqueur, and had told the rest of the team that Mario wouldn't know the difference. They all chuckled when he proved her right.

Mario immediately knew that Julie had set him up. He looked at Julie and said, "Do you know something, woman? People have called their divorce lawyers for less provocation than you have given me. Cannoli is sacred food for my people. Frangelico does not belong in cannoli."

"I guess if *you* had written *The Godfather* you'd have said, 'Take the gun, leave Julie's cannoli'," Julie joked.

"Okay, team." Mario was happy and hated to bring up business. "How can we help the folks in Michigan and Texas?"

"I know what we can do," Rosa said. "Nadene and I have already made some contacts from Washington. We can call Reverend Mackenzie and Father Messier, and ask them if they have any friends in those states. We can try to get a coalition of religions leaders together. I think non-violent protests, run by different leaders working together, would swing votes for the ban."

"Make it so," Mario said, as he patted Rosa's hand. "You get an extra cannoli for that fantastic idea."

Nadene looked at Rosa and said, "I want to work with you on this one, girl. Mario, what if we need to travel to make it work?"

"No, we stay here," Mario answered. "Let's see how good our telemarketing skills really are. I will call Father Messier before Rosa does just to say hello. I've been meaning to talk with him anyway. Rosa, then you call and tell him you'd like to meet with him. Is there any other business that we need to talk about before we go?"

"Just one thing," Seth said. "Rosa and I are getting married."

"What?" Mario was astonished.

Everyone hugged and kissed Seth and Rosa.

"I had no idea that you two decided to get married," Julie said.

"I had no idea either," Rosa said, and burst into tears.

"Is that a yes?" Seth asked.

"Yes!"

~ ~ ~

It was Thursday morning at 9:00. Two FBI agents carrying automatic weapons walked into Mario's office. David, Takeo, and Sara were with Julie at the McGuire home. The B Team was at work planning strategy for the Michigan vote. "Senator McGuire, I must ask you not to leave the building. We have agents en route to your home. Your wife and guests must not leave the house either, unless it is an absolute emergency."

Mario's phone rang. "Hello Rocco, your agents just walked in. Now what?"

"The FCC and Domestic Security are making a move in Vermont. They've shut down two radio stations in Bennington and there's activity around several cellphone towers. Two unmarked choppers have been sighted above Mount Ascutney, and there's another patrolling the towers in the vicinity of Camel's Hump. Stay put, Mario. We've given Governor Howard one of our phones, so call him at this number, 4801. I've dispatched more agents, but we haven't decided yet what to do about the choppers. There are other reports of the FCC shutting down a station in St. Albans, to your north. Maybe they're going to start at both ends and work their way toward the middle."

"Thanks, Rocco."

Mario immediately called Governor Howard at 4801. "Good morning, Brian. Looks like we are under attack from our own government. I never thought I'd live to see this day."

"This is what we are going to do," Governor Howard said. "I have put out emergency alerts to every police department in the state. They are now coordinated with the Vermont State Police. We will not let one radio station or one cellphone tower be destroyed or fall into these invaders' hands. We have already ousted them from the stations in Bennington. We will resist. I thought the full house and senate had to vote for emergency powers, and the president then had to sign the measure before the Emergency Communications Act could be put into effect."

"The president can authorize temporary action without consulting congress if there is a national emergency, like a terrorist attack."

"What terrorist attack? *They* are the terrorists! Has the president gone senile?"

"I don't know, Brian. I suspect that all of this is happening without the president's approval. I applaud your decision to resist their actions."

"Mario, I'm debating whether to call out the National Guard. What do you think?"

"That's what they want you to do. Let's see how our combined police force, along with the FBI, can handle the attacks. You can always call out the Guard later if they're needed. It's probably a good idea to get them ready just in case."

David and Takeo showed up at the office escorted by two FBI agents. "Where are Julie and Sara?" Mario asked.

"They are back at your place. Don't worry, there are heavily armed agents with them."

Mario said, "I'm not going to stay here. I'm going to WJOY in Burlington, and speak to the people. That station has the strongest signal in Vermont." He turned to one of the agents. "Make sure that either your people or the police guard the transmitter towers in South Burlington. If they're knocked out, it will take months to get back on the air."

"We're headed out there at the same time as you are, sir," one of the agents responded.

Nadene said, "I'm coming with you."

David and Takeo both said, "Me too."

Two FBI agents remained behind with Seth and Rosa, who had been ordered to stay in the office to handle communications.

Nadene drove to the broadcast offices of WJOY, and Mario McGuire introduced himself to the station manager. A small contingent of police was outside the building and two cars full of FBI agents arrived as well.

"Are we really under attack?" the manager asked.

"It does look that way," Mario answered. "Please send your entire staff home except for the technicians needed to keep the station on the air. I can't force you to do this, but I urgently request that you interrupt your regular programming and let me speak to the people."

"By all means, senator. Just let me know when you are ready."

The transmitter tower of WJOY was clearly visible from the offices. There was a picture window facing the field, and everyone in the room saw an unmarked chopper land on the ground near the tower. Seven men in dark uniforms began placing boxes of explosives at the base of each of the metal posts. An FBI agent shouted, "They're trying to blow up the towers, stop them!" David and Takeo were parked closest to the field. They ran out of the office and jumped in their four-wheel-drive Toyota Rav 4 just ahead of the FBI agents, and sped toward the invaders.

"Come back here!" Mario shouted, but they ignored him. Mario and Nadene got in a state police car that had followed the FBI cars. Both Nadene and Mario had their .45s out and clips in place. "Where's your duty weapon?" Mario asked Nadene.

"I wanted the target auto, because it's fast *and* accurate," Nadene said. "What do David and Takeo think they're doing? Two scientists attacking a paramilitary group! Mario, I hope we can get ahead of them."

"Me, too," Mario agreed. The FBI car was having a hard time getting through the muddy access road and was spinning its wheels. The other cars were behind the FBI vehicle. Four agents got out and pushed from the rear in an attempt to free it from the mud.

The invaders had finished placing the explosives around all four support posts and were running back to their chopper as David and Takeo arrived in their car. They skidded on the wet grass and stopped about two hundred feet from the chopper. They crouched behind their car, drew their weapons, and fired at the chopper. They made a lot of noise shooting dozens of rounds from their .40 caliber H & K autos. A few shots hit the side of the chopper and some deflected off the bulletproof glass windshield. One of the terrorists returned fire with an automatic weapon and totally shredded the car. David and Takeo each hit the ground behind a wheel and took cover. The two tires on the side of the car facing the chopper hissed as the air ran out of them. The gas tank was punctured and gas was spilling on the ground.

They looked at each other, and David swallowed hard. "I'm sure glad we came back to Vermont where it's safe," he said.

Takeo said, "If the gas ignites, fall straight back and keep the car between us and them. They won't be able to see us through the smoke and flames.

"Did I ever tell you that my father made me study Gikan Ryu? It's a Japanese form of Karate. When I was three years old, he taught me some of the moves. Nearly every week for fifteen years, I would do this for him. I hated it with a passion, but in Japan, children in my position did what they were told. What I wanted wasn't as important as what he wanted. I eventually became a Soke, which is a grand master."

More high-powered rounds sliced through the car body, and they returned the fire. "I don't know why I'm telling you this now, but if something happens to me, please tell my father that I'm glad he made me learn Gikan Ryu."

David and Takeo each fired another clip of ammo. They didn't hit anyone, but their fire pinned down the men and prevented them from boarding the chopper. There were seven attackers on the ground and an unknown number in the chopper. The three other cars arrived on the scene. Thanks to David and Takeo, the FBI agents and state police could get out of their vehicles. They formed a line of four cars. Mario and Nadene's car was next to David's.

Nadene shouted at David and Takeo, "You two keep down!"

The FBI agents let down a barrage of automatic-weapons fire that sent the terrorists scurrying behind the chopper. Several were hit.

Mario knew all about choppers. "Shoot the tail rotor, shoot the tail rotor!" he shouted. The officers let loose another barrage but no one hit the rotor. Nine-millimeter sub-machine guns were not very accurate at long ranges. Mario and Nadene were crouched behind their car and Mario said, "Remember our bet?"

"Shit, what are you talking about, Mario?"

"Our shooting contest. I'll bet I can hit that rotor before you do."

"You're on, senator." Nadene shot five rounds but the rotor was still spinning. Mario fired three times and pieces of the chopper's tail rotor went flying into the air.

"Time to bake brownies, Nadene. That thing will never take off now," Mario said. The attackers continued to fire at the two forward cars. Two FBI agents had been wounded, and a state police officer had been killed. Five of the invaders had been killed, and the two survivors finally surrendered along with the pilot of the chopper, who came out with his hands up.

The FBI agents shouted as they ran toward the three remaining terrorists. "On the ground, on the ground, face down, spread your arms and legs apart! Get on the ground!"

Mario shouted, "Get the detonators!"

Mario looked at the bullet holes in their car and had a flashback to Vietnam and the holes in the side of his MedEvac chopper. He turned to Nadene and said, "We stopped them. Go see how David and Takeo are. Nadene? Nadene?"

214

Nadene was slumped against the side of their bullet-riddled car. There was blood on her blouse, and on the shattered window glass. Her blood was dripping down the side of the car and onto the grass. Her .45 was still in her hand, but it was pointed straight down at the ground. She didn't move.

~ ~ ~

Best Friend would call in twenty minutes. The Roundback Mountain conference was in session. The dehumidification system had malfunctioned, and there was a musty smell from the mildew that was growing everywhere. The odor overpowered the aroma of the freshly brewed coffee. It had been 24 hours since the failed attempt to take over Vermont's communications infrastructure. Sergeant Evans, the FBI agent disguised as a Marine, had planted a recorder in the adjustable mechanism of one of the chairs. It happened to be the chair that Ludlowe Wenman now occupied.

Senator Cyrus Whitcom said, "John Peterson, will you kindly tell us what went wrong in Vermont? Good God, you do look awful."

Peterson's lip was swollen, his nose was broken and taped, and if you looked closely, you could see that two of his bottom teeth were missing. He didn't explain his appearance or the encounter with DiAngelo. "We underestimated their ability to respond to the attack. They may have been tipped off, but honestly, I don't see how that's possible."

"A little honesty is a good thing right about now, John," Whitcom said. "Am I correct in saying that all the radio stations in Vermont are still on the air?"

"Yes, sir, they are."

"You mean you had the most capable military teams in the world, with the best equipment available, you launched a surprise attack on a bunch of hillbillies, and you got whipped. Is that what you're saying?"

"Not entirely, sir. We did destroy a few towers and got several policemen and McGuire's chief of staff," Peterson answered.

"The governor did not call out the National Guard, most of the cellphone towers are still standing, and all the radio stations are still transmitting. I would call your excursion a total disaster!" Whitcom pounded the table in anger.

Slokov said, "All we have done is create a David who stood up to Goliath and won. The entire country is aware that an attempt was made to seize control of communications in Vermont. They don't know by whom, just yet. If they find out, we will be in big trouble, did you ever think of that?"

"We're already in big trouble," Peterson said. "Several of our people were captured. They were formerly your men, Skip, and were on loan from Eagle Claw Security to the FCC for this operation."

"Don't worry about a thing. There's no way they will talk. We gave them a story to use. No doubt they will be questioned separately. When they all say the same thing, they should confuse the FBI with little trouble," Skip Walsh said.

"You're underestimating the FBI," Peterson said.

"And you're underestimating my men," Walsh snapped back.

Best Friend called right on time. "I do wish we hadn't been so sloppy in Vermont. Our main purpose in going into McGuire's home state, where this whole thing started, was to agitate the people. We wanted them to be afraid, so they would force McGuire to bring back television. The people of Vermont are more agitated at the intrusion than the ban. Seven of their peace officers are dead, and their deaths have galvanized the community. We lost fifteen agents, and another ten were captured. We overestimated our own abilities, and underestimated their resources. It would be no different in South Carolina or Oregon if we tried to use force there.

"Now, we didn't succeed in destroying radio and telecommunications, but we have achieved one very fine by-product. The Vermont action is causing the legislators in other states to rethink their positions. The threat of violence is as good as an actual attack. Our analysts tell us that sentiment against the television ban is on the rise in Michigan and Texas. The majority of legislators in those two states are now going to vote with us. I'm not talking about a squeaker here, folks. I'm talking about fifty-five percent in Michigan and sixty-three percent in Texas. Speaking of Texas, Senator Whitcom, you had better deliver your state into the 'no' column or you'll never live it down."

"Yes sir, I know. I feel confident that we will win in both states. As a matter of fact, I have a meeting in Houston as soon as I leave here."

The meeting broke up, and the group took the elevator to the surface. They walked past the Marine guards and got into their cars. The two gate sentries opened the sliding steel barricade. Three FBI vehicles suddenly appeared and blocked the roadway in front of Slokov's car, which was the first one out of the complex. Peterson was sitting next to Slokov. Skip Walsh was in the car directly behind them. The rest were in the third car. The occupants of the first two cars climbed out of their vehicles, wondering what was going on.

Rocco DiAngelo and four agents walked past the first car, and DiAngelo said, "Hello John Boy, and Harold Slokov. Make sure if either of you leave town, that you give me your phone numbers. I'll be calling on both of you real soon."

He then walked over to car number two and spoke to Walsh. "Skip Walsh, you are under arrest for murder, destroying public property, and inciting to riot. You have the right to remain silent. You will be allowed to contact the attorney of your choice.

Anything you say can and will be used against you in a court of law."

An FBI agent handcuffed Walsh, and they stuck him in the back of the lead FBI car. As DiAngelo got into the second FBI car, he turned around and looked at the vehicle occupied by Beatrice and Ludlowe Wenman, and Cyrus Whitcom. They were still inside, trying to hide their faces. "Enjoy the rest of your day, gentleman and lady, and you too, Senator Whitcom."

~ ~ ~

There were three Bazookas restaurants in Houston. Whitcom was in the largest of the three, about a mile from the Astrodome. He was meeting with the governor and lieutenant governor. They had a table in the back corner of the room, and on a Sunday afternoon the crowd was light. It was so loud in the room from the TVs that nobody could hear their conversation, and if anyone could have, they wouldn't care anyway. There were 21 television screens scattered around the room, all broadcasting a baseball game between the Houston Astros and the New York Mets. The Mets were leading six to nothing in the top of the fourth.

Whitcom had made a sizeable contribution to the governor's campaign and had stumped around the state with the two men in the last election. They had both won handily. It was payback time, and all three men knew it.

"What about the state Senate? We have a majority there. Do you anticipate any trouble defeating the measure?" Whitcom asked.

"It's in the bag, Cyrus, it's in the bag," the governor said.

"Hello, boys." A Bazooka girl came over to their table. "Oh my, aren't yew the governor? Aren't yew our senator? I don't know who yew are, but yew must be someone important. Oh my, what can I get yew fellers, how 'bout a pitcher?"

She wasn't very bright, but it wasn't about brains.

~ ~ ~

When a Bermuda high sat off the east coast, a clockwise motion sent warm, moist air over the Champlain Valley in Vermont. Foul air from the eastern cities was funneled north in a trough that added to the discomfort. The high made the interior of the state ten to fifteen degrees warmer than the coast of Maine. This was the third day of the unpleasant weather. The temperature had hit ninety-three yesterday, and was supposed to reach ninety-five today. Sometimes these fronts lasted for seven days before they broke. This one was scheduled to go another two days before a dry northern front from Canada changed the pattern. It would be so welcome when it came. The temperature would drop about twenty degrees, the haze and smog would disappear, and the sky would return to a deep blue.

Today, however, the day of the funeral, the weather was oppressive. It was difficult for seniors to breathe, and a National Oceanic Weather Alert warned people with asthma and heart disease to stay indoors.

Barre, Vermont was a working class town, not too far from Montpelier, the capital. Hope Cemetery in Barre was where many of the original Italian stone carvers were buried. They had worked in the granite quarries and developed silicosis in their lungs from the dust. Granite is an unfriendly stone, unlike marble, which passes through the system without damage. Many of the quarry workers died young. In those days they didn't wear respirators. Most of the buildings in New York City were built with Vermont granite cut by these immigrants. Some were superior stone carvers.

One man, who knew he was dying, carved a likeness of himself out of solid granite, in his best Sunday suit, to place on his grave. There were several other stone portraits in the cemetery that were equally poignant and beautiful, and some that were quite unusual. There was a life-sized race car, an empty armchair, a biplane, and a soccer ball. There was an empty double bed, husband and wife finally reunited in the next world. The unique carvings reflected what had been important to the departed in *this* life.

When Mario and Stephanie were little, their father Patrick would take them to look at the monuments and the wonderful stone carvings. Mario hadn't appreciated their majesty because the cemetery always gave him the creeps.

Today, there would be a large funeral. The governor would be present. Rocco DiAngelo had traveled from Washington to be here. Many state legislators had already arrived, and Senator Benjamin Lowenstein from New York would attend.

Father Messier put his arm around Mario, and tried to comfort him. Seth and Rosa did the same. Everyone was perspiring from the heat, and little black flies were sticking to Mario's arms.

Nadene should have been at home recuperating, but she arrived with Oscar. Her shoulder was in a sling, and she had a bandage on her head from where she had bashed it against the car. If the bullet had hit her just two inches more to the right, she would now be dead, and there would have been two funerals. She was weak, but could not be kept away. The heat was enervating, and she leaned on Oscar for support. She refused to sit down, arguing constantly with Mario, Rosa, and Oscar, who tried to convince her to rest in a portable chair they had brought.

David showed Nadene his wallet. The brown leather had a crease and tear down its entire length. When he had returned home the evening after the shootout under the transmission towers, he'd noticed that there was a hole in the front of his pants pocket. He also noticed a hole in the back of his pocket. That's when he examined his wallet.

"That bullet came mighty close to the family jewels," Nadene said as she lost her balance.

David threw both arms around her.

"Don't squeeze, hon," Nadene said.

David and Takeo had rushed to her aid after she was hit and immediately stopped the bleeding. They had saved her life. They couldn't save a state trooper, and one of the FBI agents who had been stationed in Mario's building was still in intensive care with serious wounds.

"I know I'm lucky you both were there, but you're going to have to put those guns away, both of you."

"Not a chance! Takeo and I are practicing in the woods. We even bought assault rifles, 223 caliber, and we keep them in the back seats of our cars, under our raincoats."

Mario's mother Sophia Bavetta-McGuire had died in her sleep three days ago, and she was being buried next to her husband.

"I'm the only member of the family left," Mario said to Julie. "But you know, there is one thing I'm happy about."

"I know," Julie said.

"How could you possibly know?"

"You're happy because we told your mother that we're together, and very much in love. We spoke to her just two days before she died."

"You're wrong," Mario said. "I'm happy because the Mets swept three games from the Houston Astros." Mario cried in Julie's arms.

CHAPTER NINE

Violent images live forever. Whether we see them on television, in the movies, or experience them in real life, they etch themselves into our being. They disturb our sleep, change our behavior, and make us feel less human. Soldiers in combat are often shocked and horrified at the sight of their first dead body. If they survive many battles, rows of dead soldiers, or a comrade mutilated and dying, are supposed to be handled matter-of-factly, all in a day's work. But it doesn't happen that way. Most soldiers who have experienced the insanity of combat will never be the same. A piece of their humanity dies, and is left on the battlefield with their dead comrades.

Similarly, people who see a person carved up by a chain saw on a television screen will never be the same. These people choose to view the same blood and gore that soldiers are forced to see. Soldiers can become desensitized and develop post-traumatic stress disorder. They can be ruined as people, and many die from drug and alcohol abuse. Americans, including young children, are becoming desensitized and pulverized in much the same way by television violence. Like the soldier who carries many deaths inside him, our children are learning to accept violence as perfectly normal.

~~~

Seth and Rosa had been spared the death and destruction that was all around the other members of their team. They visited the female FBI agent, the one who gave them the four CDs to sign, at

Fletcher Allen hospital in Burlington. She had been wounded at the radio towers and may never walk again. If she does recover use of her legs, it will be after a year of agonizing therapy. They saw Nadene every day, weakened and shattered by her bullet wound. They all attended the funerals for the peace officers killed in the line of duty.

Takeo and David were responding to the violence differently than Seth and Rosa. Takeo and David had embraced violence as part of their vendetta against those who had killed Carol, Stephanie, Don, and Takeo's colleagues. Seth and Rosa were desperately trying to go in the other direction. They were seeking a common nonviolent ground. Perhaps it was their religious training.

Rosa was very angry at Nadene. She sat next to her and was patting her hand. Nadene's wounds were still painful, but her attitude was unchanged. Nadene made one of her vintage comments and challenged Mario to another shootout, double or nothing. Mario accepted.

Rosa gently slapped her hand and said, "You have a husband and two children. What do you want? Next time maybe your whole arm will be blown off. It's going to take you months before you can play the piano again. Stop trying to be the baddest bitch in town. Time for you to mellow out. Senator, don't you encourage her."

Nadene looked at Rosa, "Don't you hit me again, girl. I can't change the way I am."

Rosa let go of Nadene's hand. "Then don't you give me any lectures about how Seth and I can get together in spite of our differences. We can't change the way we are, either. We're going to fight and curse at each other, just to be like you."

"I said that's enough!" Nadene was angry, but she knew Rosa was right.

Seth and Rosa visited Father Messier at Saint Francis church. The priest was touchingly glad to see them. He had an elegant tea service ready with a dish full of raisin scones that one of his parishioners had baked for him.

"Father, there are two things that we would like to ask of you. One is personal, and the other isn't," Rosa said.

Father Messier raised his eyebrows. He was the kind of person who was happiest when he could be of service. "What is the personal question, dear?"

"We would like to be married in your church."

Seth said, "I agree that the ceremony can be held here, but I have something to say first, if that is all right."

"Of course, Seth."

"Father, you know a great deal about my religion. The Islamic view of marriage is different than the Catholic view. The sacramental concept of marriage is not present in my religion. There is no ceremony to give it the solemnity that it has in the Catholic Church. For us, it's a question of mutual agreements and contracts. The imam always assigns the details to a family elder, who lets the couple decide what they will do and say. Very often it is just as much the marriage of two families as it is of two people. The one thing I'm not ready to do, Father, is agree that our children will be raised as Catholics. Will this cause trouble?"

Father Messier stood up and said, "I won't tell the bishop, if you won't. This promise need not be a part of your ceremony. I feel confident that the two of you will work out what is best."

Rosa was trying hard not to cry, but her face said it all.

"What is the second question you have for me?"

Seth said, "I know you have been following all the ban-TV events, Father, and we are nearing the end of our journey. On

September fourth, the senate is going to vote on the ban. There are two important state votes next week. I don't know how you feel about the violence, and whether or not you will help us win these votes."

"I detest violence. Christ said to love your enemies, but I admit that I cannot allow anyone to destroy this church or my people. I cannot ask a person not to defend him or herself. What I object to is a policy and lifestyle of violence. Do you need my help in Michigan and Texas? Mario told me those are the next two states that will vote."

Rosa said, "Yes, we do, Father. Mario says that Texas is probably lost to us, but Michigan is very important because there's a large Muslim population there, and the rest of the Midwest may follow Michigan's lead. If they vote against the ban, it could hurt the senate vote in September."

Father Messier said, "I have an idea. Reverend Mackenzie and I have friends in Michigan who are members of the National Council of Churches, Synagogues, and Mosques. I know several imams and rabbis who might like to work with us. Seth, you could be a big help in recruiting them."

Seth said, "I will do it. The FBI wants us to remain in Vermont due to threats against our team, but Rosa and I will accompany you and Reverend Mackenzie to Michigan. We cannot sit back while other members of our group feel free to roam around the countryside shooting at others and getting shot."

Father Messier said, "There is nothing to fear in Michigan. The danger is in *not* going."

~~~

Reverend Mackenzie met Seth, Rosa, and Father Messier at the airport in Detroit. The reverend's flight from Charlotte had arrived just a half-hour later than the flight from Burlington.

"Clara sends her best to all of you. She had to stay behind to help one of our church families though a crisis."

"She is a remarkable woman," Seth said.

"And she thinks the world of you and Rosa. Oh, here's a little something we got for the both of you, with our congratulations on your engagement."

Reverend Mackenzie shook Seth's hand and kissed Rosa's cheek. He handed her a small box wrapped in silver paper and tied with silver and gold ribbons. Rosa stopped right in the middle of the busy corridor and untied the bows. Seth grabbed her around the waist and pulled her out of the traffic lane. The four of them stood in front of an empty gate as she unwrapped the tissue paper to reveal a pair of one-inch-long interlocked gold hearts. The hearts could be pulled apart, or joined together. On each there was the same inscription, "My heart is within your heart is within my heart." The piece was designed so the message read over and over again in an eternal loop.

"One of our parishioners is a jeweler. Clara and I loved this and thought of both of you."

Rosa and Seth were overjoyed and thanked the reverend. Rosa had a thought and then a prayer. She knew that she and Seth would always be together. She just felt it. She was sure they would be able to work out their differences. She prayed for life and for health. There was nothing more important for her to wish for. Seth and Rosa cared about each other and about their work. Neither of them cared at all for "things." They hardly ever shopped. Even though they now had over two million dollars between them, Rosa still drove the same car and lived in the same apartment. She had bought plenty of new books, however, and Seth had bought some new drums.

~ ~ ~

Temple Beth Israel was in an old section of Detroit. It bordered row houses, and some of the neighborhoods were rough. Father Messier, Reverend Mackenzie, Seth, and Rosa had come to see Rabbi Aaron Lieberman, a personal friend of the priest. The rabbi was glad to see them and showed them around the synagogue. There was a comely simplicity in the building, which was built in 1917. Seth put on a yarmulke and felt strange at first, but then he began to enjoy himself.

"We may have the poorest Jewish congregation in America," the rabbi said, "but we do have the best food. Eat, eat!" Rabbi Lieberman was a round, animated man. "Seth, you can be proud of your brothers. Reverend and Father, listen to what is happening here. America's biggest mosque is in Dearborn. Michigan Mosque cost fourteen million dollars, oh I'm so jealous. Imam Abdul Mohamed and I are good friends. We see each other socially, even. We have been conducting joint services. We go to the mosque and pray with them, and they come here and pray with us. I told him about your arrival here, and he wants us to visit him at the mosque. Is that okay?"

"Wow, okay!" Seth exclaimed.

On the drive to the mosque, Seth explained that Michigan might vote against the ban.

"I know, I know," the Rabbi said. "What do you expect? We haven't yet recovered from all the lost manufacturing jobs. Flint and other cities are trying their best to cope. Michigan has the hardest-working people in the world. They worked their entire lives, and then many were cast aside by a system that was ill-prepared for the changes. Everywhere are losses, losses, losses."

"What does that have to do with television?" Rosa asked.

"I'll tell you. When you are out of work and sitting in your favorite bar with a bottle of your favorite brew, what are you going to do, sit on the stool and read a copy of *Pride and Prejudice*?" The rabbi chuckled.

Father Messier laughed and said, "Very good, Aaron, when you've got nothing, you've got nothing to lose. It *is* about loss. Everything is a take-away, lower pay, or no jobs at all, no health insurance, and rising prices. Some unfortunate souls have given up hope. They sure as hell aren't going to give up their TVs."

"It's like trying to take the blonde away from King Kong," Rabbi Lieberman said as they drove up to the mosque. "I know the imam will give you a tour, but let me tell you about Michigan Mosque. Those two minarets are 110 feet tall and are decorated with crescent moons. There are three golden domes. Look at the Moorish arches and the green tiles."

When they exited from the rabbi's car, a dozen reporters mobbed them, asked questions, and took photos.

"Where did they come from?" Rosa asked.

"I called them," Father Messier said.

"You have a scheme, you have a scheme, Raymond. For a holy man, you are the cagiest SOB I've ever met," Rabbi Lieberman said.

Imam Abdul Mohamed arrived at the scene with two elders of the mosque. The reporters asked him what he was going to do about the ban.

"I stand with my Christian and Jewish brothers in opposing television. We will meet and pray for guidance."

Father Messier turned to the media group and asked them to please return to this spot in four hours, at 3:00 in the afternoon. They would have an important announcement to make.

"We will? I agree with Aaron, you are up to something," Reverend Mackenzie said.

Seth excused himself and joined the Friday morning prayers. The musalla, or prayer room, had arched portals at the entrance. It held 700 with room for another 350 people on the mezzanine.

Worshippers prayed on the exact coordinates facing Mecca, 52 degrees, 30 minutes northeast. The imam chanted prayers, and there were a surprising number of people for the middle of the day. Workers at Ford's Rouge auto plant rushed to pray on their lunch breaks. Women were kneeling on the same carpet as the men; they did not have to worship separately. There were wire racks in the hallway that held the worshippers' shoes. Seth had a hole in his left sock, at the end of his big toe, and Rosa teased him about it.

Father Messier asked Seth and Rosa to excuse the four of them for a few minutes. They were in the banquet room and the priest, rabbi, reverend, and imam huddled together in a corner of the room.

"What are they up to?" Rosa asked.

"I don't have a clue," Seth answered.

After about fifteen minutes, the four holy men walked back to Seth and Rosa. Imam Mohamed spoke for the group.

"We would like you to be married here in this banquet room, and we propose a joint service. I will say prayers, and since it is his idea, I will let Father Messier tell you what he wants to do."

"We will have a blessed Tabernacle in the room, it will be no different than any church. I will say the same blessing that I do in church. Rabbi Lieberman will have a Torah and will read from scripture, like he does at every wedding service at the synagogue. Reverend Mackenzie will give a blessing, you will love what he says."

The imam said, "The marriage license is no problem, and there's plenty of time to get the required blood tests. The Michigan legislature votes on the ban Wednesday. We would all like to marry you on Tuesday. Is this something you want to do?"

Seth and Rosa jumped up and embraced each other.

"I believe that is a yes," the rabbi said. "Oh, look at the time. It's ten minutes to three. Let's go talk to the reporters. Remember now, say nothing about the television ban, only this marriage."

After they had met with the reporters, Rosa called the B Team and told them the news. They all promised to be at the wedding. Mario asked Rosa whose idea it was and she answered, Father Messier.

Mario hung up the phone with Rosa and spoke to Julie, Nadene, and David. "Brilliant, absolutely brilliant. Father Messier knew that not only would this be a groundbreaking religious event that would be life itself to Seth and Rosa, but it would also capture the hearts of people in Michigan who may have otherwise voted against the ban. Ironically, the imam is going to allow TV coverage. Not since the Washington hearing have we used TV as a weapon against itself. I'll bet you two trays full of cannoli with orange rind and no Frangelico, that Michigan passes the ban. The wedding is the day before the vote, absolutely brilliant."

"Why do you fight this mythological battle with me about the ingredients of cannoli? Mario, is this a male-female power struggle? Are you trying to bait me?" Julie was indignant.

"Yes, I am. We have very good sex after we fight."

"Don't count your cannoli with orange rind just yet, Senator Husband, and don't even think about what else you're thinking about."

~ ~ ~

"Hello Harold, this is Julie, my cellphone recorded your number, but you didn't leave a message."

"Well, Julie, I have a picture I'm going to send you. I know the cellphone screen is small but I'm sure you can see enough detail."

Slokov transmitted a short video of Julie and Mario making love in their bedroom. His photographer had shot it from outside their South Burlington bedroom window.

"As you can see, the two of you are very animated. This doesn't look like faking, Julie, not at all. You have been playing with us, haven't you?"

"If I ever see one of your photographers outside my bedroom window, I'll shoot him and you. I've been doing exactly what's expected of me. You can't blame a girl for enjoying a little action, can you?"

"Very cute. What about the blue Mercedes convertible you bought with our money? Mario went with you to pick the fucking thing out, big secret here."

"Harold, I'm independently wealthy. I don't tell him anything about my finances. I also make lots of money selling my artwork."

"Yes, I know, Julie. As a matter of fact, you make all the money you really need. I'm finding it hard to believe that you are working against your husband. You're with him wherever he goes."

"Harold, use your brain. The FBI has me shadowed and tailed constantly, when the hell do I get some breathing room?"

"You don't. And just to give you a little more incentive to carry out the next task I have for you, here's a bit of news."

Slokov told Julie what he wanted her to do and issued a threat that greatly upset her. She agreed to meet him. He told her how to elude the FBI. She was to be on Shelburne Bay in one hour, and he would pick her up with his seaplane. If she told Mario anything about their conversation, he would make good on his threat. She would simply have to disappear for the meeting without getting caught.

~ ~ ~

Mario and Julie would travel tomorrow, August 28th, for Seth and Rosa's wedding on the 29th. Michigan would be voting on the 30th, Illinois and Indiana on August 31st. This was the last big push before the Senate vote. Several states had hearings scheduled for after that vote, but if the Senate chose to defeat the ban, it would override state decisions.

"What should I wear?" Mario asked Julie.

"How about your light gray suit? You could put a red handkerchief in the pocket."

"I know, I'll also put on my white beret with a gold Strat pin."

"If you must."

"You don't like my beret?"

"I like it fine, for your band, but this is a formal occasion with lots of media coverage."

"Good, I will wear it. What are you going to wear?"

"I don't know yet, but I promise I'll pick something and then change my mind at least three times before we leave. I will annoy you each time, and demand to know why one outfit is better than another. *And*, I can always tell if you're really listening or just trying to patronize me."

"I'm so glad I married a simple girl."

~ ~ ~

Julie was thinking about the meeting she'd had with Slokov. She had always been good at keeping secrets. She didn't share all her thoughts with her husband, and sometimes she didn't tell Mario anything. She could go through her normal day, be a loving wife, and not give him a hint of what was simmering beneath her surface.

Mario brought her violin into the living room. In his other hand was a guitar case. He opened the hard case, with travel stickers all over it, and pulled out his old Martin D18. This was the same model that Elvis Presley had used. Mario had bought his when he was a sophomore in college. It had been chipped and dinked here and there, and most of the glossy finish had been worn off the spruce top where he'd rested his forearm for thirty-eight years. There were several deep scratches around the sound hole from his flat-picking. The mahogany back and sides were still free of cracks, but his belt buckle had put marks on the finish. He had just put a new set of phosphor-bronze strings on it, and the old D18 sounded rich and sparkling.

Julie was an excellent violinist, although she hadn't practiced much lately. Her heritage was three-quarters Irish, one-quarter French, and she had been raised with the same music that Mario had. She was very good at improvising fiddle tunes, and sometimes she and Mario liked to go out on the deck and play Irish folk music. It was raining today so they sat in their living room. Julie was about to tell him that she wasn't in the mood to play, but decided to try it. She lifted a nineteenth-century German violin from its very battered case and tightened up the bow. She put some rosin on it and asked Mario for a G, then D, A, and E.

"Tomorrow we fly to Michigan for the wedding, and then on to Washington for the final vote. We've come a long way, baby, but it isn't over yet," Mario said. He grabbed *Rise Up Singing*, a book of song lyrics, and turned to the "Struggle" chapter. He propped the book open on a metal music stand and selected a song. Julie didn't sing too often, but she did like to take solos in the instrumental breaks. The chords in these songs were simple, and she was blessed with the ability to fill in all the empty spaces in the music.

"It's time for our Irish heritage, Julie, songs of struggle, songs of rebellion. You know, one of my fondest memories of my mother was at a Christmas party we had for the staff of *The Clarion*. She learned Irish dancing just to please my father. They did a jig together at the party. A Tommy Makem and the Clancy Brothers record was playing, and they danced until they were exhausted.

"Whenever I have something tough to do, I always hear that music in my head. Let's play some."

They played and sang "The Patriot Game" by Dominic Behan. Mario sang the first verse and did a fairly good job with the lyrics, displaying a touch of Irish brogue and a hint of Brooklynese. Julie would play the fiddle at the end of each verse, and bowed some great licks in a highly melodic style. If Mario didn't stop singing, she would play the lead anyway. She would not allow him to run roughshod over her playing, even though he was the vocalist. This sometimes made him mad, and when he sang the last verse about the "quislings who sold out the Patriot Game," he was almost shouting the words over the violin.

Mario was watching Julie. He knew she was up to something, but he wouldn't ask her. His experience told him that she believed in a person's "right to know." In other words, she wouldn't share her thoughts unless she felt like it. *What could she be concealing? Is it a health issue, a marriage issue, a work issue? God knows.*

The last song they did was an old rebellion song by Sean O'Reilly called "For the Emerald Green." This is a little-known, rousing drinking-song that's played in Dublin pubs on the wrong side of town. If you happen to be traveling in parts of Northern Ireland and try to sing it, you may get yourself killed. Though there have been many positive changes in Ireland with the cessation of violence, Mario felt it was best to leave these old songs unread in the book, or to sing them strictly in private.

"With the crackle of a Thompson gun,
he marched across Antrim town,
his golden ringlets seen.
They all cried the day he died,
for the green, for the emerald green."

Julie played a solo after the second verse, but then put her fiddle down and disappeared into her studio.

~ ~ ~

The B Team was in a jovial mood as they prepared to board Flight 3673 from Burlington, to Chicago, and then on to Detroit. Nadene, Julie, and the others passed through security. Mario placed his keys in the tray, along with his pocket pistol and government ID card with a metal strip. He walked through the scanner, and it beeped. The security guard asked him if he had any other metal objects in his pocket, and he said no. They told him to put his hands over his belt buckle and pass through again. The device still beeped. The guard moved a wand back and forth across the senator and stopped at his jacket pocket. He reached in and pulled out a three-inch-square foil bag.

"What is this, Senator?" The guard opened the bag and saw white powder. "I'm sorry, Senator, you will have to come with me."

"What the hell is going on here?" Mario was outraged.

"This looks like a bag of cocaine, Senator."

"You must be out of your mind. Someone must have planted that in my pocket. Use your head, why would I take cocaine and put it in a bag that would trip the metal detector?"

"I'm sorry, sir, my job is to confiscate all illegal contraband. If this is an illegal substance, you will have to be detained, sir." Four security guards surrounded Mario.

Kalie Kohn was standing with her camera crew on the other side of the gate and was photographing Mario. She shouted at the guards.

"Why are you arresting the senator? Did he try to smuggle drugs onto the plane?"

Mario looked at Julie and said, "Look who just so happens to be standing here at our gate in Burlington, Kalie Kohn from Metro Media. I wonder how many more people are involved in this setup."

The flight was scheduled to leave in fifteen minutes. Mario instructed the others to go on without him and Julie. They protested, but he said that it was important for them to be there at the wedding. "I'll find out what is going on here, and we'll take a later flight out."

Two FBI agents appeared on the scene and flashed their badges. "Let me see the evidence, please," one of agents told airport security. "Let me also see your credentials, please." The FBI agents examined the security guards' IDs. "All four of you have just been assigned to this station today?"

"Yes sir, we have."

"Where did you come from?"

"Roanoke."

"You all departed from Virginia together, just to be here in Vermont today?" the FBI agent said, looking at his partner. "Hey, Pete, looks like we have a traveling umpiring crew. This is the first time I've ever seen this, how about you?"

"First time for me, too."

"Care to change your story, boys and girl? Let me see that evidence."

The lead Domestic Security agent, disguised as airport security, handed the FBI agent the foil envelope. The head "security guard" said, "We will have to hold the senator until we can determine where he got the packet of drugs."

"I'm sorry, Mario," Julie said. "It was supposed to be a joke. It's just confectioners' sugar."

The FBI agent tasted some of the powder. "Yup, this is sugar, all right. You can go, Senator. We would like to speak to your wife, however."

Mario looked at Julie. She was the only person other than himself who had had access to his jacket pocket. For some unknown reason, she must have planted the envelope in his pocket. For some other unknown reason, she had called the FBI's attention to the powder and told them it wasn't coke. Two state policemen were also stationed at the gate. They apologized but said that they would have to hold Julie for interfering with airport security.

The FBI agent reminded the troopers that it was not illegal to carry confectioners' sugar. They could not hold Julie McGuire. The ticket clerk put them on a flight three hours later. Mario called Seth in Michigan and gave him their new arrival time. Mario couldn't wait to get Julie alone. He planned to stay calm and wait to hear what she had to say. They walked outside the terminal with the two FBI agents. Mario thanked them for their help and apologized for his wife's behavior.

One of the agents took Mario aside and said, "Someone put her up to that, Senator. See if you can find out who and why, and give us a call."

Mario and Julie were alone as they walked back to the parking terminal. Mario held out both hands with his palms up, and asked a silent question. His face was quite red, and Julie knew that he was about to erupt like Mount St. Helens.

"You will have to trust me, I can't tell you what's going on. This is something I have to do myself."

"That is bullshit, that is totally unacceptable bullshit. You will tell me right now what you're up to. If you were supposed to plant drugs on me, you did it because someone threatened you. Did you make the switch from cocaine to confectioners' sugar?"

"I can't talk about it."

"If you made the switch, whoever put you up to it will know that you double-crossed him, so you'd better tell me now so we can figure out how to protect you."

"I can't, I have to buy some time."

"Time for what? How can keeping me in the dark help you?"

"Mario, how do you know that we're not being watched? We're out here in the open. We can go back to the car, but Seth isn't here to scan it for bugs. We don't dare speak in there."

"Let's drive to Red Rocks Park. We can sit on a fucking deserted park bench facing the Adirondack Mountains. Will that satisfy you?"

They got out of Mario's white Cabrio and walked along the water. Mario's phone rang. "This is Rocco. I just heard about your airport trouble. Listen, Julie is being blackmailed. We checked the flight plans of private aircraft coming into your area in the last week and discovered that none other than Harold Slokov filed a plan yesterday from Lake George, New York where he has one of his summer homes, to Lake Champlain. I don't have proof, but I'll bet that he met with Julie. See if you can get her to level with you and call me back."

"Thanks, Rocco."

"What did he tell you?" Julie asked.

"That you probably met with Slokov, on his seaplane. Something you promised me that you would never do. Did you let him kiss you again? What the hell is going on here?" Mario was in a rage.

Julie said, "He played me a tape of Carol's voice. Then he showed me a cellphone video of her. She is alive and being held by Slokov's group, but I don't know where."

"Oh, my God, Carol!" Mario said.

"Slokov gave me a packet of cocaine and said they would kill her if I didn't plant the drugs on you. He also said they would kill her if I told you. I substituted confectioners' sugar for the drugs to buy us time. I didn't want to tell you, because I was afraid they would find out." Suddenly, she slapped his face with enough force to turn his cheek bright red.

"I should have known you'd be more concerned about whether he kissed me than if I was in danger!"

Mario tried to hold Julie close but she pushed him away. He tried again and said, "I'm sorry! I'm so happy Carol's alive. What are we going to do? Why didn't you tell me? You could have been killed." He slapped her hard enough to knock off her sunglasses.

Julie whacked Mario again, only this time not nearly as hard. She hit him three times in succession. He also hit her with less force than before. He then grabbed her and kissed her. She bit him gently on the lip. They ran into the woods and stopped behind a large sugar maple tree. Mario loosened his pants and lifted up her skirt. He ripped her blouse by accident as he tried to unbutton it. They fell to the forest floor and rolled around in the mud and leaves. Julie sat on top of Mario. A chickadee landed in the tree directly above them. Maple sap dripped from a broken branch.

They lay next to each other for fifteen minutes without saying a word. Then Mario helped Julie up and they got dressed. They were covered with mud and Julie knocked a daddy-long-legs spider from her arm. Mario had been bitten on the end of his penis by a mosquito. Julie laughed, but then looked at her watch.

"Mario, our flight is in fifty minutes. We have to go home and change." They ran back to the water's edge, retrieved Julie's sunglasses and headed back to the house. They would discuss what to do about Carol when they got there.

"This time, I am going to wear my white beret. Maybe it will bring us good luck, although I must admit, for the last hour it's been excellent."

~ ~ ~

"Look Mario, you're going to have to lock her in a closet, tie her to the bed, something. I gave you a pair of handcuffs as a souvenir, remember, from our Connecticut crime raid. Put one cuff around your wrist and one around hers. No, wait a minute, bad idea. She'll just drag you wherever she wants to go. I've told you before, man, you are pussy-whipped."

Mario was talking to Rocco from a hotel room in Dearborn. The wedding would take place tomorrow, and he'd been filling Rocco in on what Julie had done. "Mario, do not tell David and Takeo that Carol is alive, they will come unglued."

"I agree, Rocco. *I've* come unglued. I don't know what to do. Slokov will contact Julie again, because he will know why she switched the drug. He may decide to kill Carol."

"I don't think so, Mario. I'm sorry to say this, but we don't even know yet if she really is alive. We could have been mistaken about the DNA evidence that suggested three victims, but I doubt it. Slokov might have faked the tape and video, so don't get your hopes up. We will presume that she *could* be alive. If so, they need her as a bargaining chip. I agree that there will be other demands. Does it do any good if I insist that Julie keep her fine self away from them? Mario, her luck is going to run out. You will have a dead wife. Try to control her, damn it!"

"I'll try. Rocco, I have to assume that Carol is still alive, please do your best to find her."

"I'm already working on it. Let me tell you about the latest bunker meeting. First of all, I could tell by whose voice was the loudest that Sonny Boy Wenman sat in the chair with the tape recorder." Rocco played it back. Mario heard a loud fart that drowned out the speaker. "He did that three times. Poor jerk needs some Beano. I wonder why they didn't discuss Carol at the meeting. It could be that only Slokov and Peterson are in the inner circle. We did hear a message from the person they call Best Friend. His voice is vaguely familiar, but the sound bandwidth is very narrow, and I think there's a scrambler on the phone that distorts the voice. I've got people working on voice-prints, but so far they haven't come up with anything.

"They are licking their wounds after Vermont and aren't going to risk more violence. I still suggest keeping your team safe, Mario. Plans can change."

"How did you guys get Skip Walsh?"

"That was easy. We interrogated Walsh's men. Loyalty to their boss disappeared quickly when they had to choose between the electric chair for treason, or a light sentence for singing. We can't get anything yet on Whitcom. We have no direct evidence that will stand up in court."

~ ~ ~

Julie turned on the TV and draped a blanket over the screen. "Hold on a minute, Rocco, I want to hear this," Mario said. Kalie Kohn was reporting on Metro Media news.

"Senator Mario McGuire from Vermont was arrested this afternoon for possession of illegal drugs. The senator and his wife were en route to a wedding of two of his staff in Dearborn, Michigan, when he was detained at the Burlington airport.

241

"Excuse me, ladies and gentlemen, I've just been handed an update on this story. It seems that the senator was released on his own recognizance when the charges couldn't be proved."

Harold Slokov called Kalie Kohn immediately. "I told you to be sure about the facts before you opened your mouth. Now we look like a bunch of amateurs. Other professional news people will say we anticipated the event. I also told you to send another reporter and not to cover it yourself. Pack up your things and get the hell out of my station. You're fired."

Mario gave the TV his middle finger and said, "I hate that bitch," as he scratched his crotch.

"Don't do that in public," Julie said.

"My cock itches, damn it," Mario said as he picked up the phone.

"What was that, Mario?" Rocco asked. "What about your cock?"

"None of your business."

Rocco was laughing. "Mario, which side of you is in control when you talk about your cock itching? Is it the Irish or the Italian side? 'Cause if it's the Italian side, I'm going to head to a psychiatrist right after I hang up this phone. I'll bet what you have is highly contagious. My mother is from Sicily, and my father is from Florence. If my cock starts itching, I'm going to have you picked up."

Mario said, "It's definitely my Italian side. It's my bad side. Rocco, that means that you have two bad sides, and no good sides. You did marry a woman who is half Irish and half German, so at least there's hope for your children."

Mario and Rocco insulted each other back and forth like two ten-year-olds.

Julie turned down the TV volume and shouted loud enough for Rocco to hear, "Must be male bonding time again."

242

Rocco told Mario to do nothing about finding Carol. He had put out an all-points search to try to determine where she was being held. "In the meantime, proceed with the wedding as planned, do not tell David or the others about Carol, and let me know immediately if Slokov gives Julie further instructions."

~ ~ ~

Julie lifted up a corner of the blanket and changed the TV channel. Another news station announced that Margaret Zelkie, the courageous director of the Department of Health, Education, and Welfare, had been killed today in Washington by a hit and run driver. She had been on her way to work when she was broadsided by someone in a stolen SUV. The driver had fled the scene. Washington police were treating the accident as involuntary manslaughter.

"You can bet the FBI will investigate this as a murder," Julie said. "It's payback for her support of the ban."

Mario said, "I really liked Margaret. I suppose it could have been an accident, but I doubt it. Julie, please stay especially close to me for the next few days."

~ ~ ~

Rosa's mother, Elena, brought a wedding dress to Dearborn that used to belong to Rosa's grandmother. She had been married in a hand-crocheted gown of fine cotton in a lacy openwork design. Since her grandmother had been only five feet tall, the dress ended right above Rosa's knees. She wore no stockings, and her olive skin complemented the magnificent ivory-colored garment. She wore an ivory silk slip underneath. She had her mother's ivory lace mantilla instead of a veil, and Rosa being Rosa, she also wore

243

red satin shoes and carried a bouquet of red roses, red carnations, and baby's breath. Seth wore a black tux with a red cummerbund and a red rose in his buttonhole. He looked like a matador.

~ ~ ~

"Do you, Rosa Montez, take this man to be your lawfully wedded husband, to have and to hold until death do you part?"

"I do."

"Do you, Sethos Azizi, take this woman to be your lawfully wedded wife, to have and to hold until death do you part?"

"I do."

The four holy men put their hands on top of Seth and Rosa's joined hands and spoke in unison. "We now pronounce you husband and wife."

Fifty camera flashes went off as they kissed. Television crews were recording the event, which was broadcast nationally on many cable news services. All of Detroit and Chicago's local stations were there. Metro Media had boycotted the wedding, and none of their TV or print media had sent a representative.

This was not just an historical religious ceremony, but the marriage of two celebrities whose blues CD had gone platinum. They were constantly in the news because of their high-profile political activities. This ceremony was the exact opposite of what they had planned. They had wanted a small wedding with just family and friends, about forty people. Now they were being married in front of over forty million. Imam Abdul Mohamed had invited the entire population of Michigan to attend. They had had to turn away thousands of well-wishers.

After the wedding the chairs were moved to the edges of the banquet hall so everyone could dance. A Greek-Syrian band was playing a lively blend of American pop and Middle-Eastern music.

Seventy-five people including the B Team, Jews, Protestants, Catholics, and Muslims formed a big circle around Seth and Rosa and started to dance. The music got faster and faster and everyone threw their arms up in the air at the end of the song. There was no alcohol allowed inside the building, but many guests had been going back and forth to their cars, and some had smuggled in flasks of ouzo and other potent liquors.

Seth's parents had flown in from Egypt. They spoke English very well and were totally charmed by Rosa. Seth's father, Anwar Azizi, was fifty years old and every bit as good-looking as his son. He was also tall, about six-four, and towered over Mario.

"Senator McGuire, you have our support in Egypt. We are watching you carefully. Our mosque has outlawed television. All over the Middle East, television is being called the Great Satan. Unfortunately, extremists are blaming the U.S. for ruining the health of the Islamic people. Most of us do not believe this, but it would be very good if America were to pass the ban. I know you will do your best."

Mario danced with the bride, and Julie with the groom. Seth and Rosa were leaving in an hour for a two-day honeymoon. They refused to tell even the FBI where they were going. Mario tried to coax the location from Rosa, but she wouldn't tell him.

"The next time you see us will be in Washington on September second," Rosa said.

"I wish you could have a longer honeymoon," Mario said.

"Don't you worry, after the vote we are going to disappear forever," Rosa laughed.

Rosa's choice of words made Mario anxious. He had too much on his mind. He was getting only a few hours sleep a night. The rest of the time he was drawing up contingency plans, drafting statements and rebuttals, writing speeches, and worrying. He was very strong, but he knew the story about the stalwart tree that refused to bend with the wind. Suddenly it snapped. Now his energy was gone and he had to rest.

The band was playing a Misalou, and the female vocalist was singing in Greek. Seth was on stage playing two dumbeks. The entire banquet hall was loudly pulsing to the music. Mario walked to a chair in the corner of the room, sat down, and immediately fell asleep. Julie and Nadene noticed him and tried to wake him, but he was out. Luckily, the news reporters had been asked to leave after the ceremony. An hour after the last guest had left the room, Mario was finally roused.

"Do you want me to call a doctor?" Nadene asked.

"No doctor, just sleep," Mario mumbled.

Oscar and Julie had to half-carry him to the car that had been pulled right up to the entrance. The imam was upset because he had wanted Mario to sleep in the mosque. The FBI intervened, and insisted he return to the hotel for security reasons.

Julie said, "He always does this. He doesn't get it that he has to stop and recharge. He goes full tilt and then collapses from exhaustion. We'll have to make sure he doesn't get too wound up before the vote. If he stays up for two days straight, like he's done before, he's liable to fall asleep right on the Senate floor. Twenty years ago he could get away with it, but not any more."

At nine the next morning, Mario awoke and smelled fresh coffee. Julie had ordered a huge breakfast from room service.

Mario said, "I feel like Rip Van Winkle. How long have I been out?"

"Since seven last night. That's about fourteen hours," Julie said.

"I think I need a course in time management. Must have been the ouzo," Mario said.

"When I first met you, you were thirty-eight years old. I considered you somewhat immature. You rode a motorcycle, played your electric guitar too loud, couldn't control your temper, drank too much whiskey, and didn't get enough sleep. You are now fifty-eight years old. The only thing that's missing from this awful equation is your motorcycle. You are even more immature now than you were then."

Mario says, "Mmm."

Julie says, "What's mmm?"

"Nothing."

~ ~ ~

The McGuires were back in Washington. Mario and Julie were waiting for the rest of the team to arrive.

"The final vote in Michigan was 52% in favor of the ban. We just barely won, in spite of all the media attention and all the tireless efforts by our quartet of religious leaders. You know, Julie, something is bothering me. There is supposed to be a separation between church and state. I rationalize our work by saying that we aren't making laws that include or exclude religion, but we *are* using religion to influence policy."

"Everyone does that when they make a moral decision. How can you be for or against abortion, for or against stem-cell research, or capital punishment, unless you combine your spiritual and temporal beliefs?" Julie said. "Like it or not, religion impacts policy."

"Then our job is to ensure that these decisions do not deprive others, even those who don't practice any religion, of their civil rights. No, we're not doing that. Thanks, baby," Mario said.

"It's too bad about Texas, but we knew how that was going to turn out. Unfortunately, Indiana, Illinois, Nevada, and Kentucky decided to postpone their votes until after the federal vote. Momentum is shifting against the ban, Mario. It's a slight shift, but it is a shift."

"I agree, but it can turn back again very quickly. Seth and I were talking about momentum, and compared our upcoming vote to a basketball game. Looks like those states called a time-out."

~ ~ ~

The B Team arrived at the office. Takeo, Sara, and David were ready to lobby hard for the ban. Nadene had brought Oscar along. Their two children were staying with Oscar's mother. The last days before the vote would be crucial. Seth and Rosa would arrive in a few hours. Their friends couldn't wait to ask them where they had been.

A mailman stuck his head in the door and spoke to Sara. "Good morning, ma'am. We've got mail for you, where would you like us to put it?"

"On this desk will be fine," Sara said.

"We will need more space than that, ma'am."

Three postal workers carried in forty sacks of mail. They stacked them four high and ten across, along the office wall.

"Nadene, looks like you've got some reading to do," Mario said. "After the vote, let's hire some students to go through these."

Nadene said, "Mario, the last two sacks I opened showed that the letters are running two to one talking about music instead of the ban. Go figure."

"Is everybody hungry?" Julie asked.

Sara and Julie volunteered to get lunch, and they phoned Bistro Bis for a large take-out order. Bis generally didn't do lunch to go, but Mario was a hard person to say "no" to. Mario was now the most powerful and influential man in the Senate. He realized that he could use that power to bend rules and get special favors. His team's visibility and popularity had increased his power. He refused to ask for special favors, but gladly accepted one if offered, as long as it didn't compromise his integrity.

Since Nadene was much better at computer graphics than he was, Mario had her print out one of his favorite quotes in Garamond type. She bought an eleven-by-fourteen inch wood frame for the quote, printed it on parchment paper, and he hung it on the wall to the left of the front door. It was the first thing that anyone saw when entering his office.

Power is not evil. It is a sacred trust. If we are strong and lucky enough to accomplish great deeds, let them be for the good. Let us rejoice in our power, for it is the power to make our world a better place.

B. Everett Randall

Sara ran into the office empty-handed. She was out of breath. "Did Julie come back here?"

"No," Nadene answered, "We thought she was with you."

"She just disappeared. We were waiting for our order, I went into the bathroom, and when I came out she was gone. There was no one in the front of the restaurant, and when I asked the man who took our order where she was, he said he didn't know. He didn't see her leave. He said he thought she was with me. Mario, where is she?" Sara was very upset and ran to Takeo.

Nadene called Mario to the outer office. An envelope had been slipped under their door addressed to Senator McGuire. She handed him the envelope and told him to hold it by the edges.

"Julie McGuire is in safe hands. If you make an appearance on the Senate floor, you will not see her alive again. If you do not appear for the vote, she will be released unharmed. Any attempt to find or rescue Julie McGuire will also result in her death."

CHAPTER TEN

Best Friend phoned Beatrice Wenman.

"We've made some good progress in the last few days, Bea. Let me tell you what's next."

He explained his new plan.

Beatrice was overjoyed. "How many other people know about this?"

"Only you, me, and him. Bea, you and I go back twenty years. When was the last time we got it on?"

"Last January, in Aspen. Don't you remember?"

"Sure, I remember the event, but not the date. Men are more likely to remember *what* happened and women *when* it happened. I think it's time we got together again. We've grabbed Julie McGuire. That's going to change the senator's plans."

"Our relationship can only get better when the Mario McGuires of the world are thrown out. Why did we need to kidnap Julie, anyway? Your contingency plan should take care of everything," Beatrice said.

"Bea, it's important to close the loop here. Peterson and Slokov are totally expendable. I want them to go down for their 'misdeeds', preferably permanently."

"Leaving us without a scratch," Beatrice Wenman said.

"Leaving us without a scratch," the caller agreed.

~ ~ ~

"I was afraid this would happen, Mario. It's almost impossible to protect you guys in Washington."

"Rocco, it's been two days since she was kidnapped, and the vote is tomorrow. Do you think Julie and Carol are still alive?"

"I don't know, Mario. I hope so. Has the opposition tried to contact you again?"

"Nothing."

"Have you told David about Carol?"

"No, he and Takeo would become unmanageable. Rocco, I can't go on the Senate floor until she is found, I can't take that chance."

"Listen, Mario, the whole country knows that she has been kidnapped. They know your opposition is behind it. The pro-ban side may lose your vote, but your opposition will ultimately hurt their cause by attempting this intimidation."

"Bullshit, Rocco. The undecided senators will be too scared to vote for the ban. Most of these politicians aren't related to Richard the Lionheart. They'll cave under pressure."

"Mario, I know you will find this hard to believe, but we are making progress in finding Carol and Julie. We know that they are not being held in a government facility. We checked every building, every bunker, every office. We have thousands of agents searching across the country. It's just a matter of time before they spot something."

"Any specific ideas?"

"Yeah, if they are alive, I have a feeling Julie and Carol are being held close to Washington. GODS couldn't take a chance on using any type of aircraft, too easy to trace. My guess is that they are being held somewhere near Camp David."

"Why Camp David?"

"The Roundback Mountain bunker is near Camp David. The Maryland-Pennsylvania border would be a perfect place to hide them, and still have access to Washington in less than an hour and a half. I've got choppers with high-resolution cameras patrolling the entire area. I know it's hard to sit and wait. Keep that phone charged and handy, and I'll call you the minute we find her."

Mario told his staff that they would have to appear at the Senate without him. The vote was tomorrow, and he dared not test Julie's captors. He was tormented because he feared that they would kill her anyway, whether or not he voted. He asked Senator Lowenstein to call the B Team as witnesses in his absence.

Mario called Father Messier in Vermont. "Father, I want you to do me a favor. Pray for Julie and for Carol."

"I will say a Mass for both of them, for all of you. Now you must do me a favor in return. This will be one of the hardest things anyone has ever asked of you. Go back to your hotel and get some sleep. Lie down and say prayers over and over again. They will put you to sleep."

Mario prayed, fell asleep at 2:00 a.m. and was awakened at 6:05 a.m. by a phone call.

"We've found Julie! Get over here right away. I'll call Seth, and he will phone the others. Get over here, now!"

Mario phoned Nadene and instructed her to stay in the office with Oscar and Rosa. An FBI agent would also be with them. Nadene was unhappy to be left behind, but she knew she was not yet strong enough to participate. Seth, David, Takeo, and Mario sped all the way to Rocco's office.

"Here's what we've got." Rocco held up a photograph taken by a surveillance chopper. It was an aerial view of a McDonald's restaurant in Highfield, Maryland, right in the area where he had suspected they would be. In the photograph you could see a woman in handcuffs being led into the back of the restaurant. "Notice the Humvees outside. They're just like the ones Eagle Claw and Domestic Security use. Here's a closeup of the woman in handcuffs; it's Julie."

Mario grabbed the photograph from Rocco. "Hurry, let's go get her!"

Rocco insisted that Mario not mention Carol. He had no proof that she was alive. Mario would still be effective on their mission, even though he knew about Julie. Rocco was not sure about David and Takeo, and he didn't need two uncontrollable scientists on his hands.

"They chose a McDonald's because it's the last place they thought we'd look. That's probably why they carelessly parked three Humvees by the back entrance. My guess is a dozen kidnappers are guarding them, but there may be more in the area. I've dispatched every available FBI agent to the scene and gave them orders not to move in until I get there."

"Until *we* get there," Mario said. "Let's go, but I want the press along."

"What? What the hell for?"

"If we have two carloads of reporters following us, taking pictures, the kidnappers may think twice before initiating hostile action."

"I'm against it, Mario. They will only get in the way and hamper our operation."

"Too late, I already called them and they're waiting outside."

"Shit, Mario, let's roll."

There were four FBI vehicles idling outside headquarters. The lead vehicle was a black Chevrolet Suburban, a big SUV with bulletproof glass on all the windows and advanced communications equipment inside. All the FBI field agents on this raid were using the radios Seth had designed. No outsider could unscramble their transmissions. The Suburban held eight people if necessary, but on this trip there were six including the FBI agent who was driving. The three vehicles behind the SUV each held four agents who were heavily armed with automatic weapons, tear

253

gas, and a grenade launcher. Behind the FBI were two additional cars full of reporters.

There was a compartment behind the back seat of Rocco's SUV that held two H & K fully automatic submachine guns. These nine-millimeter weapons had six loaded clips with thirty rounds in each. David and Takeo had their pistols, and Rocco gave them instructions.

"Okay, here's what we're going to do. You guys are backup. Do you know what backup is? That means when we get to our target area, the FBI moves in first. After we make contact, the reporters are free to roam around at their own risk, the stupid bastards. You will carry these automatic weapons, get out of this vehicle, and watch our backs. If you see a threat, you are to let us know by radio, since you are going to be about one hundred yards behind the last FBI station. To use your weapon, insert a clip into the bottom of the weapon, pull the slide back, and fire. It's that simple. Mario and Seth, you use pistols."

"I will help, but I choose not to carry a pistol," Seth said.

"I think you have more courage than anybody," Takeo said.

The six-vehicle caravan left headquarters and traveled west on 193 for 1.6 miles. It then headed west on 495 for 6.1 miles toward northern Virginia and merged onto I-270 North via Exit 35 toward Frederick. The distance from Washington to Highfield was 68 miles. Northbound traffic was light at 7:20 a.m. The Senate vote would take place at 3:00 p.m., but the debate would begin at 10:00 a.m. The vote was the farthest thing from Mario's mind.

This was the first time Rocco and Mario had seen action together since Que Sahn in 1971. Mario was then 22 years old, and he had just plucked Rocco out of the jungle in his Huey UH1. Now Mario relived that mission. He knew all the stats. He had been part of the 326th MedEvac unit. A total of 6,632 wounded men were evacuated in the 67-day battle. 618 choppers were shot up, 55 crewmen were killed, and another 178 wounded, including

Mario. He had flown 47 missions, and ten times he brought back choppers with bullet holes in them. *The damned Huey had a maximum speed of only 135 miles per hour. You could hit it with a rock if we were low enough.*

Mario had almost been awarded the Distinguished Flying Cross, and he did receive two Special Commendations and a Purple Heart. He had a scar on his left leg from the bullet. He never thought he would be pushing sixty years old, and still be in harm's way. He had to protect David and Takeo. They must not be hurt in this action, but how could he keep them safe?

Rocco received a communication from the last FBI car. "Mr. DiAngelo, there are three Humvees following us, sir. They have top-mounted thirty-caliber machine guns. They aren't as fast as we are, sir, I suggest we increase speed."

"Thanks, Stan," Rocco said. He increased speed to 110 miles per hour. The Humvees fell one mile behind them. Nine miles from Frederick the traffic got heavier and the caravan slowed down to less than seventy miles per hour. The Humvees were only a half a mile back now.

"Those damned reporters are the first cars they will hit. Shit, Mario I knew this was a bad idea," Rocco said. "Stan, you and Julio take your cars and fall behind the press corps. Block the road and stop the Humvees. Get down behind your vehicles because they will be shooting. You are authorized to use maximum force. Repeat, maximum force."

The FBI cars jammed on their brakes and made a barricade across the road. The lead Humvee let loose with its machine gun, and the FBI agents laid down a barrage of fire aimed at the first vehicle. An FBI agent used his shoulder-fired grenade launcher and hit the first Humvee from a distance of almost two hundred feet, blowing it to pieces. The other two Humvees approached too quickly, and they passed on either side of the roadblock. Several agents were hit in the crossfire. Stan radioed Rocco.

"Sir, one Humvee destroyed, the other two got by us, repeat, the other two got by us. We took some casualties, am calling for aid now, sir. Both of our vehicles are out of action, sir. We cannot follow you, repeat, our cars are out of action."

A Domestic Security chopper was flying low over the highway, and it started shooting at Stan and his group. As it passed directly overhead, the agents returned fire and set the chopper ablaze. It crashed in a field next to the highway. Stan radioed Rocco and told him they had knocked out a chopper.

"Great work, Stan, any more of you hit?"

"Yes, sir."

"Bad?"

"Yes, sir, we may have fatalities."

There was a roadblock up ahead. Rocco was in the front seat of the SUV. He raised his anti-shake binoculars and spotted three Maryland State Police cars. He quickly dialed their frequency to order them to open the roadblock, but received no answer. He tried again.

"Turn on your damn radios," Rocco said. "I forgot to call the state police and let them know our movements."

The police were at the ready with shotguns and rifles. Rocco told the driver to flash his blue light and turn on the siren.

"You know, Mario, sometimes it's the little things that mean a lot. I knew it was a good idea to equip these vehicles with standard police warning gear."

The police held their fire but kept the road blocked, and the Humvees were again closing fast. Rocco told the driver to cross the grass median and drive on the wrong side of the road. Oncoming traffic was moderate headed toward Washington. The driver wove back and forth dodging cars, forcing several off the road. The other three cars were following close behind, and from the air the caravan looked like a giant undulating snake. Bypassing the road block, they again crossed the median and were

256

now going in the right direction. Traffic was too heavy for them to increase speed, although they were able to hit eighty miles per hour for short stretches. Highway 270 became 40 West, and then U.S. 15 North. The lead Humvee fired its machine gun from a distance of three hundred yards.

The FBI car was now last in the string, placing the two press corps cars in the middle. Bullets hit a car next to the FBI vehicle, puncturing the gas tank and setting it on fire. It pulled off the road and two men bolted from the vehicle before it exploded.

David and Seth silently prayed, and David rocked back and forth, davening in the age-old Jewish tradition. Seth remembered what Rosa had said: he and David, a Jew and a Muslim, were both praying to the same God.

Takeo took out one of the H & K weapons and studied it. "Mr. DiAngelo, how can I get one of these?"

"Join the FBI," Rocco said. "Americans can't own fully automatic weapons unless they have a license from the Bureau of Alcohol, Tobacco, and Firearms. They generally don't give them out unless you own a machine gun dealership that sells weapons to the government. Nice and tidy."

"Do I also have to get permission if I want to smoke a cigar?" Takeo asked. They laughed as Rocco received a radio message. They were only five miles from Highfield. Stan said, "Our wounded are on the way to the hospital, and four teams are waiting near the McDonald's."

"Thanks, Stan," Rocco said. "Keep me informed about your casualties."

Rocco received another message from the FBI car. "Sir, the Humvees have broken off and are no longer chasing us. Do you copy?"

"Copy. We're going to reduce speed, copy?"

"Copy."

Rocco said, "They're smart. They couldn't catch us on the open road, and they don't know what might be waiting for them at our destination. So they took off."

Rocco got another message. "Fire Leader One, this is CX 23 and CX 24, copy?"

"Copy. Where the hell have you guys been? Did you see where those two Humvees went?"

"Yes, sir, do you want us to follow them?" Two FBI choppers were now part of the task force. Rocco said, "I want one of you to follow them and coordinate ground activity. Take them out or capture them. CX 24, fly overhead with us and give us air support if necessary, copy?"

Rocco glanced at Mario. "This is weird. Here we are again, a generation after Vietnam, and we're still playing with choppers. It's about time I returned the favor, Mario."

The caravan stopped a half-mile from the McDonald's restaurant. Rocco instructed the press corps to follow them in only if there was no gunfire. If there was a standoff, they should use their own discretion.

"Mario, I have sand in my head for agreeing to do this."

"Dis will work, trust me, Rocco."

The entire team moved in. Rocco left the SUV with Seth, David, and Takeo. Mario refused to stay behind and followed Rocco.

"Mario, do you have a weapon?" Mario pulled his Kimber .45 from under his sweatshirt. "You stay back until we know what's going on here."

Forty-seven FBI agents and two cars full of reporters surrounded the restaurant. The kidnappers peered out through the broken windows. One of them shouted, "If you shoot, both women die!"

Rocco knew he had them. They were severely out-gunned. And now they knew that Carol was also alive, because he had said "both women." They would not harm their hostages or they would have murder charges added to kidnapping charges. He knew the soldier-of-fortune mentality. They weren't martyrs to a cause, they did what they did for money. They liked living as much as he did. Mario had an idea and explained it to Rocco.

"Mario, that may work." Rocco ordered one of his agents to run back to the SUV and get the bullhorn from under the back panel. Rocco's amplified voice said, "This is FBI agent Rocco DiAngelo. Your military position is completely hopeless. If you surrender, throw down your weapons, and release your captives unharmed, you will be treated as prisoners of war, not as criminals. I repeat, you will be treated as prisoners of war."

Rocco was lying, but it was a lie that the men inside the restaurant were anxious to believe. They came out with their hands up. David, Takeo, and Seth were watching, and they ran toward the restaurant. The press photographers were out snapping pictures and shooting live wireless video footage. Once again America was witnessing violence firsthand. Carol and Julie were still handcuffed as they were led outside by FBI agents.

"The keys, where are the keys, you prick?" Rocco slammed the lead guy to the ground, took the keys off the kidnapper's belt, and loosened the cuffs.

"Oh my God! Oh my God! Carol! She's alive, Takeo, she's alive! Carol!" David shouted her name over and over. Takeo smelled garlic and walked over to a blond man who had yet to be handcuffed. "Well, if it isn't the priest. Good morning, Father." Takeo kicked him in the head, breaking his nose and cheekbone. He knocked him to the pavement and was about to kick him again, when two, and then four, FBI agents finally got him under control.

Rocco said to Mario, "That's why I didn't want to tell them. My God, that man has some kick."

David carried Carol in his arms, and Mario rushed to Julie. David and Carol, Julie and Mario, were locked in each other's arms, sobbing.

Rocco turned to a reporter with a microphone and said, "The stranglehold that these criminals have had on this great nation has ended. We will question these men and find out who gave them the orders to kidnap these two women. I want everyone in America to know how courageous Senator McGuire, his wife, and his team are. I don't care if you agree or disagree with them on the TV ban. They have great courage. I'm thankful to God that we were able to get here on time and rescue them alive."

The FBI agents cheered at the end of Rocco's speech and high-fived each other.

Julie and Carol had been beaten and raped. Julie had a split lip, blood smears on her blouse, and deep scratches on her neck. Carol had a broken nose and two cracked ribs. They were filthy from being dragged across the floor, and their clothes were in rags. Carol was much thinner and was weak from the months of abuse. Takeo and David bandaged the women's wounds with Takeo's pocket medical kit, but they both needed to be in the hospital. Headquarters called for a MedEvac chopper, which had just touched down. "A MedEvac, eh, Mario? Looks like we can finally call this one even."

"No, Rocco, now I owe you. I owe you everything." The old friends embraced. "Hey look, this is an old Bell model 204. Where did it come from?"

"Bethesda Naval Hospital," Rocco answered.

David and Takeo traveled in the chopper with Julie and Carol. The women's injuries were not life-threatening, and Julie insisted that Mario return to the Capitol for the vote. The debate would have started by the time they arrived. Mario, Seth, and Rocco drove the SUV back to Washington under armed FBI escort. Seth sat in the back seat and suddenly spotted an electronic listening device in the bottom of the weapons case. He scribbled something on a small pad that he took from his pocket.

"Bug in back of car." He passed the pad to Mario and to Rocco.

Rocco wrote, "No wonder they broke off. They knew exactly what we had waiting for them."

Mario wrote, "I'm going to set a trap, play along with me, okay?"

Mario said out loud, "I'm glad we're going to get back in time for the vote. Seth, remember I told you there are five Republicans who normally vote on party lines, but are open to talking with us. We're going to break away from the floor at 11:00 to meet with them. They want some guarantees in exchange for voting to approve the ban. I believe we'll be on time. The meeting is on the third floor of the Russell Senate Office Building, in room SD 385. You go back to the office and get the material we talked about. They will want to see it. There's a good chance we can change their minds."

Although the SUV's tank was still more than half full, Rocco said, "Shit, I'm almost out of gas, let's pull in here."

"Good idea," Mario said. "I've got to take a piss."

"Me too," Seth said.

Once they were outside the vehicle, Mario explained that the Russell Building was the perfect spot for a trap because it was far away from the Senate floor. Rocco called headquarters and told Director Frank Clancy their plan. The FBI dispatched agents, who evacuated the floor and took up positions in offices surrounding room SD 385.

Seth called Mario's office. "Hello Rosa, did you hear the news?" She, Nadene, and Oscar had already heard the whole story on the radio. Rosa was limp with relief that Seth was unharmed.

The SUV arrived at the Russell Office Building at precisely 10:50 a.m. Rocco and Mario got out of the car, and Seth drove it back to headquarters. FBI agents were in room SD 385, talking loudly with the door closed. They were arguing about the ban, pretending to be senators who were about to vote.

Five hooded men with submachine guns got out of the elevator and ran to the room. One of them threw open the door. The FBI agents were all under cover and let loose a barrage at the five men. They hit them from within the room, from diagonally across the hall, and from the corridor. Rocco and Mario stood back in an adjoining room and let the agents do their jobs. All five intruders were killed within ten seconds. Rocco walked around each, and pulled off their hoods.

"Mario, here's John Boy, not looking too good. I think Peterson's boss wanted him to handle this attack personally. Setting him up, maybe? Finally some justice for Stephanie and Don.

"Let me get this call. Hello, this is DiAngelo, go ahead. Great, thanks. Looks like the kidnappers fingered Peterson and Slokov. Where is Harold Slokov? Oh yes, he's in Dallas."

Rocco gave the order to arrest Slokov.

Mario said, "Rocco, I've got to get to the Senate. Let me know what happens."

~ ~ ~

An estimated 200,000 people had massed at the Capitol. The National Guard had been called out to help the Washington police keep order. The crowd was almost evenly divided between those supporting and those opposing the ban. The guardsmen tried to run interference, but fights broke out and many people were arrested. Mario walked into the Senate, escorted by two FBI agents. He turned to one of them. "Look at the mayhem. This reminds me of the Democratic convention in Chicago in 1968."

Dozens of people were bleeding from being bashed with billy clubs. Several hundred protesters had been arrested, and as in 1968 Chicago, they had resisted violently.

Mario walked into the chamber. Many senators cheered his entrance, and several shook his hand. Seth, Rosa, and Nadene joined Mario at his table.

"Mmm, mmm," Nadene said. "Here we go again, this is for the whole pecan pie."

In Mario's absence, Senator Bruch had been arguing against the ban. He was a brilliant orator, and he spoke of working within the system. He reminded the senators that medical science had cured polio and wiped out smallpox. Science would also find a solution to the medical risks of television and computer screens.

"You don't shoot the patient, ladies and gentlemen." Bruch was traveling over old ground. Most of his comments on the Senate floor today were a rehash of what had been said many times before. He finished his speech, and the vice president recognized Mario McGuire. Mario yawned and rubbed his eyes, then snapped into sharp focus.

He spoke of the kidnapping of his wife and niece. He told the senators that John Peterson, head of the Government Office of Domestic Security, had been killed trying to raid government offices. He was part of a team of five hooded men who were shot by the FBI. Harold Slokov of Metro Media had also been implicated in the kidnappings. Mario was trying to use this new information to outrage the Senate. He spoke of the total breakdown of morality and justice.

"Point of order, Mr. Vice President! Point of order!" Cyrus Whitcom stood and raised his hand.

"Yes, Senator Whitcom." The vice president recognized his right to speak. This infuriated Mario and some of the other senators.

"Thank you, Mr. Vice President. Senator McGuire has the nerve to stand in front of this august body and talk about morality. He has the nerve to talk about morality! This is what Mario McGuire's morality looks like." Whitcom held up a 16 by 20 photograph of Mario in bed with Rosa. Seth and Rosa both jumped to their feet, but Mario grabbed their arms and pulled them back into their seats.

"Keep calm, keep calm. Don't do or say anything yet."

"The entire country was watching all teary-eyed as his two rock stars got married in Dearborn, Michigan. It looks like Senator McGuire has first bedroom rights for his staff. This is the most disgusting thing I have ever witnessed in the Senate."

The entire room was aghast. The vice president had to slam down his gavel three times to ask for order.

The vice president displayed his typical sideways smirk. He always wore the same expression no matter what was going on. "Senator McGuire, do you care to comment?"

"Yes, Mr. Vice President, I call Francine Bouchard to testify."

Francine was sworn in. She had her hair in a French twist, and looked very spiffy. Although she resembled Miss Marple, today she wasn't dressed like her. She had borrowed one of Rosa's black dresses last month and liked it so much that Rosa gave it to her, over Seth's objections.

"Miss Bouchard, please tell the Senate what you know."

Francine spoke into Mario's microphone. "I can prove to you all that the photo Senator Whitcom is holding is a fake. Here is a photograph that I took of the man who shot part of Whitcom's photograph."

"What's going on here, what does she mean, 'part' of the photograph?" Bruch said with annoyance.

"You're out of order, Senator Bruch, shut the hell up. Please continue, Ms. Bouchard," Mario said. "I didn't properly introduce Francine Bouchard. She's a reporter with the *Barre/Montpelier Times-Argus*. She has won three New England Press Association awards for her news and features writing. Francine."

"The man standing outside the Ridgeway Motel near Augusta, Maine, is John Hopper. He is an employee of Metro Media. He is outside Sethos Azizi's and Rosa Montez's room shooting through

264

the glass. At the time this photo was taken, Mario McGuire was here in Washington. Here's the hotel receipt proving that Mr. Azizi and Ms. Montez occupied that room."

Francine looked at Seth and Rosa. "Please forgive me for this. I took another photograph of Seth and Rosa from the exact same spot where Mr. Hopper stood." She opened a large mailing tube and held up the photograph.

Mario said, "I demand to see Whitcom's photograph." Whitcom had given the photo to the vice president as evidence. He in turn handed it to Mario, who held up both photographs, side by side.

"Ladies and gentlemen, you can clearly see that Ms. Montez is in the exact same position, in the same bed, with the same covers folded and creased in the exact same spots. The only difference is that Whitcom and his people put me in the photograph electronically. This is very easy to do with today's digital technology.

"My wife Julie has been working secretly with the FBI, and we have documentation in this envelope proving that she handed these photos over to Harold Slokov, who is at this very moment being arrested for murder and kidnapping. Here is a photo of me in my swimming trunks. Note the position of my body."

Mario walked back and forth down the aisles displaying both photographs. Shouts of "Shame! Shame!" reverberated on the floor. Mario walked to Cyrus Whitcom's table and held the photos directly in front of him. Whitcom grabbed both and tore them to pieces. Mario impassively allowed him to destroy the photos. He walked back to his table, and Rosa asked Mario if she could say something into the microphone. The vice president didn't recognize Rosa, but she spoke anyway.

"My husband and I have nothing to be ashamed of." She clasped Francine's hand. "I don't care if the whole world sees our joy. Senators Whitcom, Bruch, and their cronies will stop at

265

nothing to destroy this country. Please, don't be intimidated by them, good senators. They are evil men."

"The times they are a-changing." Seth sang the Bob Dylan song as he raised his fist in the air.

The Senate voted on the ban. The final tally was read by the vice president: affirmative, 52; negative, 48. The bill to outlaw television and computer screens had passed by four votes.

~ ~ ~

Metro Media Towers was bustling with activity. Five FBI agents entered the building, and the lead man showed his credentials to the receptionist in the lobby.

"FBI, ma'am. Are these the only elevators in the building?"

"No sir, Mr. Slokov has his own private elevator on the other side of the lobby, but you need a special key to use it."

"Give me the key."

"I don't know, sir. He doesn't like..."

"Give me the goddamned key! Byron, you wait by the main elevators in case he tries to come down as we're going up. Sean, you stay with the receptionist. Ma'am, you try to call him on that phone and you will do jail time, is that clear?"

Slokov had a warning light on his desk that made a loud ping as it flashed. This told him that someone was headed up in his private elevator. The receptionist *always* called him and asked if he wanted to see a visitor. She didn't do it this time. He had been watching the news, so he knew the FBI was on its way. Slokov quickly locked the door. The electronic locks were strong, and gunfire wouldn't penetrate the steel. He walked into his tropical forest and sat on the same bench that he had shared with Julie. A small violet butterfly landed on his hand. He crushed it, and flicked the powdery residue off his palm. "Lying bitch."

266

"Open the door! FBI!"

"Make it easy on yourself, don't force us to come in there after you."

The agents continued to pound on the door with no result.

"Okay, let's blow it open."

An agent drilled four, quarter-inch holes around the touch pad and filled the holes with a special explosive/acid mix. It was so powerful that they had to be back thirty feet for safety. They ignited the charge, but the door didn't budge. As they prepared another charge, Harold Slokov walked to the staircase at the end of his penthouse office.

When the weather was mild, he often climbed to the roof and tended his garden. The ornamentals were in the tropical forest, but his vegetable garden was on the roof. It was early September in Dallas, and the temperature was still ninety-two degrees at 3:00 p.m. He enjoyed going out on the roof in the mornings when the temperature was still in the low seventies.

He bent down and plucked a ripe cherry tomato. This variety was called Sugary. It loved to be put in twenty-inch pots. He had a dozen plants, and he was always bringing bags of the fruit to his meetings. He sucked on the fruit and then swallowed it.

Harold Slokov had always been in control. He decided who, what, when, where, why, and how.

He heard a second explosion at the door. He walked to the end of the roof, to the farthest point away from the staircase. In one minute the FBI would be upon him. He stood in front of the four-foot-high tile parapet on the north side of the building. There was a south wind blowing at twenty miles per hour. Slokov climbed on top of the wall and launched himself into emptiness.

~ ~ ~

Mario answered his phone. "Hello, David, we won."

"I just heard the news. Mario, don't come to the hospital. They are going to release Julie and Carol today, and we will drive them back to the hotel."

"Bless you, David. I'm all done in. Got to get some sleep."

Mario went back to his hotel room escorted by Nadene, Seth, and Rosa. He could walk under his own power, but just barely. All his friends knew that once Mario overextended himself, he needed special care. Julie lovingly called him her two-year-old Senator. Six hours later Julie came home. David had warned her that Mario would probably have done one of his classic fades.

Julie crawled next to him in bed and pulled the covers over both of them. *Should she tell him about the rapes?* Carol had told David, and David was very tender towards her. How would Mario react? Thank God neither she nor Carol had suffered permanent damage, except to their souls. *She will not tell Mario.* Julie glanced at the nightstand on Mario's side of the bed and noticed a Harley Davidson catalog. She laughed out loud and strained the stitches in her lip, but Mario didn't stir.

Nine hours later Julie woke up. It was 6:15 a.m. and Mario was still sleeping soundly. At eight o'clock, Seth and Rosa showed up with a fabulous breakfast. Mario finally awakened and put on his light gray hooded robe. He threw his arms around Julie and said, "Excuse us for a minute, don't go away, we'll be right back."

He led Julie back into the bedroom. "My poor darling, are you going to be okay?" He gently kissed her bandaged lip.

"I think so."

"I just want to say one thing. I know that you were probably abused in ways you don't want me to know about. I won't press you. Julie, I beg your forgiveness. It isn't fair for you to have had to endure such horrors. There is no cause important enough to justify that. I want you to always feel free to talk to me about what happened, if you want to, when you want to. They can torture.

They can kill and they can rape, but they can never destroy our love."

Julie hadn't expected Mario to say what he had. She knew what it must have cost him to overcome his rage so as to offer her the comfort she needed. Julie didn't often cry. Today was the first time since her mother had died.

~ ~ ~

The entire team returned to Vermont.

Julie said, "Mario, do you know what David told me? He wants to move to New England. He asked Takeo how he would feel if David gave up research and became a general practitioner. Takeo laughed and said that he was thinking of doing the same thing."

"How does Carol feel about that?"

"She loves the idea. As a matter of fact, they want to look at homes on Lake Champlain."

"Julie, wouldn't it be great if Carol and David lived here? I hope she wouldn't miss California too much."

~ ~ ~

"Hello, Bea," Best Friend said. "Did you do as I suggested?"

"I surely did. Since Whitcom is now the largest stockholder of Metro Media, he has first dibs on Slokov's stock. I spoke to him this morning, and he said he would be delighted if I bought Slokov's eighty percent. In my opinion, he could never raise the money. Are they going to come down very hard on Whitcom?"

"Not at all. He's already told the press corps that he thought the photograph was genuine. That's what Harold Slokov told him. Isn't it convenient that Slokov can no longer contradict Whitcom? The photographer, Hooper, or whatever his name is, worked for

Metro Media, and he is in jail. Whitcom is in the clear unless the FBI nails him. More important, we now have a controlling interest in the largest media company in the world. Bea, you now have the largest retail organization and the largest media organization. What *are* you going to do next?"

"I was thinking of pharmaceuticals, and perhaps sports. I'm not even considering oil, because that's your turf, dear."

"Well, thank you for leaving me something. Has Ludlowe been behaving himself?"

"He has a new girlfriend."

"Uh, oh, where did he meet her? Didn't the last one steal money from him?"

"This girl works in his favorite bakery. Now he has the best of both worlds. He can get breasts and Napoleons at the same time. Don't worry about Ludlowe, he's easy to control."

~ ~ ~

The B Team got together at Mario's house. Everyone was there, even Rocco DiAngelo and his wife Maureen. It wasn't a loud, boisterous party. It wasn't really a party at all, more like a reunion of tired combatants.

Julie and Carol had been avoiding each other. They were uncomfortable in each other's presence, and if they were in the same room, they chose opposite ends of it. Finally Julie had had enough; she followed Carol outside when she went to get her sweater from the car. "I guess we remind each other of the nightmare we survived," Julie said.

"Now I know how concentration camp victims felt. I still don't feel quite human," Carol said. "I still feel guilty about not being in the car with my mother. After I was abducted in the parking lot, I heard and saw the car explode, and for months I've been having flashbacks. Perhaps you're right. I can't make eye contact with you because I see the same pain in your eyes as I feel myself. You are very courageous and wise to know what's wrong.

"In the months they held me hostage, I was raped a dozen times by three different men. The last time I was blindfolded and gagged. I wanted to die right there. I never thought I'd be rescued. I managed to grab one of their weapons, put it to my head, and squeezed the trigger, but it wasn't loaded. There was no bullet in the chamber. I never told anyone about this, not even David," Carol said.

"I was raped by two men the day before the rescue," Julie said. "I was blindfolded, handcuffed with my hands behind me, and gagged, but I managed to knee one of them in the balls. You should have heard him yell. After they finished raping me, they slapped me around and dragged me across the floor by my hair."

"It makes me feel better knowing that those murderers and kidnappers will get the death penalty," Carol said.

"I have only one thing to say, darling," Julie said. "Time is our greatest ally. The intense pain will diminish with time. Let's make a promise to each other that we won't let them ruin the rest of our lives. If we talk about the rapes to each other, we will rob the nightmare of its power to hurt us any more." They walked arm in arm back into the house. They were both suddenly very lighthearted.

~ ~ ~

Rocco and Mario drank too much, and Mario asked Rocco a question when they went outside on the deck.

Some of the leaves in the higher elevations were already changing color. From mid-September through the end of October, Vermont was the most beautiful place on Earth, Mario often boasted. He had said it so often that Julie had begged him not to say it again this year.

"Do you know something, Rocco? From mid-September through the first week in November, Vermont is the most beautiful place on Earth. Do you still have your Harley?"

"I have three of them. I still have the blue Sportster you saw, plus a Springer, and get this, I found a mint condition 1936 Knucklehead with matching sidecar. Here, I brought some pictures. I told Maureen it was safer because it has three wheels."

"Is that Maureen in the sidecar? I can't tell with her helmet on."

"You bet. There is only one problem with the new bike, it takes up too much room. So Maureen has to park her car in the driveway, because the bikes are kept in one half of our two-car garage."

"Baloney, your car is in the driveway, not hers. Rocco, don't you bullshit me. I'm going inside and ask her right now."

"Oh yeah, if you do that, I'm going to ask Julie why she won't *allow* you to buy a motorcycle, and I'll do it in front of everybody. You're pussy-whipped, Mario."

The two men were rough-housing on the deck laughing until they knocked over one of Julie's favorite plants, shattering the pot. She opened the sliding glass door and threw a pitcher of beer on them.

"Oooo, that's cold," Rocco said.

"Behave yourselves," Julie said.

"Mario, can I borrow a shirt?"

"No."

Their antics livened up the gathering. Maureen had a fit of hysterical laughter at the sight of her husband dripping with Long Trail Ale.

"What a waste of good brew," she said.

272

Rocco said to Julie, "I should have remembered the Bistro Bis incident. You can be dangerous with food in your hands. Remind me never to come over here if you make a big pot of boiling hot Irish stew."

Just before the gathering broke up, Rocco mentioned some last minute business.

"Listen people, your regular telephones are safe to use again. Keep these other devices charged. They are to be used only to call the FBI. No other calls are to be made from these phones. Let's tell Seth what we think of his invention." Everyone clapped and cheered.

Rocco still wanted Sethos Azizi to work for the FBI.

~ ~ ~

Mario had Nadene drive him to the Harley dealer. He had bought a Dyna Super Glide Custom in Glacier White Pearl color. He had a special sissy bar installed, laced wheels, and he also had them put on a small sport windshield. He didn't like the full-face helmets so he picked one with a plastic visor on the front. Not as safe, but much more comfortable.

"Julie is going to kill me," Nadene said.

"No, she won't. I'll just tell her that I forced you."

"She knows better, and she will be pissed. When I drop you off, you're on your own. I don't want to follow you back home."

It had been over twenty years since Mario had ridden a motorcycle. The Harley was a perfect choice for him. He could ride it in an upright position. The crotch-rockets were fast, but you had to be a contortionist to sit bent forward. His old back much preferred the straight up and down position. The Harley was plenty fast enough, especially from a stoplight. He loved the sound. The chrome engine covers and the brass eagle over the battery cover were custom parts. That was another good thing about Harleys. They had a parts catalog over an inch thick. You could soup up the engines, buy any kind of cosmetic enhancement, change the seat height, the position of the pegs, and there was another whole catalog of riding apparel.

His old bike had been a four-cylinder Honda 750, and it was *very* fast. Julie had refused to ride on it. *Oh shit, she is going to be pissed.*

Nadene dropped him off and waved goodbye. The dealer had done a great job prepping the bike, and had even filled the tank with gas. It stood outside in the parking lot, waiting, pointed toward the road. Mario had done extensive research about Harleys. He knew how to turn on the fuel valve, and knew where the neutral indicator light was. It was even easier than riding a bicycle. He pressed the starter button and the engine roared to life. Once underway, he noticed that the bike's weight was no problem.

He could hide inside his helmet. Nobody recognized him. In a while that would probably change. Word would get out that Senator McGuire had a white Harley, but for now, at least, he was enjoying the anonymity. It didn't take Mario long to feel comfortable with the clutch and transmission.

He pulled into his driveway and noticed that Seth and Rosa were visiting. *Good, that will keep Julie from going off the deep end.*

The three of them ran out of the house.

"What's this, Mario? You're not too old to ride a motorcycle," Julie said, "but you're definitely too old to fall off one, you moron! I hope you just borrowed that thing. It's so loud. It's vile and repulsive. What's next, a ring pierced through your nose? You bought the wrong helmet. Where's the little piss-pot? And where are your tattoos? Did you have to take rugged individualist lessons before they let you have it?"

Seth was laughing so hard he had to turn away.

"Mario, you know the difference between a Harley and a Hoover? It's the position of the dirt bag," Julie cracked.

"Ha, ha, I've heard that one before, and it doesn't improve with repetition. This bike gets over 50 miles per gallon."

"Does it get over 50 miles per gallon in January snow, or when there's a pouring rain?"

"If I knew you felt that way about it I wouldn't have gotten that sissy bar." Mario pointed to the back of the seat.

"What sissy bar? Now you're calling me a sissy?"

"No, that's just a term for that backrest."

"Then why not say 'backrest'? Is sissy bar a Harley term?"

Rosa walked around the bike and said, "The color is very pretty."

"There, you see, very pretty," Mario said.

"They are too dangerous. At your age you don't have the reaction time you once had," Julie said.

"I'm doing just fine."

"Okay, I'm getting one too, and not one of those monstrosities. I'm going to get a motorcycle with some class. I'll buy a Moto Guzzi or a Ducati. Perhaps a lightweight Honda. Then every time I ride you can worry about *me*. I will buy one tomorrow."

"You're not serious."

"Just watch me."

"How can you be so spiteful? You pay me back by doing something dangerous?"

"Do you hear yourself? Do you hear yourself? You just admitted that riding a motorcycle is dangerous."

"Dangerous for you, but not for me."

"If you don't get that thing out of here, it's going to be dangerous for you."

Mario and Julie continued to fight about the new Harley. Seth and Rosa had never heard such a long argument between them, and they were enjoying it. Rosa was laughing when Julie came back into the house.

"Rosa, you think it's funny. Just you wait until Seth decides he wants to fly tiny jet planes for the FBI, or take up hang gliding.

"Mario, I can't even blame this on your mid-life crisis. You're too old for one and besides you already had it. That's why we have fifty guitars and amps all over the freakin' house."

~ ~ ~

The presidential news conference was one week away, and Mario called Senator Benjamin Lowenstein in New York.

"Ben, did you have any luck?"

Senator Lowenstein had planned to talk with the president. He had had great success getting access in the past, much more so than some members of the president's own party. He was going to lobby for the TV ban. Mario had planned to do that himself but decided against it. He was overexposed, so he asked Lowenstein to give it a shot.

"Mario, he's not taking calls from anybody. He's speaking only to members of his cabinet and his closest advisors."

"Including Whitcom?"

"Not including Whitcom. Even someone as aloof and basically clueless as the president knows he needs to distance himself from the likes of Whitcom. That man should be executed for treason, but he won't serve even one day's jail time. Mario, I know how this looks to the rest of the world. They see hundreds of people in this country who use money to buy power, they see them use that power in selfish, greedy ways, and they see the policies these slobs fabricate directed against the man on the street. In Europe, Asia, everywhere the story's the same. America is saying 'What's mine is mine and what's yours is negotiable.' Spreading 'Democracy' is just another way of protecting American interests."

"It's not only America that's full of this kind of corruption," Mario said.

"We've always had some corrupt leaders, as have most of the world's countries, but we knew they were corrupt, and they were usually kept under wraps. Our country's ethos was not corrupt. Now corruption is out in the open, and nobody gives a shit. Not the leaders, not the people. We've become totally cynical about government."

"Ben, you're not in a good mood."

"I'm in a terrible mood. The son of a bitch won't talk to me."

"At least you did your best. I wouldn't have gotten any further."

~ ~ ~

Mario rode his Harley down Route 116 toward Lincoln and the national forest to do some target shooting. He would take the mountain road up Mount Abraham. The autumn palette above two thousand feet was at peak color. The sky was blue, there was no wind, and the temperature was sixty-five degrees with low humidity. It was one of those rare days when it felt warm in the sun and cool in the shade. Soon it would be deer season. The ritual would again bring thousands of people into the woods. Mario fastened his canvas bag holding his gun and shooting supplies to the back seat with crisscrossed bungee cords. He turned down one of the dirt access roads leading into national forestland. It was so quiet and peaceful, he decided not to do any target shooting after all.

He sat in the sun, alongside a two-foot waterfall from one of the streams that fed Lewis Creek and took an envelope out of the breast pocket of his black and red leather jacket. He opened the envelope and pulled out an editorial written by his father, Patrick McGuire. The date was October 26, 1960. On the yellowed page with his editorial were two ads. Their newspaper was small, and he couldn't devote a full page to editorials and letters. One ad was for Three Corners Furniture Store, which had gone out of business sometime in the 1970s. The other was for Stone Theater in Montpelier. It had burned to the ground in 1983. But in 1960 those advertisers and Patrick McGuire were very much alive. Mario read his father's editorial out loud.

~ ~ ~

"Now that autumn's color cavalcade is finishing its natural cycle, from green, to red and orange, and finally to yellow, I noticed another color. Soon, November's rain and winds will render the trees bare, and there will be nothing. I closed up the paper the other night and drove up our street. It's a trip I've taken hundreds of times but I never really noticed this color before.

"From every darkened house shone a blue glow. A blue glow from a television set in my neighbors' living rooms. There are only two stations available in this part of the country, so most of the people were watching Ed Sullivan, or I Love Lucy. Forgive me, I don't know all the names of the shows and when they are on, so I just picked those two. Soon it will be winter in the North Country. The temperature will be below zero, and the snow as high as the fence tops. As the days get shorter and shorter, we will choose to live inside, unless of course we like to ski or ice-fish.

"It will be dark at 4:30 by the end of December, much earlier than today on October 26, and the blue glow will also start earlier. I remember my family would sit around our piano in wintertime. Little Mario, who was six years old, would play his miniature guitar, and his twin sister Stephanie would play the bodhran. How that child loved to use the little beaters on that drum! My brother would play the banjo, my nephew would play the pennywhistle, and my niece and I would sing and play the piano. This is how we entertained ourselves. When we finished playing music, the men withdrew to the dining room table. We played cards and talked about politics, the books we read, and how far Duke Synder clouted the ball yesterday.

"Yes, we did drink a pint or two. The women would sometimes join us, but they mostly played with the children and tended to the kitchen. When the night was over after one of these gatherings, the feeling was very different than it is in our house after television intruded. I used to think that Mario would continue playing the guitar, but now at twelve, all he and Stephanie want to do is watch television. That's why I made my decision. I will confess, right here on these pages, that my wife Sophia is not happy with it. We will not be watching television in my house, not for any reason. A poet whose name I can't recall wrote a haiku which reads:

How different are
these two silences, before
the song, and after.

"When we finished an evening of music and talk, *we* had made the music, *we* had done the talking. We had learned something about ourselves and each other. Now we let others make the music for us, and we learn only what Lucy and Ed want to tell us. How different are these two silences, after *our* songs and after *their* songs. The canned laughter on the comedy shows is created by the sponsors who are imprinting their messages on our brains. We then go out and buy the new Vegamatic, or the Dewpoint quadruple-bay, pop-up toaster. There's a Dewpoint toaster in my kitchen, for heaven's sake, and we don't need it. They are laughing at us.

"So, if you drive by our street on a cold winter evening, please knock on the door and say hello. We're the house without the blue light."

~~~

Mario folded up his father's editorial and put the envelope back in his pocket. He started the Harley and headed back to South Burlington. Halfway down the Mountain Road he decided what the title of his book would be. He would call it *Screen*.

CHAPTER ELEVEN

"I'm no better than Joe McCarthy. He was more effective than I am; at least he found a few commies. He drove his poor wife crazy, but he didn't get her kidnapped and raped."

Mario had already downed one drink and was mostly through the second. Julie and he were sitting on their deck watching the sunset. It had been warm today, hitting seventy-nine, but when the sun disappeared behind Whiteface Mountain, the temperature would drop quickly to the upper thirties.

"Julie, darlin', would you get me another drink?"

There hadn't been much left of the bottle after their party, and now after Mario's second drink only about an inch remained. Julie poured it down the drain. "All gone, Mario."

"I remember distintly, *distinctly,* that there was more in that bottle. Now what did you do with it? Stupid question. Why did you pour it down the drain?"

"You don't need it, Mario. You're feeling blue, and you don't need to go all the way to morose. Alcohol will ruin you. Listen, Mario, you are very different from Joe McCarthy, so stop trying to end up like him. Your menace is real, and for the most part his was a witchhunt."

"I got Stephanie and Don killed, you and Carol kidnapped and raped, Nadene and FBI agents shot, and Seth and Rosa humiliated by a photograph that has traveled around the world on the Internet. And that's just my family and friends. What about all the others?"

"Mario, we're playing that game again where you lean to the left and try to fall down, and I prop you up by giving you positive support. Then you lean forward, and I run forward to catch you, and then back, and on and on. Mario! You did not do those horrible things, your enemies did. Aren't you forgetting something? Your bill passed in the Senate."

"But that's as far as it will go. Don't forget, the president has veto power."

"You don't know he will do that."

"Yes, I do, and I'm upset about something else too. Takeo and Sara want to move to New Zealand. Takeo told me he's gotten used to open spaces, and cities like Tokyo and New York are just too crowded. He and Sara want to live in the country, but not this country. He dislikes American *and* Japanese cultures. David and Carol were with them; they all stopped by while you were at the hairdresser. Carol said she and David want to go with the Arais for a while, not permanently, but for a long vacation. I asked her if they were still going to buy a house here, and she said not right now. David said that he and Takeo sold their guns. They want to live in a peaceful country and heal the sick like they were trained to do. They will probably love it there and never come back. She's the only family I've got left. They'll probably get married over there." Mario was weepy.

"So that's what this is all about. I'm sorry to hear that too. I was looking forward to having them around and kind of hoping Takeo and Sara would move here also. But that might not happen right away. If Carol is happier in New Zealand than in Vermont, it will have been the right decision. We will visit them there, but I know we'll see them so rarely. Shit! Stupid girl, how could she tell that to you!" Julie realized that Mario had a right to be sad about his niece's decision. "Her timing is absolutely awful. Where are you going, Mario?"

"I'm going to get some whiskey." Julie tried to stop him because even though he had had only two drinks, his mental state would compound the effects of the alcohol. Mario ignored her, and he drove his Cabrio to the state liquor store on Shelburne Road. He bought two bottles of his favorite spirit, Redbreast Pure Pot Still Irish Whiskey, aged twelve years in oak casks. He always joked that the most impressive thing about Redbreast is that the Irish were able to keep their hands off it for twelve whole years.

The sun was just above the mountaintop when he returned home. Julie was thankful that he had made it back safely, but then she became angry.

"Mario, since you want to get good and sloppy drunk, I'll give you another excuse. Right now I was worried that you would crash, because you drove your car while under the influence. Every time you get on your goddamned motorcycle, I say a prayer. Every time you grab that stupid gun, I say another prayer. I'm sick and tired of praying just before and after you do anything, Mario! You are not the only person on the planet. Don't you care what effect you're having on me?"

"Yes I care, but this isn't about you. It's about me. I feel like I'm losing it. I'm too old and tired to be effective, and you're right, I will sell my motorcycle."

Julie paused for five seconds. "You manipulative bastard. You are good. You are *very* good. Now, I'm supposed to say, 'poor Mario is feeling old, and the motorcycle makes him feel young.' Oh no, dear, you're not too old for your motorcycle, why don't you get two more, like Rocco has. You are very, very good. I don't care if you sell your goddamned motorcycle!"

Mario laughed, "Was I really trying to do that? You know, with most people the technique would have been very effective."

"You should have been a Republican, Mario."

"I appleagiz, *apologize*, for being a manipulative bastard, and I also apologize in advance for getting shit-faced tonight. I promise I will be a totally new man, resurrected right after breakfast. A man you will be happy to spend the rest of your life with."

"Now you're playing the Christ card. Don't you have any shame?"

"What? Oh, you mean resurrected. You have to be dead before that can happen."

"You're working on it."

Mario was already into the Redbreast whiskey. "Do you know what else saddens me?" He was really slurring his words now.

"Laurel and Hardy, Sid Caesar, the Pink Panther? I would imagine that just about anything would sadden you right now."

"No, really. After we're gone, who is going to fight the Whitcoms and Wenmans of the world? What kind of a country are Seth and Rosa going to raise their children in?"

"Mario, this is where I have to leave our discussion. You stay out here and watch the sunset. I'm going inside, but I will answer your question. You would not ordinarily ask it if you were sober because you already know the answer. Your question is illogical. When we are dead, so will be Whitcom and Wenman, and all other members of the dark side who are our age. Seth and Rosa, David and Carol, will have to fight another evil group. Their children will fight yet another. The war will never, ever end.

"Good would not exist if it didn't have evil to balance it. Just as smooth would not be smooth without rough to compare it to. If it were eighty-five degrees all the time, where would the concept of cold come from? Everything moves in cycles. Sometimes evil is up, and sometimes good is up. Sometimes it's twenty below with a blizzard blowing, and sometimes you can sit out on your deck drinking good Redbreast Irish whiskey.

"Mario?" After two more drinks Mario had fallen asleep. *I hope this isn't another fade out.* She threw a blanket over him, and kissed the top of his head. At 8:00 p.m. she tried to wake him, but he didn't want to stir. He muttered "Nadene, armor piercing bullets, chopper rotor." *Whatever does that mean?*

Julie decided what to do. Mario's redwood lounge chair had wooden wheels on the back. She opened the sliding glass door, picked up the light end of the chair at his feet, and pushed it into the living room.

~ ~ ~

The day of the president's news conference had arrived. Mario, Julie, Carol, David, Oscar, Nadene, Sara, Takeo, Seth, and Rosa were crowded into the McGuires' living room. Mario had the radio tuned to WJOY.

The DJ was playing one of their songs. Seth turned up the volume. To ease the tension, everyone sang along with the seventh cut on the B Team's CD, another Nadene Johnson original.

Gonna take to the highway, see the whole U.S. of A.
Gonna take to the highway, see the whole U.S. of A.
From New Jersey to California, Gonna travel round and play.
Well it's up 89 in New Hampshire, cross 66 in old Mo,
To I-95 through Atlanta, I've got a long way to go.
West on 70 in Kansas, how do you do, what do you say?
Gonna take to the highway, see the whole U.S. of A.

Nadene said, "I have an announcement to make. Mario is going to bake brownies for all of us, so please let him know what you would like in them. I suggest pecan brownies."

"What's dis?"

"*Dis* is because you do not shoot straight with your staff."

"That's a terrible thing to say. You know I do."

"Senator McGuire, do you agree that it is very wrong to lie to someone you care about?"

"Yes."

285

"And if I ask you a question you have to tell me the truth."

"About most things, I do, but something like the size of my...."

"I don't care about that. Do you remember when we were shooting at that chopper rotor by the antenna towers? We both took the same number of shots. When I shot, nothing happened, but when you shot, it splintered. My question, Senator McGuire, is, did you, or did you not, use armor-piercing bullets?"

Mario was completely deadpan and didn't speak.

"Senator?"

"How many trays of brownies should I bake?"

Nadene shrieked with delight. Julie slapped palms with Nadene and said, "See what I have to live with?"

"How did you figure it out?" Mario asked.

Nadene just shrugged her shoulders. He quickly looked at Julie.

"A little bird called Robin Redbreast told me," Julie said.

~ ~ ~

"Ladies and gentlemen, the President of the United States." Mario turned up the volume to near maximum and everyone listened intently. Two tape recorders were running. The president chose to speak from the Oval Office, which had lately become a tradition.

"Good evening, my fellow Americans, and friends from other nations. This will not be a short news conference because I have much material to cover. When I was elected to this office, I promised never to lie to the American people. But telling a lie isn't the only way to mislead. Even though I was never asked about my shortcomings, they have caused repercussions throughout my entire administration. Let me explain.

"I have never considered myself a strong, robust leader like Teddy Roosevelt. Nor do I have the wit of Harry Truman, or the oratory skill of John Kennedy. I've always been a quiet person. My philosophy is that you lead by example. My method, after being elected to this office, was to build a cabinet full of people who were *not* like me. If they were all strong, extroverted leaders, I reasoned, that would allow me to tend to the big picture of quietly steering the ship. In some cases, my philosophy reaped great dividends. In other cases, it failed miserably. I have surrounded myself with strong people who have excluded me from their decisions, and what *they* have decided is not best for the country, only for themselves. My administration is corrupt."

The president had to pause to allow the hubbub to die down.

"John Peterson's scandalous link to the crimes against innocent American and Japanese citizens is now well documented."

~ ~ ~

"Well documented, my foot, he was shot dead trying to kill U.S. senators, for Christ's sake. What a wuss this man is," Nadene said.

~ ~ ~

"I have asked for the resignations of the Director of the Veteran's Administration and the Director of the Federal Communications Commission, and have removed Senator Cyrus Whitcom as a presidential advisor and recommended him for criminal prosecution. The Government Office of Domestic Security has been cleansed from top to bottom. I have nominated Emily Fiorenza to replace Peterson. She is the acting head until she can be confirmed by the Senate. We have nearly completed our investigation of the missile-firing incident near Tokyo. I can tell you now that the missile was launched from one of our ships. The captain of that vessel, and the person who gave him the order to fire, will be sent to Japan for prosecution under their laws. An apology and full reparations will be offered to the Japanese. We will not be above international law."

There was an outcry in the room and the president had to pause again.

~ ~ ~

"Ichiro Kobayashi!" Takeo shouted with his fist in the air.

"Now we're getting somewhere," Seth said.

"But when is he going to talk about our bill?" Rosa said.

~ ~ ~

"We have completed the interrogation of the terrorists who were arrested in New York City. Immigration and Customs Enforcement, working with the FBI, has linked this group with the one that blew up the refineries in Texas. Except for one man from Iran, they are all Saudi Arabian nationals. I have lodged a protest with the Saudi government and will ask our UN representative for sanctions against that country. We will not be blackmailed by any country because we need their oil. An alcoholic doesn't need whiskey!" The president raised his voice.

"It's time we ended our dependence on foreign oil. It's time America went off the car and on the wagon. I'm going to ask Congress for twenty billion dollars. Yes, twenty billion dollars for prize money." There were more murmurs in the room. "This prize will be awarded to the university, the consortium, or the housewife who invents an affordable means of transportation that does not use *any* oil or gasoline. I even want to see synthetic grease used on the wheels.

"If you asked any shipyard in the world today to build a Liberty ship like the ones we used during World War II, as fast as possible, sparing no expense, it would take the best builders six months to accomplish this task. Yet in the 1940s, with 1940s technology, we could build a ship in one week. Did you ever see one of those ships? They were big, magnificent, ocean-going vessels. My father served on one, the *Mirabeau B. Lamar*. We built them in one week because we had soldiers and friends on the other side who needed supplies to survive. We did it because we had to. We did it because we had the skill, because we had strength of purpose that only a united people can have.

"The world has changed. Today our biggest enemies are not other countries, but the habits that are causing the destruction of the planet. We must stop using oil for fuel, and sending our children off to wars in foreign countries to feed our habit." The president paused and took a drink of water.

~ ~ ~

"I don't believe I've ever heard him so forceful, and speaking such truth," Takeo said.

"That's what he wants you to think," Mario said. "I don't trust him. He throws us a few crumbs and keeps the whole loaf for himself. Just you wait and see how it all ends."

~ ~ ~

"Hello Bea, what do you think?" Best Friend asked.

"I think he's absolutely magnificent. Right now he could tell the country that we need to invade the Canary Islands and we would be there tomorrow morning."

"I told him that it was very important to sell himself before he tried to sell his product. I said he should make huge promises that involve billions of dollars. Congress will never pass the legislation. He's doing very well."

"Do you remember Kalie Kohn?" Beatrice Wenman asked.

"Yes, I do."

"She's there at the news briefing. I re-hired her and made her vice president and chief operating officer of television media. She asked me if she could question the president today. Of course I said yes. She will feed him just the right questions to make him look good."

Best Friend chuckled.

~ ~ ~

The president continued. "Now I'm going to read from a prepared speech. I asked a member of my administration to contract with a polling company to learn whether America is for or against the Cancer Prevention Act. We do not have binding national referendums here as they do in some other countries. I think referendums are a good idea, and we should consider it. When there are important decisions to be made, such as whether we will send your son or daughter off to war in a foreign country, it would be better if Americans had a direct say in the decision. Perhaps I'll ask the Supreme Court to look into the legalities of such a referendum.

"I wanted control over the polling process because it was going to be the most important criteria, not the only criteria, but the most important, that I used to make my decision.

"So much is at stake here. The first thing I have on my mind is the welfare of the people. I also believe that I should do what the people of the United States *want* me to do. I phrased the following question to be used by the polling company. 'Sir, or Madam, this poll has been requested by the President of the United States. How should he vote on the Cancer Prevention Act, also known as the television ban? Yes, he should sign it, or no, he should veto it. Signing the bill means that television will be eliminated. A veto means that television will be reinstated.'

"The reason I wanted this poll taken is because there is an awesome responsibility attached to this decision. If I sign the bill and pass it into law, untold millions of people will be out of work, many will lose their health insurance, we will have double-digit inflation and unemployment, and our economy will be so weakened that we won't be able to compete successfully with the rest of the world's industrial powers.

"If I veto the bill, it is highly doubtful that Congress can override my veto, because, as you know, they would need a two-thirds majority to override. The bill would be dead." The president paused again to drink more water.

~ ~ ~

"That's not the only thing that will be dead," David said. "The cancer rate in this country is up 2.2 percent this year. Next year it will be up 3.1 percent, and within a decade it will climb past 12 percent. Does a deadly threat have to move fast before anyone notices that there's a problem?"

"Right on," Seth said. "Ruin the air, little by little. Finally the problem is recognized because everyone is turning blue."

"Shush," Julie said. "Let's listen."

~ ~ ~

"If I veto the bill, then the American people will continue to be exposed to the harmful effects of screens. Many will die of cancer as a result.

"National Forum, the polling Company that was contracted to assemble my data, hired twenty-five hundred temporary workers who called people in every state, in every corner of every state. For three days they worked diligently. In the representative sampling that was taken by National Forum, the majority of Americans polled oppose the ban."

~ ~ ~

"Told you so," Mario said.

~ ~ ~

"The vote was not overwhelmingly against it, but the final tally was 2,582,418 No, and 2,219,746 Yes. I have therefore decided to veto the ban."

~ ~ ~

"What do you think, Bea?" Best Friend asked.
"Masterful, masterful, masterful! Bravo!"

~ ~ ~

"Go drown yourself!" Nadene shouted.

"Like you said, Mario, he kept the whole loaf and gave us the crumbs," Sara said sadly.

~ ~ ~

The president continued: "That was my prepared statement of five days ago. Since that time, I have learned the following facts. I wondered why we had contracted with National Forum, when in the past we used Gallup, Harris, or the network polls. I asked Director Frank Clancy of the FBI to investigate National Forum."

~ ~ ~

Mario's FBI phone rang. "Hello, Mario, listen to this, just listen to this," Rocco said.

~ ~ ~

"Director Clancy traced the ownership of National Forum to the Wentworth Corporation, a wholly owned subsidiary of the WenCo Corporation. The FBI interviewed the workers who had conducted the polls. Their results were computerized and tabulated in National Forum's home office. When the FBI tried to determine how the data had been collected and stored, they learned that the electronic trail for the original count had been destroyed. There is no backup on paper, or anywhere else. National Forum cannot verify these figures.

"On the day these findings were given to me by the FBI, the National Security Administration handed me a photograph of Beatrice Wenman and the vice president that had been taken several weeks earlier. Please forgive me, because this is a great embarrassment, they were caught, err, in the act, if you know what I mean. As you know, the vice president is a married man with six grown children. Here he is consorting with the richest woman in the world, who owns the polling company he recommended. The NSA violated the vice president's and Ms. Wenman's privacy, which is against the law, and I thank them for sticking their necks out. I will protect those patriots any way I can. But this odd couple has violated their country. They are traitors in the truest sense of the word.

"I am here and now demanding the resignation of the vice president. There is evidence to suggest that he masterminded many of these other crimes. I ask that the Justice Department prosecute him to the fullest extent of the law. They will have the complete cooperation of the White House. I have also asked the FBI to arrest Beatrice and Ludlowe Wenman for fraud, obstruction of justice, and possibly for higher crimes."

~ ~ ~

"Holy shit!" David said.
"The wicked don't flourish after all," Nadene said.
"Do you believe this?" Takeo was awestruck.
"Fuck you, Mr. Vice President!" Mario shouted.
"What about the ban?" Julie asked.

~ ~ ~

"Hello, Mother, what do we do now?"

"I knew I couldn't rely on National Forum's data, so I asked the other polling companies, as well as NBC, ABC, and CBS to conduct similar polls. The results were very different. Fifty-five percent of Americans polled are in favor of the ban. These are all first-rate polling organizations, and their results vary less than two percent.

"This is what I am proposing to the American people. I would like time for all of us to discover how to work together. I propose that Congress pass a law to seize the assets of the Wenman family that were used to buy control of Metro Media. I also propose to make it illegal for any company to own more than two types of media. This includes television, radio, cable services, theatres, newspapers, wireless, and land-based telecommunications. Right now, Metro Media owns every one of those categories. They have had too much power over the American people for too long.

"The reparations money will be used for research. I will ask those fine people at Stanford and Keio Universities, Doctors Feinstein, Arai, and their colleagues, to approach the ban differently. Solve the problem. Find the right spectral balance in moving images that will not cause cancer. I want the greatest minds in the world to work on this project. I will ask Congress to award a ten-billion-dollar prize to the person or group who succeeds."

~ ~ ~

Mario dropped his drink and the glass shattered. David and Takeo both turned white.

~ ~ ~

"But Mom, you have to take me with you!"

~ ~ ~

"I will sign the bill if the Senate agrees that one year from today, on September 21, moving screen images will be shut down entirely if a permanent solution has not been found. In the meantime, I want the Department of Health, Education, and Welfare, and the new Surgeon General...oh, by the way, I forgot to mention that I've asked Alan Drawler for his resignation. He was blackmailed into fabricating evidence. The death of Margaret Zelkie, the late Director of H.E.W., has been investigated and it is most certainly murder, by the same group that has perpetrated all the other atrocities. I will have to move quickly and install new directors in both agencies. I've asked both acting heads to prepare extensive warning literature, including television spots, to explain the dangers of watching moving images. No network or station will be allowed to refuse these spots or they will be shut down.

"I'm also going to ask that another rider be put on the bill that requires all existing television and computer screens to have the following label affixed. It must be at least three inches long and placed in the lower left corner just under the screen. It must be in fourteen-point bold type in all capital letters."

CAUTION! WATCHING THIS SCREEN IS HAZARDOUS TO YOUR HEALTH. PLEASE CONSULT YOUR DOCTOR BEFORE VIEWING TV.

The president paused. "Now I must fervently ask the American people for forgiveness. I'll get right to the most important point. I've been held hostage in the White House and threatened by people in my own cabinet. I've been forced to support their agenda or my family would have been harmed. I am now working with the FBI to root out these criminals, and it's past time for me to ask for help from the American people. In the days ahead I'll be providing you with more detail.

"We will weather this crisis as we have many others in the past. God bless America.

"I'll take questions now."

The president's news conference ended one hour later. Reporters asked him dozens of rapid-fire questions: *Who are these criminals you refer to? Are you going to resign? Where is the vice president?*

The president did not call on Kalie Kohn, in spite of her wriggling and squirming attempts to get his attention. Francine Bouchard got a special tip-of-the-hat from the president. He thanked her and Mario McGuire for their courage. He intended to invite Senator McGuire and his team to the White House.

~ ~ ~

Mario turned off WJOY. The station's call letters were intoned by the announcer, and repeated by David who shouted "JOY!" Everyone started shouting over and over, "JOY! JOY! JOY!" Then the entire team was silent for about a minute as each person prayed or sat alone with her or his thoughts. Finally Mario raised a glass of Redbreast and said, "This is for you, Mom, Pop, Steph, Don."

~ ~ ~

One by one, television stations came back on the air and commenced regular programming. Internet servers were reconfigured so there was again nationwide computer coverage. Within one week, everything was back to normal, except that there was a decline of 30% in the total television audience.

Francine Bouchard called Mario to let him know that she was interviewing people about the ban for WPBS-TV, the public station. She was a guest journalist and hoped Mario wouldn't be mad. He jokingly told her to expect a call from his lawyer. Francine had offers to be a news anchor from seven different major networks. She also got an offer to be managing editor of the *Times-Argus* newspaper, at about one-third the salary of the TV jobs. She chose the newspaper.

At the McGuires, the B Team sat down to listen to the TV. Julie had a Fender amp cover over the flat panel screen.

"Okay, I'm just going to let everyone peek to see how she looks," Julie said. Francine was wearing Rosa's black dress and dangling silver earrings. She looked great as she introduced her segment of a show called *Across the Fence.*

"Like many other citizens in America, Vermonters have experienced the off-again on-again sensation of losing and then re-gaining their television and computer screens. What are people thinking? We asked dozens of folks throughout the state this question. 'Are you glad, or are you sorry, that screens have moving images again, and what do you like best and least about TV?'

"I'm on Church Street, in downtown Burlington. What is your name and where are you from?"

"Nancy O'Shea, I'm a student at Saint Michael's College, and my home is Albany, New York."

"Are you glad or sorry to see TV back?"

"I nearly committed suicide when they took TV off the air. I moved back home to New York, because they still had it, but when New York voted against it, and New Jersey voted against it, I didn't know what to do, so I moved back to school. I had to repeat three classes."

"What are your favorite shows?"

"*American Idol* and *Dancing with the Stars*."

"Is there anything you don't like on TV?"

"I never watch football."

"How many hours do you watch in a day?"

"Not that much, really. Five or six hours."

"What is your name, sir, and are you glad or sad to see TV back?"

"I'm not going to give you my name. TV? Who the hell cares about TV? I nearly lost my business because we had to turn off our computers. You, McGuire, and everyone who thinks like you are certifiable."

"Are you afraid of cancer, sir?"

"No, but *you* scare me, lady."

"What are your names, where do you go to school, and are you glad or sad to see TV back?"

"I'm Brittany Dupont, and she's Caroline Hoffman. We're juniors at Winooski High School, and we both live in Winooski."

"At first I was very upset."

"Me too."

"Now I don't even turn it on."

"Neither do I."

"I'm learning how to play the drums."

"I'm learning how to play the bass."

"We formed a blues group, and we want to sound like the B Team."

"Who do you like best in the group?"

They shriek in unison, "Sethos!"

"What are your names, where are you from, and are you glad or sad to see TV back?"

"Sol and Freda Chandler from Grand Isle, Vermont." Mr. Chandler was speaking. "We don't miss it because we didn't have it in the first place. We stopped watching TV when I retired five years ago. We have not watched one show since then. I don't like TV, but it's here to stay. Trying to get the younger generation to do without TV is like asking us to do without electricity, or our grandparents to do without lamp-oil or candles."

"What is your name, where are you from, and are you glad or sad to see TV back?"

"My name is Florence Lovell and I live in Bristol. I'm a teacher at Mount Abraham High School. I'm a single mother, and I used to pick up my daughter from day care, come home, and turn on the TV while I made us dinner. I wouldn't even notice what was on most of the time. I barely glanced at it. It was just another voice in the room. I'll bet many lonely seniors were upset when the ban was in force, because TV was their only companion. Many do not have the resources to play or listen to music, or to read. Still, the world existed just fine before TV was invented.

"I still turn on my set, but I don't watch it. The screen is facing the wall. Most of the time I know exactly what's going on by the sound. To tell you the truth, I wish they would create some new radio shows. During the ban, I borrowed tapes from the library of *The Shadow*, *Mystery Theater*, Jack Benny, and a few others. Now we listen to them all the time. I love to watch my daughter's face when something exciting happens. She looks animated, like she's a part of the story. When she watches TV, she becomes a zombie. You don't have to stare at a box that is damaging your health to have entertainment. With radio, you can look in any direction and still have the story all around you. Most important, you are using your imagination. *You* are making the images. We just bought a subscription to XM radio. They have hundreds of stations that play everything, fifties rock, old time radio, book discussions, any kind of music. We love our radio."

"Now *there's* a teacher. I wish I'd had her in high school," Julie said. "Good job, Francine." She turned off the TV.

~ ~ ~

Mario laughed and picked up the latest issue of *Five Boroughs Magazine*. "Listen to dis." He read from the political pages.

Origins: DEM*O*CRAT

Unlike so many obscure words, the origin of this one is clearly documented. In England during the Middle Ages, there was a ruling class of bureaucrats who terribly abused the citizenry by over-taxing the poor.

They were in power for many, many years and would go door to door demanding shillings from people who could not afford to give. They were Collectors of Revenue Authorized by the Tax System. People called them CRATS.

Then one night, in an ale house, a citizen whose name is now lost forever, sat dejected. He desperately wanted a plate of stew and a pint of stout. His friend asked him why he wasn't eating, and he

301

replied that he had no money. "Dem ol' CRATS took me last shilling," he was heard to lament.

From that night forward, whenever the good people spoke of sadistic tax collectors, they used the term DEM*O*CRATS.

"What about Republicans?" Rosa asked.

Origins: RE*PUB*LI*CAN

This is an interesting word, and its origins are well documented. During the Middle Ages in London, there were two classes of people who visited the ale houses or pubs. The first group was well behaved, would visit the pub once a week, have a meal and a pint of ale, then call it a night and go home to their families.

The second group was not well behaved. They would drink until intoxicated and return again to do the same thing every night. This returning over and over got them the name of REPUBS.

Since eventually most of these people fell into dire straits and became derelicts, they were often found in the narrow alleys in back of the pubs licking garbage cans.

So when the police arrested the worst offenders for vagrancy, they labeled them RE*PUB*LI*CANS.

"Oh baby, these are wicked. I'm glad I'm an Independent," Mario said. He put the magazine down and had one of his "aha" moments. *Five Boroughs is free to print "Origins," and I'm free to read it.*

"Listen folks," Mario said. "Until now, the president hasn't been an effective leader, and I strongly suspected he was corrupt. I'll say one thing, he sure knows how to use platitudes and make big promises. I still don't trust him. We'll have to wait and see how it all goes down. I'll bet the FBI will look in every corner for evidence.

"All politicians use platitudes. It's like a fundamentalist Christian speaking in tongues. They are part of a politician's catechism. If you are in the sewing business, you probably use words like *spool, needle, thread, yarn, yard, bobbin*, and others that are unique to the trade.

"We use words like *nation, security, liberty, freedom, prosperity, progress, democracy, social welfare*, and others so often that few people even react to them any more.

"But if we stop and analyze just one of those words, a word like *freedom*, and speak it from the heart about what it really means to us, that's a different story. When a politician finishes his or her speech with the phrase 'God bless America', like the president did, the politician thinks it's a done deal.

"That politician is wrong. Saying 'God bless America' doesn't guarantee He will. It's a prayer, remember? God's blessing has to be earned. Some of the biggest, most corrupt liars will stand up at the podium and ask God to bless America. Those liars had better be careful, because God is listening. He will do his best to get rid of that corrupt politician.

"I've created my share of wind and noise, and I know I rant now and then. If I've learned anything from this experience, it's how preciously important words are. If you speak them, you've got to mean them. So, let me say something now, because I mean it. God bless America."

"Rocco, this is Mario. There's something I've been meaning to mention. Did Clancy ask you to keep quiet about the FBI's probe of National Forum and the case against the vice president? Do you have anything on the president?"

"Nothing yet on the president, and Clancy didn't *ask* me. He told me that if I opened my mouth, it would stay open with a fishhook in it, and I would be stuffed and mounted on a large wooden plaque. I would then be given as a gift to the vice president.

"Of course he told me! Look, Mario, I used up my allotted screw-up allowance when I punched Peterson. By the way, we are about to close our case against Lyle Sinton of Supreme Oil. We have a definite go on money laundering and conspiracy."

"Isn't that nice! Rocco, I'm selling my motorcycle. Julie is frightened every time I ride it, and I can't do that to her. She's a good sport about everything else."

"Pussy-whipped, Mario. Just kidding, I agree with you. The pleasure you get from riding has to be balanced against the agida it gives her. If I were in your position I'd do the same thing. Why don't you keep the Cabrio, and buy a fast sports car, like a Corvette?"

"Ooo, good idea. Do you remember dose 1958s, with the V8s? You could put in a 327 engine with two four-barrel carbs..."

"Or rebuild a 427 with a fuel-injected engine. It would be much faster than the Harley."

"Great, either one would drive Julie even crazier than the Harley! Thanks Rocco, I'll let you know what I decide."

Mario then phoned the Director of Chittenden County United Way and donated his Glacier Pearl White Harley to them for auction. The gas tank had been signed by him and the rest of the B

Team. United Way took out an ad on e-Bay and romanced the bike. It was a seven-day auction, and by the third day the bids reached one hundred thousand dollars. The winning bid at the end of day seven was three-hundred and seventy-five thousand dollars.

The high bidder was Ludlowe Wenman, who was out on bail. United Way shipped him the bike, and Wenman called the local TV station and had them film him setting the bike on fire. With his new girlfriend, Kristie McMuffin, standing by his side, the gas tank blew up and the heavy chrome cap flew off, hitting a cameraman a glancing blow on the side of the head. He needed twenty stitches and suffered a concussion. The police re-arrested Wenman for reckless endangerment, and the FBI told them to hold him without bail for questioning on money laundering and being an accessory to murder.

~ ~ ~

Reverend Mackenzie, Imam Mohamed, Rabbi Lieberman, and Father Messier met in Charlotte, North Carolina to plan strategy. They discussed the moral dilemma facing the country. The National Council of Churches, Synagogues, and Mosques had approved substantial funding for TV commercials. Federal regulations required that equal air time be given to opposing views, so the stations had no choice but to play these spots. The four holy men went to the TransCarolina ad agency and shot four thirty-second ads that would air before shows that had high sexual or violent content.

There were no moving images in their commercials. There was a still color photo of the four of them, dressed in their ceremonial garb, surrounded by children. Each cleric's name appeared on the screen directly above his head. Rabbi Lieberman's spot was the last to be shot. It was scheduled to go on just before an episode of *The Gottinelli Family*, an extremely violent mob saga watched by millions of people.

"Hello, my name is Aaron Lieberman. I'm the third guy from the left, the handsome one. Do us a favor, get up out of that chair and turn your TV off. Go play with your son or your daughter, talk to a friend, make love to your mate. When you are dead, believe me, you are dead for a long time. Real death isn't quick and easy, like they show you in this program. When someone is shot, it can take many agonizing hours for them to die. It's not fun and it's not healthy to watch these bozos kill each other. The violent images you are watching will stay with you forever. Why not live a little right now? Turn off the TV and go get a pizza. Turn this garbage off."

"This message was brought to you by the National Council of Churches, Synagogues, and Mosques."

~ ~ ~

"Hello Bea, don't forget the time. We have only a small window here."

The vice president had been in hiding for several weeks, holed up on a ranch right outside Taos, New Mexico. The ranch belonged to his largest campaign contributor, an oilman named Bud Mertin. Mertin had received a great deal of help from the vice president, who had made sure that legislation got passed that enriched both of them by many millions of dollars. Mertin had a one-mile-long asphalt runway on his ranch from which he flew his personal jet.

Today, however, Beatrice Wenman was flying in from Mexico on a twin-engine Lear. She had bought the plane overseas and hired the pilot and co-pilot in Mexico City. The FBI and Domestic

Security had no record of the serial number on any terrorist watch lists. The pilot filed a flight pattern that took him into Tijuana, and then he turned north undetected, and landed in Taos.

Beatrice had left Ludlowe behind. He would just have to do the best he could. The vice president was ready. The jet refueled, and they immediately took off back across the border. They planned to fly to a private strip outside Valladolid on the Yucatan Peninsula. From there they would fly to Sao Paulo, Brazil. The large city would hide them well. The vice president had dyed his hair black and wore a false beard. Beatrice Wenman had custom theatrical makeup and wore a red wig. From a distance of ten feet she looked to be about 35 years old.

The plane arrived in Mexico and taxied down the private strip to a shabby, simple farmhouse. The landing was very rough because the grass and dirt strip had not been well maintained. The house had been stocked with supplies, had electricity and running water, and even two Chinese-made air conditioners. Bottled drinking water had been brought in for the Americans. The nearest houses were one quarter of a mile away, and the locals never ventured into this area because they knew it was the property of banditos. The house also sat three hundred yards from the dirt road.

The outside stucco was rough, and many of the half-round roof tiles were cracked or broken. This was not the sort of dwelling anyone would expect to find them in. There was dense growth around all four sides, overgrown actually, except around the front door and two windows.

Inside was a different story. An average American family would have been glad to live in such conditions. There was two thousand square feet of living space, satellite TV, and modern appliances, including laundry facilities. The house was surrounded by two hundred and fifty acres and was owned by Raul Ensenada. Senor Ensenada was currently serving ten years in an Arizona prison for human trafficking. In his absence, the property manager made the place available to high-powered folks who needed a safe house to hide from the authorities, for a price, of course. The last time it was used was four months ago to house a drug lord on the run.

With Beatrice Wenman shelling out two million dollars up front, the house had been refurbished pronto.

The two fugitives congratulated each other on their good fortune. The pilot and co-pilot helped them with six sizeable pieces of luggage and collected their half-million cash each, in U.S. funds. They would get an additional one million cash each when they took the pair to Sao Paulo. The home in Brazil was being prepared in much the same way the Valladolid house had been.

Beatrice sat on the leather couch. The inside temperature was eighty-eight degrees, so the vice president turned both air conditioners on high.

"Held hostage, that's bullshit. I knew I should have killed the bastard when I had the chance."

"What happened? Did the president get religion at the last minute?" Beatrice asked.

"He's a miserable double-crosser who threw us to the sharks. He knew it would get more difficult to keep his hands looking clean, because too many people were involved in our power play. He was afraid that someone would implicate him."

"So he launched a pre-emptive strike against us," Beatrice said.

"He'll get his. As soon as we get to Brazil, I'll let America know who was running the show."

"Do you think we can ever go home?" Beatrice asked.

"For Christ's sake, Bea, we killed off government agents, top scientists, a federal department head, and an entire jetliner full of Japs. Every law enforcement agency in the United States is after us. No, we can't go back. What would you rather do, be executed for treason, or live in Brazil?"

"They won't get their hands on *all* our assets. We have over twenty million dollars right in that suitcase," Beatrice said.

She heard a sound in the hall, looked up, and screamed. Four armed men stood in the doorway.

"Don't either of you move, please. I am Inspector Hector Gonzales, representing the Government of Mexico."

"I'm FBI agent Carlos Juarez. You are under arrest for crimes against the people of the United States."

Gonzales, Juarez, and two other FBI agents had been hiding in a small bedroom. They were hot and sweaty, and agent Juarez was heartbroken at having to arrest his own vice president. The other FBI agents, John Tilliston and Michael Long, removed the weapons from the vice president's jacket and Beatrice Wenman's purse. Agent Juarez also removed a credit-card-sized tape recorder from a light fixture in the living room. It was the same type the FBI had used in the Maryland bunker and was completely indestructible.

"Ms. Wenman, your son Ludlowe said you might be using this safe house. He was kind enough to get into your computer for us. It would have taken us some time to bypass your security," Juarez said.

"You piece of government trash! You plea-bargained my boy." She turned to her lover. "Did you hear, darling, they plea-bargained my baby boy."

Agent Juarez read them their rights as a Mexican military chopper landed on the airstrip. "We are all going back to the USA," he informed them.

The agents placed both fugitives in handcuffs. The hot conditions caused the vice president's fake beard to work loose on the left side. It was peeling away from his temple and hung downward. He tried to shake it off but couldn't.

"Mr. Vice President, you look like a half-assed Abe Lincoln," agent Long said.

"He wouldn't come up to Abe's ankles," agent Tilliston said.

Beatrice Wenman was breathing heavily and shouted, "Pain in chest, pain in chest!" She was faking a heart attack.

Juarez was not fooled. "Ms. Wenman, try to stay alive until we reach Mexico City. If you die before that, we will just have to ship your body across the border, and it's extra paperwork."

"How much money do you want? Just name the amount. I can give you and your family happiness and security forever. I can give you billions, just name your price."

"Okay, Ms. Wenman, time to board the aircraft." Juarez and his fellow agents climbed into the chopper after their captives. "Senor Gonzales, would you like to take some photographs for your records?"

"Si, si, gracias for reminding me. I am happy to be a part of getting justice for your people."

"It will also be justice for your people, Hector, because this man does not care about Hispanics like you and me." The two men pounded each other on the shoulder.

"You think I was in charge? The president gave me orders, and as soon as we reach American soil, I'm going to tell the whole country. I was only following his orders!"

The FBI recorder captured every word of the vice president's accusation. Agent Juarez stuck it in his jacket pocket.

The chopper revved its engine and flew straight up off the grass strip. When it reached an altitude of 500 feet, a Stinger missile fired from the jungle hit it amidships. It exploded into tiny fragments, killing all those inside. The tape recorder spiraled downward and landed in some brush alongside the airstrip with the rest of the debris.

~ ~ ~

At the same time, Takeo and Sara were in New York. David, Carol, Seth, and Rosa were with Mario and Julie at Junior's Italian Restaurant in Colchester, Vermont. David announced that neither they nor the Arais would be going to New Zealand, although they all might visit the country later on. David and Takeo intended to find solutions to the screen problems long before the year was up. When they did succeed, both couples would move to Vermont. David and Carol planned to be married in California and wanted everyone to attend.

"Do you know something, Sethos and Rosa," Carol said, "David and I are going to face the same problem you did. Do we get married by a rabbi or a priest? Do we raise our children to be Christians or Jews?"

"Neither," Seth said. "You get married in a Mosque and raise your children in Islam."

Mario said, "I knew that was coming."

"Why don't you get our favorite holy quartet together and get married in Dearborn like Seth and Rosa? Airfare for the Father and Reverend wouldn't be that expensive, and I'll bet they would do it," Julie said.

"That's a good idea, but I think we want to do something different. We want to create our own service and have it on the beach as the sun sets over the Pacific Ocean," Carol said.

"How California," Mario kidded his niece.

The waitress asked if they wanted dessert, but Julie said she had something for them at home. Mario paid the check and they all left together. "Why do I always get stuck with the check?" Mario asked.

"Because it's a business expense. You're supposed to charge it to the US government," Rosa said.

"But we didn't discuss any government business, only personal business. Very happy personal business, I might add. So, next time it will be someone else who pays, unless, of course you want to spend the entire meal working."

"May I ask you something, Uncle Mario?"

"Yes?"

"Have you ever cheated the government or used your position for your own gain?"

"Carol, you do ask a blunt question," Julie said.

"It's easy for me to answer that one. I have never once asked for special favors or treatment. I must admit that our recent popularity opens doors that would normally be closed. I get my dry cleaning fast, restaurant food delivered, that sort of thing. My job is a sacred trust. To abuse that trust is to deceive the people who depend on me to look out for their interests.

"And it's about time I changed all that. I need a new Corvette. I need a swimming pool. Bring on the lobbyists who want favors. I'll stick it to them. Does anyone need a new car or a house?" Mario joked.

"Uncle Mario, if we have a girl, we're going to name her Stephanie. If it's a boy, David and I have decided to name him Mario."

Mario blushed, and Julie laughed.

"What's so funny?" Mario asked.

"I think it's beautiful, it's just that..."

"What?"

"Poor Mario can't get his names to match. Mario McGuire, now Mario Feinstein. What's next, Mario Arai?" Julie said.

David laughed. "So help me God, that is exactly what Takeo told me he and Sara were going to do. He gave me the idea. Would it help if I changed my last name to DiMaggio, or DiAngelo, or DiBartolo?"

Nadene and Oscar joined them at the McGuire's place, and Nadene announced that she would like to quit before Christmas.

"It's time for me to be with my family. I'm going to record more music, and I want to teach high school."

Rosa was especially happy because she wanted Nadene to stop acting like Wonder Woman.

~ ~ ~

Julie entered the living room carrying an eighteen-inch-long silver-plated tray that had once belonged to her grandmother. It had a lace doily on it and a large oval china platter with fancy cloth napkins folded to one side. On the other side was a stack of a dozen five-inch dessert plates in the same pattern, and a dozen small silver forks. The platter held two dozen cannoli.

Mario looked at the plate, and then at Julie.

"Don't even ask."

THE McGUIRES' CANNOLI RECIPE

One box of 6 cannoli shells (approx. 3 oz. total weight)

15 oz. container ricotta cheese

½ cup sifted confectioners' sugar

1 oz. semisweet chocolate, chopped coarsely

5 teaspoons Frangelico (hazelnut liqueur)

1 teaspoon grated orange rind

¼ teaspoon pure vanilla extract

Set the cannoli shells aside while you prepare the filling.

Drain the ricotta of any liquid that may have accumulated. Add remaining ingredients and beat together well. Using a pastry tube or narrow-bowl spoon, fill the shells with the ricotta mixture. Arrange cannoli on a decorative platter and keep refrigerated until ready to serve.

Makes 6 cannoli.

Joe Randazzo has traveled extensively and writes about what he's seen. He believes in the heroism of the ordinary working person, the transformative power of love, and the rejuvenating effects of a truly fine pizza. To support his writing passion he worked as a Case Resolution Specialist for Homeland Security in Vermont, and has a secret clearance from the US government. He has lived some of the scenes in his book, *Screen*.

www.ingramcontent.com/pod-product-compliance
Lightning Source LLC
Chambersburg PA
CBHW020908200626
46814CB00001BA/241